CROWNS

BLOOD KING
PART I

NICOLA TYCHE

COLUMBIA RIVER
PUBLISHING

COLUMBIA RIVER PUBLISHING

Vancouver, WA 98685

COLUMBIA RIVER
PUBLISHING

First published in the United States

Copyright © 2025 by Nicola Tyche

All rights reserved.

ISBN: PB: 978-1-959615-13-2; eBook: 978-1-959615-12-5

HC: 978-1-959615-14-9; Audio: 978-1-959615-15-6

Cover design by Saint Jupiter Graphic

3D art created by Harry Osborn Art

Edited by Kate Studer

Edited by Hanna Richards

Proofread by Kate Studer

This one's mine.

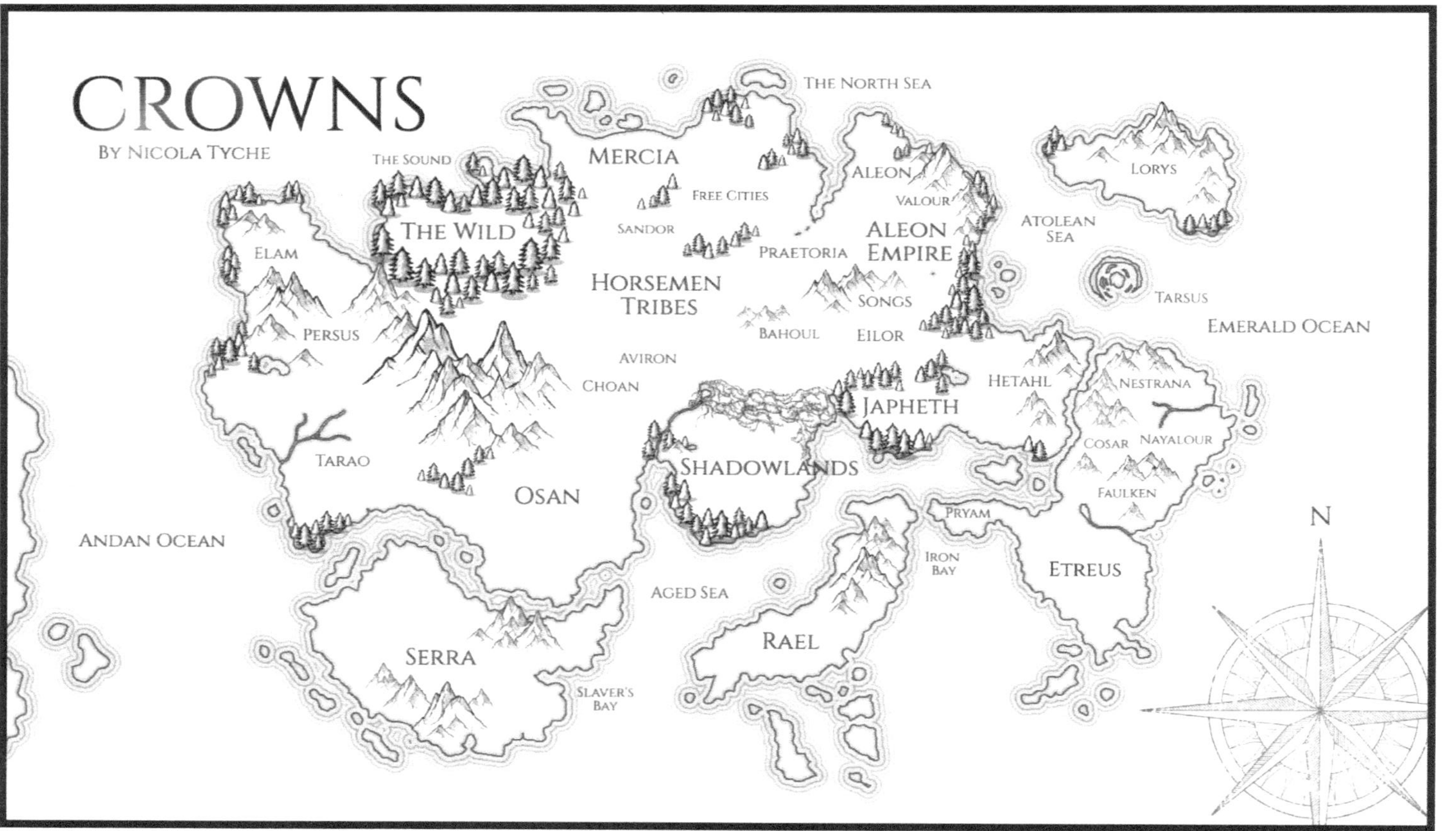

CROWNS
By Nicola Tyche
THE NORTH SEA
THE SOUND
MERCIA
ALEON
VALOUR
LORYS
Free Cities
Sandor
ALEON EMPIRE
ATOLEAN SEA
THE WILD
Praetoria
Elam
Songs
Tarsus
Persus
Bahoul
Eilor
EMERALD OCEAN
HORSEMEN TRIBES
Aviron
Choan
Hetahl
Nestrana
Japheth
Tarao
Cosar
Nayalour
Osan
Shadowlands
Faulken
Pryam
Andan Ocean
Iron Bay
Etreus
Aged Sea
Serra
Rael
Slaver's Bay
N

Blood King
Part I

CHAPTER ONE

The thirsty sands of the arena drank up the blood before it could even pool, leaving nothing more than a trail of crimson stain—the only thing left of the life that once was. Another soul sacrificed. To nothing but the roar of the crowd. As if he'd existed only for that moment of entertainment.

This was the bloodsport.

Cyrus stared at the gate in front of him, through which another body had just been carried out from the arena. A drop of blood trailed down the iron end bar, and he caught it, brushing it between his fingertips. Cyrus would likely share the same end. They all would.

"Eternal rest, brother," he prayed bitterly.

He glanced at his friend Everan beside him, whose eyes were dark under his helm. Everan tapped his fingertips against his chest and then his forehead—a sign of tribute for someone passed.

The arena guard dogs snarled along the hold line, and Cyrus jostled Everan back. While the guards themselves weren't to be trifled with, it was the dogs that one really needed to watch out for, if one could even call them dogs. They were dark-haired beasts with their ears and tails removed, fanged abominations that stood the height of a man's hip. Their heads spanned the length from elbow to fingertip, and their growl was their only warning. If fighters didn't mind the line, the animals attacked without mercy. If a man didn't do as he was told, they made sure that he quickly ceased to be a man at all.

The dogs passed, and Everan's gaze shifted out across the arena, to where a new group of fighters had just entered. Among them, an ox of a man threw his head back and bellowed a challenge into the air. The spectators roared.

Cyrus let his eyes sweep the stands—so many people packed together that he couldn't tell where one tier ended and another began. Sun canopies stretched over the center sections, offering protection from the sweltering heat for those wealthy enough to afford premium seating. Red flags lined the top round of the arena above them.

The color of the kingdom of Rael.

The color of blood.

Cyrus would give them blood. Not for the glory of the arena. Not because the masses called for it—he'd serve them up their own blood if he could. But he had only one goal, and he waited for a single opportunity. Until then, he'd do what he needed to stay alive and to keep his men alive.

A horn sounded, and the top chains of the entry gates pulled taut, raising the iron bars in front of them. Cyrus called over his shoulder, "Four!"

"Four!" echoed Everan and the two fighters with them, Manus and Kieve.

"Four!" the wall guard bellowed up to the sport scribes.

Four. It was how many men were entering the arena. With luck, four would walk out.

Competing teams were always equally sized, generally teams of four, sometimes six, sometimes two. Cyrus's team had a method, and years together had perfected this method. Their strategy was to focus on eliminating one man from the opposing team as quickly as possible, giving them a numbers advantage, then using their extra man to float where needed to finish the rest. It wasn't a unique strategy; many teams took this approach. The difference—speed. Cyrus's team always used their top two fighters to focus on the first kill. Together, they brought a fast death.

Cyrus led this run. Not only was he the top fighter of this team, but he was the best out of all his men, arguably the best in all of Rael, and he was the fighting head of House Pyro. When he fought, he always led.

His team kicked out into a charge, and Cyrus set his sight on the man closest on his left.

Everan followed.

They thundered down on the man, their blades singing through the air. This was the moment that Cyrus looked forward to in each fight—not the blood, not the kill, but the calm before the chaos of the clash. He could hear his heartbeat in his ears as his senses sharpened. It beat in harmony with his intent, like a ballad—the aria of the arena.

Then came the violence.

Cyrus cut high, and Everan went low. The man met Cyrus's blade with a high counter, but the steel of Everan's sword severed his leg. His scream was cut short as Cyrus swung again and took his head.

There was no time for celebration, and Cyrus's attention cut to his team around him. Kieve took the man on the far right. Everan went after a second, and Cyrus turned and joined Manus against the third ox of a man, who wielded both an axe and a sword. As Cyrus and Manus attacked, the massive man swung his battle-axe with his right hand to counter. The clash vibrated through Cyrus's whole body. Manus swung for a leg, but the brute blocked it with the short sword in his left hand.

Their opponent then launched his own attack, swinging out with both weapons. Cyrus and Manus jumped back. It was a narrow miss, reminding Cyrus just how near death always was.

From the corner of his eye, Cyrus kept watch on the side gates of the arena. He tried to drown out the roar of the crowd to focus. His heart beat faster. He and Manus were too close—too close to what was hidden behind those gates. They had only blinks of time left. They needed to get to the center of the arena, but the brute blocked their way. The large man was better than Cyrus had expected, with more stamina. He drove Cyrus and Manus back with merciless swings.

Cyrus glanced at the gates again. *They were too close.* They had to get to the center.

The brute swung again, and Manus couldn't clear it fast enough. His shield took the brunt of the blow, but it knocked him backward to the ground. The massive man swung his axe up and heaved it down in a strike for Manus's head, but Cyrus leapt forward with his own upswing to block it. The force of the blow radiated pain to his elbows and up into his shoulders. Cyrus gritted his teeth and held with every ounce of strength he had as Manus rolled away.

Metal grated against metal, and the side gates started to rise. *Fuck.* Cyrus wasn't focused on their opponent anymore. He jerked Manus back to his feet and pushed him toward the center of the arena. "Go!" he snapped. They were out of time. He needed to get to the center too, but the brute blocked his path. The large man snarled and heaved another swing of his axe. Cyrus knocked it to the side.

Chains clinked together deep within the darkness behind the rising gates at Cyrus's back—not loud, barely audible above the fighting and the crowd.

But he heard it.

And he knew what waited inside that darkness, with its claws and its teeth.

His opponent lunged toward him with another attack. Cyrus threw his shield. Its thick edge hit the man in the chest, stunning the giant for a moment, but a moment was all Cyrus needed. He darted forward, slipping past the man, and raced toward the center of the arena, not looking back at the vicious roar behind him—the roar of the animal that was no longer held back by the gates.

The brute screamed as claws found flesh. A snarl. A wet snap. Then silence.

It was good to be quicker.

Cyrus dared a glance back and saw their opponent was now a bloodied mess under the weight of a black lion. The massive cat sprang toward Cyrus, and he moved even faster. Safety was at the center of the arena.

He reached it just as the beast hit the end of its chain and was snapped to a roaring stop.

Cyrus's eyes found Everan, who was pulling his sword from a downed man on the east side of the arena. One more kill achieved, but they were still one away from a finish, and the stakes had just been raised.

At the far end of the arena, a man with a horned helm pushed Kieve back toward a closed gate. Behind it, a snarling, striped cat reached through the bars, trying to snag a victim in its claws. Manus raced toward him to help but suddenly staggered and fell, a javelin protruding from his thigh. Cyrus hissed and cut his gaze back to the cheering crowd in the stands. For extra amusement, paying spectators could purchase short spears to throw at the fighters. It wasn't often that someone was hit. *Fuck fortune*—it wasn't on their side today.

Cyrus raced to his side, but Manus shoved him off.

"Help Kieve!" Manus shouted.

Cyrus's eyes darted to find his friend still at the far end of the arena. The gate behind Kieve started to open, and the striped cat clawed impatiently at the bottom as it slowly rose. Unaware, Kieve continued to battle his opponent.

"Kieve!" Cyrus bellowed.

But Kieve didn't hear him over the clash of their weapons and the roar of the crowd. Cyrus and Everan both raced toward their teammate. Cyrus cursed as dread coursed through him—they wouldn't make it in time. He pushed himself faster. He had to get to Kieve.

With a bladed staff, the horn-helmed man delivered a low strike, splintering the bone just below Kieve's knee with a sickening crunch. Kieve dropped to the ground.

"Kieve!" Cyrus thundered.

From under the gate, the cat finally sprang free.

And it leapt at Kieve.

Cyrus barreled into the animal that was over twice his size, and in a tumult of man and beast, they crashed to the ground. He tried to roll away, but the big cat twisted and clawed at him, catching him across the chest and tearing open his skin. Pain ripped through him, but he ignored it and scrambled to his feet.

He'd lost his sword on the impact; he had nothing to fight with. Still, he put himself between the massive beast and Kieve. The cat gave a snarling threat of intent. Its lips peeled back, flashing its teeth.

"Leave me!" Kieve yelled from behind him. "Get to the center!"

The animal was chained, but they were still within its reach. With his leg, Kieve wouldn't make it to safety.

And Cyrus wouldn't leave him.

The only thing that could save them now was if Everan killed the last man. It would stop the fight, and the chains would drag the cats back behind the gates. Somewhere to his left, he heard the clang of swords—Everan battling the final opponent—but Cyrus couldn't take his eyes from the cat. The animal swiped at him again, and he jumped back, narrowly missing it.

They'd had close calls in the arena before, but not many were truly bad. *This* was bad. Cyrus was a gold-tier fighter, one of the best, but even he couldn't take on a striped cat with no weapon, no protection. He'd never feared dying in the arena. Perhaps he should have.

The cat struck again, and Cyrus used the thick slave cuff on his forearm to shield himself. It wasn't enough, and pain sliced down his arm.

"Cyrus!" Kieve shouted from behind him. "Go!"

But still, Cyrus refused to leave him. From the corner of his eye, he saw his sword on the ground. Not far. And yet too far. The animal crouched, lining up for its kill...

Then the cat lunged.

Cyrus threw his arms up, bracing himself.

But the attack never came.

The chain pulled tight, choking the animal back. It took Cyrus a moment to understand what was happening, but then he whirled to see Everan pulling his blade from the final opponent.

The crowd roared.

It was over.

Cyrus stood, his body still quaking with fight. The deep gashes across his chest and arm burned, but as air filled his lungs, his racing heart slowed. He turned back to Kieve.

"What the fuck is wrong with you?" Kieve yelled. "That cat could have killed you!"

That was the point of the bloodsport. Cyrus ignored the rebuke and pulled Kieve up. He shouldered himself under Kieve's arm to hold his weight. Across the arena, Everan did the same for Manus, who still struggled with the lance through his thigh.

"Cyrus," Kieve said, pulling them both still. There was a break in his voice. He couldn't get his words out, but he didn't need to. Neither of them had to say how close it had been this time.

"I know," Cyrus said, and cuffed him on the back.

They staggered back to their gate.

"Four!" the gate guard called out.

Four to live another day.

Everan and Cyrus carried Manus and Kieve down the long, narrow corridor under the arena toward their holding room. Blood poured down Cyrus's front and arm. He gritted his teeth through the pain that came with each step under Kieve's weight. The injured fighter was the same height as Cyrus, a little thicker, but a lot heavier. With his light skin and blond hair, the two could pass as brothers. Cyrus considered him so. He considered all of them brothers—brothers born of the womb of the arena.

Guards barked orders for them to get out of the way as the arena was readied for the next fight. They made it to the holding room and laid Manus and Kieve down on the dirt floor. It was nearly impossible to keep from bumping the lance in Manus's thigh, and the fighter hissed in pain with each movement. Blood spilled out and soaked into the dirt underneath him. Too much blood.

Everan pulled off his bloodstained tunic, looking for a relatively clean section, then tore a strip off. "Breathe," he told Manus before wrapping it around his thigh and the protruding javelin to stabilize it.

Manus groaned through his clenched teeth. Sweat beaded his brow. Everan fastened his belt over the cloth and pulled it tight to slow the bleeding. He eyed his handiwork after he'd finished.

"That looks like shit," Cyrus jested. Humor was all they had in times like these.

"You look like shit," Everan told him.

Cyrus snorted.

Everan ripped off another piece of his tunic and pressed it to Cyrus's gaping chest, but Cyrus pulled back. "Don't touch it." He couldn't let Everan touch his blood. He couldn't let anyone touch his blood.

"There's nothing in my mind you haven't already seen."

While Everan's tone was light and he'd meant it in jest, his words were heavy. It was true—there was nothing in Everan's mind Cyrus hadn't already seen, just as with many of his brothers when his blood had accidentally touched them. Cyrus avoided it when he could, but it wasn't a choice. Where his blood touched, his mind followed. It was a chain pulling him to places he didn't always want to go. There were dreams to be held privately, memories he wasn't meant to see. He hated it, but he couldn't stop it. This was the nature of his curse, and only those closest to him knew: Everan, Kieve, Manus, and a few others.

"He'd like not to be in your mind when you use your hand tonight," Kieve said to Everan, grinning through his own pain.

Everan laughed. "No hand for me. I got two kills. Pyro will let me have Visa."

Cyrus stiffened at the mention of their master, hating the way his name lingered. *Pyro.* He was the man who owned them, forced them to fight, profited from their blood. But Cyrus tried to push that from his mind. He was happy for his brother. Everan had taken the final kill. He'd scored two marks, finished the match, and Pyro would give him a woman for the night as a reward. Everan would choose Visa—the slave woman he loved more than life. Cyrus had married them in secret four months ago, with only the stars and gods to witness.

A guard announced the wagon for House Pyro, and they stepped out and down the narrow corridor. They followed it to an adjoining hall, which took them to the back area of the arena, where live men were unloaded, and dead men loaded.

There was already a body in their wagon when they reached it. Dade had lost his one-on-one bout a few fights before Cyrus's match. He'd been a newer fighter to House Pyro. Cyrus hadn't known him for long, but Dade's death still angered him. Cyrus was angered by all the lives this wretched sport took. But anger wasn't enough.

Everan placed what was left of his tattered shirt over Dade's face.

It wasn't a long ride back to the villa. As the wealthiest lord of Rael, Pyro had the convenience of quartering his bloodsport fighters near the city center, where many nobles couldn't even afford to live. Cyrus was grateful for the short travel time as he watched Manus and Kieve groan from their injuries under the shifting of the cart. Each jolt drew a painful grimace from them. Despite Everan's handiwork, blood seeped from Manus's thigh and soaked into the wooden cart bed underneath him. Cyrus was glad they hadn't tried to remove the javelin. They might have lost him. But now if they could get Kieve and Manus to Teron, the healer back at the villa, they'd both be all right.

They passed through the gates of the villa and under the columned pathway of blooming wisteria that stretched forty wagon lengths at least. Many thought the villa was beautiful, and it was. But it was the kind of beauty that masked the rot of morality—marble floors built on bloodstained earth, where silk sheets covered the backs of wicked men.

Golden chains were still chains. Cyrus hated this place, this city, this kingdom.

He hated this life.

Well, most of it. He looked around at his friends. He cared for these men. He would die for these men.

Cyrus and Everan helped Manus and Kieve to the healing quarters. The men's faces were pale, their bodies weak, but with Teron's magic, they'd be better by morning.

"Rest well, brothers," Cyrus told them after he and Everan had laid them on the worktables. He could finally breathe easy. They'd made it. He didn't have to worry about them now. He clapped Everan on the back in parting and walked to his own chamber.

He was too tired to bathe, too tired to eat, but he forced himself to. He needed strength. His chest and arm burned as he pulled the linen from the wounds. The dried blood had melded the cloth to his torn skin, and new blood beaded as he stripped it away. The gashes were deep. He needed Teron's healing power too, but Kieve's and Manus's injuries begged more urgent attention, and he'd have them tended first.

Having finally washed and eaten, Cyrus sank down onto his bed, but sleep didn't come. Instead, his mind wandered. Sometimes it brought him dreams of people he didn't know, places he'd never been.

But on days like today, days when his blood had been spilled, his mind traveled.

To everywhere his blood had touched.

He found Manus's mind. His friend was now finished with the healer and lying in his own room, resting; the same with Kieve. Cyrus hadn't realized he'd gotten blood on the both of them—*by the gods, that shit got everywhere.* They couldn't feel his presence, he knew. If their minds were quiet, perhaps Cyrus would have been happy to stay, to rest in their peace. But like Cyrus, they felt no peace, only the horrors of the life that plagued their days.

Cyrus pushed his mind to move on. He couldn't entirely control it. Wherever his blood touched called him. It pulled him in. Rarely could he wrestle himself out, but he could usually move from one mind to another, if there was another mind to move to.

He found Everan. Visa had made it to him, and Cyrus smiled. He lingered for a moment, looking at her through Everan's eyes. She was a beautiful woman. Her skin was dark, but not as dark as Everan's, the color of night. Her high cheekbones sat below her large brown eyes and tapered softly to the fullness of her lips, all framed by a thick mane of black curls.

Everan slipped the linen gown from her shoulders, and she smiled. Cyrus struggled to pull himself from his brother's mind. He hadn't meant to stay that long; he hadn't meant to intrude.

He pushed his mind to drift out beyond, to anywhere else his blood called.

And then he found what he was hoping for.

The big cat lay in its cage, sated and lazy. It wasn't often Cyrus could travel to one of the animals—it wasn't often they scored his blood. But as recompense, he could enjoy the aftermath. Their minds were peaceful. After the carnage and rage of the fight, animals forgot everything and fell back on simple needs: eating, drinking, sleeping.

As the cat slept, Cyrus let himself stay in the quiet of its mind, where there were no dreams, no memories to haunt him. His body relaxed.

Finally, sleep came for him too.

Chapter Two

Cyrus had just finished tightening the leather straps of his treads as his chamber door swung open. Pyro stepped inside. Disgust rippled through Cyrus. He hated this man—this man who owned him, who mistook that ownership to mean he controlled him. And perhaps he did.

For now.

"You just sit there in the presence of your master?" Pyro snarled.

Heat coursed through Cyrus's veins, and he clenched his fists. *Master.* Cyrus had no master, but slowly, he stood.

"And if you pull another stunt like the one you did yesterday, you won't be able to sit at all," Pyro added.

Cyrus knew what Pyro was referring to. He'd put himself in harm's way for a lesser-ranked fighter. As lead of House Pyro, he was expected to protect Pyro's assets, including himself, and make the necessary sacrifices to keep House Pyro on top. Sometimes that meant accepting the loss of a lesser fighter. But Cyrus would never abandon Kieve, or any of the other fighters for that matter. If Cyrus did have any reservations about putting his own life at risk, it wouldn't be for Pyro's reasons. It would be because Cyrus was the only one who might be able to kill Pyro one day.

No. Not *might*. *Would*, he corrected himself. He *would* kill Pyro one day.

Pyro wasn't a usual lord. He wasn't fattened by gluttony—his indulgences were of a different nature. He was a large man, larger than Cyrus, well muscled and highly skilled in leisure sport wrestling. Cyrus could kill him, but not easily, not with his bare hands, and certainly not while guards trailed the lord everywhere he went. But one day there would be an opportunity, and Cyrus needed to ensure he'd be able to take it.

The malicious lord eyed him and scowled. He stepped closer, running his gaze down Cyrus's injuries, then he reached out and poked at the swollen flesh around the gashes across his chest. "You haven't seen the healer."

A sharp pain shot through Cyrus with each prod, but he didn't let himself show it. The lord liked inflicting pain. Cyrus wouldn't give him the satisfaction. "Manus and Kieve needed him more," he said.

"Manus and Kieve aren't gold-tier fighters!" Pyro snapped. He grabbed Cyrus by the throat, just under his jaw, and clutched him tightly. Pyro's anger was cruel and abusive. Few withstood it unscathed.

Cyrus tensed with his own fury against Pyro's hold, cracking open the wounds on his chest. The broken gashes wept fresh trails of blood down his skin. Cyrus prayed to the gods—the gods that had forsaken him—that Pyro wouldn't touch it. He hated this man's mind, and he couldn't control his curse enough to stay out of it.

Pyro loosened his hold, only slightly, and ran his hand down the base of Cyrus's throat. "You're the most valuable man I have." He paused, and his eyes dropped to Cyrus's stomach.

Every fiber of Cyrus's body tightened. The trail of blood from his chest now reached his navel, and he knew the lord's bloodlust wouldn't let him ignore it.

Pyro brought his eyes back up, locking his gaze with Cyrus's as the corners of his mouth drew up. Then he dropped his free hand to Cyrus's stomach and swiped his thumb up the trail of blood.

Cyrus blinked slowly as another wave of disgust rippled through him. *Fuck the gods. All of them.*

Pyro brought his thumb to his mouth and drew it between his lips. Cyrus felt it—the moment his blood touched the lord's tongue. He felt the link in his mind, and it sickened him more than Pyro's physical hold.

These were the times that Cyrus silently vowed, over and over, that he would kill this man.

He'd kill him.

He'd kill him.

He'd kill him.

It was his mantra. His only solace.

Pyro's smile grew as he savored Cyrus's blood. He didn't know about the curse, the affliction that trapped Cyrus in a chaos from which he couldn't break free. Pyro could never know—the lord lived to torment, and Cyrus was tormented enough.

Cyrus forced himself still as the lord stepped around behind him. Pyro's hand stayed on his neck. His grip tightened, pulling Cyrus back against him. Cyrus could feel the hard length of male arousal. Bile rose in his throat.

Pyro chuckled into his ear. "If you won't take care of yourself, you'll make me do it." He ran his free hand down Cyrus's stomach to his groin and gripped him roughly. "And you won't like it when I do it."

Cyrus trembled with rage, but he could only stand there, his eyes burning into the guards at his door, who refused to meet his gaze.

The lord snorted. "Or maybe you will like it."

Every muscle of Cyrus's body coiled with fight, and Pyro chuckled again. With a final rough squeeze, he released him and stepped toward the door. "Get to the healer," he snarled over his shoulder. "Now." And then he was gone.

It took a few moments for Cyrus's death-lust to pass enough for him to move. One guard still held the door open but didn't dare press Cyrus to move quicker, and didn't dare look at him. It was a wise decision.

Finally, Cyrus stepped out of his chamber, reluctantly doing as he was bid. It wasn't that he didn't think he needed healing, but he'd wanted to give Teron more time. He was an old man, and healing took energy. While scrapes and gashes didn't take much, injuries like the ones Manus and Kieve had would have taken every ounce of power the old man could muster. Had Cyrus gone the evening prior, Teron wouldn't have had the strength to heal him too. He hoped the old man had recovered somewhat.

Trying to collect himself, Cyrus breathed in the morning air. It helped that the guard didn't follow. Only gold-tier fighters were free to move around the villa unsupervised. Pyro believed in incentives to motivate his fighters to rise through the ranks. It wasn't the wisest idea to allow those most capable of killing the freedom to roam. But Cyrus certainly wouldn't object. It would be to his advantage. One day.

The healer's workroom wasn't a far walk. Teron was Rael's best-kept secret—speaking about him outside the villa was punishable by death. He was the world's only known healer. Pyro had procured him for King Orrid but asked that he remain at the villa to heal his fighters and simply travel to the palace when needed. Orrid, certain Teron would choose the palace, had given the old healer the choice. Cyrus had always wondered why Teron had chosen the villa. It certainly gave Pyro a premier advantage against the other fighting houses.

Cyrus reached the workroom, which was plain and simple, like Teron himself. Despite having access to every instrument, every physic, and every herb, the old healer kept only a few things, all meticulously stored in cabinets along the wall. Two large slab worktables filled the center of the room, where Cyrus and Everan had laid Manus and Kieve the night before. In the corner was a small side table and chair, which was exactly where Teron now sat eating a bowl of dumplings in broth. He moved to rise when he saw Cyrus.

"No, no," Cyrus told him. "Sit. Finish first."

The old man relaxed and took another spoonful of broth. "I thought you'd come last night," he said after he swallowed.

"I knew you had your hands full," Cyrus replied as Teron took another bite. "And it's not that bad."

The old man eyed Cyrus's chest, and he tilted his head. "It looks bad."

"Do you need more time?" A night might not have been enough.

Teron picked up his bowl and drained it, then shook his head as he set it back on the table. "Come." He stood and moved to one of the slab worktables.

Cyrus knew the process, and he stepped to it, sitting down and lying back. He didn't close his eyes as he normally did. He didn't dare. He feared where he'd find himself—in Pyro's mind—and the thought haunted him. The lord had done more than touch his blood, he'd consumed it, and Cyrus would have to guard his mind longer than usual. There'd be no sleep tonight.

Teron drew close, leaning over him, inspecting the wounds across his chest and then his arm. He pressed the swollen flesh around the crusted tears of skin. It was painful, but Cyrus didn't move. The healer spread his fingers wide across the gash on his arm; it was less severe and would be the easier of the two.

Cyrus tried to settle himself, tried to relax. The process wasn't painful, but he hated it. He'd rather suffer the injury itself. Of all the minds, Teron's was the hardest to endure—all the things the old man had seen, all the things he'd healed. What had been done to men in bloodsport, what had been done to men under Pyro, were things that haunted Teron's mind. And when he touched Cyrus's blood, they haunted Cyrus too.

Warmth pulsed over his arm, soothing the sting. Teron's touch took away the pain, at least the pain of the flesh. Nothing could heal the soul.

As the healer worked, so did Cyrus, struggling against the pull of Teron's mind. But he couldn't help the glimpses of the memories that coursed through him: Manus lying on the table, splinters of the javelin still in his thigh, and Kieve, writhing with a strip of leather between his teeth as his leg was reset. Broken bones were some of the worst injuries, needing to be aligned before Teron was able to start the healing. There were limits, of course. Shattered bones couldn't be healed at all; Teron could only dull the pain.

The warmth lifted, and Cyrus didn't have to look at his arm to know the wound was gone, as if it had never existed. Teron moved to the gashes on his chest and spread his hands across them. The warmth returned.

"Do you ever get tired?" Cyrus asked as Teron worked. "Not the kind of tired that makes you need a break, but the tired that makes you feel like you just can't do this anymore?"

"Healing is a gift that I am proud to share with the world."

Cyrus almost snorted. *Share with the world.* The world knew nothing about Teron. "Your gift only lines Pyro's purse."

"My gift might save the man who will change the fate of Rael."

"Some bloodsport fighter? We can't even change our own fates."

The old man smiled, more to himself than to Cyrus. "I think you are destined for greatness."

"The only thing I'm destined for is an early grave, and I suppose we'll see how great that really is."

It was a slow process, with the morning waning, and Teron was tiring. Cyrus glanced down. The outer edges of the ripped skin had mostly healed, but the deep gashes toward the center still remained. However, new skin had threaded over, and the injury wasn't as bad as it had been.

He put his hand over Teron's. "That's good enough. The rest can heal on its own."

The old man frowned. "Come back this evening, and I'll finish."

Cyrus gave him an appreciative nod, but he wouldn't come back. Teron had a lot to manage without Cyrus adding to his burden, and he'd healed him enough; the rest would scab quickly and mend on its own. He had another fight in the morning, but he'd cover the wound, and it would be fine.

Cyrus pushed himself up and swung off the table. He gave Teron another nod of thanks and left the healer's workroom.

It was late morning now. Normally, Cyrus would be on his way to the practice fields, but not today. The day before a fight was a rest day. It wasn't often he had fights so close together, but the king was celebrating a reign of twenty-five years, and the city was alive with activity. Cyrus and his men would have many fights this week. Hopefully they'd live through them. But he knew...

Some of them wouldn't.

They had good odds, though. Pyro had more gold-tier fighters than any other house, making their teams strong and formidable. And they had Cyrus. While it was Pyro who basked under the accolades of victories, it was Cyrus who achieved them. It was Cyrus who made the men—trained them, grew them, led them. It was Cyrus who fought most against losing anything more in this forsaken hell of a kingdom.

Of course, those who survived the arena still had to deal with the cruel perversions of their lord. Pyro loved his fighters, not just for the bloodsport. He loved their bodies. He loved doing wicked things to them.

Cyrus had been fortunate, if ever he considered himself so. Pyro didn't abuse his gold-tier fighters or fighters that were progressing quickly up the tiers—he wouldn't risk breaking their spirits.

Pyro had broken many men's spirits.

Cyrus made his way across the courtyard toward the meal hall. It was well after breakfast, but there should still be something left to eat. If not, Portia would make up a meal for him. The broad-shouldered slave woman could have been a fighter herself, Cyrus was sure, but her responsibility was to fill their bellies, and she did a good job of it.

As he made his way across the courtyard, he noticed a caged cart on the cobbled mainway, and he slowed. It was the kind of cart that brought Pyro's new purchases—the kind of cart that Cyrus had arrived in when Pyro had bought him four years ago.

Over a dozen guards stood around it, more than usually accompanied a new purchase. Breakfast forgotten, Cyrus drew closer. It was likely another bloodsport fighter, although sometimes it was someone or something else: a unique animal, a person with special abilities. Pyro was a procurer, with a talent for obtaining rare and precious things. It was what had gained him favor with the king, and what had made him the wealthiest man in all of Rael.

Cyrus came around the back side of the cart, his gaze shifting between the guards to see what the cage held. He was usually the one to first look over new fighters and assess them. He'd be the one to oversee this man's training.

Except it wasn't a man, and Cyrus stopped.

It was a woman. She was on her knees, with her wrists bound, as purchases always arrived. Only she was held with chains instead of rope, and more chains than any man ever wore. Blood stained the wagon underneath her, but he couldn't tell from where it came.

Her head hung low, with her long, dark hair falling forward and hiding her face. He stepped closer.

Hephain, the lead guard and nearest to the cage door, tilted his spear to block him. "No closer, Cyrus."

Cyrus shifted his gaze to the guard. He could rip that spear from his hands and run him through with it before he even knew what had happened. But Hephain was one of the kinder guards, and he wouldn't be Cyrus's first choice to kill.

Cyrus let his eyes travel back to the woman. She raised her head in hearing the exchange. The prominent show of her cheekbones sharpened the roundness of her face. Her skin was light, like his own—too light to be from Rael. She'd been beaten but not broken. There was a wildness to her despite being chained. Her eyes shone bright like emeralds. They skimmed his face, then dropped to the bloodied wounds across his chest. Her nostrils flared, and her eyes flashed black.

Cyrus took a step back but then found only green eyes staring back at him again. Had he just imagined that? Perhaps the light...

Her cracked lips parted slightly. "A drink," she said, little more than a whisper. "Please."

But the guards didn't move.

He glanced at Hephain.

The lead guard shook his head. "We've been ordered to give her nothing. And to say nothing to her."

Cyrus looked back at the woman.

"Please," she said hoarsely. She was a small thing—if she stood to her full height, he doubted she'd reach his shoulder.

"Not even water?" Cyrus pressed.

Hephain's lips thinned. "Lord Pyro—"

Fuck Pyro. Maybe it was his spite that fueled him more than concern for the woman, but regardless, Cyrus turned and strode across the courtyard to the side waterspout, where fighters often drank their fill after returning from the arena, and he pumped water into the bucket that sat beside it. Bringing the bucket back to the cage, he pulled the ladle up and held it through the bars. The guards didn't move to stop him.

The woman reached forward, but she couldn't lift her hands much. Whether from the weakness of neglect or the weight of the chains, her arms trembled. Curse all mankind who could do this to another. Cyrus stepped closer, reaching his hand farther through the bars to bring the ladle nearer to her.

"Cy—" Hephain warned, but before the name could even fully leave his lips, the woman lunged and grabbed Cyrus's arm. Her fingers curled, and her nails raked his skin.

She was fast, but Cyrus was fast too, and he snapped away and out of her reach. He glanced down at his arm. While she'd been quick enough to catch him, she hadn't broken the skin.

"Get back!" Hephain ordered. He shoved the woman with the butt of his spear and pushed Cyrus away. "Get back!"

Cyrus could only stare at her. Her emerald eyes stared back at him, full of fire. Any weakness he'd assumed of her was gone.

"You tried," Hephain said to him. "Now move on." Glancing back at the woman, the guard's brow dropped. "That's what you pull with someone showing you kindness?" the guard spat angrily at her. "What are you doing?"

But Cyrus knew exactly what she'd been doing...

Trying to draw his blood.

Chapter Three

The melodies of night insects filled the evening air. Cyrus lay in his bed, his mind still on the woman in the cage. He'd tried to talk himself into believing she'd had a fit of madness, but her gaze had gone right to his chest. She'd seen the blood. Her eyes had darkened to black. He was sure of it now; he hadn't imagined it. Then she'd clawed him. Did she know about him? *No.* She couldn't. But even if she did, why would she want his blood? It only benefited *him*. Or, rather, cursed him...

He let his eyes drift closed for a moment, forgetting...

And it hit him like a punch to the gut, nearly taking the wind from him—Pyro's mind. Cyrus thrashed in his bed, unable to pull himself out, unable to pull himself free.

Through Pyro's eyes, he could see.

And he didn't have the control to *unsee.*

A man hung in chains that stretched from the ceiling. It was a striking contrast to the finery of Pyro's chamber, which was adorned in gold and rich purples. The man's body hung limply. Cyrus saw him as Pyro did: from behind. The man's back was marked with bloodied whip lines, the skin of his buttocks broken and raw. Blood ran down his legs and pooled on the floor.

Cyrus couldn't see the man's face, but his eyes caught the short-cut blond hair, the palm-size birthmark on the man's side, and the scar that ran from behind his ear to his shoulder—the scar he'd gotten when Cyrus had barely kicked him out of the way in time to miss the axe aimed for his head during a bloodsport match.

Cyrus shook as a sickness washed over him. This wasn't just any man.

He sucked in a breath as he bolted up in his bed, panting, his fists clenched. He bared his teeth with a rage.

Pyro had Kieve.

Cyrus stumbled to his feet, blind to everything around him. He felt his body in his own chamber, but he couldn't break his mind from the dreamscape. A sweat broke over his skin. He tried to pull out of Pyro's head, but he couldn't. He couldn't control the curse, especially when the blood was consumed. When he was calm, he could push himself to another mind if it was open to him, but there was nowhere else for him to go now, and Cyrus wasn't calm.

He grasped around blindly and hit a chair, knocking it over. Stumbling back, he flailed until he found the wall. He followed it to the window and clenched his hands around the iron bars, supporting himself. Then he tucked his head into the fold of his elbow and struggled against the hold on his mind. He needed out—he was desperate to get out. But he couldn't escape the image as Pyro relished it.

Their last fight had been the third in a row where Kieve had failed for a kill, and he'd dropped status within his tier. Pyro was punishing him—a punishment the depraved lord lived for.

Another wave of sickness rippled through Cyrus. Pyro stared at Kieve's body as if taking a moment to savor the sight. From the manacles that bound his hands overhead, over the trails of blood that wept down his arms, across the broken skin of his back and buttocks, down to Kieve's legs, which no longer supported his weight.

Pyro just stared with a sick fascination.

Cyrus couldn't tell if Kieve was conscious or not. He prayed he wasn't, but as Pyro reached and clasped his shoulder, Kieve's flinch told him he was very much awake.

The horrible things he'd already endured, what Pyro had already done to him... the horrible things Pyro would yet do...

White-hot rage flooded Cyrus, and he roared.

Pyro.

Cyrus would kill him.

He'd kill him.

And for a moment, Pyro stopped. Cyrus saw through Pyro's eyes as the lord looked around the room, as if he'd heard something. Had he felt Cyrus in his mind? Did he know he was watching now?

Pyro's gaze stopped on the doors that stood open into the hall from his chamber. Cyrus wished more than anything he could have willed himself there, to be standing in that doorway, sword in hand. But he had no such power, only this curse that plagued him with sight.

The depraved lord stepped away from Kieve and crossed the room to the doors. Taking one last look down the empty hall, Pyro closed them and latched the lock—to shut out the world from what he was about to do.

But he couldn't shut out Cyrus.

CHAPTER FOUR

The wagon hit a deep rut in the road, jarring them all, but Cyrus didn't feel it. He stared at the floorboards, although he wasn't looking at anything in particular.

Sitting beside him, Everan shouldered him lightly. "You well, brother?"

He'd never be well. He'd gone to Kieve's chamber before they'd left the villa for the arena. Kieve lay in his bed, facing the wall. He didn't move when Cyrus called to him. The skin of his back was free of the torturous evidence, by Teron's healing touch. But Teron wasn't able to heal what ailed his friend now.

When he'd put his hand on Kieve's shoulder, Kieve had trembled.

"Cyrus."

Everan's voice brought him back, and he straightened. He gave a stiff nod, but Everan knew him better. Cyrus glanced up at the other men in the wagon looking back at him: Haddick, Jaem, Bash, and Kord. They all knew him better, and they all knew Kieve had been carried back to his chamber early that morning. Pyro didn't mind them knowing—incentive for them to keep their tiering and status. And to stay out of Pyro's chamber. They all held the same disgust and loathing for their master and the same worry for Kieve, but they didn't really know what it was like. They hadn't seen what Cyrus had. They hadn't seen the way Kieve had been abused. They hadn't felt the pain and rage that came from having to watch a person they loved suffer while knowing that there was nothing they could do to stop it. They didn't *really* know.

"Cyrus," Everan said again, quietly.

Cyrus followed Everan's gaze down to where he gripped the bench of the wagon. His knuckles were white. He released it but clasped his hands together to keep them from shaking.

They reached the arena, a monument of blood and spectacle, a marvel of the human hunger for violence. It had taken King Orrid nearly six years to build it, and it was one of the largest structures in Rael, second only to the palace.

Cyrus's men jumped down from the wagon. The air was thick with the tang of blood and sweat, and as Cyrus followed them, it clung to the back of his throat.

The unloading area was as it always was—a chaotic flurry between those coming and those going. Departing teams loaded their dead as arena handlers barked commands at incoming fighters. Cyrus and his men took the shadowed corridors down into the dark underbelly of the sport that killed more men than war.

It was a six-man fight today. The Sport Authority determined the fight cards, the tiering matches, and the schedule, which they posted weekly. However, they frequently made changes, so Cyrus checked it daily.

Everan and Kord were both gold-tier fighters, Jaem was silver, and Haddick, copper. Bash wasn't yet ranked. He hadn't come from a house trade. Instead, he'd been purchased directly from the slaving kingdom, Serra. He'd been marketed as a laborer, but Pyro had noticed Bash's size and tried him in the sparring fields, where he proved to be a naturally good fighter.

Most fighters came from Serran slavers, who'd either bought them as prisoners of war or stolen them from their homelands. Cyrus was no exception, although he'd been only a child at the time. He was raised in the bloodsport. He'd been sold as a servant boy to House Devon, where he helped tend the fighters. He knew how to kill a man before he knew how to read. But he tried not to think about that now.

He turned his focus back to Bash. This was an important fight for him—he needed a team win and another kill to reach the first level of the bronze tier. And to stay in Pyro's good graces. Cyrus was determined to get him there. Bash had come a long way in his training. His skill was there; now he just needed the numbers. His only weakness—honor. He believed in a fair fight, but this world was anything but fair. It worried Cyrus. Honor would get Bash killed.

And this would be a difficult fight. With additional men in the arena, it was more likely the cats would claim a kill and less likely their team would get their numbers. They needed to be fast.

Cyrus tried to push Kieve from his mind. His men needed his full focus today if they were to stay alive. He checked the wrap around his chest that he'd put over the dressing earlier that morning, making sure it was secure.

"You didn't get Teron to finish healing that for you?" Everan asked, nodding to his chest.

Teron had done enough healing that morning. "It's fine," he mumbled. He rolled his shoulders, testing the binding, making sure he still had the range to move properly.

Everan watched him with a frown.

Cyrus picked up his sword. "Bash needs a kill."

Everan nodded. "He'll get it."

The crowd roared in the arena above, with a thunder that sent plumes of dust through the tunneled halls and into their holding chamber. A fight had just finished.

"House Pyro!" came the call.

It was time.

Cyrus led the way out and down the hall. They passed the holding chambers of other fighters. Some were waiting for their fights. Some had already finished and were tending their wounded. Some weren't waiting at all; they were just dead.

He would help Bash get his kill, he committed to himself. One more—he already had nine. Ten would get him to bronze. Cyrus kept track of all his fighters' numbers. He felt equally responsible in helping them level up. In this sport, a man couldn't survive alone. Each needed the power of the team. It was the downfall of so many—chasing status and tiering at the cost of their teammates. Veteran fighters knew. Cyrus knew.

He'd had his own mentors who'd looked out for him as a younger fighter, men who had helped him learn and survive, men who had helped him rise. Now, at the age of twenty-nine, he was one of the oldest fighters in the sport, and he had his own men to take care of.

They waited at the gates, watching while bodies from the previous match were still being pulled from the arena. The victors stood in its center, reveling in their win. Their team lead held his sword high, urging the crowd to cheer louder, and they did. Cyrus knew him. Bravat was his name.

Bravat, and fighters like him, irritated Cyrus. He disliked those who played the crowd, but he understood why they did it. The crowd could call for death despite a win. And they could call for a life to be spared.

Cyrus couldn't bring himself to charm the crowd, not in the face of those who'd been slain. Was blood not enough? *No.* It was never enough for the masses who sat fat in their gluttony, perfumed in the rot of their greed, and cheered as the arena sands drank up the lifeblood of men condemned to this carnage. He couldn't bring himself to entertain them more than death already did. He refused. Yet, by the fickle grace of the gods, Cyrus somehow remained a crowd favorite.

Bravat took one final turn, his arms spread wide to the roar of spectators, and his eyes stopped on Cyrus. The brute smiled. A cocksure smile.

Cyrus didn't understand how Bravat could feel victorious. Yes, they'd won, but at the cost of two men on his team. Two lives lost. Did that mean nothing to him? He tried to shake it off as he watched Bravat follow his men out of the arena. Cyrus had his own team to focus on.

The gates rose.

"Six!" Cyrus bellowed over his shoulder as he strode through.

"Six!" his men echoed behind him.

"Six!" called the gate guard atop the wall.

They were the first to enter the arena. Cyrus hated being first. He'd rather the other teams enter before them, as they usually tended to spread out, allowing Cyrus to choose the first kill and set up the charge. Now the first kill would be the man that first reached them, which was generally the fastest and most nimble, not the quickest to end. And time wasn't a luxury they had.

Cyrus glanced at his men. Everan gave him a slight nod. Bash did as well. Cyrus could see the anxiousness weighing on him.

The gates on the far side of the arena rose, and six men charged forward. Cyrus recognized them—fighters from House Aramine. They were good men, ones he'd kill with regret.

He set his sight on the first man that would reach them and broke into a run. Everan veered to the right, a ruse for the flank of the opposing team, who drifted out more to meet him. Cyrus bared his teeth and focused: hot sand beneath his feet, the taste of metal, the smell of blood. Time slowed, and his senses drank everything in—the feel of the charge.

A blink before he reached his opponent, Cyrus leapt high, attacking from above to pull the man's attention up so Everan's sword could strike low to the legs. He didn't need to look to see if Everan had cut back hard and fast at the last moment to join him. He knew he was there. Everan was always there.

The man blocked Cyrus's attack with an upswing, as they'd hoped, then screamed and fell forward, like everyone who had their legs severed underneath them. Cyrus finished him with a backswing of his blade before the man even hit the ground.

It was a faster kill than he'd expected, and he puffed a small breath in relief, but there was no time to pause in that relief.

Everan sprang up and charged back toward his original target as the rest of the men clashed with matching opponents. They had only moments before the side gates rose, risking losing their kills to the cats or becoming kills themselves. Now at a one-man advantage, Cyrus whipped his attention to Bash.

The fighter was squaring against a man above his tier, but he fought with equal vigor. Cyrus hoped it was enough.

The chains of the side gates rattled. Time was running out. Bash advanced with a lethal combination of strikes, and on an upswing, his opponent stumbled back, losing his balance, and hit the ground.

"Finish him!" Cyrus roared as he raced toward them, fearing Bash would falter.

Don't falter.

Finish him!

But Bash paused, just like Cyrus feared he would. The hesitation of killing a man on the ground.

And that hesitation cost him.

Bash's opponent flung a handful of sand in his face, blinding him, then sprang to his feet with a fatal thrust toward the gut. But Cyrus barreled into the man, careening him sideways. He could have ended him there, taking his head with a backhanded swing, but he pulled back. Bash needed this kill. Instead, Cyrus dropped and raked his blade along the man's side, slowing him.

The side gates rose.

They were out of time.

"Get to the center!" Cyrus bellowed.

Bash clawed at his face, still struggling to see, as a giant striped cat lunged from the darkness of its keep. Cyrus jerked Bash sideways, just in time, and pulled him toward the center of the arena as the beast sprang again, but this time onto Bash's unfortunate opponent.

Cyrus swore. That kill was lost.

He shoved Bash, who was finally managing to regain his sight, toward the center, where Jaem fought another man. Cyrus slid in and overtook the match, redirecting Jaem to join Everan. But Cyrus didn't keep the opponent for himself. Instead, he fell back for Bash to try again.

Bash's eyes were tearing and red, but they focused on his target.

A scream rang out, and Cyrus glanced over his shoulder to see another man from the Aramine team—Kord's opponent—snagged and being dragged to his death by the black lion. Cyrus hadn't even realized the second beast's gate had been opened. At least they were outside the perimeter. They needed to finish quickly, though. When the third gate opened, the perimeters would overlap, and there would be no safety.

"Time!" he bellowed.

His team raced to finish. Everan set up Jaem to take a kill, and Jaem did so beautifully. *Two remaining.*

Bash attacked, a second effort at his own kill, weaving through another set of skilled moves—moves Cyrus had taught him. But this was a silver-tier opponent, and Bash still suffered from troubled vision. Tears trailed his dusted face as he blinked rapidly to clear his bloodshot eyes. It would be a challenge for him to win against this opponent at his best, and he certainly wasn't at his best. He needed help.

Cyrus saw an opportunity and lunged forward, drawing the man's focus with an elbow to the face. As the Aramine fighter blocked it,

Cyrus dropped his opposite arm and ripped his blade across the man's thigh, slicing to the bone.

The man didn't scream, perhaps he didn't even feel the lightning cut of Cyrus's sword, but his leg wouldn't hold him, and he stumbled forward.

Bash's blade finally found home as he sank it into the man's chest. The Aramine fighter collapsed to the ground. Cyrus growled in triumph and turned to scan the rest of the arena. But his joy was cut short as he saw Haddick on his knees—having been run through by his opponent's sword.

"No!" he roared, and then charged toward him. Kord beat him there and, with two swings of his sword, cut down the Aramine fighter, claiming the last kill for the team win and stopping the fight. The chains of the cats tightened, and they were dragged back into the darkness of their dens.

The crowd cheered. Of course they fucking cheered.

Cyrus reached Haddick and dropped down beside him. Blood poured from his lower stomach. "You'll be all right, brother," he assured him. Cyrus quickly assessed his men. Everan, Bash, Kord, Jaem. While bloody, they were all uninjured.

Haddick struggled to speak.

"Save your strength," Cyrus said as he looped an arm underneath him. A sword through the stomach would have been fatal for a fighter in any other fighting house, but not House Pyro. Not with Teron. Cyrus breathed an air of thanks that it hadn't been to the chest—they had time to get him back to the villa. "Let's get you to Teron. You'll be fine."

Everan moved to Haddick's other side, and Kord and Jaem took his feet. Together they lifted and carried their friend from the arena.

"Six!" Cyrus bellowed out as they stepped through the gate.

"Six!" the gate guard called.

They made their way down the long tunneled hall from the arena, carrying Haddick. The tightness of his body lessened as they went. He was losing consciousness. Perhaps that was better than suffering through the pain. Cyrus was grateful the villa wasn't far. With luck, Teron would heal him quickly, and when Haddick woke again, it would be as if this had never happened.

They wove through the corridors, doing their best to keep from jostling their friend, but as they passed a side hall, a woman's voice called out.

It was the faintest of calls.

"Lucien."

Cyrus stopped abruptly. Prickles rose up along the back of his spine.

Kord grunted as they all staggered to a stop. "What the f—"

"Did you hear that?"

"Hear what?"

But Cyrus just stared down into the darkness of the side hall. His hearing sharpened.

That name...

Everan said something to him, but he didn't catch it.

That name...

Maybe he'd imagined it. No. He'd worked hard to forget that name, to strip it from every piece of himself, from every dark corner of his mind—to erase it as though it had never existed.

"Lucien," came the voice again, jarring him just as much as the first time.

"That. Did you hear it?"

Everan gave an ever-so-slight shake of his head.

Then the voice came again, quieter now, but somehow more powerful. The whisper of a sinister siren.

"Lucien."

His breaths came faster. No one knew that name. Not Everan, not Kord, not Kieve. No one. Yet *someone* did.

And she was calling to him.

"Take him," Cyrus said to Bash.

"But what are you—"

"Take him."

Bash quickly moved to take his place carrying Haddick. Cyrus nodded for the small group to keep on. "Go. Get Haddick to Teron. I'll follow."

"Wait—what are you going to do?" Everan asked.

"Just go."

Everan glanced down the dark hallway, then back at him. "Cyrus," he said warily.

"Go on. I'll see you back at the villa."

Reluctantly, they moved off again down the hall toward the exit and the cart that would take them to the villa and to Teron. Cyrus watched them go. Waiting. His heart pounding.

When they disappeared, he turned back toward the hall.

Back toward the voice.

CHAPTER FIVE

Cyrus eyed the dark corridor. His pulse thrummed in his ears. The voice that had called him didn't come again, but it still echoed in his mind. It wove itself into memories long buried, threatening to pull them to the surface. He wouldn't let it. He shook his head, forcing those memories back down. But the call—it held him. It wouldn't let him go.

It beckoned him.

Slowly, he started down the hall.

Closed cells lined the sides. These weren't the normal holding chambers for waiting fighters. The doors to these cells were solid, with barred center openings barely large enough to put a hand through.

He passed the first cell, pausing to look inside. It was empty.

He kept on.

The second cell wasn't empty. It held a small person curled in a corner. A man or a woman, he couldn't tell. Was this who had called to him?

Two guards and their dogs passed in the main hall, and Cyrus pressed himself against the shadowed wall to keep from being seen. The arena guards were relatively lenient with team leads, like Cyrus, but they wouldn't be if they found him here. And the dogs absolutely wouldn't be.

"A drink?" came the voice again, from farther down the hall.

Cyrus's head snapped toward it. He couldn't yet see her. *The woman from the cage?* No. It couldn't be. But she'd said the same thing, with the same voice, when he'd seen her at the villa. What was she doing at the arena? In a cell like this?

He glanced back toward the main hall, checking for guards. Seeing none, he continued on. He passed two more cells, not bothering to look inside. The voice hadn't come from them. When he reached the far chamber, he paused, then slowly peered through the small barred opening of the door.

It *was* the woman.

She hung in chains in the center of the cell, her arms stretched above her head. Around her lay a circle of white powder. Flour? Chalk? Her head rested against her manacled arm, tired and weak, but her green eyes almost seemed to smile.

"Lucien," she said again.

He'd already heard her say it, but hearing it again still stopped his breath. His pulse raced, faster than before a fight. "Why do you call me that?" How could she know?

The smile in her eyes moved to her lips. "It's your name."

He'd had many names over his lifetime, a new one with each master until he'd reached gold-tier status. Now no one dared change his name, not even Pyro. It was a name known to every lover of the bloodsport. And he liked the name Cyrus.

But *Lucien*...

"I can smell you," she said. "I smell the power in you."

So, she was also plagued with madness. "I don't have power."

She gave snort of amusement. "Give me a drink." Her voice was seductive. Smoky.

But he shook his head. "I don't think you're thirsty."

"Not water. Give me your hand."

Not water. *Blood.*

At least she was honest this time, but... "Based on our last encounter, I'm going to have to say *no*."

Her smile dropped. "Lucien, please."

The door was locked. He couldn't reach her even if he wanted to. But he didn't want to. He certainly didn't want to be caught in this woman's mind. "That's not my name," he said, "and still—no."

Her eyes flashed black, then back to green.

"How did you do that?" he asked. "Your eyes."

"Give me your hand and I'll tell you."

Right. "I don't care to know that much." He moved to leave.

"Seer!"

He stopped. "I'm not a seer." Seers saw the future. He saw... not the future. He didn't see anything. He merely had dreams. About weird, worthless shit.

She fought against her manacles, betraying her desperation now.

He couldn't help his curiosity, though. "You want my blood. Why?"

Her face tightened and her lips thinned.

This was a waste of time. Cyrus turned again to leave.

"Please," she called. "I'm sorry."

He paused and, leaning close against the barred opening in the door, gave a small scoff. "Here's the thing. I'm not sure you actually mean that."

Her face darkened. "This isn't a game, seer."

"I told you, I'm not a seer."

"How long have you had the visions? Or do you still think they're dreams?"

He stilled.

"Do you find yourself in the minds of others?" she asked.

His pulse quickened again, and his breaths came faster. "How do you know this?"

"I told you. I smell you."

This was some kind of trick. "You smell blood and sweat."

"And power. I can give you more power. Just give me your blood."

He ran his eyes up the chains that held her. "You don't look like you have any power to give."

"I can destroy this arena and everyone in it!" she hissed at him.

He took a step back. He almost believed her. *No.* He didn't. He wanted to. He'd give anything to bring this arena to the ground, with everyone in it, but these were only the ramblings of a mad woman, or a woman trying to manipulate him. What did she want? Or perhaps an even more puzzling question... "Why are you here?"

She scowled. "Have you not heard? The grand finale. Six days' time. They're going to burn the witches."

He hadn't heard that, and he tilted his head to the side. "Is that what you are? A witch?" He didn't believe in witches.

"Give me your hand and I'll show you what I am," she snapped, all efforts at nicety now gone.

He snorted. "Forgive me if I don't trust you."

"I don't have time for this."

"It sounds like you have six days." He moved from the door and turned back down the hall.

"Lucien!" she called after him.

It sent a prickle up his spine, but he kept walking.

"Seer!"

Still, he ignored her. He reached the end of the side hall, and as he rounded the corner into the main corridor, he almost collided with a guard.

He stiffened, but when he saw that it wasn't an arena guard with a dog, he eased. It was the lead guard of House Pyro   Hephain.

"Where were you?" Hephain asked him. "Why didn't you come with the others?"

Cyrus shrugged. "I stayed to watch the next fight." Fighters weren't allowed to watch the fights, although there were a few secret pockets in the arena that Cyrus took advantage of from time to time. Still, he didn't mind telling Hephain this. What would he do? Nothing. Hephain wasn't one for punishment.

The guard's eyes narrowed. He didn't believe him anyway. "Who was it?"

"If you wanted to see it, you should have been here," Cyrus quipped back. He kept moving and stepped outside to the loading area. Everan and the team had already taken the wagon back to the villa.

Hephain followed Cyrus out into the late-afternoon sun and mounted his horse, his eyes still filled with suspicion. Two additional guards sat mounted, waiting. The rest had gone with the wagon.

Cyrus sighed. Three horses, three guards. He'd have to walk. Fortunately, it wasn't too far.

The setting sun did little to break the heat. Sand stuck to his damp skin, rubbing him raw on the edges of the wrap around his chest as he moved. Thankfully, a wagon from House Lycus stopped, offering him a ride. While bloodsport fighters showed no mercy in a match, they tended to look after one another outside the arena. Cyrus was appreciative.

As he jumped up and took a seat, his eyes trailed the chain running the length of the wagon that was clipped to each fighter's manacles. Although this was normal, Cyrus often forgot. While fighters of House Pyro also wore manacles—thick cuffs of metal fitted around each wrist, covering half their forearms—rarely were they chained. Most men took it as lenience, but Cyrus knew exactly what it was. Pyro was daring them to run. Because he liked to punish them.

Perhaps he hoped Cyrus would run.

Cyrus had never even considered it. Nor would he. He wouldn't abandon his brothers, and he wouldn't abandon a potential opportunity to take down Pyro.

"Is your man gonna be all right?" Ryman, the House Lycus lead, asked him.

Haddick. Cyrus nodded. "Yeah, he'll be fine."

"Good," Ryman said with a nod back. "Good."

"Hey…" Cyrus paused, then asked, "Have you heard anything about witches? Being brought to the arena?"

"Witches?" Ryman snorted. "You believin' in all that?"

Cyrus shook his head. "No."

"Good," Ryman said again. "They're just trying to throw us off our game."

Right.

When they reached the villa, Cyrus cuffed Ryman on the shoulder in thanks before dropping down off the wagon and then striding through the gates of the villa. He headed straight to Teron's work chamber, but when he arrived, the room was empty. Where was Haddick? Teron couldn't have healed him that quickly; the injury was too severe. He stepped back out into the hall. It was also empty. Too empty. And quiet. Too quiet.

He followed the hall down and back outside. The courtyard was vacant as he made his way across it. Where was everyone?

Then he spotted Bash in the practice corral, a lone figure leaning against the fence.

"Bash," Cyrus called out. "Where's Haddick? And Everan?"

Bash turned when he heard him. His forehead was etched in pain, his eyes red.

Unease grew heavy in his stomach. "Bash?"

Tears streamed down the fighter's face, and he drew a ragged breath through his mouth. But no words came.

"What's happened?" Cyrus asked him.

Bash drew in another ragged breath. "Haddick..."

No. Cyrus's stomach dropped.

Bash's lip trembled. "It's my fault."

Cyrus shook his head. "What? No—"

"If I'd have made that first kill, you would have been free to help him. It's my fault he—"

His words broke on a sob.

Cyrus reached out and gripped the fighter's shoulders. Bash crumbled, and Cyrus pulled him close. The wounds of his chest burned under his wrap as he held him, but he ignored it as he fought his own emotion.

"You said he'd be all right," Bash cried.

Those words were like a dagger. He had said that. He'd believed it. And Haddick wasn't all right.

No matter how well Cyrus battled or how hard he tried, he couldn't save them all. These people he loved.

He couldn't escape the loss.

This was the bloodsport.

Every muscle of his body ached. Cyrus lay in a tub of water that had long run cold, trying to soak the linen wrap from where it had melded to the torn skin of his chest. It hurt, but he didn't have the energy to deal with it, or the will. He almost wanted the pain to distract him from the chaos of a day that had exhausted him with every emotion—happiness for Bash reaching the bronze tier, utter loss and sorrow for Haddick, thankfulness for Everan, who'd overseen Haddick's body being taken to the pyre, and complete rage at Pyro for spitting on it.

There was the overwhelming need for revenge, and to *avenge*, with a hate that threatened to consume him. It was always on the verge of consuming him. Not just hate for Pyro. Hate for everyone in every kingdom who fed this world of violence.

Rael.

The Shadowlands.

Serra.

Hate for everyone who'd put him here. Hate for everyone who'd abandoned him.

His mother, even though she was dead.

His father, who he could only wish was dead.

And then there was the person who'd hurt him most of all...

His fingers curled under the water. Somewhere inside, a memory stirred. Blond hair. Blue eyes. A brother who'd once been his whole world.

Outside, wagons rattled through the courtyard, snapping him back. He was too tired to rise and look. Instead, he just listened to the snorts and harness chinks of horses. Guards barked orders, although he couldn't make out their words. Then came the creak and latching of metal cage doors.

It was likely the late delivery of another of Pyro's purchases. Maybe it was another witch bound for the arena.

His mind shifted to the woman. The *witch*. Cyrus had never met a witch. *Because they weren't real.* He'd never met anyone with abilities apart from himself and Teron. But if there were witches, and the king wanted them, it would be Pyro he would ask to acquire them.

How did one catch a witch? And how did one keep her? Was she still there, in her cell?

With her green eyes.

She'd called him by a name he hadn't heard since he was a boy. A name he had tried to forget. He'd nearly succeeded. Until now.

She'd also called him a seer. She'd known about his dreams—she'd called them visions. Were they visions? Were they to come true? Cyrus hadn't known any of his dreams to come true, but he also never knew the people he saw. Maybe she was wrong. Maybe they were just simple dreams. But she'd known about his ability to enter the minds of others.

What did she want from him? His blood, although he couldn't guess why.

He didn't care. He wasn't cruel enough to be without pity for her circumstance, but he had his own challenges to deal with. And if she was truly a witch, she'd have power—she could figure out the means to help herself. There wasn't anything he could do. He couldn't even help the people he truly cared about.

He'd stopped by Kieve's chamber before returning to his own. Kieve was the same as when Cyrus had seen him that morning—he hadn't moved from his bed. He didn't answer when Cyrus called to him, but when Cyrus had put his hand on his shoulder, he'd trembled.

"Rest, then, brother," Cyrus had told him. He didn't know what else to say. He didn't know how to fix a broken man.

Rage built in his core at the hell of a world that showed no mercy.

Cyrus would have no mercy for this world.

Chapter Six

Cold. It was so cold. He couldn't feel his feet. Snow fell around him. He couldn't run anymore. He couldn't follow her.

She'd left him.

Alone.

To die.

He had a sickness, she'd said—an evil inside him. And she'd left him. But still, he called for her.

"Mother!" he screamed.

His tears froze on his cheeks. He knew she wasn't coming back, but he couldn't stop himself. "Mother!" he screamed again.

The biting wind howled through the trees, mocking him.

She wasn't coming.

"Alexander!" he called.

Blood of his blood, flesh of his flesh. No closer had two brothers been. But Alexander wasn't coming for him either.

No one was coming for him.

Cyrus sat up with a start, gasping for breath. His skin was ice-cold, yet sweat covered him. He looked around—he was in his chamber. He swallowed as his breaths calmed. It had been over twenty years since that day in the forest, and at least ten since he'd last been haunted by it in his dreams.

The witch. This was her fault—reminding him...

Cyrus raked his hands through his hair and over his face, solidifying himself in the present. That memory—it had been a long time ago. He was no longer that boy, no longer that weak.

He kicked himself up and off the bed and splashed water over his face from the basin on the side table. He had another fight today; he needed to focus. His mind wanted to drift back, to linger in the past that haunted him, but he couldn't let it. The *fight*, he told himself, and he forced his focus.

Four on four. It would be Cyrus, Kord, Ram, and Sergen. Sergen was a copper-tier fighter and new to House Pyro. Cyrus was still feeling him out, learning his strengths and weaknesses. He had confidence in him, though—he was showing all the right signs of a team fighter. He was a little soft, perhaps, but that was better than the alternative.

Sometimes men weren't team fighters. They didn't have it in them, or their habits were too hard to break. If they put other men in the house at risk, Cyrus had to eliminate them. An accident during training at the villa, or a poor setup in the arena—there were many ways to get rid of a man. Fortunately, it didn't have to happen often, but occasionally, there came a fighter that didn't fit, a fighter that jeopardized them all.

Cyrus understood the singular drive, the selfish focus. It came from the desperation to stay alive, but the only way to stay alive was with the team. It was a cruel world, and Cyrus didn't want to make it crueler, but he did what he had to do to protect *all* the fighters in the house.

The sun hadn't yet risen, and he didn't expect many men in the dining hall when he arrived, but there were a few. Perhaps they'd had nightmares too. Cyrus wondered if there was a man in the villa who *didn't* have nightmares. Perhaps Pyro. Pyro *was* the nightmare.

Cyrus noticed Kieve sitting at the end of one of the long tables. It brought a small rush of relief. He was happy to see him finally up and out. Kieve needed to get back to normal—or normal enough to fight. A man who couldn't fight in House Pyro was a dead man.

Kieve kept his eyes down on his uneaten food as Cyrus took the seat across from him.

"Are you back on the schedule?" Cyrus asked him.

A delicate arm set a plate of steaming pork and eggs in front of him, and Cyrus looked up to find Visa's smiling face.

"You're up early," she said.

He gave an appreciative nod to Everan's woman. She often helped Portia in the kitchen and tended the fighters. "Thank you," he told her.

She raised a brow. "Did you get any sleep last night?"

"Enough." He never got enough sleep.

Her eyes told him she didn't buy his answer. "Can I get you anything else?"

He shook his head as he picked up his fork. "This is good."

She smiled again and swept back into the kitchen.

Cyrus turned his gaze back on Kieve. His friend still wasn't well. He hadn't touched his food, there was no color in his face, and the dark circles under his eyes gave a haunted look. He was a haunted man.

"You need to eat something," Cyrus told him. "Are you on the schedule?" he asked again. Kieve would have had to get sign-off by a Sport Authority physician. It wasn't something difficult, but looking at the despondent fighter... everything might be difficult for Kieve now.

Kieve sat blankly as he thumbed his fork in his fist.

"You need to get back on the fight card." Cyrus hated pushing him, but he had no choice.

The fighter only stared down at his plate.

"Kieve."

Still, Kieve said nothing.

Cyrus didn't know what to do. He wanted to support him with gentle kindness, give him time, but they didn't have time. He rose abruptly and snapped out his hand, grabbing Kieve's face and making him look at him.

Kieve tried to shrink away, his eyes wide, his breaths short, but Cyrus held him.

"Don't let that bastard break you," Cyrus said between his teeth, leaning closer over the table. "There will come a day that he will answer for everything he's done. But you have to stay strong." Cyrus would make him stay strong.

When Kieve finally spoke, his voice came in barely a whisper. "You don't know. You don't know what he did."

"I know." Cyrus released Kieve's face but shifted his hand back around the nape of his friend's neck, still holding him tightly. "I saw from his mind. I was right there with you."

Kieve's eyes welled.

"I'm still with you," Cyrus told him. He saw the doubt in Kieve's face, the brokenness, the lack of hope. Cyrus squeezed him tighter. "I will get you out of this place. I swear to you. Do you hear me?"

Slowly, Kieve nodded.

"But you have to get back on the schedule. Can you do that?"

Again, Kieve gave ever the faintest nod.

Cyrus nodded back. "Now eat," he said.

Sweat dripped down his brow. Cyrus gritted his teeth as he stood at the gate of the arena. Kord, a gold-tier fighter and one of his closest friends, stood beside him. It was a four-man match: Cyrus and one of his younger fighters, Ram; Kord; and Sergen, the new guy. Together they'd face four men from House Flavian.

There were about two hundred fighting houses serving Rael's arena, each with a couple hundred fighters. Cyrus didn't know them all, but he knew most house leads, and many of the gold- and silver-tier fighters, as well as a few others. Then there were the countless churn houses. People who couldn't afford regular arena entry often turned to churn-house fights—unregulated houses that pitted untrained, even unfit, men against each other during off-peak hours. They didn't bother with tiering—their fighters didn't live long enough for that, or promising ones were picked up by a noble house. Sergen had been a churn-house fighter, bought by House Malek before being sold to House Pyro.

Sergen needed a kill today, and Cyrus was feeling confident. They'd run through their strategy multiple times that morning, even though it was quite simple. Cyrus and Kord would make the first kill, then Cyrus would pair with Sergen to help set him up. If needed, Kord would join after he finished his opponent, unless Ram needed help.

The gate rose, and Cyrus strode through. "Four!" he called.

"Four!" came the echo behind him.

"Four!" the gate guard bellowed.

Cyrus and his men were the second team into the arena. Cyrus chose his target and broke into a run. Kord split slightly to his right, just as Everan always did. Everan and Kord were his closest friends, and Cyrus relied on them both with complete faith, and not just in the arena. Out of all the men, Cyrus had known Kord the longest. Of the five houses he'd belonged to, he'd been with Kord in three. Pyro had purchased them from House Parvil, where they'd both gained their gold-tier status. Together they'd come a long way, and they'd go a long way still.

Cyrus set his charge and focused.

He saw every detail of his target—every piece of armor, every scrap of fabric, every part of exposed flesh. Each footfall across the burning sand came like thunder in his ears. His nostrils flared, breathing deep the blood-laden air.

Time slowed.

To nearly a stop.

Then it sped forward, hurling him into the clash.

His target swept up with his sword, expecting Cyrus to leap and rain an attack from above. Instead, Cyrus dropped low, slicing through a leg and bringing him down. Blood sprayed his shoulder as Kord's sword claimed the man's head.

Cyrus and Kord worked fluidly, extensions of each other. They knew each other's moves like their own. Years of practice had made them perfect in their dance. Divinely perfect. But they didn't have time for pride, and they swung their attention back to the fight.

There were three men left from House Flavian. Ram and Sergen each quickly took an opponent, and Kord careened to meet a third before the man could join a two-on-one against Ram. Cyrus turned his focus on Sergen.

His copper-tier teammate was skilled, but Cyrus quickly realized Sergen's opponent was better. Sergen would need help. Cyrus maneuvered to the side to put their opponent between them, but the man backed toward the cats' side gates, using them as a defensive advantage.

He wouldn't be able to do that for long. Sergen and Cyrus pressed him back farther.

The man wore a half-face helm—his peripheral would be hindered, as would his hearing. Would he catch when the cats' gates started to rise? Cyrus swore under his breath. Damned if he had to end up saving this man just so Sergen could kill him.

Sergen launched forward in a clean series of moves—a little too calculated and stiff for Cyrus's taste. They'd need to work on that more in practice. The man drove a skilled counter. Their blades locked, and the Flavian fighter shoved Sergen back.

This was taking too long.

Cyrus looked for an opportunity to deliver a debilitating strike, but their opponent was quick and defended himself well. Was this a silver-tier fighter? Cyrus didn't know him.

A snarl came from the shadows behind the gates. The restless cats knew their release was near.

They needed to end this.

The Flavian fighter again locked blades with Sergen, and Cyrus saw his opportunity. He lunged forward, ripping his blade along the man's hamstring. When the fighter buckled and jerked sideways, Cyrus delivered a blow with his elbow that knocked the helm from his head. But when he saw the man underneath, he stumbled backward.

The Flavian fighter staring back at him was blond. Like Cyrus.

Too much like him.

It was Cyrus's hair.

And the face looking back at him—Cyrus's face.

No, not Cyrus's face.

Alexander's face.

Alexander. It was his brother.

CHAPTER SEVEN

All reason left him.

Cyrus's blood heated as he stood in the center of the arena, staring back at his brother. Fury welled in his core.

He'd kill him.

He'd kill him right here.

Cyrus surged forward.

Alexander tried to launch a defense on one leg, but he never stood a chance. Cyrus arced his sword out with a force that knocked Alexander's weapon from his hand. Then he spun, using the momentum, and drove his blade through Alexander's chest.

As Alexander gaped up at him, Cyrus pushed his blade deeper. To the hilt. Then he grabbed him by the throat. It wasn't enough to watch Alexander die. He had to feel it. And he needed Alexander to look at him. Cyrus needed to be the last person he saw. So many things he'd wanted to say over the years, so many things Alexander needed to know, but in the moment, words wouldn't come.

"Cyrus!"

He heard his name, but he couldn't peel his eyes away. As Alexander's weight sank, Cyrus could only stare as the life left him.

Hands grabbed Cyrus, shaking him. Kord's hands. Kord's voice.

"Get to the center!" Kord yelled.

Cyrus looked back to the man on his blade, still a blond man, but the dead eyes looking back at him weren't deep cerulean blue. In fact, the face looking back at him wasn't anything like his own. Cyrus pushed him off his sword, and the body collapsed to the ground.

It wasn't Alexander.

Cyrus blinked, his heart still hammering. His fingers were numb against the hilt of his sword. *It wasn't Alexander.*

Kord grabbed him again, jerking him out of the way as a flash of black ripped past. The claws that reached for him just barely missed. Cyrus stumbled back.

He hadn't realized the cat had been released. Cyrus finally found his wits, and he, Kord, and Sergen bolted toward the center of the arena, reaching it just as the cat snapped to the end of its chain with a snarl.

Kord raced into action. "Sergen!" he bellowed as he tore toward Ram, who was fighting the last of the Flavian men. Cyrus glanced around. He hadn't noticed Kord had killed a third man, but he *did* notice a second cat was now free on the other side of the arena. They had only moments before the third would be released.

Kord slipped in and took over Ram's opponent. A lower-tier fighter—it was only a short exchange before Kord had him clipped at the calves, setting Sergen up for a sure kill. This time, Sergen got it.

The fight was over. Cheers deafened the arena.

The cats' chains tightened, and the beasts were dragged back to their cages as Cyrus stood, still in a daze, grasping for his senses. He looked around. The Flavian fighters were dead. Ram and Kord stared back at him, as did Sergen.

What had just happened? A deep crease of confusion lay between Sergen's brows. Cyrus gave him an apologetic tilt of his head. "I'm sorry," he told him. "That was your kill."

Sergen was quiet for a moment, then gave a short nod. "It's all right. I got it in the end. I know you were trying to help set it up."

Cyrus glanced back at the dead Flavian fighter he'd thought was Alexander.

"Did you know him?" Sergen asked.

Cyrus shook his head. He didn't know this man, and he didn't know what had come over him. He'd never lost his focus in a fight. But he'd thought he'd seen—

A rough hand grabbed him again. "What the fuck was that?" Kord spat.

Cyrus shook his head again. "Nothing," he muttered. But it wasn't nothing. He needed to get out of here. He staggered back and started toward the exit.

Kord followed him. "Hey. Are you all right?"

He ignored the question. Of course he wasn't all right. "Four!" he shouted to the gate guard as they passed through.

"Four!" came the echo.

His mind was still in a fog. What was going on with him? Was the witch doing this to him? Or maybe she'd just stirred his long-dead memories, which were now coming back to haunt him.

"Cyrus!" Kord called after him.

As they made their way through the narrow corridor, a passing man shouldered by him. Hard. Cyrus nearly lost his balance but caught himself against the wall and snapped his head to see Bravat, the crowd-pleasing mountain of a man who fought for House Massus.

"An off day, Cyrus?" Bravat goaded. "That was a close one."

Had he been watching?

Bravat was a silver-tier fighter, but he'd had a lightning rise through the levels, one of the fastest in arena history, no doubt contributing to his intolerable ego. Cyrus tried to ignore him.

Bravat gave a hearty chuckle. "I would have been disappointed if you'd died before our house match in two days."

House Pyro would fight House Massus in two days? When Cyrus had checked earlier that morning, he hadn't seen that. It must be a change. But no matter—his men would take it as any other match. And be victorious.

Cyrus didn't say a word; he only kept walking.

"See you in the arena, Cyrus," Bravat called after him.

Cyrus didn't fear a fight with a team from House Massus, but it wouldn't be an easy one if he wasn't at his best, and right now, he wasn't at his best. He was still unsettled by the stir of memories. The witch was messing with him, and the heat of anger flashed inside him.

He paused in the main corridor at the witch's hall, glancing down into its darkness. There was no voice this time, but still she called to him.

"Cyrus?" Kord said, stopping as well. "What's going on with you?"

"You go ahead. I'll meet you at the wagon."

"Not this again—"

"I won't be long."

"You know, you're being really fucking weird."

"Just... I'll meet you back at the wagon."

Kord's lips thinned, but he nodded for Ram and Sergen to follow and kept down the hall that would lead them out to the loading area.

Cyrus did a quick glance for any guards and their dogs, then slipped down the dark side hall. The first chamber, which had been empty before, now held another woman. She hung from chains in the center of the cell with a white circle around her, the same as the witch. Was this woman a witch too?

He passed the second chamber, which held a different occupant than it had before—another woman, chained in the same manner. The women said nothing, but their eyes followed him as he passed. Unease needled him.

Cyrus set his attention on the witch's chamber ahead. The hall was quiet. Was she still in there? When he reached the door, he looked through the small, barred opening.

The witch was there. She hung from the center, limp, as though dead. But her emerald eyes stared back at him.

"Ah, the seer not named Lucien," she said.

That name again. His skin prickled. Was she the one tormenting his mind? Trying to manipulate him...

"Are you haunting me?" he asked.

"That's more your ability than mine," she answered.

What did that mean? "Stop your games."

Her eyes narrowed. "I don't play games."

He didn't believe her.

"What do you want, seer?" Her voice sweetened. "Couldn't stop thinking about me?" Was she goading him?

The heat of anger tinged his skin. "Just checking to see if they burned you at the stake yet," he quipped back. Perhaps after they did, this nonsense would stop.

Her smirk fell, and she glared back at him.

Cyrus turned to catch up with Kord and the others.

Chapter Eight

The evening gave little reprieve from the heat. Sweat slicked his skin despite the cold bath he'd just taken after returning from the arena. Cyrus's mind was still on the fight earlier that day. On Alexander's face. Or what he'd thought was Alexander's face.

Every time he closed his eyes, the flashes of images returned. It was a face he'd never seen as an adult, but he knew it was just like his own. As children, Cyrus and his twin brother had been indistinguishable. Probably not so much anymore. A man wore his past on his face, and his brother's life had been very different from his own. Alexander had a life of privilege, while Cyrus rotted away in this hell.

Cyrus could *feel* him, feel his power. All the time. They were the same. He knew Alexander could feel him too. Yet he never came. He never came to bring Cyrus home. It was a weight in his chest, reminding him daily of those who'd abandoned him, forsaken him—those he'd loved most. His brother. His father. But now his love for them was gone. It had festered and died and rotted into the burning hatred that fueled his fight. The hurt that nearly broke him was now what made him strong.

And if he ever broke free from this hell—

A noise outside caught his attention and drew him to the window. Whoever had come was just around the corner, beyond his sight, but he heard them—horses, men. Another purchase, maybe. More deliveries than usual had come over the past several days, some at odd hours of the night, and not all of them fighters. But whatever this was, it was louder.

A laugh carried through the air.

Who the fuck would be laughing?

Cyrus quickly pulled on his boots and strode out of his chamber, past the guard to see the commotion.

Three supply wagons were in the courtyard. Servants unloaded bags of rice and grain to the cellars. Portia, Visa, and three other women worked to carry meats and vegetables into the kitchen. Nothing unusual.

Then Cyrus spotted another wagon at the end, with Pyro standing beside it. It wasn't a supply wagon—it was a purchase wagon—and Cyrus stiffened when he saw the men.

Bravat, the crowd-riling fighter, dropped down to the ground, followed by another dozen men. He wore a large grin as Pyro cuffed him on the shoulder.

Cyrus's chest tightened. Pyro had bought Bravat? If there was one thing worse than having to fight against Bravat in the arena, it would be fighting *with* him on the same team.

"It's a great risk to make a buy before a fight, and you cost me quite a fortune, but I knew it was a risk to take," Pyro said with glee. "Now your win today is a win for House Pyro!"

Bravat and his men had prevailed in their fight after Cyrus's team had finished earlier in the day, but Cyrus hardly considered it a win. Bravat's team had lost two men in the match, one of them a gold-tier fighter. Not that a gold-tier fighter's life was worth more—or maybe it was—but to have come so far, to have survived so much... Cyrus's stomach soured. Perhaps it was a blessing, for both Bravat's dead men and Haddick, that they no longer had to face the hell that was House Pyro.

Cyrus's eyes found Everan, who stood across the courtyard with Kord. His face was heavy. The loss of Haddick and now the purchase of Bravat and his team—it was a difficult week for him too. It wasn't that the fighters of the house minded new purchases. They welcomed them, even. Fighters didn't have a choice; they were all forced into this life. They were all at the mercy of the masters who bought and sold them like livestock, but fighters like Bravat put themselves before their brothers. They couldn't be trusted and were a liability. As lead of House Pyro, Cyrus now had to deal with this liability.

Cyrus watched Bravat as he and his men looked around the courtyard with grins on their faces. Yes, House Pyro was beautiful. It was the most lavish villa in Rael's capital city of Carn, one of the most lavish villas in all of Rael, and Pyro's fighters had almost any luxury. Bravat and his men thought they'd reached the top of bloodsport success.

How quickly they'd learn...

"Show them to their rooms," Pyro told a nearby servant. He waved his hand at Bravat and his men. "You fought well today. Take a woman, your pick. Rest. And tomorrow—another win!"

Bravat's smile grew, and his eyes landed on Visa, who was just finishing helping Portia with the kitchen delivery. His smile widened. "Her."

Visa froze.

Everan rocked off the post he'd been leaning against, and his body tightened. No one ever claimed Visa. Everyone knew she was Everan's—all but Pyro, who'd use it against him if he did.

Pyro grunted with a nod, oblivious and uncaring.

Everan could say nothing. He hadn't fought today; he had no right to a reward, and he couldn't expose his heart or his marriage—it would mean death for them both. But as Everan stepped forward with a dark fire of fight in his eyes, Cyrus worried that his friend wasn't thinking of what he couldn't or shouldn't do.

"I've already claimed her," Cyrus called out.

Everan's head twisted toward him. Cyrus never asked for women, although there were a couple that occasionally came to his chamber.

Pleasures of the flesh did help everyone forget everything, for a little while.

Bravat snorted his objection, and Pyro's eyes narrowed.

"Do I not get first choice?" Cyrus challenged. Not only was he the house lead, but he was Pyro's top fighter with the most team wins in the history of the bloodsport. With or without a kill, it was unlikely Pyro would refuse him, but he *had* gotten a kill, and a team win. Bravat had suffered two losses, making Cyrus all the bolder.

Pyro looked at Bravat, then back at Cyrus. He frowned. "Fine, take the bitch," he told Cyrus. Then he waved to the servant and said, "See Bravat gets another."

Cyrus cut Bravat a warning eye before he crossed the courtyard and clasped Visa's upper arm. He pulled her roughly back toward the fighters' side of the villa. When they reached his chamber, he jerked her inside and kicked the door shut behind him. It was a little early to be retiring for the evening, but it wasn't like he'd had anything else planned.

Now alone, he released Visa. He hadn't wanted to be rough with her, but his claim needed to be seen as a show of power, not him favoring her, which would make her a target for both Bravat and Pyro. "Did I hurt you?" he asked as he moved to the side table to pour himself a cup of water.

She shook her head. "Not really, no."

He nodded and drained his cup.

She gave him an appreciative smile. "Thank you. You could have taken Cassia or Gemma and had a real reward. And I know they were looking forward to maybe spending time with you."

Cassia and Gemma—he would have liked spending time with them too. But this was more important. For Everan. And for Visa.

Fuck the gods, it was hot. He stripped down to his braies and dropped onto the bed. "I'm tired. And the best reward would be some sleep." Maybe an early evening wasn't the worst thing. He let out a long sigh as he shifted his arm up and over his head, covering his eyes with his forearm. He'd left a strip of bed open for Visa. If he were a gentleman, he'd offer her the whole bed and sleep on the floor. But he wasn't a gentleman—he was a man with a fight in the morning, and he needed sleep. And regardless of what he did or didn't offer her, it would still be better than an evening with Bravat.

Quiet settled in the room, but not in his mind. His thoughts were on the day—on the fight, on Alexander. He shifted to his side, then again to his back. Frustration barbed him as he realized sleep wouldn't come.

The bed dipped as Visa sat down on its edge. "Can I help you?" she asked softly.

He lifted his arm from over his eyes and looked at her.

She *could* help him. He shouldn't let her—he'd told himself he wouldn't do this again, at least not with Visa. This was Everan's woman, not someone he should indulge to meet his own needs. But he desperately wanted to escape the torment of his mind, and slowly, he nodded.

Visa smiled and shifted closer to him.

He reached above the headboard to the bottom corner of the window, where the small tip of a nail protruded. He pricked his thumb against it, drawing blood, then he brought the swell to her forehead and gently pressed a crimson droplet to her skin. And he closed his eyes.

He let his blood transport him, and when he opened his eyes again, he stood in the middle of a sprawling field, with the grass as high as his hips. Rolling hills spread as far as he could see, and as the sun set on the horizon, it lit the grass in gold. A homestead sat in the distance. This had been Visa's home before she'd been stolen away, but she kept its memory alive in her heart, and she was sharing it with him. Cyrus dropped down and lay on his back, his arms outstretched above his head, looking up at the sky. He couldn't hear the grasses whisper as they swayed in the breeze around him—he could never hear while in someone's memories. But he could imagine, and he could enjoy it all the same.

These were the best of friends—those who gave him the quiet of their minds, those who helped him rest.

He felt Visa's fingers run through his hair, helping him relax. The tension in his shoulders faded, and his body grew heavy.

And finally, in the field of high golden grass, sleep came.

Cyrus pulled on his leathers to the sounds of morning. When he'd woken, Visa had already gone; she was probably helping Portia with breakfast.

The basin water was cold, and his skin prickled as he splashed it over his face. It was the only cool he'd feel all day, and he relished it. But then intrusive thoughts of the day before came flowing back. He tried to push them from his mind—all the memories, memories from when he was young. When he was weak.

Why were they coming back? And why now?

Cyrus stood, letting the water trickle down his neck and chest as he gripped the edge of the side table and used it to support his weight. He couldn't afford to be weak.

Voices outside carried through his window and brought him back, and he settled.

He wasn't weak anymore, he reminded himself. He was the lead fighter of the greatest fighting house in Rael, and the most famed man in the bloodsport.

Cyrus snapped the towel from where it hung near the side table and dried his skin, then pulled on his boots and stepped out into the day.

By the time he made it to the meal hall, most of the fighters had eaten and left already. Kord and Everan were still there and sat toward the end of one of the long tables. Cyrus took the seat across from them.

"We thought you'd taken your eternal rest, brother," Kord said with a grin. "We were starting to get worried that we'd have to find another man for today, which means we'd be feeding the cats this afternoon."

Kord joked, but it wasn't a joking matter. They had another fight in the late afternoon. Cyrus hated late-afternoon fights, when the sun was at its hottest and the arena was already covered in the blood of all those who'd fought before. The cats also tended to be the most agitated in the afternoon, as the guards inside poked them with spikes to rouse them from their day slumber.

But sometimes joking was all one could do.

Everan smiled at Cyrus as he swallowed the last bite of food from his plate. "Visa said she was able to help you get some sleep."

Cyrus nodded. Everan didn't look at it the same, but Cyrus viewed being in one's mind as more intimate than being in one's bed. He was always wary of intruding, but he was appreciative of both Everan and Visa.

"The most sleep I've had in months," he said, and it was true, even with the haunts of his past. He cut Everan a wry smile. "I must confess, the more she lets me in, the more I want to keep her. She has"—he held up his hands and gripped the air like flesh—"the biggest grass fields."

Everan let out a hearty laugh, and Cyrus couldn't help but join him. Then Everan's laugh faded, and his face slightly sobered. He swallowed. "Thank you for what you did. With Bravat."

Cyrus shook his head. "No need. I also benefited."

"But you didn't do it for that. And I'm grateful. We both are."

Visa stepped out of the back kitchen with a plate of steaming meat over rice and set it down in front of Cyrus with a grin. "About time you showed up. I nearly had to have a bloodsport match myself to save you some choice cuts of meat."

He dipped his head appreciatively. "Then I owe you double."

"We'll call it even." She winked at Everan and then disappeared back through the doors. Cyrus and Everan both watched her until she was gone.

Cyrus looked back at Everan, serious now, and he leaned forward onto his elbows, lowering his voice. "There will come a day that you will live the life you choose, and you won't have to fight for your time."

Everan shook his head. "I can't let myself hope for that."

"You have to. It's true. I'll get us out of this. You, Visa, Kieve, Bash..." He glanced at Kord beside Everan. "All of us."

Everan and Kord both looked at him, not wanting to hope, not wanting to risk the disappointment. False hope could kill, but real hope was the only thing that would keep them from the darkness of despair. Cyrus wouldn't let it be false.

He stabbed a piece of marinated beef and took a bite, careful not to pick up any of the rice with it—not a single grain. He knew where it came from.

The Shadowlands.

It had been Shadowmen who'd found him after his mother had abandoned him. It had been Shadowmen who'd sold him to the Serran slavers, specifically the Shadow King. And as if it weren't enough for them to profit from putting men in chains, the Shadowlands also supported the slave trade with their rice. To look at it on his plate, the continued evidence of their profit in his suffering... He'd see it rot before he let it nourish him.

Everan watched him. He said nothing, but Cyrus knew he wanted to. He'd say the same thing he'd said many times over the years. *You can't live on meat alone. You need your energy.*

But between the fresh fruits and vegetables and breads delivered to his chamber, and with meals of marinated meats, Cyrus had all he needed. He would accept nothing from the Shadowlands.

Everan kept quiet, even though his eyes didn't.

After they finished, they headed toward the central part of the villa. They'd soak in the pool for a while and rest more before the afternoon sport.

"Have you seen Kieve?" Cyrus asked as they walked. A wave of guilt hit him that he hadn't gone to see him when he'd returned from the arena the evening before.

Everan shook his head. "Visa said he took his meal in his chamber."

Cyrus frowned. He hoped Kieve wasn't regressing.

"He's still not on the schedule," Everan added.

"He's going to be," Cyrus replied. "He told me he'd get back on."

Kord shrugged. "Let's see if he'll come to the pool with us."

They headed toward his chamber, only to be met by Hephain along the way.

"Get to the arena," the lead guard told them. "House Balsam didn't show this morning. The schedule's been moved up."

"Damn," Kord muttered in disappointment, but not for missing the pool. When fighters didn't make their matches, they faced severe consequences, usually worse than the fight itself. That also meant they all had to hurry. They wouldn't be shown lenience for being late either, even if the times had changed.

Cyrus nodded to Everan and Kord. "Let's go, then."

"Not you," Hephain said to Everan and Kord. Then to Cyrus: "You'll take Bravat."

Cyrus tilted his head toward the lead guard. "What?" He couldn't have heard that right.

"With Bravat now scoring for House Pyro, the cards have changed. You, Ram, Bravat, and Val."

"What about Everan and Kord?" Cyrus asked.

"Moved to tomorrow," Hephain replied.

Cyrus glanced at both Everan and Kord in surprise. This was where Pyro's ignorance of their team dynamics really showed. He'd pushed the Sport Authority into pairing the two crowd favorites together, no doubt to draw more attention with a dream team, thinking it would be a clean win and easy money. But that wasn't how it worked. The team's practice made them perfect. Their trust made them perfect. Little did Pyro know—he'd probably just damned his top fighters.

Everan and Kord were quiet.

"We'll wait for you," Everan said grimly. "Gods keep you, brother."

CHAPTER NINE

Pyro was a fucking fool—a fool who was about to unwittingly get his two most famed fighters killed.

Cyrus and Bravat stood at the arena's gate entry, waiting. They hadn't had a single spar together. They didn't know each other's strengths to use them, or each other's weaknesses to guard them. They didn't know how to protect each other. Cyrus wasn't sure if he even wanted to protect Bravat, and he was pretty sure Bravat felt likewise.

It was a four-man fight: Cyrus and one of his younger fighters, Ram, together with Bravat and a man from Bravat's purchased team, Val. Together they'd face four men from House Camden. Ram was well settled into the bronze tier, and having already met his kill requirements, he needed only to build team wins to progress. They didn't need the numbers, which took some of the pressure off. They just needed to stay alive. Easy enough. He cast Bravat a glance from the corner of his eye. At least, he hoped it was easy enough. He didn't trust Bravat.

The gates rose. "Follow my lead," Cyrus told him.

Bravat shouldered him backward. "Stay the fuck out of my way." Then he entered first.

Cyrus glanced back at Ram, and the young fighter shook his head. This was exactly what Cyrus was worried about. He pursed his lips and followed. "Four!" he called as he stepped into the arena.

"Four!" Ram and Bravat's man, Val, both echoed.

"Four!" the gate guard confirmed.

They were the second team into the arena. Cyrus chose his target and broke into a run. Ram spread slightly to his right. This was the first time the young fighter was taking the position of Cyrus's co-sword, but Ram had seen Everan and Kord do it plenty of times, and they'd practiced it repeatedly in the sparring fields.

Cyrus gained speed, focusing. At the clash, Ram executed the sequence beautifully. Just as they'd practiced. As their opponent fell, he gave Ram a click of his tongue in approval. That had been impressively fast. Ram flashed him a grin.

This opening move was getting old, but it kept working, mostly thanks to fighters not being able to watch and study other teams. But sooner or later, their opponents would catch on, and they'd have to come up with something different. Until then...

Cyrus and Ram swung their attention back to the fight. Bravat dropped another man from the opposing team, then there were only two left from House Camden.

Three javelins lodged themselves into the sand several paces away—thrown by paying spectators. Cyrus appreciated that they were typically poor shots. What he wouldn't give to launch them back.

Now that was a thought—

The side gate of the arena rose, pulling Cyrus's attention. The cats. *Talk about a play that was getting old*, but the crowd loved the cats, and they were released almost every fight.

"Center!" Cyrus bellowed, just as the gleam of a sword came for his head. He knocked it away. High and low, left and right, he drew the man's focus to his every move and drove him back, letting Ram calculate a silent strike. When Ram saw the opening, he took it, getting the third kill.

Cyrus spun to continue but stopped when he saw the last man hanging from Bravat's sword. Bravat kicked him back and off, letting the body drop to the ground.

The arena roared with cheers from the crowd.

The chains pulled the cats back into their cages, and the gates lowered. Cyrus let out a breath of relief that the fight hadn't gone as poorly as he'd feared. In fact, it had gone exceptionally well. They'd been lucky.

Bravat held his arms high, encouraging the crowd to be louder, and they responded. Cyrus glanced at Ram with a dark brow. He hated fighting, but he hated this even more, and he turned and headed for the exit. Ram followed.

"Four!" Cyrus bellowed to the gate guard, not waiting for Bravat and Val.

"Four!" came the echo.

Cyrus was annoyed. More than annoyed. Was this how fights would be when he and Bravat were paired? It was a dangerous thing. He'd have to figure out what to do about it—how to handle Bravat.

Bravat and Val caught up, and Cyrus heard a shuffle behind him. He glanced at them over his shoulder.

"What the fuck?" Val spat, shoving Bravat.

Bravat snorted. "Be faster, and you might get one next time."

Cyrus slowed. "What's going on?" he called.

"None of your fucking business," Bravat told him.

And that was enough to send Cyrus over. He spun, nearly making Bravat run into him as he confronted him nose to nose. "I'm the lead of House Pyro," Cyrus snarled. "Everything is my fucking business." He'd drop this man here and now.

Bravat bristled, and for a minute, Cyrus thought they might actually spill blood in the transfer hall. It would gain them a severe punishment, but Cyrus didn't care about that right now.

But to Cyrus's surprise, Bravat took a wary step back. He didn't lose his attitude, though. "Val's just pissed because he needed a kill this fight," he sneered. Then he shrugged. "Now he needs two in the next, so he doesn't drop status."

Cyrus felt his lips thin and his brows drop even lower. "Why did you take two kills if he needed one?"

Bravat shrugged again. "He'll get it on the next one."

Cyrus lunged, grabbed Bravat, and shoved him against the wall. "And what if there isn't a next one?"

Bravat shoved him back. "What the fuck? Get off me!"

"Hey, what's going on?" an arena guard yelled from down the hall.

Ram grabbed Cyrus's arm. "Let him go."

"He'll damn his own men!" Cyrus spat. "And us with him!"

"Cyrus," Ram said, gripping him tighter.

Rage seeped from Cyrus's pores as his blazing stare stayed locked with Bravat's.

"Hey!" the arena guard bellowed again, and started toward them, a dog at his side.

"Cyrus," Ram called, more firmly this time.

Bravat shoved Cyrus back, then shouldered by and continued down the corridor, past another guard that had come to see what the commotion was about.

Cyrus knew there was nothing more he could do. At least, not right now. He looked at Val. "How many do you need? Two?"

Val shook his head, clearly not wanting Cyrus's support. "Don't worry about it," he said sharply. "I'm fine. I'll get them."

Except it wasn't fine, and there might not be a next time. Val followed after Bravat, and Cyrus could only watch him go.

"Come on," Ram said. "We'll figure this out back at the villa." Cyrus wasn't so sure, but he nodded, and they both headed toward the loading area and the waiting wagon that would take them back.

The water of the pool drew the heat from Cyrus's body. He'd stopped by Kieve's chamber to get him to join, but the fighter had been asleep. Cyrus had left him. It wasn't often that those who were haunted got such relief.

He sat languidly now, facing Everan and Kord, who relaxed across from him. He'd shared with them what had happened with Bravat in the arena. Neither of them was surprised, but now the question was what to do about it all.

Their discussion was cut short by the subject himself, as Bravat stepped into the pool house. A couple of his men, Arns and Bevin, followed in after him.

The big fighter was laughing. "The fucks think they—"

Bravat's voice cut when he saw Cyrus.

The teams didn't say a word to each other, but Bravat wore a smirk as he entered the water on the far side of the pool. Cyrus watched him. How ignorant this man was.

"What, you got something to say?" Bravat challenged as he sank down into the water.

Cyrus forgot sometimes that he wore his thoughts on his face. He might as well tell them. They needed to know. "You need to start looking out for one another here," he said to them. "Pyro isn't a lord you can afford to disappoint."

"Worry about yourself," Bravat sneered back. "I can handle Pyro just fine."

Cyrus snorted. "You? Handle Pyro? Do you know what he does to men who fail to make tier, or worse—lose status?"

"From where I see it, you're the only one who needs to be worried about that."

What did that mean? "I'm lead of House Pyro," Cyrus said.

"For how long?" Bravat gave a crooked smile. "You know my purchase was the most expensive one in bloodsport history?" he boasted. Like it was something to be proud of. "You don't spend that much on a man without having a plan for him."

"Don't listen to him," Kord told Cyrus. "Pyro would have to be mad to remove you as lead."

Mad, or completely ignorant of how everything worked, which Pyro was. Cyrus and Bravat were paired again for a two-on-two fight in the morning. The crowd had loved them together, and Pyro always gave the crowd what they wanted. Kord and Everan had been bumped yet another day, to a three-on-three that would again include Cyrus.

"This is the life, yeah?" Bravat said to his companions. They all wore stupid grins as they relaxed against the sides of the pool.

They had no idea what this life was.

Cyrus watched the arrogant fighter. He needed to get rid of him. Not for himself. Cyrus didn't care about being lead. He did care about his men, and Bravat would put every single one of them in jeopardy. It would be difficult to stage an accident with a silver-tier fighter that called a lot of attention to himself, but perhaps tomorrow there would be an opportunity...

Bravat looked around. "Hey, where's Val?"

His words pulled Cyrus from his plotting.

"Haven't seen him," Bevin said.

Arns snorted. "Probably sleeping."

Bravat shrugged. "He's probably still pissed at me for taking his kill. He's gotta be faster."

They all chuckled.

But there was nothing to chuckle about.

Cyrus wanted to leave; however, leaving right now would send the wrong message. So he stayed, forcing a front of indifference through their boorish banter. And the unpeaceful pools became even more so.

Kord shifted, stretching his arms out on either side of him along the pool's edge. "How's Bash?" he asked Cyrus, picking the conversation back up between the three of them.

Cyrus sighed. It had been two days since Haddick's death, for which Bash still blamed himself, but he'd make it through. "A little better. He just needs some time." Hopefully not much more time, though. The fighter was on the roster for another fight in three days, and he needed to be ready.

Bravat stood and rose from the water. "It's too crowded," he said shortly as he eyed Cyrus.

It gave Cyrus a small sense of satisfaction that his presence bothered Bravat enough to make him leave. He almost smiled.

Benly, the pool-house servant, stepped forward and handed him a towel, and Bravat snapped it from his hands and dried off. Bravat's two men stepped out as well, also taking towels.

"I'm hungry," Bravat added. "Let's go get something to eat." The three men headed toward the door. As Bravat passed Cyrus, he dropped his wet towel on the ground less than a pace from where Cyrus rested his arm against the edge. Then they exited.

Everan's eyes followed them out as Benly scrambled forward and collected the soiled towel.

"He's a risk," Kord said when they were gone.

Bravat *was* a risk, a risk that would cost them all. He had to be dealt with. "I'll take care of him," Cyrus told them.

"You'll need to be careful," Everan warned. "He's got a lot of attention on him right now."

The three of them rose from the pool and toweled off before donning their robes. Then they headed back toward their chambers to dress. As they walked, Cyrus spotted Bravat, Bevin, and Arns at the edge of the courtyard, laughing. They'd run into a couple more of Bravat's men on the way to the meal hall.

Great. More of them. Cyrus considered opting for his meal in his chamber.

Suddenly, everyone quieted.

On the far side of the courtyard, from Pyro's end of the villa, two guards dragged an unrecognizable, bloodied body past them, toward Teron's workroom.

Bravat and his men stared in confusion and dismay. Then they looked at one another.

"Who was that?" Bravat called across to Cyrus as the guards disappeared with the unconscious man around the corner. "What happened to him?"

Cyrus didn't need to recognize him to know who he was.

"Do you know who that was?" Bravat asked him again, walking toward him. His voice held a ring of annoyance.

"Where's your man who missed his kill?" Cyrus asked him, and he watched Bravat's face change.

"Val?" Bravat looked down the way toward Teron's workroom. "Val!" He moved to follow, but Everan reached out and caught him.

"Let the healer tend him," Everan said. "You can see him later."

Bravat pushed Everan off, and his face twisted. "What fucking happened to him?" he raged.

"What is it you said before?" Cyrus asked him. "This is the life."

Bravat stared at him, struck with horror.

And Cyrus left for his chamber, letting Bravat discover the hell he was in now.

CHAPTER TEN

Bravat stood silently beside him. Cyrus glanced at the fighter out of the corner of his eye as they waited at the gate for their match. There was no goading, no taunting, no roasting from the big fighter this time. No doubt the memory of Val's bloody body was still on his mind.

Cyrus had looked into Bravat's numbers. The fighter was close to gold. He needed only three more kills, and his sober countenance told Cyrus he was intent on getting one today.

The crowd roared as the match before them finished. Cyrus tightened his grip on his sword. "On my lead," he told Bravat.

"Fuck your lead," Bravat spat back. "You worry about your man, I'll worry about mine."

Cyrus's lips tightened. This was how teams lost. "We need to drop the first man quickly."

Bravat snorted. "I'll drop mine, then I'll take care of yours. How does that sound, eh?"

Cyrus clenched his teeth. *Arrogant bastard.* It was just the two of them, and they'd be lucky to get through this one.

The gates rose, and arena guards dragged the unfortunate souls who had fallen in the previous fight through, to be hauled out.

Another roar of the crowd told Cyrus their opponents had entered. The guard nodded to him, and he stepped through the gate.

"Two!" Cyrus called out.

Bravat didn't repeat it. No one was required to, but it was a usual practice. Cyrus wasn't sure why—perhaps it was how it had always been—but it felt like more of a commitment that the number of lives they entered with would be the same as when they left. The team number was a sacred number—a prayer. And everyone spoke it.

Except Bravat.

"Two!" the wall guard shouted to the scorekeepers.

Cyrus settled his sights on their opponents—a gold and silver fighter from House Rysil. House Rysil was almost as famed as House Pyro, with excellent fighters pushing the bounds of their levels. They wouldn't be easy to take down. Fights would also get progressively harder as they neared the king's celebration finale. Cyrus was just thankful they were still fighting men. The gods only knew what they'd be facing in the final days. Something told him the cats wouldn't be the worst of it.

Bravat took off at a run toward the man on the right. Cyrus swore—Bravat wasn't one for research, and he'd gone after the gold-tier fighter.

Perhaps his problem with Bravat would take care of itself.

Cyrus focused on the second man.

Swords rang out as Bravat attacked, but Cyrus kept his eyes on his own opponent. He struck. The man threw back a series of counters. He was a silver-tier fighter, and good. His footwork was quick, and his sword work clean. On a defensive return, the man spun with a fake strike and then a follow-through, grazing Cyrus's shoulder.

Cyrus paused for a moment, glancing at the thin line of blood that now started to bead along the cut. That had been smooth. He'd be proud if his silver fighters fought this well.

But he didn't have time to dally and admire. With the second sequence, he launched a full assault. On the closing move, his sword found home, between the man's ribs and into his heart. It was a merciful death. As the fighter fell from his sword, Cyrus turned his attention back to Bravat, who wasn't faring so well.

By now, Bravat had discovered he'd picked the wrong opponent, and he was fighting for his life. Leander was his opponent's name. Cyrus trotted toward them—not fast—debating how much he really wanted to engage. If Cyrus let Bravat be killed, there would be consequences. But how severe would the consequences be if Cyrus won after? A win with two kills, and with several other high-profile fights scheduled through the week—Pyro likely wouldn't do anything.

Bravat was fading. His strikes were slower now, his breathing ragged. Cyrus didn't look to see if Pyro was watching from where he sat in the top viewing box with the king and royal family. He never acknowledged the lord's presence while he was in the arena—a dangerous thing, but his spite wouldn't let him. He was sure Pyro was watching, though. Watching Bravat struggle. The most expensive purchase in the history of bloodsport. Cyrus couldn't have planned this better...

Leander delivered a sharp kick to Bravat's chest that landed him on his back. It was all over now. The Rysil fighter drove forward with a downswing for the kill.

Cyrus didn't know what made him do it; it certainly wasn't an action of a rational mind, but before he could think, he barreled forward and met Leander's blade with his own. Leander was a strong man, and the clash jolted Cyrus, driving a pain up his arms to his shoulders. But Cyrus pushed through and served a series of moves that drove Leander back, giving Bravat a chance to scramble to his feet.

He checked the gates from the corner of his eye. They had a little more time yet before the cats were released, although not much.

Leander launched a counter. It was a desperate one, made under pressure.

And he made mistakes.

Cyrus saw his opportunity. As they passed back-to-back on a spin, he flung out his blade low and wide.

Leander stopped midcounter and looked down.

All was still for a moment. Then blood rushed from Leander's severed hamstrings. Cyrus didn't finish him. Instead, he waited, a silent offering to Bravat to take the kill he so desperately needed.

Leander stumbled forward, and Bravat drove his sword through for the win. Cyrus's eyes met Bravat's, and the big fighter's stare pierced him back.

The crowd roared.

Bravat's eyes were still on him. His face was stone. He was probably livid, his ego not allowing him to appreciate an act of charity.

With the fight finally over, Cyrus turned and walked from the arena. He'd let the hot-headed fighter bask in the crowd's approval by himself. Maybe soaking in some of the glory would stay a confrontation, at least until they got back to the villa.

"Two!" Cyrus called out as he passed through the gate.

"Two!" the gate guard echoed.

But as he stepped into the corridor, Bravat grabbed his arm from behind. "I didn't ask you to set me up."

And Cyrus shouldn't have. He regretted doing it now. Bravat posed a danger to all the men in House Pyro. Cyrus should have let the arena take care of him. He cursed himself.

Bravat swallowed. "Thank you."

Oh. That was new.

A silence sat between them for a moment. Bravat's eyes shifted to the ground before meeting Cyrus's again. "On your lead now," he said, but with his fists clenched, as if the words tasted bitter.

The large fighter turned and continued down the hall, leaving Cyrus still trying to wrap his mind around what had just happened.

"Clear the hall!" a guard called, snapping Cyrus back to the present.

He moved quickly to catch up to Bravat. He wasn't entirely sure what to do with this man now. If he partnered him with—

Wait, was he seriously considering sparing Bravat? This man was arrogant and reckless. But he was also a strong fighter. He could be a strong member of the team, if he minded his place. Time would tell, and suddenly Cyrus found himself a little more willing to give him that time.

They headed toward the exit where they'd meet their wagon. As Cyrus passed the witch's hall, he paused. Was she still there?

Bravat glanced down the dark and silent corridor. "What's down there?"

Cyrus shook his head. "Nothing." And he kept going.

The wagon ride back to the villa was quiet. Bravat didn't say anything more to Cyrus, but the air was different between them—an air of respect. However, despite things settling, Cyrus had had enough of Bravat for the day, and he was looking forward to the quiet of his own chamber. He also had things to tend to and wanted to check on Kieve. He needed to make sure he got back on the schedule.

Cyrus slid off the wagon before it even reached the end of the wisteria entry into the courtyard, slipping between the columns and heading toward his chamber. When he reached it, he exhaled a tired breath as he pulled off his leathers, letting them drop to the floor. He washed the blood and dirt from his skin in the tepid water of the basin on the side table. He needed a bath, but he'd do that later, when he could soak and fall asleep.

Now, relatively clean and dressed in fresh clothing, he stepped back outside. The corner of his mouth turned up when he saw his friend walking toward him.

"What did you do to Bravat?" Everan asked.

Cyrus dipped his brows. "Why do you ask?"

"Because he's being tolerable."

Cyrus snorted. He wondered how long that would last. Still, he hoped Bravat understood now. He was a strong fighter, and he'd make a good addition to the team if he could be a team*mate*.

"Where are you headed?" Everan said.

"To talk to Kieve." Cyrus hadn't seen his name show up on the schedule, but plenty of slots hadn't yet been posted. Depending on when Kieve got the sign-off from the Sport Authority physician, he might not be listed until later in the week.

"I'll go with you."

Clouds covered the sky, giving a small reprieve from the heat. Maybe the fickle gods would favor the fighters and give them clouds for tomorrow's match.

They neared Kieve's chamber, and a guard shifted uneasily as they passed, refusing to meet his eye.

Cyrus slowed and glanced at Everan

His friend cut him a wary eye back.

When they reached Kieve's door, he knocked.

There was no answer.

Cyrus knocked again.

Still, Kieve didn't answer.

He looked back at the guard, whose gaze was focused away from him, in the opposite direction.

Cyrus swung the door open. The room was empty. He looked at Everan.

"I haven't seen him out today," Everan said.

Cyrus hadn't either, but Everan had been at the villa all day—if Kieve was around, he would have seen him. A sinking weight pulled at his stomach.

Something wasn't right.

Cyrus stepped back out into the hall and called to the guard, "Where's Kieve?"

The guard ignored him.

The weight in his stomach grew heavier.

Cyrus stalked toward him. "Where's Kieve?" he demanded.

The guard tightened his hold on his spear.

Everan grabbed Cyrus's arm and pulled him back toward the courtyard. "We'll find him. Come on."

Cyrus ripped his arm from Everan's hold, his daggered glare still on the guard, then he turned and strode toward the main hall, where he knew the lead guard, Hephain, would be. His pulse thrummed in his ears, quickening his step. He needed to find Kieve.

They passed Bash and Ram.

"Is something wrong?" Bash asked.

But Cyrus's focus was on Hephain, who was exactly where Cyrus had expected—by the main hall, his spear in hand.

"Where's Kieve?" Cyrus demanded before he even reached him.

Hephain's head turned, and as his gaze fell on Cyrus, he shifted.

Cyrus lengthened his stride toward him. "Where is he?"

Hephain lowered his grip on his spear.

Cyrus's voice dropped. Became colder. "Where is Kieve?" he demanded again as he reached him.

Kord was passing through the columns in the courtyard, and he started toward them upon hearing Cyrus. "What's going on?" he called.

"Go back to your chambers," Hephain told them all.

"Where is he?" Cyrus snarled. His blood ran cold, and his hands curled into fists.

"Cyrus," Everan said, trying to calm him, but Cyrus was beyond calming.

His body was moving before he could stop it. He nearly collided with Hephain, grabbing the guard's breastplate. "Where is he?!"

Laying hands on a guard earned a man a lashing, or worse. But Hephain made no move to defend himself, no move to call for help. He only gripped Cyrus back. "Cyrus," he said firmly. "Go back to your chamber."

"Did Pyro take him?"

Hephain gripped him tighter.

"Tell me!" Cyrus demanded. "Did Pyro take him again?"

"Cyrus—"

"Answer me!"

Everan grabbed him, but Cyrus pushed him off, not letting go of Hephain. "Answer me," he pleaded, desperate now.

But Hephain didn't have to respond for him to know. Anywhere else Kieve might have been, Hephain would have just told him. Hephain's silence answered for him.

Fire rippled over his skin, and Cyrus spun toward Pyro's residence.

"Don't," the guard warned, grabbing him, but Cyrus shoved him off.

Hephain moved after him. "Cyrus! Don't do something stupid!"

Everan caught his arm again, and he tried to jerk away.

"Let me go!" Cyrus snapped.

"Kord!" Everan shouted.

Kord was already there, grabbing his left arm.

Cyrus struggled to rip free. "I'll kill him!"

Everan swept Cyrus's legs out from underneath him with a swift kick, dropping him, and pinned him to the ground with a firm hand over his mouth. "Shut your mouth. You'll get us all killed."

Cyrus still fought, but Hephain and Kord had hold of him now as well.

"Let me go!" he thundered from underneath Everan's hand. He wrenched his head free. "Kieve!"

Everan clutched Cyrus just underneath his jaw, forcing him still. "You can't do anything for him right now, except get him killed, get yourself killed, and all of us with you."

The rage swelled so hard within Cyrus's chest that his eyes watered. "You don't know what Pyro's doing to him!" he yelled hoarsely.

Everan still gripped him. "I know Kieve is strong. And we can't help him right now. Not like this."

"Let's get him to his chamber," Hephain said.

"Kieve!" Cyrus bellowed.

They pulled him up off the ground. He fought them the whole way, but he couldn't overpower the three of them to get away.

When they reached his room, Everan and Kord muscled him inside. They held him tightly.

"Kieve!" Cyrus thundered again as Hephain closed the door behind them and locked it.

CHAPTER ELEVEN

Cyrus drifted in and out of dreams. When he woke, he couldn't move. Or maybe he wasn't awake. He struggled against the invisible force that held him.

"Easy," came Everan's voice.

He tried to open his eyes, but he couldn't. All around him was darkness.

"Should I give him more?" Kord asked from somewhere close by, but Cyrus couldn't pinpoint exactly where.

"No. We've already given him enough to drop a horse."

Their voices faded, and Cyrus fell back into darkness. Shadows coiled around him, and cold seeped into his bones. Cyrus found himself in a dark corridor, standing. He looked down. How had he gotten to his feet? Where were Everan and Kord?

Was he still in his room? No...

He glanced around but could see nothing through the shadows.

He started walking. Light followed him; from where, he wasn't sure. It wasn't much, just enough to see a few paces ahead.

Cyrus heard nothing, and he kept walking.

The corridor opened into a large room, with a little more light. It was a throne room. Two black thrones sat centered on a dais.

Black. Everywhere was black—the stone walls, the tapestries that covered them.

His pulse quickened.

There was only one kingdom of black.

The Shadowlands.

Cyrus stilled. He'd seen this before. It had been a long time. Ten years? More? Less? This was an old dream, one he'd almost forgotten.

He caught movement from the corner of his eye, and he turned to see a woman. He knew this woman—he knew her moon-spun hair. She looked a lot different from how he remembered her, as a child. He hadn't known her well then, but still he recognized her.

The Mercian princess.

She was unaware he was even there. His gaze followed her as she walked down the center of the room to the throne, where she turned and sat, alone. Her alabaster skin contrasted sharply against the shadows. Her dress of white and silver boasted Mercia's colors, and her eyes burned with a blue fire.

As she sat on the throne of the Shadow King.

Then the darkness swallowed him again.

Cyrus stood in a side hall of the arena—the hall of the witch. He wasn't sure what had made him come. He'd left Manus, Everan, and Kord in the holding chamber, where they waited for their fights.

He'd been in a rage when he'd woken in his chamber that morning. Not at Everan or at Kord. He understood that they'd done what they'd had to. Cyrus had been on the verge of rebellion, and it would have killed them all. Pyro employed an army of guards at the villa—Cyrus wouldn't have even made it through the threshold of the lord's residence.

They'd been lucky with Hephain, one of the few guards with a soul. He'd helped get Cyrus to his room, where Everan and Kord had sedated him with tanon oil, then locked them inside while keeping the other guards away.

Visa brewed several pots of runik tea, which Everan and Kord forced down Cyrus's throat in intervals too frequent to count, to purge the effects of the tanon by morning—before they had to be at the arena. By the time Cyrus had regained full control of himself, the worst had passed. Kieve was in his room, again healed by Teron's touch.

Everyone acted as though things were back to normal.

But things weren't normal.

Kieve wasn't normal.

The reality was that Kieve would likely never fight again.

And Pyro would kill him.

Cyrus continued warily down the hall, and when he reached the witch's cell, he looked through the barred opening of the door.

But she wasn't there.

How many days had it been? Two? Three? Had they burned her? *No.* She'd said six days. It hadn't been six days.

Where was sh—

Her face suddenly appeared in front of him on the other side of the bars, and he stumbled backward with a curse.

She gave him a close-lipped smile. "Did I scare you?"

"No," he said quickly. A little too quickly to be believable. "I'm not afraid of you." She probably wasn't even a witch. But how had she escaped her chains?

Her green eyes shined bright. "That's what they all say. Before I make them scream."

Looking closer, he could see what she'd done. There was no magic at play. She'd worked her chains off the ceiling hooks. She still had them locked around her wrists, but with the length of the chain, she could move freely in her cell now. She could reach the door.

"And how do you typically make them scream?" he asked.

"If you're here to help me, you're running out of time." Her impatience was showing now.

"*You're* running out of time. And no, I'm not here to help you." He didn't trust this woman.

She turned colder. "Then why are you here?"

That was a good question. Why *was* he here?

She pursed her lips, and her nostrils flared. "We can help each other," she told him. "I can free you."

He narrowed his eyes. "You can't even free yourself." And freedom was a dream—a hopeless dream. He should go. This was pointless.

But still, he lingered. He eyed her. "You said you can give me power."

"I can," she answered quickly.

"What kind of power? And how much?" He couldn't believe he was even asking this. She couldn't give him power.

She cocked her head to the side. "It depends on what you want to do."

"I want to kill a man. A powerful man."

The line of her lips curved at the corners. "Is that all?"

"What can you do?" he pressed.

"I can give you control of the beasts."

His brow dipped. "I don't want a fucking animal. I want blood."

"They'll answer to your thoughts, to your every command."

That was it? There were only four cats, and they were chained. Even if what she said was true, they would be of no help. "What about men?"

She scoffed. "If I could control men, I wouldn't be here." Her green eyes flashed. "But I can bring this arena to the ground."

"How?" he pressed.

"Give me your blood and I'll show you."

He wasn't so easily fooled. "My blood will free you, won't it?"

She frowned.

"Answer me," he demanded.

"Yes," she said finally. "It will let me free myself."

"How? What does it do?"

"It will allow me to channel the Aether, to tap into a power greater than anything else in this world."

He didn't know what she meant by *the Aether*, but he understood enough. She thought he could give her the power to break the bonds of her chains. She was wrong—he couldn't. And even if what she said were true, even if she could get some kind of power from him, how did he know she would help him in return?

"How do I know you won't just escape this arena once you're free?" he asked.

"When I'm free, this arena will want to escape *me*." She spoke with the fire of hungry vengeance. "And I want access to your power after. I need it. So, I'll make you a deal, seer. Free me, and I'll help you. You give *me* power, I give *you* power."

But she was wrong about him. "I'm not a seer."

"You have no idea what you are," she snapped back. "But I do. I smell it on you. I feel it radiating off you. Free me, and I'll make you the most powerful man in the world."

That wasn't what he was after. "I don't want to be the most powerful man in the world. I don't care about being a powerful man at all. I want the blood of powerful men."

"You want blood, then give me yours," she said. "Is it a king you want? I'll give you a world of kings."

Now that sounded like madness.

"Give me your blood," she begged. She gripped the iron bars on the door tighter, leaning into them. Sweat of desperation hung on her brow.

If she was desperate, she'd tell him anything he wanted to hear. Even if she did have power, he didn't. She was either lying or wrong. Neither would help him. He took a step back.

"Lucien!"

A prickle ran up his spine. "I told you that's not my name."

A roar from the crowd came from the arena—a fight was ending. Manus would be up for his one-on-one match. Cyrus had to go; he'd wasted enough time. He turned to leave.

"Please!" she begged. "I need your help!"

There was a part of him that wanted to help. But his blood would do nothing but bring chaos to his mind, and he couldn't afford that. So he couldn't help her. He couldn't even help his own men.

"Seer!" she called.

He wasn't a seer. He backed away from the door, turned, and made his way back down the hall the way he'd come.

Chapter Twelve

The crowd's roar was almost deafening. They loved solo fights. Cyrus stood with Manus by the gate to the arena and gripped the side of the fighter's neck encouragingly.

"We've practiced this a hundred times," Cyrus told him. "Work him high, then drop low. Sweep and end. You get this kill, and you'll move to starred silver. It will put you in sight for gold."

Manus drew in a deep breath and nodded. A bronze lock of hair fell over his forehead, not long enough to hinder his sight. It had been longer, but Cyrus had gotten Visa to cut it a few days prior.

Cyrus clutched his shoulders, looking him in the eye. "You *will* get this."

Manus nodded again, and the gate rose.

Cyrus cuffed him on the shoulder. "One!" he roared.

"One!" the wall guard echoed.

Manus gripped the hilt of his short sword and trotted to the center of the arena to wait for his opponent.

Why hadn't he repeated it?

He was nervous.

It was fine.

Cyrus moved quickly and slipped down a narrow circular hall and around to the next gate to secretly watch the fight.

The tiered side seating was packed with throngs of spectators. Cyrus's eyes traveled over the top observation box in the center stand and stopped when they found the king.

King Orrid—a man as vile as his name sounded—lounged under a draped canopy to shield himself from the harsh sun. The king considered himself a pious man, having converted to the religion of the Northern kingdoms of Mercia and Aleon. He'd built temples and pulled down statues of the old gods and erected those of the new. But he didn't stop his bloodsport. Did the gods want blood as much as men did? Mercia and Aleon had no such games, but like most religious men, this king chose what suited his own agenda.

The king's daughter sat beside him, flashing colored ribbons of her favored fighting houses and clapping gleefully. She was as sordid as her father. The queen rarely made an appearance but frequently hosted private matches at the palace. The whole family disgusted Cyrus.

He swept his gaze to the far side of the king's platform, and hate rippled over his skin. There, he saw Pyro. Pyro was a usual guest in the royal box, as the king's premier supplier of the most sought-after luxuries from around the world. And the king and Pyro shared common appetites.

Cyrus kept his gaze on Pyro. When in the arena, he never looked up at him; he never acknowledged him. However, he let himself look now as he made his silent vow again—the only vow that gave him the strength to keep going, to keep fighting. He'd find a way to kill this man.

The excited crowd cheered, and Cyrus shifted his attention back to his friend. Manus was good—a good fighter with a good heart. He'd make a good lead one day.

Manus glanced around the arena. When he found Cyrus watching him, he nodded. Cyrus gave a nod of encouragement back.

The cross gate opened, and Manus's opponent came out at a run. But instead of breaking into a return run to meet him, Manus widened his stance, as they'd practiced.

The man leapt forward with a deadly initial blow, and Manus caught it with an upswing, knocking it to the side. He used his opponent's momentum to spin them so that Manus was now on the forward advance, with the challenger forced to fight moving backward.

Manus drove a series of strikes, one after the other. Cyrus's body tightened in tandem with each move, knowing each play, each blow. Yes. *Yes.*

Still moving backward, the opponent stumbled. Even at a distance, Cyrus could see his confidence starting to waver. *Good.* Don't let up, Cyrus prayed. Manus didn't. He pressed harder, forcing the sequence higher.

Good. Higher.

Manus drove the exchange to chest level, and higher still. His opponent worked his own counter higher.

And... now.

In a split, Manus delivered a sweeping kick that dropped the other fighter to the ground. He was on him in an instant. The man didn't even know what hit him as Manus served the lethal strike, finishing him, and the fight.

Flawless. Fucking flawless.

It was a quick kill, a merciful one, just as they had practiced. *Better* than they'd practiced.

Cyrus panted with relief as a grin spread across his face. Manus did it. He would move to starred silver. Then with ten more team wins with personal kills, he'd get gold.

But the chant from the crowd made him still. The smile fell from Cyrus's face.

No.

His eyes swept the stands.

No. *NO.*

The crowd was in bloodlust. It had happened too fast. They wanted more. Manus didn't have the support of the masses like Cyrus did to get away with quick kills. Cyrus should have known. *He should have known.*

They chanted for the cats.

Cyrus's heart hammered against his ribs. It was up to the king. King Orrid smiled as his gaze moved around the arena. Then he looked to Pyro. Of course he'd give the decision to the lord. Pyro was the master—the master of Manus, of his fate.

No. Manus had just made starred silver and was on the cusp of gold. It had been a flawless kill, one Cyrus had choreographed himself. It was a perfect kill by a perfect fighter—Pyro couldn't allow a crowd call.

Pyro looked back at the king, and Cyrus's heartbeat nearly choked him.

Pyro nodded.

"No!" Cyrus bellowed, but his voice was drowned in the cheers of the crowd.

Manus turned, and his eyes found Cyrus's. He lowered his sword, and just stood, staring at his friend. His eyes were full of defeat, full of fear. He'd done everything to perfection, and still, this was what fate gave to him.

"Manus!" Cyrus thundered as the cats' gates opened with their chains slack, and they leapt for the spent fighter.

Seconds. It was only seconds before Manus's body was torn and mangled to different corners of the arena.

Cyrus sobbed with rage.

But he could only watch.

Cyrus stumbled blindly through the dark corridor, his face wet with tears and his body aflame with the heat of manic fury. The roars of the crowd shook the arena—calls for blood. More blood. Endless blood.

He found the cell.

The witch said nothing when she saw him, only stared at him with her eyes wide.

"You said you can bring this arena to the ground." His voice shook as he spoke. "You can kill them?"

Her chains clinked as she gripped the bars of the cell door, drawing as close as she could to him. "I can."

"All of them?"

"All of them," she promised.

He had no blade to draw his blood—fighters weren't given weapons until they lined up to enter the area—but he reached out to her. At this point, he didn't care what she needed to do to get it. She grabbed his hand and pulled it through the bars, then bit into the flesh of his forearm.

He bared his teeth against the pain but held still.

Then it hit him.

The connection was unlike anything he'd ever felt before. It didn't take him into her mind or into her thoughts. No, it brought *her* into *him*. He could taste her on his tongue, something sweet, and her scent of smoky earth filled his nose. She flooded him—his senses, his body, his mind—all of him. Icy fire rippled over his skin. Every hair rose on end.

When she pulled back, releasing him, he could still feel her—everything and everywhere inside him, all at once. And he felt like he could crush the earth. Was this the power she spoke of? Was it her power? Was it his?

His blood coated her lips and chin, and her green eyes were now black as night. She tilted her head up toward the ceiling and breathed foreign words into the air.

And then came the pull.

As quickly as she'd spread herself through every fiber of his being, she withdrew, and a new surge of power coursed through him. *Through* him. She inhaled sharply. He could still feel her—drawing it from him, breathing it from his lungs, prizing it from his veins.

The floor tremored beneath his feet, sending plumes of dust up around them, and the cell doors rattled on their hinges.

She swayed, just for a moment, her breath ragged. Then she laughed. Softly at first, then louder.

"Oh, the power you have," she whispered.

Her fingers twitched, and the air heated around them. Hotter and hotter, to an inferno—but it didn't burn him. Suddenly, the chains disintegrated from her hands and feet. Like ash. *She turned iron into ash.*

Her eyes found his again, and her smile grew. The door to her cell unlocked and swung open on its own.

Cyrus stood frozen. If he hadn't believed she was a witch before, he certainly believed it now.

She grabbed him and pulled him inside, and the door swung closed behind him. Before he could object, she brought his bleeding forearm to her mouth once more, drinking deeply. Then she closed her eyes, her hands gripping his wrists, and whispered more words he couldn't understand.

He wasn't sure what was about to happen. Would things just start to collapse? Or...

The roars of the arena crowd carried through the hall, signaling a kill, and it brought him back to the present. Then he remembered—Kord, Everan. If this was really happening, he needed to get them out.

"Hurry it up," he said.

"Shut up," she told him. "You can't rush the spell." She kept chanting.

The cheers sounded again. Another kill. Cyrus didn't know how many men were in the current fight, or how long he had to get back to Everan and Kord. *Not long.* If they entered the arena, he wasn't sure how he could get them out, and if they were forced to go without him...

"Hurry it up, witch," he hissed.

Suddenly, a searing pain shot up his arms, and he gritted his teeth to keep from growling. Fire—his veins were on fire—and it spread from her hands up his wrists to his shoulders. He tried to jerk away, but she held on to him. Dark patterns bled from his skin, forming markings up his arms—symbols of some sort.

Then she released him.

The burn subsided, and he looked down at the ink patterns on his arms. "What is this?" he asked through his teeth.

"Your own power is enough to kill you if you don't use it carefully, which you won't because you're completely ignorant of it." He was about to object before she added, "Combined with mine, well... You're no good to me dead. These markings will protect you from yourself."

He glanced down at his arms again. Why did he need markings? What—

She grasped the base of his jaw and forced his eyes back to her. "Listen to me very carefully, seer. When the beasts are let loose into the arena, they'll be free of their chains. But your blood has to touch them for you to take control. Until then, they act on their own instinct. You *must* take care."

"I'm still going into the arena? And I don't want the animals. What am I supposed to even do with them?"

"You only need to have a thought," she told him, "and they'll follow."

What the fuck? "What are *you* going to do?"

She smiled. "They wanted a burning. I'm going to burn this arena to the ground."

Cyrus paused. "Wait—I have men with me."

"Then get them out. Because everyone here is going to die."

CHAPTER THIRTEEN

Cyrus staggered back to the holding chamber in a daze. All he could see was blood. All he could feel was blood.

Pyro's blood.

Rael's blood.

Had he set something in motion that would give him that blood? Or only spill his own?

As he neared the holding room, he slowed. Through the open door, Everan paced back and forth, with Kord leaning against the far wall.

When Kord noticed Cyrus, he rocked forward off the wall. "What the fuck?" he called out. His eyes were rimmed red. "Where have you been? They fucking ripped Manus apart!"

It was a vision Cyrus would never be able to erase. His mind still reeled from the way Manus had looked at him, after doing exactly what Cyrus had taught him and doing it flawlessly, before he was killed for it. Guilt daggered him. Cyrus knew the crowd's bloodlust, but with his own loathing for entertaining them, for satisfying them—he was responsible for Manus's death. He'd given Manus the skill to win the fight, but not the balance to please the crowd and stay alive.

And Cyrus had been so quick to judge Bravat for his theatrics and his playing to the masses. But Bravat had been right...

"Cyrus," Everan called, snapping him back. "Where have you been? What's going on?"

What *was* going on? Cyrus paused. In leaving the witch, he'd had the irrational confidence that only rage fueled. But now... now he found that confidence waning as logic took hold. What was he really going to do? What the witch had promised him and what they'd discussed wasn't exactly a plan. In fact, far from it. And he wasn't even sure where she was now. He thought she'd followed him, but she was nowhere to be seen.

He tried to recall what she'd said. He would have the cats for whatever plan he created along the way. *If they didn't kill him first.* And he still wasn't sure what the witch was going to do.

Kord and Everan's gazes dropped to the markings on Cyrus's arms.

"What..." Kord started, but he couldn't finish.

"What's on your arms?" Everan asked.

Cyrus's mind raced. What had she said the markings were for? To protect him from himself? He still wasn't sure what that even meant.

"Cyrus," Everan pressed.

The markings didn't matter. What did matter: Everan and Kord needed to leave. Even if the witch had lied about bringing the arena down, Cyrus's own actions would damn them. He didn't know exactly what he was going to do, only that he was going after Pyro. If he failed, he'd be executed, as would anyone with him. If he didn't fail, they'd still be executed.

Cyrus closed the distance between them and pulled Everan and Kord close, dropping his voice low. "I'm going in alone."

"What?" Everan balked. "It's three-on-three, gold."

Kord's brows dipped. "You're good but not that good."

"I said I'm going alone. Whoever goes into that arena is not coming out. And I won't have it be the two of you."

Everan shook his head. "No, I'm not letting you go in by yourself."

Cyrus clutched them tightly. "I need you to get out of here. Tell the guards your lead sent you home."

"House Pyro!" came the call at the arena entry, summoning them to the gate.

Cyrus's eyes burned into Everan's. "If I succeed, House Pyro will fall into chaos. Get Visa, get as many as you can, and run. If you can make it across the Aged Sea to Osan, they'll grant refuge—they don't believe in the slavery of men."

"Succeed in what?" Everan shook his head again. "Cyrus, what are you going to do?"

"Pyro! House Pyro!" came the call again.

Cyrus glanced between Everan and Kord. "Distance yourself from me as much as you can. We are not brothers. We are not friends. You will not mourn me."

Everan's face twisted. "Cyrus—"

"Now get out of here," Cyrus said between his teeth. Then he turned and strode from the holding chamber. The gate was open when he reached it. "One!" he bellowed as he passed through.

The wall guard paused for a moment, confused, but then reluctantly echoed, "One!"

The sand of the arena was hot under his feet. Crimson stains lay scattered from end to end—blood of the fallen. Manus's blood. Cyrus gripped his sword. His eyes found the king, and Cyrus looked at him directly from the arena for the first time. Then Cyrus's gaze moved to Pyro, who rose from his seat in surprise and confusion. Pyro glanced at the king, then his worried eyes moved back to Cyrus.

Good. He should be worried.

The gate rose for his opponents, and Cyrus gripped his sword tighter. His eyes darted to the gates of the cats, but they remained closed. He didn't know what to expect—that the witch would release them right away?

Or perhaps she had no power to release them at all. He wasn't sure how she'd even be able to get close to them—the king's most prized possessions. She'd already managed to be caught herself; how strong could she be?

Suddenly, Cyrus started to feel very much like a fool. Had he just damned himself?

Even if what she'd said were true, what would he do with the beasts? He glanced back at Pyro and the king. His heart thrummed heavier in his chest. Had he acted too hastily? And now what? He'd die for nothing.

No... He believed she wanted revenge. She'd burn this arena to the ground. Perhaps she'd lied to him about his role. It bordered on insanity—that he'd be able to control the cats. And for what? What would that do?

No. She intended to use him only as a distraction.

The realization sank in, but a calm came with it.

He was okay being a distraction. He was okay with sacrificing himself, so long as Pyro died too.

He turned to face the three opponents sprinting toward him. If he was to be the distraction, he'd do a fine job of it.

When they saw it was only Cyrus, they slowed, looking at one another.

Cyrus immediately recognized them: Brant, Reed, and Kade, all gold-tier fighters. Brant had once been part of House Pyro, where Cyrus had helped him reach both silver and gold. Now he led House Akim.

Rarely were words spoken in a fight, but Brant called out to Cyrus, "What is this? Where are your other two men?"

Cyrus held out his arms. "It's only me."

The fighters of House Akim looked at one another again.

Shouts rang from the crowd. They were thirsty for more blood and wanted the fighters to get on with it.

"I don't want to fight you," Cyrus called.

Kade snorted. "Then you're in an unfortunate job."

Cyrus wouldn't argue with that. His mind raced with what to do next. Perhaps he should just fight—he could hold out a little while, even against three gold-tier fighters. He probably should have thought this through a little more, and he cursed himself. This wasn't the type of thing one did without a plan. Yet here he was, *without a plan*, as were most actions fueled by rage.

The crowd's boos grew louder.

Cyrus glanced at the cats' gates again from the corner of his eye. He just needed to make it to their release. That time always came too soon. Now he feared it might not come soon enough. And even when the beasts were released, he wasn't sure they'd be his deliverance.

"Brant, listen to me," Cyrus called. If only he could delay them for a little longer...

"Do *not* listen to him!" Reed yelled as he stalked forward, preparing to attack.

The cats' gates remained closed. Cyrus cut a quick look around the arena—nothing was caving in, nothing was on fire. Maybe she *had* escaped. *Fucking witch...*

The crowd started their boos again.

"This isn't personal, Cyrus," Brant said, tightening his grip on his sword.

"I'm asking you to make it personal," Cyrus called back. "You know me, Brant."

"And what would you have us do?"

The crowd's boos thundered louder.

Cyrus held out a hand. "Nothing. Just wait." Just like he was waiting... on a witch that had likely abandoned him.

The men looked at one another again.

"Fuck him, Brant," Reed said. "Let's kill him and go home." Cyrus didn't blame him—if fighters refused to fight, they died.

But Brant made no move to advance.

Shouts rang from the crowd—demands for the cats. Not far from Cyrus, a javelin thrown from the stands buried itself into the sand.

Chains clinked, and the cats' gates started to rise as the arena guards engaged the pulleys. It wasn't some magic release. And these cats were *not* going to be in a mind to obey him. Cyrus cursed as the realization set in—the witch had lied. She wasn't coming, and he was a fool to have even believed her. There would be no raining hellfire on the arena. He was alone and out of time. The only path to survival now was to kill Brant and his men. And there was no path to Pyro.

Reed and Kade charged forward in attack. Cyrus kicked Reed back and ripped his blade along his sword arm, disabling the Akim fighter, then spun to meet Kade. But Kade was closer than he'd thought, and the large man delivered an elbow that almost dropped Cyrus to the ground.

Cyrus scrambled back, expecting Kade's immediate assault, but when it didn't come, he paused. His brow dipped in confusion at Kade and Brant, who had paused too.

He followed their gazes to all four cats' gates rising. The guards rarely let out all four. The beasts' perimeters would overlap. There would be no safety—their punishment for delaying the fight.

The gates clanged as they opened, and four cats leapt out.

Kade turned and set his murderous intent back on Cyrus. Cyrus cursed the witch under his breath. He'd definitely die now.

But before Kade charged, Brant's bellow came. "Cyrus!"

Cyrus snapped his head up and noticed—no chains.

The animals had no chains.

Shouts rose in the arena as the crowd realized the same.

The cats prowled toward them. Now it didn't matter who won; there would be no calling the animals back, no being saved from them.

One lunged for Reed. The injured Akim fighter had no means to protect himself, and his scream was cut off sharply as he was taken down.

"Reed!" Brant yelled. But there was nothing he could do. Kade and Brant both backed toward Cyrus. No one had ever tried fighting the cats, but that seemed the only option now.

As the animals set their sights on the three men, Cyrus thought of another wild possibility.

The beasts stalked toward them.

He held... waiting... waiting...

The cats leapt.

Cyrus swept out a kick, followed immediately by a second one, dropping both Brant and Kade to the ground from behind. Then in a single movement, he ripped his sword across his own left hand and flung his arm out, arcing a wide spray of blood around the three of them and onto the animals.

As his blood found the beasts, a tremor rippled through him.

A fog.

Then it cleared.

And he could see.

Not just from his own eyes but from eyes looking back at him—eyes of the beasts. And more, he could feel them. Their hunger for blood clawed at him, their wildness fought against him. He gritted his teeth, forcing his will battled theirs. It wasn't as easy as the witch had made it out to be, and for a moment, he wasn't sure who was in control—him or the beasts.

Finally, the animals dropped back, ceasing their attack, but he could still feel their hunger to kill.

Cyrus clutched his head, trying to get his bearings as an energy rushed through him. It made him lightheaded yet all his senses sharper, almost painfully so. He became aware of everything around him—the crowd that had fallen nearly silent, the smell of blood, the taste of it...

He opened his eyes. At his feet, Brant and Kade lay on the sand, looking up at him with fear and confusion in their eyes. Cyrus swayed slightly as he straightened and drew his gaze back over the stands. The spectators were on their feet, but the arena was as silent as a temple hall.

The king stood in his viewing box, his mouth agape, as did Pyro next to him.

The need to kill coursed through Cyrus, but he didn't know if it belonged to him or to the cats. Probably both. And he saw his chance.

He sprung to the javelin protruding from the sand and pulled it free. Then with the most earnest of prayers, he hurled it toward the royal viewing box—at Pyro.

Never had he begged the gods so ardently. He begged his aim to hit true.

Hit this man.

Kill this man.

Cyrus begged the gods to give him this. *Please give him this.*

But the javelin missed.

And instead impaled the king.

The arena fell silent.

Everything, silent.

Then the screams started.

Pyro gaped at the king, then back to Cyrus, and his eyes widened more.

Cyrus swore on all things holy. He raised his sword, pointing to Pyro—a promise long made—and with every thought, every wish, every fiber of his being, he called through the bonds to the cats for the lord's blood.

The beasts jumped forward and leapt up the arena wall into the stands with lethal grace. They mauled everyone in their path. More screams tore through the air, and the shouts of guards rang out. Cyrus knew he had only moments before they came for him, only moments to seize his opportunity, and he pushed his call for Pyro through the bonds, again and again.

Pyro stumbled backward in the royal viewing box and fell. He stumbled again as he rose, but as he tried to flee, the surge of the panicked crowd blocked him in. He clambered over the dead king and raced toward the other side. Cyrus followed him with the cats.

Guards poured into the arena toward Cyrus. He ignored them and pushed the cats faster. The animals clawed over the bodies of spectators, racing toward their target. All he cared about was getting Pyro.

A set of eyes in his mind went dark, and one of the striped cats fell back into the arena, a spear protruding from its side. But Cyrus still had three more animals, and he drove them with every fiber of his will.

Two guards barreled toward him, but he didn't break his concentration. Just a little more—

A sword arced toward his head. He let it come as the black lion sprang on Pyro, its claws out and jaws wide. And Cyrus gave into the cold of death that would now claim him.

Except it didn't come.

Brant and Kade, now on their feet, met the guards' attack, driving them back, away from Cyrus. It wouldn't be enough, though. Guards swarmed around them. Brant dropped to his knees as a spear pierced his side.

"Brant!" Kade called.

They'd all die now.

Suddenly, thunder shook the arena—not from the sky but from the ground. The west wall shuddered, then buckled with a roar, collapsing the tiered seating in an avalanche of stone and dust. Bloodsport fighters poured in. They collided with the guards in a thick battle clash. In the stands, more fighters went after the spectators. The air was filled with the screams of the dying. The crowd surged in panic—shoving, trampling, clawing to escape.

None of them would.

And then there was fire. He wasn't sure from where it came...

The witch.

Flames spread through the air, setting ablaze everything and everyone in its path. The screams came louder.

Cyrus paid no attention to the dying. His eyes were on one man—the only man that mattered—the man that the black lion dragged through the stands back toward the arena. Back toward Cyrus.

Pyro.

The lion leapt from the top of the wall into the arena, pulling Pyro with him. It was a long drop, and Pyro's legs gave out from underneath him with a sickening crunch as he landed.

He screamed.

Cyrus had no compassion for him, no mercy. He stalked toward the lord with a hatred in his heart that no vengeance could heal. He'd take that vengeance anyway.

Pyro cowered on his knees, weeping.

Cyrus drew the lord's chin up with the tip of his sword to look at him.

"P-please," wept Pyro. "I'll give you whatever you want."

Cyrus slid the tip of his sword to Pyro's throat. "What I want is to see you die," he said, pressing the tip into his skin. And he'd get what he wanted now.

"Will you really kill him here?" came a voice behind him. "So quickly?"

Cyrus turned to see the witch.

She stood at ease in the center of the chaos, her hair wind-tossed, a smear of ash on one cheek. There was blood on her hands and firelight in her eyes. No dismay. No alarm. Only sharp and alive, untouched by the panic that surrounded them.

"This man deserves a lot of things," she said, "but a quick death isn't one of them."

Cyrus didn't disagree, but... "I don't have much time," he said, and he turned back to the whimpering Pyro.

"What makes you say that? The city will be yours by nightfall. You have all the time you could want."

Cyrus drew his brows together. "What?"

"You killed the king. Your men are taking the city."

He still didn't understand. "My men? What men?" Men of House Pyro?

"Look around you," she said with a wave of her arm. "Did you not intend to start a rebellion?"

He could only stare at her.

"Look around," she said again.

He peeled his eyes from her and swept them over the chaos. Thousands of bloodsport fighters attacked the fleeing crowd in swarms, killing the nobles and guards, cutting down spectators.

The arena was burning.

The flags of Rael were burning.

The king was dead.

But a rebellion hadn't been the plan. *This* hadn't been the plan.

The witch flashed him a smile. "Well done, seer."

"My name is Cyrus." His voice was hoarse, barely above a whisper.

She raised a brow. "You mean *King* Cyrus."

Chapter Fourteen

Billows of smoke filled the sky, stinging the nose and needling the lungs. Cyrus stood, breathing it in. Embers and ash of a fallen Rael fueled him more than the air itself.

With fighters from over two hundred fighting houses, they amassed an army, and Cyrus rallied them like an army. The screams of the dying had mostly faded—not because the fighting had stopped, but because, as it progressed through the capital, they were now too far to hear.

The witch had left him without explanation, not that he cared where she went. She'd held her promise, and she could do what she pleased. And Cyrus's mind was consumed with something else. He returned to the arena, where a few of his men held Pyro for him.

The merciless rays of the sun broke through the clouds of smoke and beat down on the ruined and condemned lord, as did Cyrus's merciless gaze. "Walk," Cyrus commanded. His throat was dry and nearly hoarse from bellowing orders to the bloodsport fighters as they overtook the city, but he had no problem delivering one more order.

Pyro whimpered. His once-gilded robes hung in tatters, coated in blood and dust. Deep claw marks stretched across his chest and shoulder, already crusted with filth. One leg bent at a sickening angle beneath him, and his face was bruised and swollen.

His voice shook, clipping the ends of his words. "My leg is broken."

Cyrus almost didn't recognize this vile craven cowering before him. It said a lot about a man—the way he faced death. Pyro was no man.

Cyrus glanced up at Kord and Everan, who stood on either side of this shitpot coward. Of course they hadn't left for safety before the chaos, like Cyrus had ordered, because they were insubordinate, loyal bastards. And he loved them for it.

His eyes found Pyro's again. "If they have to carry you, they'll cut your leg off to make the burden easier on themselves."

Kord and Everan put their hands on the hilts of their blades.

Pyro's eyes widened. He panted with sobbing breaths, then slowly hobbled up onto one leg. Kord and Everan would take him back to the villa—the villa that Cyrus now claimed—and Pyro would be held there until Cyrus was able to deal with him, which he was very much looking forward to. Brant, who'd suffered a spear to the side defending Cyrus from the initial rush of arena guards, had already been taken back. Cyrus hoped Teron could heal him.

Kord grabbed Pyro by his soiled tunic and shoved him toward the exit.

"Don't let him die before I get back," Cyrus told them.

"We'll keep him alive enough," Everan said. He tossed him a small linen wrap of dried meat. "Here—I know you've eaten next to nothing all day."

Cyrus wasn't hungry, but he accepted it. It was easier than arguing. He gave Everan a nod, and watched his friend follow after Kord. Then he tucked the meat away. There was still work to do.

He left the empty arena and strode down the inside corridor that led to the grandstand stairs and took them two at a time to the top, then followed the railed walkway to the royal viewing box. King Orrid lay where Cyrus has speared him. The princess was gone. Perhaps she'd escaped. He turned his attention back to the king. Orrid's dead eyes were still open, his mouth still agape. Blood and piss soaked the layers of his embroidered tunics, staining them the color of crimson and death. It was an inglorious and wretched end for a king.

Yet it wasn't enough.

Orrid had created this hell. He'd started the bloodsport shortly after he'd taken the crown twenty-five years ago. Then he'd spent six long years building the arena. Countless men had died in the effort, only for even more to die for its glory after. For death to be his legacy, his own demise had been too quick, too merciful. Cyrus trembled as rage rippled through him. How could fate not punish him?

If fate wouldn't, Cyrus would.

He grasped Orrid's body and dragged him to the railing, tossing him over, down to the sands of the arena below. Then he swung over the railing himself, hanging as far as he could before letting go and dropping to the ground. Pain splintered up his shins, but he ignored it. Grasping Orrid again, he dragged the disgraced king's body through the gates, over the dead that now littered the ground, down the center corridor, and through the columns to the grand main entrance outside.

Sweat drenched him, and exhaustion wrecked his body, but he wasn't finished. He searched for binding. It wasn't hard to find, as it had been cut from those held in some of the cells, but it *was* hard to find binding long enough to string a body to the entry gate. He managed.

With Orrid's body now on display, Cyrus stepped back to admire his work.

But it wasn't enough.

He pulled a dagger from a dead guard nearby and sliced open the king's stomach, spilling his entrails to the ground.

It wasn't enough.

He plunged the dagger in again. And again. His arms shook, as did his breaths.

It *still* wasn't enough.

Cyrus bared his teeth as he stabbed him again. *Why wasn't it enough?* Letting out a roar, he sank the dagger into Orrid's eye. Then he released it and stepped back.

He stood—his chest heaving, his heart pounding. Panting. Staring.

At the dagger. At the body. At the blood.

Blood. He looked down at himself. It covered him. Its metallic tang coated his tongue, its iron mist still hung in the air. The scent was a common one of the arena, but it was different now. With it mingled the acrid scent of burning flesh, burning banners, a burning kingdom—the scent of freedom.

He was free.

They were all free.

But that notion felt hollow.

And suddenly, he was overwhelmed. He swayed and had to catch himself. His eyes stung, and his vision blurred. He sucked in a quaking breath as his chest tightened.

He was free.

Yet why didn't he feel free? Why was the weight still there? It was supposed to be gone.

What else did he have to do?

Cyrus lifted his chin to the sky. Clouds of smoke still blocked the sun—the sun that beat down relentlessly day after day after day. The sun that heated the sands to burn their feet, and the blades to burn their skin as the life was sliced from them for Rael's mere entertainment.

If only he could bring down the sun.

He straightened. He might not have been able to bring down the sun, but he had erased it from the sky and replaced its orange hues with the glowing embers of this wretched kingdom.

Cyrus closed his eyes and breathed deeply, filling his lungs again with the scent of destruction. This was victory. He should relish it, take heart in it. But as low growls came from behind him, he stilled.

Slowly, he turned.

Two arena guard dogs stalked toward him, their thick heads low, their hackles raised. The whites of their teeth flashed in warning—teeth that loved ripping men apart. A third stepped out from behind another column. Blood matted their black brindle coats. Their short leather leashes hung from their collars, not quite reaching the ground. The animals moved freely now, with their handlers most likely dead.

Cyrus took a slow step back.

While these weren't cats, they were just as deadly, and Cyrus had nothing to defend himself with. He glanced at the dagger protruding from the dead king's eye socket, but it was too far to reach. He took another step back.

The dog closest to him growled.

Cyrus fumbled and found the dried meat that Everan had given him. Slowly, he pulled it from the linen, ever so careful to not make a sudden move, and tossed it away from him. With luck, they'd go for the meat, and he'd make his escape.

But the dogs didn't even look at the meat. Their eyes stayed locked on him as they spread to surround him.

His mind raced for what to do. Then his pulse quickened. The cats. He called them through the link in his mind, willing them to come, begging them to come.

But he felt nothing.

Were they still connected? Were they still alive?

As the dogs moved closer, he realized he didn't even have time for the cats. He took another step back, his heart pounding.

The first dog lunged, teeth bared, snapping for his throat. These animals were trained to kill. Cyrus flung up his arm. His manacle stopped the animal's crushing jaws, but past the edge of the metal, teeth still tore into his flesh. Cyrus roared in pain. Hot breath hit his neck, those teeth just a hand's width away.

A second dog caught his thigh, crunching down to the bone, and the third dog went for his calf. That was it for his left leg. Still, he wrenched against them, struggling to stay up. If he fell, he was dead. But the beasts were too powerful, and he bellowed as he was pulled to the ground. Out of all the ways he thought he'd die today, this hadn't been one of them.

But as he hit the cobbled mainway, a tremor rippled through him—the bond of the blood—tugging at the edges of his mind. He latched onto it, still struggling, clawing, fighting. He battled the animals' want to kill with his own determination to live.

The dogs' aggression started to crack beneath his will. He fought harder, taking control. As the dogs' attack ebbed, Cyrus raked his eyes around him and spotted a sword on a dead guard a few yards away—the same guard he'd lifted the dagger from. But he stopped as the dogs shuffled off him. They only stood now, waiting.

Waiting for what?

Then he knew.

He no longer needed a sword.

Cyrus rolled to his side, panting, and held his torn forearm against his chest. Despite the mild protection of the manacle, the bone was likely broken. Pain coursed through his left leg, which seemed even worse. He pushed himself up to sit.

One of the dogs growled.

Calm, Cyrus pushed through the bond, if that was what one could call it. *Everyone, calm.* Even himself.

The dogs quieted.

Cyrus eyed them. Could he control them now? He willed them to lie down, and they did. Like the cats, he could feel them, although this connection was deeper somehow—maybe because his blood was *in* them, not just *on* them.

He wasn't sure what made him do it, but he reached out his hand to the closest one, his eyes locking with the animal's. The dog lowered its head, but as Cyrus put his hand on top of it, it didn't just yield. The dog rolled its head into his hand, seeking physical attention, and Cyrus couldn't control the sudden need to scratch the animal just behind the nub of what was left of its ear. It pushed even closer to him.

The other two dogs crept forward, their ends wagging as though they still had tails.

Cyrus wasn't fond of animals, but there was a connection with these beasts that was beyond the blood. They'd been dealt the cruel hand of fate, as he had. Now they'd be free too.

He wanted to explore this more—understand what was happening to him, what this all meant, but now wasn't the time. His injuries were significant, and the light was fading. Cyrus looked to the sky. He needed to get himself back to the villa, where Teron could heal him. But first, he had one last task. He needed to ensure no slave had been left behind, make sure no noble had been left alive. He gritted his teeth through the pain and pushed himself to stand. Still gripping his injured arm close to him, he started back into the arena.

The dogs trailed him as he limped through the corridors, checking that no one had been left locked in a cell, that no one had been left chained. If the other fighters were like him, they'd have no intention of returning.

It didn't take him long. Cyrus was relieved to find everyone had been cleared, save for a few wounded guards—the dogs finished them off. As he watched their pleas for mercy ripped from their throats, he wasn't sure if it was his will or the animals'. It didn't matter. It didn't dull the satisfaction. After, he made his way to the back loading area outside, hoping to find a horse or a cart; he'd lost a lot of blood and was weakening, and he didn't think he'd be able to walk back.

He found none, and leaned against a column for a moment, panting, before forcing himself to start back to the villa on foot. He hoped he'd make it.

The air was quiet. Where was everyone? Dead littered the ground. In the distance, plumes of smoke billowed into the sky. Were they still fighting? He still had fight within him, but his strength was waning. Each step sent a jolt of pain through him. His arm throbbed, dripping blood steadily down his front. His legs couldn't hold him much longer. He had to get to Teron. Suddenly, everything seemed to spin around him, and he had to stop. The villa was too far. He couldn't make it. Each breath dragged him closer to collapse. Curling forward, he grasped a dog to keep from falling.

But his strength gave out, and he dropped to his knees. A wave of disappointment washed over him. He wasn't sure why. He'd done more than anything he'd ever dreamed of doing. Maybe it was because he hadn't been able to kill Pyro himself. More than anything, he'd wanted that satisfaction. Maybe it was because Alexander was still out there—living, laughing, enjoying all the pleasures of a privileged life.

Would his brother feel him die?

Would he be happy?

The world tilted and dimmed, then blurred at the edges. He collapsed onto his side.

Not yet, he prayed. There was still so much more he wanted to do. So much more he needed to do.

But the gods weren't listening.

They never had.

His breath slowed, and for the first time in this cursed hell of a kingdom, he felt cold.

So, this was it. This was the end.

He couldn't fight the darkness as it swallowed him.

145

Chapter Fifteen

Night hung around him. Cyrus cracked open his eyes at a faint flicker of light. His gaze caught and sharpened on the candle flame across the room on a small side table. *His* side table. *In his chamber.* Except, he didn't remember returning to the villa...

Then everything came rushing back.

The arena.

The king.

Pyro.

He sat up with a start. Pain shot through his arm, and he winced. It was bandaged, and it hurt something fierce. He gingerly tested the rest of his body and found his left leg fully mended. Teron's work. That was good. The old healer obviously didn't have the strength to heal him all in one sitting, but that was fine. Cyrus was healed enough.

His clothing had been stripped from him. Not a surprise. Teron always gave him a thorough check-over.

Cyrus rose from the bed slowly but still a little too fast, darkening his vision to near blindness. He gripped the edge to steady himself until the sensation passed. Recovered, he picked up the single candle and lit two more with it.

When he turned, he found three glowing sets of eyes looking back at him.

The dogs. Slowly, they stepped from the shadows.

Cyrus froze. He couldn't feel them anymore, or he didn't think he could feel them. Chaos still spiraled through his mind, through his body, but nothing he could make sense of.

Down, he commanded through the bond. If there was still a bond.

The dogs stepped toward him, their heads low, their mouths open. He knew animals only in the context of using them, but he didn't take this for the best sign. Unease weighted his stomach. Would they spare him only when his blood demanded it?

The dogs stared at Cyrus, and Cyrus stared back.

Was there any connection still at all? He reached out his hand. The dog closest to him stretched its neck toward him, its nose testing the air.

Cyrus reached farther.

It was a stupid thing to do—he already couldn't use his sword arm. If he lost the ability in both arms with still so much fighting left to do…

But it wasn't a swift bite that came. In a surprising move, the dog bumped its head up under Cyrus's hand, the same as it had done at the arena.

Cyrus puffed an air of relief and swallowed, giving himself a few breaths as his beating heart slowed. He'd assumed the animal had done that before under the confines of control, but he wasn't controlling it now.

The dog, not finding satisfactory scratches, pushed his hand harder, and Cyrus gave in. Its short brindle coat was surprisingly soft, and petting it had a calming effect... for them both. The dog's tailless hind shook from side to side, and Cyrus chuckled. Within moments, all three animals were vying for his attention.

Then he knew—these dogs belonged to him now. He wasn't sure what he'd do with them. He'd never had a dog before. Now he had three.

Giving each animal one last pat, he moved to the sideboard and lit another candle. The water in the basin darkened as he sloppily washed his face and hands. He desperately needed a bath, but he wouldn't bother now. It would be another day of blood—he'd clean up later.

As he pulled a towel, he paused. The markings on his arms that the witch had given him were still there. Were they permanent? Did they still protect him? From what?

He spied his leathers in a heap on the floor. He pulled them on. They were still covered in blood, but he didn't care enough to find clean ones. In fact, he didn't mind at all. Most of the blood was likely the king's, who he hoped was still strung up at the entry of the arena. Cyrus was happy to wear his blood for a little while longer.

"He lives," a voice called from the door.

Cyrus looked over his shoulder to see Everan. His friend grinned at him as Jaem and Bash shuffled in behind.

"How did I get here?" Cyrus asked.

"Bash found you, brought you back." He tipped his head to the large fighter behind him.

Cyrus gave Bash an appreciative nod, and Bash smiled.

Everan cast the dogs a wary glance. "They followed you back. We tried containing them, but they weren't too keen on the idea. Kord nearly lost a hand. So, we just left them. They seemed friendly toward you, with your... magic."

Cyrus snorted. "It's not magic."

Everan raised a brow. "What do you call floating around in people's minds?"

"I don't float."

"Fine. *Entering* minds, then. And the thing back at the arena with the cats?" He nodded at Cyrus's marked arms. "Now that. When are you going to tell us what's going on?"

Cyrus looked down at the markings again. "There was a woman."

"Oh, yeah. We know. The witch."

Cyrus's eyes darted up. "Where is she?"

"That I don't know," Everan said.

"Haven't seen her since we left the arena," Bash added.

She was probably long gone by now. Cyrus didn't blame her. He'd have left already too, if he could.

"How long have I been out?" he asked.

Everan shrugged. "A few hours."

Teron entered the room. Cyrus was happy to see him, although he didn't want any more healing. With the events of the last day, all that Teron had seen and felt, the suffering of those who'd fought for their freedom, the ones Teron couldn't save—Cyrus didn't want to see it. Perhaps it was cowardly, but he didn't think he could carry it. He barely had the strength for himself. Plus, he knew Teron was tired. There were still plenty of men who needed healing, and the old man obviously hadn't rested himself.

Teron stepped toward him, rolling up the sleeves of his robe.

"I'm fine," Cyrus told him, shifting back. "You've done enough."

"But I'm not finished."

"The rest will heal fine on its—"

"Cyrus, let him finish," Everan said. "The men need you. They're awaiting your orders."

Cyrus paused. "My orders?"

"You're our lead."

"Well... not anymore."

Teron reached for the bandaging on his arm, and Cyrus pulled it back, raising his hand to pause the old man.

"Why would you think that?" Everan asked. "Of course you're still our lead."

In fairness, Cyrus wasn't exactly sure what he was thinking. It wasn't like he'd given any thought to what would happen after the arena fell. He hadn't even believed that *could* happen. "Um..." He really just needed some time to figure things out. "Tell them to get some sleep."

"Who cares about sleep?" Jaem said.

That was true. Who cared about sleep after tasting freedom? "Well, I don't have orders for them."

"Then what are they to do?" Everan asked. "What's your plan?"

Cyrus gave a half-hearted shrug. "I don't have a plan. And they can do whatever they'd like, so long as they burn this place to the ground."

The space between Everan's brows creased. "You can't just let it all go now."

"Yes, I can."

Everan side-dipped his head at Bash and Jaem, and they exited the room.

Teron moved toward Cyrus again.

"No," Cyrus told the old healer. "I'm fine." Except he wasn't fine. The pain was excruciating.

"People need a leader," Everan said.

Cyrus reared his head in surprise. "You mean me?" He snorted as Everan raised a brow. "I'm not meant to lead." He wasn't worthy of such a responsibility.

Teron waved Cyrus back toward his bed. "I've been waiting for you to wake to finish," he told him. "Come. Lie down."

"I said I'm fine."

"What do you think you've been doing for the last four years?" Everan asked.

Teron shook a finger at Cyrus. "I'm the one that wrapped that arm, and I know you're not fine."

"Cyrus," Everan pressed. "Everyone's looking to you."

"They shouldn't be!" Cyrus snapped. "I didn't ask them to."

"Cyrus." Teron reached for him again.

He ripped his arm back, and a searing pain tore through it. "I said I'm fine," he gritted through his teeth.

The dogs let out a low growl, and the room quieted. Cyrus drew in a breath and let it out slowly. He wiped his hand over his face. He hadn't meant to lash out. Not at Everan, and certainly not at Teron. Collecting himself, he said, "Even if I did want to lead them, which I don't, there are many more qualified than I am."

The corner of Everan's mouth twitched. "Who?" He shook his head. "Cyrus, you've turned a nation."

"But I can't do anything more for them." Cyrus ran a hand through his hair. "You talk to me like I'm the promise of a new hope. I can't be their hope."

Everan stepped close and put his hand on Cyrus's shoulder. "Then be their justice. There's still so much more to do. Help us finish this."

CHAPTER SIXTEEN

Cyrus made his way through the courtyard toward the main hall of the villa where his men had gathered. He'd checked on Pyro as soon as he'd left his chamber, not because he was worried that the pile of shit had escaped but because others might not have been able to resist their need for retribution. He'd found him a little worse for wear but still fit to face the demise planned for him. Cyrus let Pyro beg for his life, then left him without a word. He wanted to take his time when he killed this man, relish it, and right now, he didn't have that time.

Dawn broke over the horizon, and Cyrus quickened his pace. He ignored the pain that knifed through his arm. Perhaps he should have let Teron finish healing him. No—it didn't hurt enough for that. At least, not when he wasn't using it, or walking, or standing, or breathing.

Everan walked beside him. "What are you going to name them?" he asked.

Cyrus had no idea what he was talking about. "What?"

Everan nodded over his shoulder at the dogs that followed. "Them. What are you going to name them?"

"Oh." Cyrus glanced back at the dogs. "I'm not."

Everan snorted. "You've got to call them something."

"No, I don't." He also had more important things to focus his mind on, more important things that worried him, things that bothered him. Things like the fact they were all free, but Cyrus didn't feel free. He saw his men with a new light in their eyes, new breath in their lungs, new power in their strides, but something inside him still bound him. It snapped its taloned clutch tight around his spirit, clawing him back and holding him in darkness.

He filled his lungs against the pressure building in his chest—the same feeling he got just before stepping into the arena. It was as though he were there now. The tightness stretched from shoulder to shoulder, the fight rippling under his skin, building with each step.

Building.

Building.

His hand tightened around the hilt of his sword at his waist. Pain shot up his arm, and again he cursed himself for not letting Teron finish healing him. But pain was good. Pain brought him back.

"Are you all right?" Everan asked.

No. He straightened, dropping his hand. "Yeah."

They slowed as they reached the main hall. Rows of guards were on their knees—Pyro's guards, their hands bound. This wasn't surprising, as they all had to die. What *was* surprising was that there were so many still alive. Cyrus knew Pyro had a lot of guards, but he'd never realized quite how many. Cyrus's men surrounded them, or what were mostly Cyrus's men. It appeared a few more had joined them from the arena.

Bravat moved between the guards, systematically eliminating them. He pulled back their heads, slit their throats, then pushed them to the ground to bleed out.

Pull. Slit. Push.

Next.

Pull. Slit. Push.

"You gonna let him kill them all?" Everan asked Cyrus.

Pull.

Slit.

Push.

"Yes," Cyrus answered.

He left Bravat to his task and took the stairs up to the main hall's double doors, but as he swung them open, he wasn't prepared for what he found.

There was standing room only. The great hall of House Pyro was one of the largest in the capital, outside of the palace. Men of money held extravagant affairs here—weddings, banquets—although few affairs truly filled the room.

It was filled now.

All eyes turned on Cyrus.

Everyone grew quiet.

Men parted as he walked through, bowing their heads. Cyrus wasn't quite sure what was happening. Everan was still beside him, although he'd fallen back slightly.

Had all these men been waiting on *him*? His gaze swept over their faces. Their expectation. Their reverence. They were looking at him like he was the answer. Now he really didn't feel worthy.

And then he saw Brant. The Akim House fighter showed no sign of injury from the spear he'd taken in the arena. Cyrus was glad of it.

Brant crossed the space between them and reached out his arm. His lips held a smile.

Cyrus clasped his arm in return. Brant's mouth opened to speak, but as his eyes welled, he closed it again without saying anything.

"Welcome, brother," Cyrus told him. "Glad to see you well. What about the rest of House Akim?"

Brant blinked back his emotion and shifted his gaze through the masses, where pockets of men briefly lifted their hands. "We're all here. But there is no more House Akim, just as there is no more House Pyro."

"The houses have fallen," Ram said, coming up behind him, "and all the men are headed here."

Cyrus shifted in surprise. "We've taken the capital?"

"No, but we've taken the palace."

"The royal family?"

"Dead."

"All of them? Are you sure?" That would have been Cyrus's next move. Anyone left of the royal family could rally defensive forces.

"It was confirmed by many of the fighters coming in," Everan said.

"Have you seen it with your own eyes?" Cyrus would trust the news only if it came from his men directly.

Everan shook his head. "I have not."

Cyrus needed to be sure. "I'll head there now, then."

"What do you want the men here to do while—"

Commotion outside pulled his attention, Kord's voice specifically. Cyrus stepped back out through the main doors to find Kord with his sword drawn a few paces from where Bravat held a guard.

"You spill his blood, I spill yours," Kord warned the large fighter.

"I'd like to see you try," Bravat goaded. It probably wasn't the wisest thing to do. Kord wasn't just a gold-tier fighter. He was a starred gold—the best there was. He would gut Bravat in the blink of an eye, but Bravat hadn't yet shown himself to be a man of awareness.

"What's going on?" Cyrus asked them.

"Release him," Kord ordered Bravat.

And Cyrus saw it wasn't just any guard Bravat held. It was Hephain, the lead guard.

"Cyrus," Kord said, soliciting his support.

But Cyrus wasn't sure yet if he wanted to give it. Yes, Hephain had shown kindness over the years, but he was the villa's lead guard. He'd protected Pyro. He'd allowed this life.

"You'd kill him?" Kord challenged. "A man who's shown mercy, a man who's shown kindness to you personally. How is this fair? How is this honorable?"

Cyrus had never promised fairness. Or honor. He didn't know if he could trust Hephain, and trust wasn't a luxury he could afford right now.

Bravat read his silence as denial of mercy and grabbed a fist full of Hephain's hair, pulling his head back.

Kord surged forward.

"Stop," Cyrus ordered. He sighed. Despite being a decorated bloodsport fighter, Kord had always detested violence, especially when he felt it unjust or unnecessary. And maybe killing Hephain was both of those things.

Cyrus moved stiffly in front of the guard, who kept his eyes boldly on him. "Why should I let you live?" Cyrus asked him.

Hephain didn't blink. "Maybe you shouldn't."

Bravat wrenched his head back again. Hephain bared his teeth but didn't fight. He accepted his fate without fear.

"Do you not *want* to live?" Cyrus asked him.

"Not if I'm now to be *your* slave, not if you intend the roles to be reversed, to punish me for what's been done to you."

Cyrus crouched down so that their eyes were level. "There's not enough punishment for what's been done to us." It wouldn't keep him from exacting that punishment, though.

Hephain still didn't cower.

Cyrus stood. "But there will be no more slaves," he said. "Only free men and dead men." He eyed Hephain, trying to determine to which he belonged. This man could be useful. He wasn't just any guard. He'd accompanied Pyro regularly to the palace, guarded him through various meetings with royals and nobles. He'd been exposed to countless powerful men and matters of state.

He'd been exposed to secrets—secrets that might benefit Cyrus now.

"Will you join me?" Cyrus asked him. "Not as a slave, but as a free man of your own free will."

"Are you fucking kidding me?" Bravat challenged. "You can't trust any of these men now. Let me finish the lot of them."

Kord cut him a daggered glare.

But Cyrus ignored them both and kept his eyes on Hephain. The guard wore an expression he couldn't read.

"Let him up," Cyrus told Bravat.

The big fighter snorted in protest, but he pulled Hephain to his feet.

"The call is yours," Cyrus told Hephain. Bravat was right—he couldn't trust a man facing an ultimatum of death. But Kord was asking for mercy, and if Cyrus had to kill Hephain later, he could.

The guard glanced at Kord before bringing his gaze back to Cyrus. Then, slowly, he sank to one knee, bowing his head. "I recognize you as Rael's new king and will serve you accordingly."

Cyrus didn't want to be recognized as the new king, nor did he want to be served, but he would accept Hephain's loyalty. For now.

"Let him go," he said to Bravat.

Bravat's hand tightened on his blade, the leather hilt creaking under his grip. Anger still simmered in his eyes, but he didn't argue further. He cut the guard's hands free.

Hephain rubbed his wrists.

"What about the rest of them?" Kord asked.

The rest of them. Cyrus had no intention of adjudicating the rest—he didn't know most of these men, nor did he care enough to try to. He simply didn't have time.

"I'll let Hephain decide," he said.

There were some guards Cyrus *did* know, men who weren't keeping their heads no matter who spoke on their behalf. Hephain's decisions would answer Bravat's question—whether Cyrus could trust him.

Despite Hephain having been spared, Kord didn't sheath his sword. His eyes were still shadowed, and his nostrils flared with each breath.

It wasn't often Cyrus saw him this bothered, even in the arena. "What's going on with you?" he asked. "Are you all ri—"

"I just came from city center," Kord said, changing the subject. "The nobles are fleeing. Should we pursue?" His shift was cold, still filled with anger. Cyrus didn't fault him. This entire circumstance was bringing out strong emotions in all of them.

Cyrus set his focus on what mattered. The nobles were fleeing. *Nobles like Pyro.* As much as he wanted to pursue them, they weren't organized enough for this. "No. Not yet. Secure the capital."

"I'll need more men."

"Well, you're in luck," Cyrus told him. "I have a whole hall of them, and they need something to do."

Kord nodded. "We're only going after the nobles. We're leaving the citizens."

Cyrus was fine with that. Most of Rael's citizens lived on the brink of poverty and were uninvolved in the wrongdoings of their government.

"What do you want us to do with nobles we capture?" Kord asked.

He rocked back slightly. "Capture? Why would you capture anyone?"

Kord glanced at the men around them, then back to Cyrus. "You want us to kill them all?"

"What else would you do with them?" He had patience for what weighed on his men's hearts, more patience for Kord in particular, but Cyrus needed him to be strong now. This was a war. "Do you pity them? Do you want to grant everyone mercy? When they had no mercy for us?"

Kord stared at him for a moment, then shook his head. "No." He paused. "But what about those who didn't own slaves?"

"Show me a noble in Rael who didn't own a slave," Cyrus said.

The sun was just peeking over the horizon, and while daylight misted the capital, the palace was still dark.

Cyrus gripped his sword tighter as he walked. His skin was sticky with the blood of nobles that he'd executed on the way to the palace. There were fewer now in the capital, given most had fled, and those who'd thought they could still fight back—he'd showed them they could not. The general masses he'd left alone, those with no status, disadvantaged by the class system, living in poverty and squalor. They could take what they wanted now, for all he cared.

His footsteps echoed as he strode through the high-arched main hall of the palace. It was quiet. Too quiet. He walked as if in a dream, not a dream of glory and victory but a dream where one finds himself in a place he doesn't know. A place he doesn't belong. But Cyrus had no intention of belonging. He was here only to ensure all who had needed to die had done so. Killing the king wasn't enough. His mangled body still welcomed anyone who entered the arena. His blood was still on Cyrus's skin.

But it wasn't enough, and Cyrus was here to take it all.

The dogs had followed him from the villa, and they trotted off to look around. He let them go. He took the stairs up to the royal wing, passing bodies that had been left where they'd fallen. Various weapons lay scattered across the floor. He'd have his men come back for these later.

The rooms were mostly empty, save a few that held what was left of their unfortunate occupants. He continued down the hall, but when he reached an alcove with two double doors slightly ajar, he paused.

Blood marked the entry. This chamber was larger than the others. Perhaps the king's.

He stepped inside.

Floral draperies hung long over the sets of double doors leading to a balcony, and a large vanity topped with perfumes and jewelry sat along the far wall. The open door of the adjacent dressing room held gowns upon gowns and shelves of shoes.

No, this wasn't the king's chamber, but it certainly belonged to a royal. A female royal.

Cyrus's eyes traveled the room and landed on a four-poster bed. In the center of the bed lay a woman. He drew nearer. He knew this woman, with her deep auburn locks and heart-shaped face.

It was the princess.

She hadn't escaped.

Her throat had been slit.

He didn't feel sorry for her. She'd often accompanied her father to the bloodsport matches. She had cheered for those she'd wagered on and worn colored ribbons of her favorite houses. She'd enjoyed blood.

And she'd gotten it.

Cyrus turned and stepped from the room. Where was the queen?

His question was answered at the cross section of another hall, where he found not only her body but also the body of the king's mother.

It was true, then. The royal family was dead. *All of them.*

And Cyrus had Pyro back at the villa. So why could he still not escape the clawing need inside him? The need for what? There was a hunger he couldn't satisfy, a thirst he couldn't quench.

His eyes drifted to the last alcove at the end of the hall. He wasn't sure why he bothered, but he moved to it, pushed the doors open, and stepped inside.

The chamber reeked of male power. *This* was the king's chamber.

His eyes traveled the room. Nearly everything had been overturned—the armoire thrown open and emptied, drawers pulled from the long dresser and their contents spilled onto the floor. However, jewels and valuables still lay strewn about. Strange that not much seemed to have been taken, but someone had been looking for something...

The largest bed he'd ever seen sat in the center. He stepped to the corner and ran his fingers over the down cover and silken sheets. His brow dipped. This was Rael—a cesspool of a kingdom festering in the sun. Who needed a fucking down cover?

Who needed any of this?

No one. That was who.

Cyrus pulled a candle from a wall candelabra and dipped its flame toward the silk.

"You'd burn it?" came a voice from behind him.

He whirled around.

It was the witch. He stared at her for a moment, at a loss for words. He hadn't seen her since she'd left him with Pyro in the center of the arena. He'd thought she'd gone.

"You don't think I should?" he asked.

She flicked her fingers, and the candle's flame disappeared.

Cyrus snorted. He supposed that was his answer.

She stepped closer to him. "The front of the arena—was that your doing?"

She must have seen King Orrid.

"What if it was?"

A hint of a smile passed over her lips. "And you're still not satisfied? You'd destroy everything here sooner than you'd take it for your own?"

"Why would I want what he had? What he touched? What he defiled with his very being?"

She stepped closer. "His kingdom is now your kingdom. His palace, your palace. Is that not the ultimate feeling of victory—taking all the spoils, knowing he writhes in the hells as he watches you enjoy his fall?"

Cyrus didn't know if he even believed in gods anymore, or their hells. He did like the idea of Orrid seeing him now, but he'd stabbed him through the fucking eye.

"Burn it," he told her.

Her eyes narrowed. "No."

"You want this palace?" he asked her. "This chamber?"

"I absolutely want this chamber."

"You'd sleep in his bed?"

She stepped closer. "I'll do more than sleep in it."

He wasn't quite sure what that meant, but then she loosened the dress from her shoulders and dropped it to the floor. Underneath she wore a chemise, but it hugged her body closely and left little to the imagination.

The chained woman he'd seen in the cart, the helpless woman strung in the cell—she was gone. The woman that stood before him now was pure power. Her alabaster skin was flawless, and her dark hair hung long over her breasts. She was beautiful. More than beautiful, and it stirred his arousal. But he pulled his eyes away.

He was pretty sure he now knew what she'd meant. "I don't require this of you," he said. "The bargain we made when I freed you, I laid out my full intentions. I have no expectations of you outside of that."

Her eyes narrowed, and her lips parted slightly as the corners of her mouth turned up. "Oh, this isn't about you." She put a hand on his chest and pushed him back toward the bed.

"What are you doing?"

"If you can't guess the answer to that, you're an idiot." She pushed him farther back. "Is this not what we agreed? That we could use each other?"

The back of his knees bumped the bed. "Yes, but..." Still? And did she really want to use him this way?

"Do you not want me to?" she asked.

He expected a question like that to come with a pause, for her to wait for his answer, but she didn't. She only pushed him more forcefully, until he found himself on his back on the bed. And he wasn't exactly sure what he wanted. This witch was a beautiful woman, but he had no connection with her. Of course he'd lain with women he hadn't felt connected to before, but that was... different. Cassia, Gemma—at least he'd known them, and they'd all been very aware of what they were doing, allowing pleasures of the flesh to distract them from this hell of a kingdom. Here with the witch... Well, he didn't know what this was, but as she climbed on top of him with her eyes dark and prowling, he was pretty sure it wasn't for pleasure. At least not his pleasure.

However, he couldn't shake the want she pulled from him. He wasn't sure why she wanted *him*, though. "I am covered in blood," he said.

"Exactly," she breathed.

Then he understood. This was a thread of spite in a tapestry of revenge. This king had tried to kill her. Now she'd take his palace, his chamber, his bed, and fuck his bloody usurper in it.

And Cyrus had no problems with this. Actually, it made him want her even more. He let her straddle him. Pain shot up his injured arm, but he ignored it. If anything, it confirmed he wasn't imagining this absolute madness.

The witch pulled at his belt. He grasped her hip with his good hand, but she pushed it off. "Don't touch me," she said.

Perhaps he should have been offended, but he wasn't. She wasn't letting him *have* her. She wasn't giving herself to him. This wasn't *for* him, or even about him. A wave of power flowed over Cyrus—an unseen force holding him down. He couldn't move.

He wouldn't have tried to touch her again, but she seemed intent on making sure of it. He didn't fight—he wasn't upset by it—he only watched her.

She pulled his cock free, her warm hands quickly making him hard, and angled herself above him. She didn't even bother looking at him as she pulled the bottom of her chemise just out of the way to take him inside her.

Cyrus groaned as the wave of sensation rippled through him. It was different from anything he'd experienced before—better. Maybe it was the surprise of it all, or because there was something profoundly erotic about being held unmoving, able only to watch. Whatever it was, every sensation was heightened, every fiber of his body begged for more. And then she began to move.

She didn't look at him or touch him beyond their joining, but her breaths came faster as she gripped the silken sheets in her fists, and she let her head fall back.

Cyrus tried to roll his hips to meet her, but he couldn't, and it piqued a desperation in him. He wanted more. He needed more. Regardless of whether she felt his need or was driven by a need of her own, she quickened her pace.

The wall candelabras grew brighter, and hotter, as did the inferno between them. He was going to lose himself—

"Witch," he rasped.

She rode him harder, lost in her own vengeful pleasure, not hearing him.

"Witch, I'm close."

She needed to stop. But there was no stopping her. He couldn't move. And then it was too late. Release hit him hard, and he surged with a growl. His body desperately tried to buck against the force that pinned him, but the invisible force still held. "Witch!" he roared.

She let out a gasp, curling forward as she quaked on top of him in her own release. Her warmth pulsed around him. Her pace slowed until she came to a stop, her breaths short and heavy, and finally, she looked at him.

"Get off me," he panted.

Confusion etched across her brow, but she pulled herself off. The invisible force let him go.

"What's wrong with you?" she asked.

He staggered up from the bed, away from her, still panting. "I released inside you." He raked his hand through his hair. How had he been so foolish? "I can't have a child."

"Do you really think I'd let myself be seeded with a child? By *you*?"

Her emerald eyes stared back at him. She almost looked offended. He didn't care about her insult, only the implication of her words. "You have the power to prevent it?"

"Of course I do."

Relief filled him.

Her eyes narrowed. "Have you never climaxed in a woman before?"

The question caught him off guard. "I can't want to bring a child into this world."

Her tongue flicked across her teeth, and a cruel smile pulled at her lips. "Well, did you at least enjoy it?"

He snorted. This woman was bold. "I was a little preoccupied trying to hold, so I have to admit I didn't appreciate it to its fullest."

"Well now you know for next time."

Again, it took him a moment to find his reply. "There will be a next time?"

She slipped off the bed. "You were actually enjoyable."

He felt like that might be a compliment. But wait... "I'm not looking for a relationship," he said.

"Neither am I."

Confusion flooded him. "You want me only to sleep in here, then?"

"No. Find your own room."

Cyrus chuckled in disbelief. "So... you're just going to call on me? To visit you at your whim?"

She tilted her head to the side. "Does that work for you?"

He was speechless.

She didn't wait for his answer, only picked up his sword and belt and pushed them into his arms. Then she herded him back toward the door.

"That's it?" he asked.

"That's it."

What a strange woman. He stumbled backward as she pushed him again.

Then she paused. "Oh, wait." She took a small bowl and dagger from the side table. Working quickly, she sliced across his palm with the blade, holding his wrist tightly to allow the blood to drip into the bowl. It was his injured arm, and he gritted his teeth. Still, he didn't stop her.

When she was finished, she shoved him backward again. "Now get out of my room," she told him.

"Wait—"

But she didn't wait. She pushed him out into the hall.

"What's—"

She closed the door, and the slide bolt clicked into place.

Cyrus stood, his clothing still undone, staring at the locked door in front of him and holding his belt and his sword as blood dripped from his hand.

He didn't even know her name.

CHAPTER SEVENTEEN

Cyrus lay in his bed, unmoving, staring at the thick ceiling beam running the length of his chamber. The morning sun poured through his window. He should have been up before dawn, but he'd let himself rest. However, despite the tiredness that blanketed him, he hadn't slept.

The bizarre encounter with the witch still had him reeling. After collecting himself and leaving the palace, he'd joined the men of House Miro and House Ander to secure the western hills, another wealthy district of the capital where several nobles and their small private armies were trying to hold their ground—unsuccessfully.

It was there Cyrus had discovered the power of presence.

He'd stormed villa after villa, not even needing to lift his sword. As soon as his small group of men pushed through the gates, the slaves within were emboldened to stand.

And they did.

They moved from villa to villa, systematically breaching each hold, systematically overwhelming and eliminating the nobles and their men. And with each victory, their numbers grew. Bloodsport fighters, freed slaves, impoverished citizens—it didn't matter. They all came together, and by nightfall, the capital was theirs.

It was late by the time he returned to his chamber, where he was surprised to find the dogs waiting for him. He'd left them wandering the palace. He wasn't sure how they'd found their way back to the villa or to his chamber, but he was too tired to care.

He wanted to drop straight onto his bed, but he desperately needed a bath, and he forced himself to take one. Exhaustion pervaded his every pore—he could have slept in the tub of brown water—yet when he finally let himself lie down atop his mattress, sleep wouldn't come. And so he found himself staring at the ceiling beam well into the night and the early hours of morning. It was the same ceiling beam he'd stared at the past four years. He couldn't stomach the thought of moving into Pyro's bed chamber. It didn't matter anyway; he wouldn't be here much longer.

Pyro was still held in the basement cells. Today, Cyrus promised—today he'd take the lord's life. A gift to himself. Maybe that would satiate the clawing hunger inside him—listening to Pyro's screams as Cyrus flayed the skin from his body. Maybe the real healing would finally come when Cyrus took the life from him, one piece at a time. He'd make it slow. He'd make it last.

Maybe then he'd be able to sleep.

The thought gave Cyrus enough energy to push himself out of bed. He splashed water onto his face from the sideboard basin. It was cold and felt good. He closed his eyes and lingered in the moment. But as he opened them again, he paused at his reflection staring back at him.

The blond hair.

That face.

The face he shared with another.

Oh, to be this close to Alexander...

The constant weight in his chest grew even heavier. "Do you feel me, brother?" he whispered. "The way I feel you?"

The water rippled, as if in answer.

"Of course you do."

Cyrus had dreamed of killing Alexander, although not over and over, as he had with Pyro. He tried not to allow himself to think and hope for things that weren't actually possible.

But now, suddenly, he was realizing how possible they truly were. Maybe this was the reason he didn't feel sated. This was the reason he didn't feel free. Two more men had to die.

His father.

His brother.

"Do you feel me?" he asked the reflection again, leaning closer. "Because I'm coming for you."

The promise breathed new life into him. He pulled on his leathers and boots and stepped out into the morning. He was quickly met by Ram, who bowed his head respectfully before greeting him.

"Don't do that," Cyrus told him.

"I know, but I—"

"I *want* you to *not* do it," he stressed.

Ram swallowed. "Okay." The young fighter picked up his step beside him. "Everan is waiting for you in the dining hall."

"Good." He was headed there now.

Ram glanced back at the dogs that followed. "So, what did you end up naming them?"

"I didn't," he answered, not breaking stride.

"Well, what do you call them, then?"

Cyrus felt his patience waning. "Dogs. I call them dogs." And enough about them. "Go get Jaem and Sergen. I want Pyro brought up."

"Where do you want him?"

Cyrus paused. Should he kill Pyro publicly? No. This was something he'd long dreamed about, something that had given him the will to live when he'd had none. Pyro was his alone. "In his old chamber, you'll find a corner with chains from the ceiling. String him up there."

Pyro had used the space to break men; now Cyrus would use it to break *him*.

Ram nodded and trotted off to do as he was bid.

Cyrus kept toward the dining hall. When he reached it, he was surprised to see every table filled, with even more men standing and holding their plates.

Everyone stood when he walked in, including Everan and Brant, who were seated with their meals on the far side of the hall.

"Don't stand for me," Cyrus said as he reached them and took a seat beside Everan.

Everan snorted with a grin. "You're king now."

"I haven't agreed to that," Cyrus snapped. "And I said don't stand. Not you, not any of our men."

The smile fell from Everan's mouth, and he and Brant seated themselves again.

Cyrus pushed a long breath out. "I'm sorry. This is just a lot."

"Well, you're not doing it alone," Everan assured him.

One of the dogs nudged the side of his leg, and Cyrus put his hand on the animal's head. He'd wondered if these animals might be a nuisance following him around, but he found them somewhat calming.

"What did you name them?" Brant asked.

Everan chuckled.

Cyrus cut him a side-eye. "I didn't. They're dogs. They don't need names."

"Well, how do you call them apart from each other?"

"Why would I ever need to do that?"

Brant frowned, then his eyes shifted, and Cyrus followed them to see Kord approaching.

Kord gave an exaggerated bow when he reached them. "My king," he said to Cyrus with a grin.

"I swear to the fucking gods," Cyrus mumbled under his breath.

Kord laughed and took a seat beside him.

Cyrus wasn't too annoyed. Kord was in good spirits, very different from the last time he'd had seen him. Cyrus was glad of it, even if it did come at the cost of a little teasing.

Anisi, a young girl who often worked the kitchen with Portia, set two plates of food in front of Cyrus and Kord with a smile, then stepped carefully over the dogs who lay in the middle of the walkway between the tables, before flitting off again back to the kitchen. Cyrus paused, watching her disappear, then glanced around the dining hall at the regular kitchen servants, all tending the men who'd come for breakfast.

"What?" Everan asked. "You have a weird look on your face."

"It's just..." Cyrus drew his gaze around the dining hall again. "They're all still working. They're free, but they're still working."

"Everyone's working. No one knows what to do now, so they're all just doing what they normally do until you tell them otherwise."

Cyrus rested his forearms on the table and leaned his weight onto them as he let out a deep sigh. "I don't know what I want them to do." What did they want to do? Would they not be the best ones to define that? But there was only the weight of their hopes pressing down on him.

"Well, what are *you* going to do?" Everan asked him.

Cyrus's eyes traveled the hall again, this time not looking at the people but at the hand-hewn rosewood arches that sprung from marble columns along the wall and peaked at least ten men tall. From their centers hung wrought iron chandeliers, requiring the efforts of no less than forty people to light them each night. Tearflower-stained glass, a precious commodity because of the hazard to create it, stretched the length of the hall, from the black rhodium-studded doors to the double halls leading to the kitchens that held a staff of more than thirty. It was beautiful. Luxurious. But luxury was a trap.

"I'm going to tear it all down," he said.

Everan's head jerked up. "What?"

"I'm going to tear it down."

Everan and Kord looked at each other and then back at Cyrus.

"All of it?" Kord asked.

"All of it."

"Cyrus," Everan said, "don't make a rash decision."

Cyrus dropped his brow. "Are you serious? This place was built on the backs of slaves. Men have died for it."

"And you'll reduce that work to nothing?"

Cyrus stared at him.

"Use it," Kord told him.

Cyrus snorted. "For what?"

"To give people a beautiful life here."

"How can life be beautiful here after everything that's been done?"

"Look around you," Kord told him. "Men are celebrating, they're smiling. They're the happiest they've ever been. Would you take that from them? What would they do then? Where would they go? If you destroy it, that only serves yourself."

Cyrus sat back in his chair. Was that true? Was he the only one who wanted to tear this kingdom to the ground? He looked around the hall again—the men talking, laughing, clasping one another on the shoulders, smiles on their faces.

Cyrus stilled as his eyes landed on Kieve.

The fighter had just entered, seemingly bewildered at the sight of the overflowing hall. He stumbled in a circle, his eyes wide and his mouth open. Cyrus hadn't seen him for a couple of days, especially not out of his chamber, and he quickly rose to meet him.

"Brother," he called, crossing the space between them and clasping his friend's shoulders. Kieve was pale and looked unsteady. Cyrus wasn't sure the last time he'd eaten.

"Is it true?" Kieve asked him. "Have we taken the palace?"

"We've taken the whole city."

Kieve gaped at him, then his eyes welled. "Are we... Are we free?"

Cyrus squeezed Kieve's shoulders tighter. His own eyes stung. "You're free."

Kieve's breaths came faster, and he swayed.

"Here," Cyrus said, pulling him toward the table. "Sit." He pushed his own plate in front of him. "Eat."

Kieve looked at Everan, still in disbelief, and Everan gave him a warm nod.

"Eat," Cyrus encouraged him again.

The broad-shouldered fighter only stared at him. The fork trembled in his hand. "But I haven't..." His words came unevenly. "I haven't done anything to help."

Cyrus straddled the bench next to him and gripped his arm. "You survived." He gripped him harder. "You survived," he said again. "That's enough. Now eat."

Kieve took a bite of the eggs and ham, chewing slowly. Then he ate more. Cyrus told him about what had happened in the arena, about Manus, and about the witch. Everan and Kord listened intently too—Cyrus hadn't told them *everything*, and their eyes grew wide with what had happened in the king's chamber.

Kieve finished his plate, then ate another, pausing only to interject questions. It was the best Cyrus had seen his friend in weeks. What he wouldn't give for Kieve to be better, and suddenly he found himself saying, "I have something for you."

Cyrus led Kieve from the dining hall to the east side of the villa and main residence, but as they reached Pyro's chamber, he paused when he noticed Kieve had stopped in the doorway. Cyrus cursed himself. He hadn't thought of how Kieve might feel returning here. Was this a mistake?

But slowly, Kieve stepped inside, where his eyes found Pyro gagged and hanging in chains. Sweat drenched the ill-fated lord, probably from struggling to free himself. Or from what he knew was to come. He struggled again when he saw Cyrus, but he should have known there was no escaping these chains.

Kieve shot an astonished look at Cyrus before looking back to Pyro.

This had been a moment that Cyrus had dreamed of, a moment he'd waited for. A moment he'd wanted for himself. But if it would heal Kieve, he'd give it to him. He drew his dagger from his belt and held it out, handle first.

"He's yours," he said, his voice low.

Kieve took the blade without a word, his face pale. His hands were as cold as stone. He stepped forward, slow and measured, until he stood before the man that had broken him.

Pyro's swollen eyes fell on him, struggling to focus. Recognition dawned slowly. Then terror.

"P-please," Pyro whimpered.

Cyrus stepped back to watch. Everything Pyro had done, all the pain he'd caused, all the suffering—now he'd be the one who suffered. He'd scream. He'd beg. But there would be no mercy.

Kieve stood still. He stared at Pyro for a long, quiet moment. Perhaps he was planning what he'd do to this man. Perhaps he was relishing the anticipation of it all.

But then, without warning, before Cyrus could react, he drove the dagger clean into Pyro's chest—fast and precise. Directly into the heart.

Pyro gasped once, then sagged against the chains, dead before he'd even realized what had struck him.

Cyrus blinked, the violence too brief. "That's... That's it? You just... ended him?"

Kieve turned, his face unreadable. "I just want it to be over."

Cyrus's jaw clenched. "You could have made him suffer. You could have made him *feel* what he did to you."

"But it wouldn't change anything," Kieve whispered.

He pressed the bloodied dagger back into Cyrus's palm. Then he left, leaving Cyrus alone with the body of the man who'd caused so much suffering, and with the hollow echo of an ending that didn't feel like victory.

Chapter Eighteen

The dark green topiaries sat in stark contrast to the golden sands of the villa grounds. Anything growing in this cursed kingdom was a miracle. Pyro owned the only true gardens in Rael—even the palace gardens were made of stone statues—and while the villa gardens were certainly beautiful, Cyrus hated them. He hated everything about this place, but he wasn't walking the gardens to love them or hate them. It was merely where he could be alone. The villa was overrun now with men flocking to it—coming in droves with their misplaced loyalty and their hopes.

And he hated that too. He hated that people looked to him now. He hated how people called him king. He had wanted to free them, not rule them. He'd wanted revenge, not a throne. He'd exchanged the chains of the arena for the chains of obligation.

Knee-high hedges lined the flagstone walkway, curving the path around to a central fountain. Here, Teron sat quietly on a bench, staring at the plumes of water that shot up into the air and then cascaded down the tiered pools to the catch below. Cyrus slowed.

When Teron noticed him, he gave a small smile. "Sire." He moved to stand, but Cyrus waved for him to stay.

Cyrus sighed and sat down beside him. "Please, Teron, not you too."

"That is the sound of an unhappy man."

"I can be happy and still not want people to call me king."

"That's true. *Are* you happy, though?"

Cyrus opened his mouth to speak, but no words came. Of course he was happy. He'd killed Orrid, taken Pyro, held the capital, freed his men. How could one not be happy with that?

Because he still had more to do...

He cleared his throat. "How long have you been out here?"

"Since just before dawn."

Cyrus shifted in surprise. Dawn had been some time ago. "Couldn't sleep?"

"I slept wonderfully," the old man replied. "But I wanted to watch the sunrise. I can't remember the last time I did so."

Cyrus couldn't remember the last time he'd enjoyed a sunrise either. The morning light arced a rainbow through the mist of the fountain, and he also couldn't remember the last time he'd seen a rainbow. He thought the sight might stir something within him—peace. Hope. Joy. But there was nothing.

It didn't take away the weight.

"I don't want to be king," he said.

"You don't choose fate; fate chooses you."

Cyrus shook his head. He wasn't sure he believed in fate. Even if he did... "I don't think fate is choosing me to be king. These people—I can't be what they need. I can't do anything for them. I can't heal them; I can't even heal myself."

"You do so much more than you know. You give them the dream and opportunity of a new life." The old man quieted. Then he turned. His brown eyes studied Cyrus. "You give them justice. Maybe that's what you need too."

Cyrus let himself hang on that thought. *Justice.* Wasn't that what Everan had said? Yes. He could deliver that. He could right the wrong. But he didn't need to be king to do that.

Teron reached for his bandaged arm, but Cyrus pulled back.

"Cyrus," the old man scolded fondly.

Resignation washed over him, and finally, he let Teron pull off the bandaging. His wounds were starting to sour; he needed the healer's touch. And the witch had cut him across his sword hand. He needed that healed as well. He wanted to tell Teron about her too, but what would he say? That he'd found the most beautiful woman who'd completely confounded him? No—he'd sound like a fool. He didn't even know if he'd see her again. He'd do better to forget her.

Teron finished pulling off the linen. Blood beaded where pieces of the wrap had melded to his skin, and Cyrus grimaced against the sting. He braced for the rush of Teron's mind, but as Teron touched him, there was no flood of horror and pain. No nightmares of darkness and blood. These memories remained, yes, but inside Teron's mind was something Cyrus had never seen before.

Peace.

For the first time since Cyrus had known him, the old man was at peace.

Cyrus watched him work—healing, rocking slightly to what might have been a melody in his own head. When the last stitch of flesh was healed, Teron released him.

They sat quietly in the calm of the morning.

"Can I ask you something?" Cyrus said after a time. "Why did you never live in the palace? You had the choice, but you chose to stay here, with the man who captured you."

"I was captured long before Pyro came along. I've been owned by powerful men for well over half a century now." Teron smiled at the sunrise. "But a seer once told me that there would be a man who would come—a fighter, under a purple banner—not born of nobility but of blood and wrath. This man would change the fate of Rael. Forever."

A purple banner.

Pyro's banner.

Teron turned to him. "That man is you."

Cyrus shook his head. "That prophecy could mean anyone."

"Cyrus," Teron chided. "You cannot say things like that as a smart man. Look what you have just done."

He stared at Teron, his pulse quickening. "Well, it doesn't mean I would change Rael for the better. I could change it for the worse."

"Worse than Orrid? Worse than Pyro?"

"I've already changed the fate of Rael; this doesn't mean that I have to also become king." Cyrus was sweating. Why was he sweating? It wasn't even that hot yet. And why did everything suddenly feel so overwhelming?

This was a choice.

He had a *choice*.

He could say no.

His voice came quietly now. "Would you be disappointed in me if I said no?"

Teron shook his head. "I could never be disappointed in you."

Cyrus stared back out at the red horizon, blinking back the blur that came to his eyes. "I'm going to be terrible at it," he said finally.

"But you're already the best that's ever been." The old man smiled. "King Cyrus."

CHAPTER NINETEEN

The sun beat down mercilessly as Cyrus slipped off his horse outside the palace.

"Feels weird to be here," Kord said as he dropped down from his own mount.

"I bet it will feel a whole lot weirder inside," Everan said.

Kord snorted.

They let their horses drink from the center fountain. It wasn't a place for horses, but that didn't matter now. The dogs lapped up their fill as well. Strange that they still chose to stay with him. Cyrus wondered if the cats would return, but no one had seen them.

"What did you name them?" Kord asked, eyeing the animals.

Everan gave a hearty laugh.

"Why does everyone keep asking me that?"

Kord shrugged. "Because that's what you do with a dog."

"I don't have to name them. They're just dogs. They don't speak; they don't understand."

"A dog knows its name," Everan said. "I had one as a kid; it came when it was called. They're quite clever. Well, some of them."

Kord smiled. "I'll name them."

"You're not naming my dogs."

"Cyrus," Kord pestered.

"Fine. Fucking fine." Cyrus looked at the dogs. "One, Two, Three," he said, and pointed at each one.

"Those are terrible names."

"Well, that's what you're getting."

After drinking their fill in the fountain, the dogs trotted off, and Cyrus, Everan, and Kord started up the stairs to the main double doors of the palace.

"Fuck, that's bright," Kord said. The white marble reflected the light and was nearly blinding. Cyrus's own eyes teared up in protest.

Once inside, his vision settled, but he didn't *feel* settled. He already regretted letting Teron talk him into moving into the palace. He didn't need a palace, or want one, but he'd given the villa to Kieve, and while Kieve had wanted him to stay, it would be strange for a king to live in a villa owned by another.

But then he'd also given the palace to the witch. Well, *had* he given it to her? Or just the king's chamber? He couldn't remember. He couldn't remember anything he'd said or agreed to during the last time they'd met.

Was she even still here?

"Wow," said Kord, letting his eyes travel the hall.

It dwarfed them—just the three of them, although Cyrus had invited more than just Everan and Kord to join him. He'd welcomed all his men, and more. Within a few days, the palace would be filled with people. He'd need help rebuilding a kingdom, and anyone who'd give that help would share in Rael's riches.

"There you are," a woman's voice called.

They all turned.

It was the witch. She stood at the top of the wide marble staircase. Her dark hair hung long and unbound, the same as when he'd last seen her. She wore an emerald dress, the color of her eyes, and although it stretched down her arms and up her neck, there was something strangely provocative about it.

"Is that her?" Kord asked quietly, although his voice echoed through the hall.

"I am," she answered for him.

Cyrus narrowed his eyes. "I could have been talking about another woman."

"You weren't."

Both Everan and Kord looked at him with smiles of bewilderment. Clearly, they were entertained. If Cyrus were honest with himself, he was too. This woman was bold. Brazen. Did he like it? No. *Yes?*

"Come," she said. "I'll show you where your chamber is." She turned as if assuming he'd just follow.

"Who says I'm staying here?"

"Are you not?" she asked without turning back.

Everan and Kord chuckled.

"Go on," Everan said. "I've promised Visa a room with a window. I'm sure your witch hasn't assigned servants' quarters yet—I'm going to stake a claim."

"You're not staying in servants' quarters," Cyrus objected.

"Don't worry. I'll find a suitable place."

"I'll go with him," Kord said.

Cyrus tightened his scowl.

Kord shrugged. "What? You need to let go of a little more stress. If you're lucky, she might help you with that." He winked.

Everan laughed, and he and Kord struck out toward the south end, leaving Cyrus alone in the great hall.

Cyrus looked up at the stairs and, with a sigh, started up after the witch. His footfalls on the white marble echoed off the empty walls.

The walls.

He paused. When he'd been here a couple of days ago, there had been paintings of the royal family. Now the walls were bare. The paintings were gone. As were the bodies in the hall.

"Are you coming?" the witch called, and she disappeared around a corner. She walked quickly, and he had to take long strides to catch up with her.

"You're still here," he said.

"Of course I'm still here, for a little while anyway, until I find what I'm looking for."

"What are you looking for?"

"That's not your business."

He almost quipped back but stopped himself. He didn't really care what she was looking for. She could have her secrecy. He *did* need to know about something else, though. He still bore the markings on his arms, although he wasn't sure what purpose they still served. "I wanted to ask you, when will these go away?" He flashed the markings.

"They won't. And you don't want them to. You'll need them for our deal."

"Our deal?"

The witch led him to an adjoining hall.

"Look, I'll be honest," he said. "I really don't remember what even happened the last two times we met."

She turned and stopped. "You don't remember me fucking you?"

Well, that... "No, I-I, uh, definitely remember that." He almost laughed, still at the disbelief of it all. "I meant, uh, the conversation."

She stopped in front of the chamber at the end of the hall. "Our deal is that you give me power, I give you power." She waved a hand at the room. "This is your chamber." She swung the door open, and her eyes traveled the space. His eyes stayed on her.

"But I don't want power," he said. "I don't need it now."

"Everyone wants power, whether they need it or not." She turned back to him. "And I'm only here until I find what I'm looking for. Then I'm leaving. Take advantage while you can."

Right. "So, what all can you do? Can you heal?"

"Witches don't have healing power."

"Teron does."

"He's not a witch."

Cyrus knew that. Maybe.

"What's your name?" he asked.

Her lips thinned as they tightened. "Essandra," she said finally.

"Essandra," he repeated. He nodded slowly, mulling. "So, how's this going to work—you're just going to be by my side, helping me out?"

"Don't mistake me for an ally," she said sharply. "Or a friend. But as long as I'm here and I have your blood, you'll have the power of my whole coven."

"Where is your coven?"

"That's also not your business."

Right.

It was another night of staring at the ceiling, albeit now a ceiling of crossbeam craftsmanship and elegant crown molding inside his palace chamber.

The pull of power from within him had ceased. He'd quickly come to recognize it as Essandra using his blood. The witch had come with her dagger and a bowl earlier that evening, drawing a steady stream from him again. He'd made her take from his arm this time, so he could still use his hands until he saw Teron again. He wondered what she was using the blood for. She was searching for something, although she refused to tell him what, but that was the least of his worries. He had a kingdom to look after now.

He didn't know why he'd agreed to this—to be… He still couldn't say it, even to himself. The thought soured his stomach. He stretched his aching body. He was used to bloodsport fighting. How did the weight of this new responsibility tire him so much? But it wasn't the kind of tired that helped him sleep. He didn't know why he still couldn't sleep.

It wasn't the bed, which was plush and comfortable. Or maybe it *was* the bed—maybe it was *too* plush and *too* comfortable.

What was he doing?

He shouldn't be here.

He didn't belong here.

No. It was this palace that didn't belong. Why had he agreed to leave it standing? Cyrus closed his eyes and inhaled deeply. Maybe if he—

"Mama!"

A girl's scream shook him from his thoughts, and he bolted up in the bed, reaching for his sword. He quickly found it. His hand curved around the hilt, bringing a confident calm with it, and he paused before pulling the blade from the scabbard.

Cyrus listened for the sound to come again.

The full moon outside the windows did little to light the room. His eyes moved over the shadows around him as he strained his ears. Still nothing. He steadied his breaths and stilled to listen closer.

But everything was quiet.

He heard nothing. He saw nothing.

It was his mind playing tricks on him.

Slowly, Cyrus lowered his sword and rested it back on the floor against the wall, but still within reach. He let himself sink back onto the bed, and his beating heart slowed, but as he closed his eyes again, it hit him.

"Mama!" came the scream. "Mama!"

He bolted up once more, and his hand flew to his head—it was a scream from inside him, but it wasn't his own.

A vision? No, not a vision... A memory? Not a memory—he could hear. How could he hear? He found himself in the middle of a village—a village on fire. Thatch-roofed houses sat ablaze, black smoke climbing high into the air. People ran by him as they were attacked from all sides. Men mounted on armored horses chased them.

He could hear the dying, smell their burning flesh, taste it in the air. How was this possible?

"Mama!" came the scream within him again. His own panic rose, but he tried to push it down. This wasn't his memory; this wasn't real.

"Mama!"

Smoke filled his lungs, and he coughed. It *was* real.

The fear of abandonment flooded him.

"Mama!"

She'd left.

She'd left him.

She—

A hand grabbed him, and he spun. A woman clasped his cheeks and pulled him to a stop. Her brown eyes bore into him. "Sabine, I'm here!"

A sob of relief escaped his lips. He tried to calm himself—this wasn't his dream.

"Listen to me!" The woman's voice was thick with fear. "Do you remember how to get to Abiniah's?"

"I th-think so," the voice within him stammered.

"Take the forest trail, go up the stream to cover your tracks. You can make it there before night. Get there, and she'll know what to do. Don't let anyone see you. Go!"

"Where's Indira?"

"I'll find her, but you need to go!"

"I can't go by myself!"

"I'll be right behind you after I find your sister."

Fear swelled within him.

"Be brave, my strong girl." Tears filled the woman's eyes. She held him tight and kissed his cheek fiercely. "I love you. Now go!"

Cyrus tore open his eyes, panting. This wasn't him. *This wasn't him.* Sweat beaded his brow. How was he hearing this? How was he feeling it? Tasting it? Smoke and ash.

Because it wasn't a vision. Visions didn't do that.

He swung his legs over the edge of the bed and hunched forward to catch his breath. It had been a nightmare—nothing like he'd ever had before. However, still a nightmare. A very strange nightmare, but nightmares usually made no sense.

Maybe it was the stress getting to him, the burden of the crown. He'd never done anything like this before, and he was afraid. He was afraid of failing. Ruling a kingdom brought a host of fears different from those of the arena. Fighting was easy—he knew what to do. Ruling was hard. And he was alone.

He needed help.

Yes—*that was it*—he'd get help.

Cyrus lay back, and his heart calmed. That was what he'd do. He knew a lot of smart people. He closed his eyes and let his mind drift again.

More visions came, but easier ones this time. Simple battles, men killing one another—visions he could fall asleep to.

Chapter Twenty

Cyrus walked with purpose. He had a plan. He turned a corner to find Kord, Sergen, and Hephain walking toward him.

"I need you to come with me," he said to Kord. Then his gaze paused on Hephain.

The ex-guard gave a small bow of his head.

"How many men did you keep?" Cyrus asked him. The last Cyrus had seen him, he'd charged Hephain with determining the fate of the remainder of Pyro's guards.

"About a quarter, Sire."

The title grated him, but Cyrus was too caught up in his answer to really be bothered. "A quarter?" That was certainly less than he'd expected Hephain to keep of the men he'd once led. His eyes narrowed. "Seifer? Pollock? Beal?" he asked.

Hephain shook his head. "I kept only those sympathetic to your cause, those I knew would be loyal to your rule."

That was a surprise. Cyrus eyed him a little longer. The ex-guard had already stripped the rich purple—Pyro's sigil color—from his armor accents and replaced it with a flat black and red. Cyrus had seen these colors more and more among the men, although he wasn't sure from where they'd come, or what had inspired them. Perhaps it was the black ash of a fallen kingdom, the red blood of a fallen sovereign. Cyrus didn't have the time or the care to think about things like colors or sigils or symbols, but he also knew men needed things to bond them, to unify them and rally their spirits. So black and red it was.

Finally, Cyrus said, "You come with me too."

Sergen gave a bow of his head and left them, and Cyrus led Kord and Hephain to a room where more of his men had gathered: Everan, Jaem, Brant, Ram, and Bash. There were so many more he could have invited, but these were the men he trusted most. These were a good start. Cyrus was also pleased to see Kieve had come.

Kieve had abandoned the villa and now stayed in a room at the far south end of the palace, a small room that he rarely left. He'd said he was better, but he didn't seem better. He remained quiet and withdrawn. He was quiet now, and his silence hung heavy in the room, a reminder of what they'd all escaped from, of what they were fighting for. Cyrus didn't burden him with attention—Kieve didn't like attention—but he was glad to see him here.

Cyrus took up a side drawing room for his makeshift council chamber, with a hastily found table and mismatched chairs. There was a palace council room of grandeur, but somehow this pragmatism felt more natural and fitting.

Essandra had come too. Cyrus was surprised she'd obliged him. He wasn't sure what he needed a witch for yet, or even what she could do, but she'd offered him power in exchange for power, and he planned to take advantage of that while he could. He wondered if she felt uncomfortable in a room full of bloodsport fighters. Her face gave away nothing.

Cyrus put his hands on the table and leaned his weight forward, looking around at everyone. "Brothers."

All eyes were on him.

"If I'm going to do this, I need help," he told them. "I need a council."

The men all glanced at one another.

Cyrus's eyes stopped on Everan and Kord. On Kieve. On Brant. "Some of you know me well." Then they moved to Hephain. "Some of you don't, but you will." His gaze swept around the room. "But all of you are men I'm choosing to put my trust in for the future."

"Wait," Essandra interrupted. "A council entirely of bloodsport fighters?"

"Are you inquiring for yourself?" Kord asked her.

She didn't bother to look at him as she flicked her hand. "I have neither the time nor the desire." Her eyes were on Cyrus. "But you need a mix of others, not just fighters."

"Others?" Kord asked. "We've served him well so far. What will others provide that we cannot?"

Essandra tilted her head, finally shifting her gaze to him. "You know the sword, but are you versed in history, or economics? Trade?" Her stare sharped on him. "Are *you* going to negotiate a treaty? Do you know what Rael needs? What Rael has to offer?"

Kord didn't answer. She cast her eyes around the rest of the table. "Any of you? Does anyone know law? Finances, taxation?" She shook her head. "A king also needs people around him with diverse thought," she pressed. "He needs a council who thinks differently from one another, and who will debate properly."

"You made your point," Kord gruffed.

Cyrus sighed, but he couldn't argue. She wasn't wrong. If anything, it was even more of an indication that he wasn't the right person to do this. He needed expertise beyond what any of them had. But how to get that expertise...

He mulled for a moment, then said, "I need a man to deliver a message."

"I can at least do that," Kord replied.

"I need scholars. Go to the university. Ask for those with knowledge in these fields. Ask if they want to contribute to the new Rael. If so, tell them to come speak to me."

Kord nodded.

Cyrus paused for a moment. Then he said, "Hephain."

The lead guard shifted in surprise. "My sword is yours, Sire," he answered.

"You'll call me Cyrus. All of you." To Hephain, he said, "As lead guard, you accompanied Pyro here often and are familiar with many of Orrid's court. You know Rael and who can be trusted. Is there anyone I should look to retain?"

Hephain paused for a moment, thinking. "Fatim Tavoy, master of coin; Murius Sinlane, master of law; and Verin Faulk, merchant councillor. They all held loyalty to the kingdom over loyalty to the king."

"Find these men," Cyrus said.

"I also have a few additional proposals," Hephain added, "for a master of records, master of ships, and master of public works. All men exceptional at their craft who would serve you well."

Cyrus turned to Jaem. "Go with Hephain to see if any of these men are still alive. If they are, bring them here."

Jaem gave a nod.

Cyrus leaned back in his chair. *That* was a start. He just hoped it was the right one. As much as he didn't want to do this, he *was* committed to trying to do it right. If everything fell apart, it wouldn't just be his failure—it would be the end to everything they'd fought for.

Cyrus hated the massive dining hall, with its six-tier chandeliers hanging from ceilings higher than eight men tall. He hated its tapestries and gilded wall reliefs, its corner candelabras and golden inlays set into the marble floor. He hated the table that sat at least fifty people.

But he didn't hate the excited smile on Visa's face as she shuffled him to sit at the head of the table, before a fully prepared feast. Everan took the chair to Cyrus's left.

"Fucking hells," Kord said as he walked in with Brant, Ram, and Bash just behind him.

Brant stared with his eyes wide at the spread on the table. "This is the most food I've ever seen."

"The *best* food I've ever seen," Jaem added as he slid into the seat beside Ram.

"Don't tell that to me, tell it to Portia," Visa said with a grin. "She's happier than a bee in a poppy field in that kitchen. Make sure you save room for dessert."

"Get her in here to eat with us," Cyrus said.

"She won't. She said she's never leaving it." Visa shook her head with a laugh. "I think she wants to sleep in there too."

They all laughed.

But the laughter quieted as Essandra stepped through the door.

She wore a midnight-blue gown with her hair swept up off her neck—very formal. She glanced at all of them, and the faintest flicker of unease flashed across her face.

"Who invited her?" Kord muttered.

"I did," Visa said. She jumped up from where she was sitting beside Everan and ran to Essandra, linking their arms and pulling her toward the table. "I'm glad you came!"

"I feel a little overdressed," Essandra whispered to her, too faintly for the room to hear. Almost too faintly for Cyrus to hear. But not quite.

Visa gave her a reassuring smile. "I think you look beautiful!"

She did look beautiful. Cyrus stood and pulled out the chair to his right. "Lady Essandra," he said.

Her eyes narrowed as she reached him, and she paused. "Are you mocking me?"

He shifted back. *What?* "No. Of course not."

She softened slightly. "Oh," she said.

Did she really think he would mock her?

Her face snapped back to a cool countenance as she seated herself, and Cyrus took his own chair again.

But then he glanced around. "Wait, where's Kieve?"

"I tried to get him to come," Visa said. "But he just wanted to eat in his chamber. I thought you'd be fine with that."

He sighed but nodded. Whatever Kieve wanted. "What about Teron?" he asked.

"He's still packing his books," Visa told him. "He's decided to stay at the villa tonight. He said he'll try to come tomorrow. I did drop him off some dinner, though."

Cyrus had convinced the healer to move into the palace with him. If Cyrus was going to live here, so would Teron. However, the old man refused to let anyone pack his books—he insisted on doing that himself.

"Should we invite Hephain?" Kord asked.

Visa gasped. "Oh! I didn't even think of him. I'm so sorry."

"If that's all right with you?" Kord asked Cyrus.

"Fine," Cyrus told him. He glanced around the table. "We can work out who else might join us. You see there's plenty of room. But for now—eat, brothers." He nodded and smiled at Visa. "Sister."

Happy laughter and clapping echoed around the table.

Everan raised his glass. "Before we do that, I'd like to say a few words."

They all quieted.

He drew in a breath. "I don't want to bring up the horrors that we've been through, but without acknowledging them, we can't truly appreciate how far we've come." He leveled his gaze on Cyrus. "Cyrus, you brought us through our darkest times. Sometimes, the only hope I had was the promise you made to me—the promise you made to us all—that you would get us out. I'm alive today because of you." His eyes welled. "I'm free today because of you." He took Visa's hand. "I have happiness because of you. My friend. My brother. My king."

Everyone nodded their heads.

Everan raised his glass higher. "Here's to our new king." He nodded to Essandra. "To our new friends." With his glass even higher, he said, "To our new life."

A cheer rang through the hall, and they heartily passed around the plates of food as they fell into lively conversation.

Cyrus looked at Essandra.

"You are so loved," she said. "Well done, seer."

He snorted. "You're as much to thank for this as I am."

"No." She shook her head. "You built this—the hearts you have here." She gave a sad smile. "Enjoy it. Happiness is so fleeting."

The food was the best that Cyrus had ever tasted, the conversation the best he'd ever had, the jokes the funniest he'd ever heard. It didn't matter that it was in a palace. It could have been on a dirt floor around a pot of unflavored broth. What mattered was that they were together, like this. Free. Safe. This was what they'd dreamed of. What they fought for.

The door to the hall swung open, and Hephain barged in. "Cyrus!" His voice was grave and urgent. "The palace is under attack!"

CHAPTER TWENTY-ONE

There had been no warning. No time.

Cyrus and his men raced down the dimly lit halls, their footsteps thundering through the palace. Torchlight flickered violently as they passed, casting twisted shadows along the stone walls. More men joined them as they went.

They spilled outside to find the courtyard in chaos. Men were scrambling to close the front gates as the nobles' army tried to fight their way through. Cyrus wasn't sure how big their army was—a couple hundred or a couple thousand—but it certainly felt on the larger side.

Oil-fed fires scattered the capital, curling smoke into the night sky and choking out the stars. Flaming arrows streaked the sky, hissing into roofs and alley structures, igniting them one by one. The clash of swords and shouting men filled the air. Someone called out Cyrus's name, but he could barely hear anything above the noise.

Suddenly, Ryman appeared beside him, breathless with blood streaked across his face. Cyrus pulled the Lycus House lead closer to hear him.

"They hit fast," Ryman shouted into his ear. "We stopped them from coming through on the south side, but we're outnumbered. They're pushing for the palace doors!"

Cyrus's eyes traveled around him. He had thousands of men, but hardly any of them were here. They'd been working to secure the outer reaches and the rest of the kingdom. The palace was exposed. They hadn't expected a raid. And this wasn't just a raid; this was a reclamation. The nobles had come to retake the capital.

He couldn't let that happen.

"Together!" he bellowed to his men. "Defend the doors!"

They swarmed to join him at the base of the palace stairs, their backs to the doors. This was for more than just the palace. The women were inside. Everan fought with a ferociousness Cyrus rarely saw, even in the arena. Visa was inside.

Steel clashed against steel. His fighters moved with precision. Kill after kill after kill. Yet the noble army kept coming.

Cyrus fought at the front, carving through the enemy, but every man who fell was replaced by two more. The tide against him pressed harder. He cut down a man, pivoted, and dropped another.

And he was realizing...

It wasn't enough. He didn't have the men.

He glanced back at the doors. He wasn't going to be able to hold the palace. And if they lost the palace, they'd lose the capital. If they lost the capital, they'd lose Rael. But there was nothing he could do. It was too much to hold. It was going to fall.

He grabbed Everan. "Get everyone from inside the palace and flee through the south gates!"

"I'm not leaving you!"

"We're not going to hold. We have to save as many as we can."

"No, Cyrus—"

Cyrus gripped him harder. "Get Visa out."

Everan stilled.

"Get Visa," Cyrus said again. "Get Essandra. Get as many as you can and get out. Once you make it to the outer reaches, you'll find more of our men. Then you can figure out where to go from there."

"What about you?"

Cyrus cut a quick glance to Kord and Ryman, who each gave a small salute between blows. "We'll give you as much time as we can."

Everan shook his head through gritted teeth.

"Go, brother," Cyrus told him. If one of them might live, let it be the best among them.

Suddenly, the wind shifted, and a biting chill swept through the courtyard. The torchlights flickered wildly along the outer walls and then were snuffed out, plunging them all into darkness. The battle ebbed as the men paused in confusion, and an eerie quiet settled over them. Uneasy. Unnatural.

A hand touched Cyrus's shoulder, and he spun.

It was the witch. She held a small flame in one hand as she reached out to him with the other.

He knew what she wanted.

"Not the palm," he warned. He needed to be able to keep fighting.

Her fingers curled around his wrist, and her flame disappeared. He was again surrounded by darkness. Cyrus couldn't see her now, but he could feel her. She sliced a clean cut across his forearm. The sting barely registered. Then the feel of her lips.

The instant his blood touched her tongue, he felt the pull. Not the pull of his mind but of his power. Through his chest, through his lungs, through his veins.

The air gusted from ice to fire, and the torches along the walls flamed alive again, flooding the courtyard in light. The nobles' men staggered back. Cyrus's men did the same.

Confusion rocked both sides.

Cyrus's eyes darted to Essandra, but her focus was on the fountain.

A pale glow bled from around the edges of the bronze statue at its center. It pulsed lightly before growing brighter.

Then it exploded.

Shards, sharp as knives, shot outward, tearing armor, slicing flesh, felling men like wheat. Cyrus flung up his arm to shield himself, but nothing hit him. Nothing hit his men.

Another explosion boomed as the fountain itself shattered and burst apart, crippling yet another wave of noble forces. Still, his fighters were spared.

Cyrus didn't waste the moment. "Push them back!" He rallied his men. The courtyard burst alive again with battle.

Then came the fire.

Burning spheres of witch-flame slammed into the enemy, setting them ablaze. Screams of the nobles' army rose above the clash of steel.

His men faltered slightly, first in fear. Then that fear turned to awe.

"Push them back!" Cyrus roared again.

They charged forward.

A swarm of the nobles' men attacked from the left, and a wall of rock erupted from the ground to block them. Cyrus glanced back at Essandra. Figures appeared from the shadows around her, cloaked in smoke. More witches. More power.

A male witch beside Essandra ripped up a wall from the ground, then shattered it, flinging shards of stone as she'd done with the fountain.

The witches fanned out. To Essandra's right, a woman threshed blows of power through the air. Men buckled midstride, writhing in agony without even being touched.

Another witch slammed her hands against the ground, and the earth trembled beneath Cyrus's feet. Cracks spidered through the cobbled courtyard. The earth buckled and cracked, then swallowed men where they stood. More screams cut through the night.

Emboldened by the witches, Cyrus rallied his men forward, pressing deeper into the fray. He cut down man after man, slashing through armor and flesh. The scent of blood and burning leather filled his lungs. Through the storm of violence, he kept his eye on Essandra, careful not to get too far from her. It wasn't that he didn't trust her power to keep her safe. He just trusted his sword more.

She moved through the battle like it was a dance—graceful, lethal, calm amid the madness. More witches joined her, and he felt the pull of power through him grow even more. The enemy fought harder, desperate now. They did their best to push toward the palace, but the witches were relentless, and so were his men.

The enemy ranks faltered. Fear took root.

"Drive them back!" Cyrus bellowed, his voice raw, his sword dripping with blood.

Essandra sent a bolt of black flame that reduced everything in its path to mere ash. The air around her shook.

Finally, the nobles broke, scattering into the darkness. Cyrus paused just outside the gates, his chest heaving. Flames broke the night. The courtyard was littered with bodies. The stone beneath his boots was slick with blood.

He turned back to his men. Their eyes moved from him to the scene around them, then to the witches who'd regrouped with Essandra. No one spoke. They only stood with their eyes wide, their mouths open.

What did one even say after witnessing power like that? Perhaps they were all struck with the question of whether it had even been real, as he was. But the devastation of the courtyard told them it was very real.

Apparently Everan was the first to gather his senses. "The nobles are retreating," he said to Cyrus. "Do you want us to follow?"

They didn't have enough men for that. Cyrus shook his head. His eyes searched for Ryman. Finding him, he said, "Go to the outer reaches and call men back to the palace. At least a thousand. More if we have them."

"You think the nobles will try again?"

"I'm sure they will. And they'll be more strategic about it next time."

Ryman nodded and left to do as he was bid. Cyrus turned back to Kord's wary gaze.

"What?" he asked. "You disagree? You question if the nobles will return?"

Kord's eyes traveled to the witches. His voice came low for only Cyrus to hear. "I question if we've bound ourselves to something even darker."

CHAPTER TWENTY-TWO

The nobles didn't try for the capital again that night. Or the next. Or the next. But Cyrus wasn't foolish enough to think they weren't coming.

Within a week, he'd assembled his new council. It was surprising he was able to get them to come to the palace, given it wasn't exactly the safest place in Rael right now. Not only had he found the six men Hephain had recommended, but he'd also secured a number of scholars from the university willing to share their expertise. They'd managed to talk Cyrus into a few more councilmen as well. Now he had a philosopher, although he wasn't sure why he needed a philosopher. He'd also appointed a chief architect and a chief physician. Cyrus already considered Teron his chief physician, but Teron was the only one who possessed real power, and he couldn't heal everyone, nor did he have the time or energy to direct others. This new chief physician was to lead health and welfare for the masses. He didn't have power, but he had knowledge and a network of doctors.

With Rael's council now mostly formed, the makeshift meeting room wouldn't hold them all, and to Cyrus's dismay, they had to move into the official royal council chamber—a room built more for display than discussion. Polished gold leaf trimmed every molding. At the center stood an absurdly long table, flanked by velvet-backed thrones instead of chairs. The room reeked of old power, old arrogance. A tightness ran between his shoulders. Cyrus shifted in his high-backed seat, uncomfortable, and began to wonder if he now had too large a council.

And needing this many councilmen was also more evidence that he wasn't the right person to lead this kingdom. What was he doing other than employing men who knew better than him? All the while, Essandra sat quietly, watching him. Judging him. They were probably all judging him; it was just worse when she did it. He didn't even know why he'd had her attend.

He tapped the letter that Everan had handed him as he'd entered on the edge of the table. It bore a half-red, half-yellow seal. A letter from Osan, the kingdom across the Aged Sea. It was the first official letter he'd received as king, yet he didn't find himself entirely eager to open it. As he broke the seal and read the words, he almost wished he hadn't.

"It's a marriage proposal," he said, and he tossed the letter to the center for the others to read.

"What?" Essandra said in surprise.

He almost picked it back up to read it over again, still in disbelief himself.

"It's an invitation from King Tagasi to discuss the potential for an alliance," Murius, his new master of law, said as he read over the letter. "His daughter, Daiyona, is unwed." He said this as if it were different from what Cyrus had just stated.

Kord snorted. "This king moves fast."

King Orrid's corpse still hung from the entry gates of the arena.

"Osan has had strained relations with Rael for over twenty years," Murius said. "I wouldn't go so far as to call them enemies, but they certainly weren't friends. It doesn't surprise me he would seek this opportunity as quickly as he could. He borders Kharav and has no other allies."

Kharav. That was what some people called the Shadowlands. A prickle of violence ran up Cyrus's spine, but he pushed it down. He had to focus. "I haven't even secured Rael yet."

"He's assuming you will. But, regardless, King Orrid is dead. You can expect many kingdoms to now start looking for opportunities with Rael."

"I'm not interested in marriage."

"You should be interested in what marriage brings—security, capabilities we don't possess, trade, to name a few. King Tagasi is an excellent consideration for—"

"You said I can expect many kingdoms to start reaching out," Cyrus said. "I won't be so hasty to accept the first one. Again, I have other things to focus on, like securing Rael."

"Then what will you tell King Tagasi?"

"I'll tell him I've received his letter."

"That's all?"

"That's all."

"But we should—"

"*That's all*," Cyrus said, more firmly. And that *was* all.

They spent the remainder of the morning reviewing assets of the crown and recommendations for even more council roles to fill, which Cyrus was quickly tiring of, then the conversation drifted to more potential allies to consider. But Cyrus didn't want to rehash their conversation about Osan.

"We'll deal with that later," Cyrus found himself saying as he stood. He'd had enough for the day—at least enough of this council. He'd pick back up with Everan and Kord separately to discuss where to deploy men next to advance against the kingdom's remaining nobles, whom he fully expected to make another attempt at the capital. But as he moved to leave, Naik, his chief physician, spoke up.

"Sire, what will you do about the dead?"

Cyrus still hated the address, but he hadn't managed to get people to stop using it. The question made him pause, though. "What about them?" They'd already been clearing bodies and burning them to prevent vermin and disease.

"King Orrid is still strung up on the gates of the arena."

He eyed the councilman. "I don't see the problem," he said. It hadn't even been two weeks. He could hang there a little while longer.

"Cyrus," Everan said quietly beside him. "Everyone has seen him; it's enough."

Nothing was enough, but… "Fine. Pull him down," he said. He was tired, and had no more energy for debate, or anything else for that matter. "We're done for today."

"Sire," Fatim, his master of coin, said. "We have one more matter to discuss."

Cyrus clasped the ends of the table and rested his weight on his arms, drawing every ounce of patience he could. "What?"

"Food. Provisions are low."

He mulled for a moment. "Take the royal supply. We won't feast in a palace if there isn't enough for everyone."

"That will make only a temporary difference."

Verin, his merchant councillor, interjected. "We can look to negotiate the same terms with the Shadowlands that Orrid had—"

"Nothing from the Shadowlands," Cyrus said abruptly. The thought brought such a vile reaction within him.

"But trade with the Shadowlands accounts for over half of our provisions," Fatim argued.

"I said no food from the Shadowlands." Cyrus wouldn't budge on this.

"So, you'll have us starve?"

"I'll have us figure out another way. Rael has farmlands."

"A few, yes, but not the climate to support mass farming."

Cyrus raked his hand through his hair in frustration. "Do I not have a room full of scholars here?"

"Not scholars of agriculture," Verin said.

Cyrus could feel it—his frustration turning to anger, getting the better of him. And why? Trade was an expected topic, and provisions were a necessary challenge to solve. Why was he getting angry? This needed his attention—this was his job. Maybe it was because he didn't want this job. And every day he spent building Rael was a day denying him the opportunity that fate had given him to set things right. Against his father. Against Alexander. And he was tired—not the tired that comes with lack of sleep, but the deep exhaustion that comes from being pushed beyond one's limits.

He could handle the arena but not the crown—what sense did that make? None. But he couldn't focus on what made sense and what didn't; he needed to get out of this room, out of this place.

"Get me a master of agriculture," he demanded, then turned and strode from the council room. It wasn't his finest demonstration of leadership, he knew, but he couldn't think about that either right now.

Cyrus reached his chamber and pushed through the door, which felt much heavier than he remembered. The whole world felt heavier now. He collapsed onto his bed. The dogs whined for attention, but he couldn't give it to them. He had nothing left. If only sleep would come. But he wasn't that fortunate.

The sun shone bright through the window, and he dropped his arm over his face to shield himself from it. He tried to push everything from his mind, letting himself fall into his inner darkness and walk the edge of where consciousness ended and sleep began.

And then he saw her.

The Mercian princess.

This was the second dream in which she'd come to him recently. Cyrus had seen her many times in many dreams over the years, but not for the past three years. He didn't think much of it; he hadn't really known her as a child, and she'd meant little to him then. He hadn't even realized her absence, but for her sudden return.

And now came the return of the dreams—dreams that didn't feel like dreams.

Rose petals fell around her as she rode under the banner of Aleon—a warm welcome for the Mercian queen. She was smiling. A monster of a man rode beside her, with markings across his chest and down his arms. His face was covered. He looked like a Shadowman, but that couldn't be possible.

A knock on the chamber door ripped him from the depths of his mind. His thoughts evaporated as the dogs jumped to their feet.

The door swung open without giving him an opportunity to answer. It was the witch.

He sighed and let his head fall back onto the bed. She was here for one of two things, neither of which he had the energy to give.

"Be warned, witch," he said. "I'm not in my best form."

"I've yet to see you in your best form," she replied shortly.

Witty, this one, but he wasn't in the mood. What had he just been thinking about? It escaped him now, but it had felt important.

"Get up," she told him.

"Now's not the time," he said.

"Not the time for a solution to your food shortage and dependence on the Shadowlands?"

Cyrus sat up. "What did you say?"

"I said *get up*." Then she turned and swept out of the room.

He pushed himself off the bed. This woman... He walked quickly to catch up with her as she made her way through the palace and outside. The dogs followed.

"What is this solution?" he pressed. Where were they going? What were they doing? He followed her through the gardens, where tall statues stood in place of topiaries, stacked stone breaking the barren landscape into artful tiers of carefully curated natural rock and marble sculptures.

Essandra moved fast for one so small, and he quickened his pace to keep up with her. The heat of the sun beat down on them. He was about to push her for an answer, but his eyes caught on two figures standing near a coveted water fountain—a man and a woman. He wasn't sure if he'd seen them before. Both had honey-colored hair, although they didn't appear to be related, and they wore similarly styled clothing to others in Essandra's coven. Clearly, they were waiting.

When Cyrus and Essandra reached them, she stopped abruptly and turned to him, drawing a thin knife and a palm-size copper bowl from the folds of her gown. He didn't object as she took his hand and didn't flinch as she dragged the blade across his flesh. The lines of her high cheekbones were sharp, as were her eyes, and she showed no hesitation in slicing open his hand. But as she watched the blood trail from his palm and down his forearm to his elbow, she paused. The angles of her face became a little less sharp. Her lips parted slightly, and their eyes met. Perhaps she didn't enjoy cutting him as much as he thought she did.

But whatever she was thinking, she quickly pushed it off and focused back on her task. When she'd filled the bowl to her satisfaction, she turned and stepped between the honey-haired man and woman.

For a moment, he thought she might offer his blood to them and was on the verge of intervening, but Essandra only brought the bowl to her own lips and drank deeply.

The pull of power within him was immediate, but not startling. He knew it now. The connection with the witch was different from the connection with anyone else. He wasn't pulled into her mind. It was like she had the ability to shut him out. There was also a weight to the bond—something more than just a bridge—something that rooted them together. He wondered if she felt it too.

She certainly felt something as she closed her eyes, letting her head fall back. She lifted her hands as she spoke words that he didn't understand into the air.

The eyes of the honey-haired woman beside her turned black, and the woman knelt to the ground. Pushing her fingers into the sand, she spoke the same words as Essandra. Their voices rose in unison.

The sand darkened.

Green shoots sprang up, and Cyrus took a step back. The woman rocked back and forth, continuing to breathe the words, but Cyrus's eyes were on the sprouting greens—row upon row. It was a narrow strip of space, but a mature crop here could feed a small family for several days.

How were they doing this? He wouldn't have believed it if he weren't seeing it himself. In fact, he still wasn't sure he believed it.

Essandra turned back to Cyrus. "If you don't want food from the Shadowlands, you won't need food from the Shadowlands," she said. "This will take time, but it will be weeks, not months."

Cyrus shook his head, still in disbelief. This was too good to be true. He glanced up, squinting against the harsh sun above them. Even if they could start crops in fields, one week in this heat would reduce a plant to nothing.

"How can you sustain it?" he asked. "Can you bring the rain?"

"The coven doesn't possess a weather witch, but..." She nodded to the man beside her, who reached out and put his hand on the fountain. The marble split, and a trench ripped its way around the small plot, forking water through the greens. "If there is a water source, Necross has the power to move earth and rock to provide irrigation."

There were wells and ephemeral pools they could source from. His pulse thrummed faster at the thought that this might actually be a possibility. This was beyond anything he could have ever imagined.

"But you must get others to harvest," she added, "because that is *not* a witch's work."

A smile tugged at the corners of his lips. "I'll get others to harvest," he promised.

"And I'll need more blood. A lot more."

He nodded. "You'll have it." This witch was proving herself to be quite useful. He thought he almost saw a smile of her own, but it might have been his imagination.

She turned and started back to the palace, with the man and woman following behind her. Cyrus watched them go. Then his eyes found Kord, who stood by the far stone wall, watching.

Cyrus crossed the garden to meet him, grinning. "Did you see that?" he asked when he reached him.

His friend had a strange look on his face—not one of awe, as Cyrus had expected.

"What?" Cyrus asked.

Kord's eyes were fixed on Cyrus's bloodied arm, and his lips held a firm frown. "I don't like it."

"What do you mean? Did you not see what she just did?"

"Yeah, and I saw what she did against the nobles too. She's using your power to augment hers."

"She's helping us."

"Yeah, but why? What does she have to gain?" Kord cast a wary look back at the witch, just as she disappeared inside the palace. "Be careful of her, Cyrus."

225

Chapter Twenty-Three

Within two weeks, crops speckled the barren lands surrounding Rael's dense capital. The coven had three hedge witches, and together, with Cyrus lending the power through his blood, they were able to increase harvest speed fivefold. Still, it would take time to build a yield that could sustain an entire kingdom.

The coven kept to themselves in the west wing of the palace. However, the more time Cyrus spent with Essandra, the more he learned about them: Each witch held their own unique power, and as leader of the coven, Essandra was able to wield each of their powers as her own. Their abilities were beyond what he'd already seen, and what he could have ever imagined. In addition to the hedge witches, the geomancer, and the fire witch, the coven also had an illusionist, a forge witch, and a pain witch, among several others. Cyrus had remembered seeing the pain witch in the fight against the nobles, and she was a little too obliging when he'd asked about the power, dropping him to his knees. However, despite what the witches shared, they were guarded with him, no doubt protecting their own agenda. Cyrus was guarded with them as well, because who could really trust a witch?

Beyond the power of his blood, Cyrus felt useless. He didn't know how to tap into his power, what it even was, how to use it, what it could do, what *he* could do. If it weren't for the draw that he felt when Essandra used his blood and his ability to travel to the minds of others when his blood touched their skin, he'd have thought he didn't have any power at all. He couldn't just freely wield it. And while Essandra was certainly more knowledgeable about magic, she didn't have all the answers. And she was a woman full of secrets.

Her coven had limits too. There was only one geomancer, a witch who could move earth and stone, and he was needed to assist with infrastructure as well, which slowed both their speed in establishing irrigation for the new crops and their ability to rebuild essential parts of the city that had been damaged during the rebellion.

Cyrus was hesitant to issue orders requiring the labor of men, but where he called, people came. They used their backs to lift stone, worked their hands to move raw earth, but this time, they did so of their own accord. Within a few weeks, all roads had been cleared and public buildings made ready to be reoccupied, all except the arena. Cyrus left it as it was—the bodies had been burned and cleared but the commemorative statues remained toppled, the wooden spectator seating burned to ash, the gates of the fighters' holding chambers ripped from their hinges. He wasn't sure what to do with the arena—a place he hated but a place that now stood as a reminder of what he'd accomplished and had overcome. He felt he should keep it, like he'd kept his manacles, although they were tucked away privately in his chamber.

The manacles were different. They didn't bring with them a sense of accomplishment but rather a reminder of what had been done to him. Where the arena gave him confidence, the manacles gave him fuel. They were painful to look at, but he would sit and hold them almost every day. He'd run his fingers over the edges that used to cut into his skin, and he'd remember—what it was to wear them, how they felt, not just on his arms but inside himself. He'd let the anger and hate fill him all over again until he thought he'd catch fire. And then he'd think about what he still had left to do, those he still had left to face.

His father.

His brother.

That time was coming.

He just needed to wait for an opportunity.

Within another few weeks, the council had reappropriated the crown's assets and had transitioned all those working on infrastructure and public services to paid labor. Cyrus gave land to those committed to managing it, and two months post rebellion, Rael was a drastically different kingdom than it was before.

But it still *looked* the same. Cyrus hated it. He wanted to rip down everything and start fresh. How could anyone begin a new life here when everything old still remained? It was the same palace of the old king, the same temples where King Orrid had paid homage to the gods of blood.

And it was in just such a temple where he found himself now. He wasn't sure what had brought him here. His eyes traveled the expanse of golden marble that spanned wall to wall under his feet and swept upward in massive columns to a ceiling so intricately carved that it looked like the lace of a gown. How many men had it taken to build this? How many men had died for it?

Cyrus wasn't unfamiliar with temples, especially temples of the Northern religion, which Orrid had proclaimed as Rael's state religion. But as a child of Mercia, Cyrus found Rael's translation nothing like the North's. Mercia didn't own slaves or hold bloodsport games. Cyrus had seen priestesses of Rael's temples when they blessed the arena and the fighters at each New Year's celebration, their gowns draped from their shoulders in a way that exposed their left breasts. Mercia had neither priestesses nor an affinity for exposing women's flesh. This was a perversion of the Northern religion, but it had gained Orrid tithings from the people, and the arena games had flooded him with gold. But Cyrus saw religion for what it was—a way to manipulate the masses, bend them to the depraved will of the power hungry, all under the guise of glory. And the gods—the gods were just as broken as the men who built their temples.

This temple was a mess. Cyrus stepped over the embroidered silk that had been pulled from the altar, through the treasures scattered across the floor—golden goblets inset with jewels, bracelets and necklaces left as offerings by worshippers. Tithing bowls were overturned with their coin now spilled across the marble. Strange these things hadn't been taken.

A rustle behind him caught his ear, and he spun.

It was Essandra. With her dagger at his neck. Her green eyes held a dark ferocity. Was she angry? Frustrated, maybe. Had the mess in the temple been her doing?

"Redecorating?" he asked.

She needled the point of the dagger against his skin.

His eyes dropped to her hand wrapped around the hilt. "Do you not use that on me enough?"

Essandra put more pressure on the blade, and he felt a trickle of blood down his neck. She wasn't in the mood for his teasing.

"What are you doing here?" he asked her.

"What are *you* doing here?" she quipped back.

What *was* he doing here? He didn't even know. "I came to pray," he said, not bothering to hide the flippancy in his voice. He glanced at the disarray around them. "Which doesn't appear to be what *you're* doing." He titled his head. She'd left several rooms of the palace in a similar way. "I take it you're having trouble finding what you're looking for."

Her lips thinned.

"What *are* you looking for?" he asked.

And they thinned even more.

He glanced around the destroyed temple. "Do you not fear angering the gods?" he asked.

Her fiery eyes narrowed. "The gods should fear angering *me*."

Then the corner of her mouth twitched, and an expression flickered across her face that he couldn't read. She drew the tip of the knife down his chest to his stomach and stopped just above his belt. Her eyes met his again, still full of fire. Did she want his body? Here? Now?

She hadn't taken him since their encounter in the palace almost two months ago. He'd assumed she'd lost interest in him. Perhaps she had, but maybe with this opportunity to desecrate a holy place of an unholy land... He could understand the appeal.

It was more than that, though. She was angry, and her angry eyes flashed as her angry hands pushed the blade more firmly against his stomach and ripped at his belt. She wasn't asking. He didn't need to be asked; he held out his open hands at his sides in reply.

She pivoted and turned them so her back was against the altar now. Without thinking, he grasped her waist and lifted her up onto it, but then he caught himself and quickly released her. He was surprised she'd let him do that. He knew his role in this arrangement, and it wasn't one of freedom with her body. Again, this wasn't for him.

He let her pull his cock free and waited for her to ruffle up her skirts and guide him before sinking inside her. The pleasure swept through him, and it was all he could do to not wrap his arms around her and pull her close, to not drop his head in the curve of her neck and breathe her in. To not touch his lips to her skin. To her mouth. Her body called to him, but he reminded himself it was just the desires of the flesh. He gave himself a moment to gain control. Then he started to move.

Cyrus was cautious with his hands, not particularly wanting to be bound by the witch's magic again, and although he didn't see the dagger now, she still had it, and she wasn't shy about using it. He kept himself from gripping her hips and instead reached over her shoulder to grasp the edge of the altar, using it to pull himself deeper.

She reached down between her thighs, up under her skirts, rubbing herself as he moved, and her breaths quickened. He wished he could see her. The ruffle of her gown covered her, even where they were joined.

It wasn't a wide altar, and her head hung back over the edge, elongating her neck. He wanted to wrap his hand around it—not to hurt her but to feel her pulse under his palm. Surely it was beating quickly, as his was now. But he didn't touch her; he only watched. There was something seductive about not being able to see her body—to have to imagine her skin underneath her dress and what her fingers were doing.

He pushed deeper, and deeper still. Her breaths came faster. Cyrus felt his control slipping.

"If you don't want me to finish inside you, I need to stop," he warned.

"If you stop, I'll set you on fire." Her words came between panting breaths.

He focused on the cold marble altar underneath them. On the stitching of her gown. On the cadence of his own breaths. But he couldn't keep his eyes from moving back to her heaving breasts. As she tightened around him in climax, he couldn't hold himself any longer, and his own release came—deep and feverish, with a primal ferocity. Raw and consuming, pulling everything from him.

Cyrus caught himself before he collapsed on top of her, hovering over her, his hands splayed on the altar. They lay still joined, their breaths heaving in unison.

Suddenly, she stopped breathing, and her body stiffened. Cyrus glanced down and found her head still hanging over the edge of the altar, but her attention focused on the wall. He followed her gaze to a small trunk on an alcove shelf behind the altar.

Pushing him off, she rolled onto her stomach, her eyes still on the trunk.

"Is that what you're looking for?" he asked as he stowed himself and refastened his leathers.

She slipped down off the altar.

"What is it?" he pressed.

Essandra looked back at him. Her eyes held a warning as her body coiled. She was going to spring for it.

But not if he got it first. He darted around the altar as she scrambled after him.

"Don't you dare!" she snapped, and she flicked out her hand. A searing pain spiked through him.

He bellowed and dropped to his knee, and she tore past him. She ripped the trunk from the inset shelf, clawing at the clasp.

The pain that had dropped him abated, but Cyrus still struggled for breath. He staggered to his feet, his eagerness to see what this trunk held pushing him up.

But as the witch opened it, her face slacked, and she puffed out a breath. "No," she whispered. She stood, staring at it.

"No!" Her voice held an unearthly thunder, and her eyes flashed black. She slammed it onto the center of the altar, and a crack split through the stone to the floor, sending out a burst that knocked him back with a large plume of dust.

Apparently, whatever she was looking for wasn't there.

Her face turned from anger to despair. She closed her eyes and pursed her lips tight. He knew defeat when he saw it. Whatever this thing was, she was desperate for it... and she would hurt him over it, no matter what was between them.

"Are you ever going to tell me what you're looking for?" he asked.

She turned away, wiping her face and crossing her arms as her eyes swept over the temple again.

Cyrus eyed the small trunk. It didn't have what she was searching for, but he was curious as to what it did have. He stepped up to the cracked altar and pushed open the lid to find it full of jewels and gold, rings and... bones? Hand bones, from the looks of them. In a temple? Religion was so strange sometimes.

"Cyrus," a voice called him from the entry of the temple. He looked up to see Ram.

The young fighter's eyes drifted over Cyrus and the blood on his neck, to Essandra, who stood with her back still turned, then over the mess strewn across the floor, before moving back to Cyrus. "Is everything all right?" Ram asked.

Cyrus snapped the trunk closed. "Everything's fine," he said. "What do you need?"

"The council is asking you to come. It's about the nobles. And there's news from Mercia."

Cyrus stilled. "What about Mercia?"

Ram shook his head. "I don't know yet. They just asked that you come. Quickly."

Chapter Twenty-Four

Cyrus reached the council room just as Everan and Kord did, and they all stepped inside, where more men were waiting than he remembered appointing. Bravat was also there. Cyrus cut a surprised glance at Everan and Kord, who both returned leery frowns.

"Sire," one of the councilmen greeted him from where he stood beside Bravat. "Thank you for coming so quickly. You need to see this." He held out a rolled parchment.

Essandra had slipped in as well, moving quietly around, and took a seat at the far side of the table. The councilmen followed her with wary eyes, but they said nothing.

Cyrus unrolled the parchment and scanned the words. It was an invitation to the masses. The ousted Raelean nobles were looking for additional people to join their army to take back the capital.

"My men found several of these," Bravat told him. "They're being distributed throughout the capital." He held out another parchment and said, "And they also found this."

My men. Bravat spoke as if he were in a position of command. But Cyrus immediately forgot about that annoyance as he took the second parchment and looked at it. It was a drawing of a woman that closely resembled Essandra, except her eyes were like those of a snake, and her teeth were sharper. An attempt to make her look scarier. There was a backdrop of flames around her, and across the bottom, it read, *BURN THE WITCHES.*

Heat coursed through his veins. "Who did this?" He tossed the parchments onto the table. Everan picked up the nobles' recruitment notice, and Kord the picture of Essandra.

Fatim, his master of coin, cleared his throat. "Well, obviously the nobles are the ones who are seeking men to join—"

"I'm not talking about the call for an army, I'm talking about the picture."

"Likely the same," Everan said. "It looks like they were both done on the same kind of parchment."

"The nobles have seen what we can do," Essandra said stiffly. "We're more of a threat to them now than your army."

"Clearly it's propaganda, though," Kord said.

"People believe propaganda all the time," she cut back. "And act on it."

Cyrus met her eyes squarely. "I would never let anything happen. No one will harm the witches." He looked back at the council. "What is the news of Mercia?"

"But are you not concerned at all about the nobles?" Fatim asked.

"Not particularly. What about Mercia?"

"But, Sire, they're trying to rally forces against you."

He felt his patience slipping. "With the disparity that used to exist between the rich and poor, I seriously doubt going back to old ways will appeal to people at all. Now, Mercia."

"But what changes will they see under your rule?" Fatim asked. "They might find the nobles' offer enticing. We have nothing for them. Our storehouses are dwindling."

"The coven is working on that." His patience slid even further.

"We can only do so much," Essandra interjected. Her eyes on Cyrus were sharp. "And our solution for you is temporary." *Until she found whatever she was looking for.*

His merchant councillor leaned forward. "Purchasing rice from the Shadowlands still remains a viable—"

"We will not buy from the Shadowlands," Cyrus snapped. "That's final." He cut his gaze around the room. "Now, what about Mercia?" he demanded.

His council stared back at him.

"Nothing consequential," Murius, his master of law, finally said. "A new lord justice has been named."

Cyrus stilled as his heart tripped, then quickened.

Murius glanced down at a piece of parchment in his hands. "And the Mercian queen—"

"What do you mean *a new lord justice*?" The words tasted bitter on his tongue. *Lord justice.* The position his father held... His heart beat faster. And heavier.

"Well, not exactly a new justice, I suppose. It's the same man that has been serving the regent, but with the coronation of the queen, he's been officially appointed."

But wait... "What happened to the old one?" What happened to his father?

Murius frowned. "Beurnat the Bear fell in battle a couple years back—three or so? It's his son that now holds the position."

Cyrus froze. His mouth went dry, and his throat tightened.

"He has two sons, I believe," Murius added.

Cyrus gaped at him in surprise. Two sons? They acknowledged Cyrus still? They so openly knew about him yet let him be trapped in this hell. *For over twenty years.*

And his father was dead?

He leaned his weight on the table, gripping its edges as though he could crush it. His skin burned.

"There's more," Murius said. "The Mercian queen is to wed the king of Aleon."

"As expected," another councilman added.

But Cyrus didn't care about the Mercian queen.

His father was dead.

And Alexander was justice.

The perfect son, in the place of their father, all the while Cyrus rotted in this hell.

The councilman said something else, but his words were lost to Cyrus. *Years* had passed—*years* that he hadn't known about his father, *years* that he'd bled on the sands of the arena as his brother basked in status.

He wasn't sure how long he stood there, but he looked up to find all eyes on him.

"So, my father's dead," he said quietly, "and my brother has taken his place." Did Alexander wear his father's armor now? The thought sent another surge of bitterness through him.

Murius gaped at him as murmurs rippled through the room. "The Mercian justice is your brother? You're the son of Beurnat the Bear?"

Only Cyrus's most trusted men of House Pyro had known.

The room grew louder.

"H-how can this be?" the councilman stammered. A man of your class, from such a prevalent family—how did you even get here?"

"A story for another day," Everan said, politely closing that conversation. He looked back at Cyrus, his face grim. "I'm sorry about your father."

Cyrus released the table and straightened. "Don't be," he said sourly. "My only regret is that I didn't get to do it myself." But then he stilled as the whisper of a thought came to him. "The Mercian queen is to marry the king of Aleon?"

Murius nodded, still reeling. "She's probably traveling now."

He paused, his pulse quickening. "I had a dream of the queen going to Aleon."

"You saw them?" It was Essandra who spoke now. Her eyes were curiously fixed on him. "Are you sure? It was her?"

He nodded, pushing his mind to remember more. "Under the banner of Aleon." His paused, the realization hitting him. "It wasn't a dream, was it?"

Her eager eyes told him it was so much more than that.

"If Alexander is her justice, he'll be with her," he thought aloud. "He'll be with his queen. I have to go. I might still be able to intercept him."

"In-intercept the queen of Mercia?" Murius stammered again, still not recovered from the prior news. "Are you serious?"

"Visions lack the context of time," Essandra added. "You might have seen her, but you don't know *when* you've seen her. It could be now; it could be months in the future."

"It doesn't matter," he said. And he didn't care. Even without the dream, this news came directly from Mercia. He looked back at Murius. "Mercia sent this directly, yes?"

"Well, it's a royal proclamation. Most likely every kingdom received the same thing, but yes, it came directly from Mercia. Still, you can't possibly—"

"How long would it have taken the news to travel?" Cyrus asked, an urgency rising in him.

Another councilman shook his head. "A week for a messenger to Hestershire, a bird to Savoy, another bird to Rodine, and then here. If the queen was departing for Aleon when this was sent, she's halfway there already, at least."

"You can't attack the queen of Mercia," a balding man in a neatly pressed tunic said. "They are not an enemy, and we can't risk war should they discover you. We don't even hold the full kingdom of Rael yet—the nobles are literally trying to rally an army against you as we speak."

"Who even are you?" Cyrus challenged. He'd never seen this man. What was he even doing here? And why did he presume he had the right to have an opinion on this?

"Pontil, Sire. Your chief architect."

Cyrus stared at him for a moment and suddenly remembered he did know this man. He'd actually appointed him. Mild embarrassment swept through him, further fueling his frustration. "Well, we're not talking about architecture," he said angrily, "and I don't really give a fuck about the nobles."

"Cyrus," Kord said, "you're king now. You have to think of Rael."

"All I've been doing is thinking of Rael!" he snapped. "For months now!"

His friend quieted, shaking his head, and Cyrus immediately regretted his tone. He rested his weight back on the edge of the table. "If fate has let me live this long, it means I'm not finished."

Kord's brows dipped. "But that doesn't mean this is fate's purpose for you."

"To be handed this opportunity—what else would it be, then?"

Kord gestured around the room. "*This.* Rebuilding. Healing for our people."

He dropped his voice. "What about my healing?" His eyes traveled between Kord and Everan. "Please, brothers," he said.

"You can't seriously be thinking of actually going," Murius said. "Now? And with so little information?"

Cyrus ignored the councilman and kept his eyes on Everan and Kord. Kord glanced at Everan.

"I'll go with you," Bravat said, cracking the silence that now weighted the room. "I'll go with you to kill a justice."

He snapped his head to Bravat in surprise. The large fighter wore a crooked smile. Cyrus wasn't foolish enough to believe this was an offer out of loyalty—it came too quickly, his tone was too eager—but Cyrus didn't particularly care. Bravat could fight, and that was what he needed right now.

Ram gave a nod. "I'll go too."

Cyrus looked back at Everan and Kord. "Brothers," he pleaded. This was his chance at Alexander, and he didn't know if he'd get another. He had to take it, but he couldn't do it without them.

Everan pursed his lips, then swore. "All right," he said. "But the council is right—the Mercian queen *can't* know who we are. You'd put Rael at risk."

"We put Rael at risk just thinking about this," Murius said, growing flustered.

Cyrus ignored him.

"How are we even going to get there?" Kord asked. "Do you know how far that is? By the time we make it, we'll have missed her."

"Sire, I beg you to think this through," Murius pressed.

Cyrus leveled his eyes on Essandra. "There's got to be something you can do."

Essandra's gaze on him grew even sharper. She probably hadn't intended for him to make use of the coven's power outside of Rael. He didn't care. *Power for power*, she'd said. He'd hold her to that. She'd probably revoke the terms after this. He didn't care about that either. Alexander had taken everything from him. Now Cyrus would take it back, no matter what it cost him.

His voice dropped lower as he spoke only to her now. "I want you to think about whatever it is you're looking for here. And how badly you want it. How you'll do whatever it takes to get it. You think about that, and you might come close to understanding how I feel right now."

Her expression changed, but he couldn't read it.

"I just need to intercept him," he said. "Can you slow the queen somehow? Buy us time?"

"No," she answered finally.

The air left his lungs.

But then she said, "I can do something better."

Chapter Twenty-Five

"A fucking *what*?" Kord asked. Everan said nothing but was equally confused. They'd followed Cyrus and Essandra from the council room into a chamber that Cyrus had taken over as a study.

Essandra stood with her arms crossed. "A portal witch."

It was the third time she'd said it, but Cyrus was still trying to get his head around what that meant.

"Tomel has the power to bridge two places together. This will allow us to simply pass from one to another, without actually having to travel the distance between them."

Cyrus could only stare at her. "So, you have the power to just take me to Mercia?" His heart raced faster. This could change everything.

She pursed her lips. "Basically, yes."

"Why didn't you tell me you could do this before?"

"Because it's an easily abused power, and it's dangerous. It has to be guarded and used sparingly."

Which meant she likely wouldn't be keen on allowing him to use it again. That was fine. Even if she gave him only one opportunity, this was what he'd use it on—going after Alexander.

"How quickly can we go?" he asked.

"As quickly as you're ready."

Despite Essandra telling him she could *take him to Mercia*, he didn't actually think it was as easy as her saying a spell and whisking him there. Except it was. And as his eyes traveled the rocky terrain of the Mercian outer reaches, he was still struggling to believe it. Travel wasn't exact—Tomel's power could get them only to a general area on a map. There was also risk. Having not been sure where the portal would exit, they had no way of knowing if they were walking into a dangerous place or situation. However, Essandra was able to lessen this risk by drawing on the power of illusion from another witch in the coven to hide them. It was impressive, like a cloak of invisibility draped over them. The only giveaway was a slight ripple where the illusion met reality—noticeable only to someone specifically looking.

Nearly five hundred bloodsport fighters accompanied him. Even Kieve came. Thinking about it brought a wave of emotion. This wasn't even a mission for their people; this was a mission for Cyrus. They'd come to help him get what he needed, and he was beyond grateful.

He'd been surprised Rael had received news about the Mercian queen's marriage alliance from the Mercian council after Cyrus had overthrown the king that Mercia had apparently been friends with, or at least friendly acquaintances with. It didn't matter that it had been a general proclamation. They wouldn't have sent it to *everyone*. They wouldn't have sent it to the Shadowlands. He suspected either Mercia was testing a new friendship, or—more likely—it was a warning under the guise of politeness to inform him, as the new king of Rael, that Mercia and Aleon still stood together. He smiled to himself. If he ever met the Mercian council after this, he'd thank them. A recheck of messenger times gave him confidence that they'd intercept the queen before she reached Aleon, but it was a guess as to where she'd be along the route. Cyrus chose a portal location closer to Aleon, hopefully ahead of her caravan, then they'd work their way back to meet her.

Every man knew the plan—when they found the queen's caravan, they would go after Alexander, separate him, and steal him back to Rael. If that failed, Cyrus would kill him there, but only Cyrus. No other man was to touch his brother. The queen wasn't the target, but if she were harmed, it would be an acceptable loss.

They wore nothing identifiable to Rael, carried no correspondence. Mercia would have no idea who they were. Cyrus's men came from many lands, their skin colors and languages as varied as the places they'd been stolen from. They now joined together to form an army that represented all yet none.

They traveled under the illusion that covered them. Their only challenge was in keeping quiet, as there was nothing the witch could do to mask their sounds, and an army of five hundred men with horses was not silent. However, the outer reaches that they traveled were less inhabited, save scatterings of villages that were easy enough to steer clear of.

"I can't feel my fucking feet," Kord told Cyrus as they made camp that evening.

Everan snorted, joining them. "I can't feel my face."

Cyrus was cold too. While it had initially been a relief to escape the eternal heat of Rael, he couldn't say this was better. He might have been born in the North, but he wasn't accustomed to winter. None of them were. He wished they'd brought more layers. The cold crept from the earth, up his legs, and the wind swept through his too few layers, chilling him to his core, but nothing could make him turn back.

Nearby, Essandra pulled her bedroll from her saddle.

Cyrus paused for a moment, watching her. "You have something for this cold, witch?"

Her icy gaze fell on him. "Do you think I have a power for everything?"

"Not everything. Just whatever keeps you from having to wear gloves and not much more than a loose cloak."

She glanced down at her bare hands and back at him. The lines of her face grew sharper.

"Fine." She stepped to Kord and put a hand on his arm. He moved to pull away, but then stopped, his eyes widening. Then she touched Everan, who reacted the same way and gaped at Cyrus.

She then stepped in front of Cyrus, but paused for a moment—was something wrong? Whatever it was, she seemed to shake it off, and she reached out her hand to his chest. Warmth flooded him. From her hand through his layers, into his core, and down his arms and his legs. It was like being touched by the gods, and he let his eyelids fall closed. When he opened them again, he was met by the depths of her emerald eyes.

"How did you do that?" he asked.

"Merene, my fire witch."

"She doesn't have to be here?" The portal witch and the illusion witch had been the only ones to come with them. Cyrus had just assumed other witches had to be present to take advantage of their powers.

She frowned. "No. In fact, if she were here, she wouldn't be happy about me using her power for the comforts of simple men."

A faint smile tugged at the corners of his mouth. "Well, thank you."

She gave a mild shrug. "I'm tired of listening to all your teeth chattering anyway. If anything's going to give us away—it's that."

Traveling was easier when he didn't feel like he was going to freeze to death, but by the fourth day, Cyrus had larger concerns than the cold. He'd expected to have come upon the queen's caravan by now, yet there was no sign, and he was starting to lose confidence. Had they arrived behind her, and were they now traveling the wrong way to intercept her? No—that couldn't be. There was no sign a caravan had passed through, and he was confident they were on the route she'd take to Aleon. They continued.

Cyrus woke the next morning to the air crisp and clean. As he stepped out of his tent, he was struck for a moment. The earth had disappeared under a sea of glittering white. He dropped down to scoop up a fistful. It had been so long since he'd seen snow, since he had touched it, and he was instantly transported to his childhood.

Cyrus and Alexander balled the snow tightly in their fists. They gathered it nearer to the edges of the isle, where it was wet and they could compact it hard enough to sting when it hit. Alexander was always wary of that and threw them lightly, which defeated the point of getting it near the ice in the first place. Cyrus didn't throw so lightly.

Alexander would hit their friends, harmlessly in the back and in good fun, garnering laughs all around.

Cyrus would hit rivals, in the head—hard—garnering laughs on one side, then usually a fight.

But regardless of their different targets, they always threw at others, never at each other. They were a team.

Cyrus pushed the memory from his mind. That had been a lifetime ago, before Alexander had left him to rot in Rael. Alexander knew Cyrus was alive. But he didn't come. He didn't care. They were no longer a team. Alexander was no longer his brother.

He stood to find Essandra now watching him. She was shorter than he was, yet always seemed to be looking down on him.

"You should send scouts ahead," she said. "We need to make sure we're not wasting our time."

"I already thought of that, but by the time they travel out and then return with news, it won't save us much."

A line formed between her brows. "Give them your blood to take with them."

"What?"

"Your blood. Give it to them to take with them."

Rearranging the words didn't make any more sense to him.

She rolled her eyes. "They can call to you when they find something. You can talk to them through the bond."

He opened his mouth, then closed it. He could do that? No, he couldn't. "That's not how it works."

She let out a small scoff. "That *is* how it works." Then she shook her head, and her eyes narrowed. "Do you not know how to travel to others' minds?"

"Of course I do. Kind of." He just couldn't always control it. And he couldn't speak.

Her lips parted more. "You don't, do you?"

"Well, it's not like you've shown me how," he replied angrily.

"I didn't think I had to teach you the most basic abilities of a traveler. These are things that should come *naturally*."

"They don't," he snapped back. Then he paused. "What's a traveler?"

She pursed her lips just as Everan and Kord approached.

"Give me your hand," she told Cyrus. Then she cut Everan a demanding look. "Get over here."

Everan glanced at Kord, then stepped closer as she'd instructed.

She made a small prick in Cyrus's finger with the tip of her dagger, then swept the swelling drop of blood toward Everan.

"Wait," Cyrus said. Over the past couple of months, he'd learned that the blood connection with the witch was very different from the blood connection with others. She could control what he saw in her mind, limit him, but Everan didn't have this ability.

"You need to learn to communicate through the bond," she told him. "It will make things so much easier. For all of us."

"It's all right," Everan said, catching on to what they were trying to do.

Cyrus relented, and Essandra pressed the blood against Everan's forehead. Cyrus drew a breath as he felt the pull.

"Focus," she told him. "You should feel both of us."

He did feel them both, but only Everan's mind was open to him.

"Now, close your eyes, and you can do one of two things. You can travel to him, *as a traveler*, or you can pull him into your own mind, but—"

"I can pull him into *my* mind?" That was better than infringing on Everan's thoughts.

"I want you to focus on traveling to *him*—it's easier to start."

"How can I pull him into mine?"

"We're not doing that right now." Her voice became firm.

"Cyrus, it's fine," Everan said. "You know every corner of my mind anyway."

Cyrus sighed and closed his eyes. He let the call of his blood pull him through the chaos, like a tide sweeping him to sea, and found himself in Everan's mind. He stared back at Essandra through Everan's eyes.

"Now say something to him," Essandra said.

Wait—that was all? He just needed to speak? Suddenly, he felt very foolish. It was so simple.

"Say something," Essandra prompted again.

"Everan."

"Not *out loud*," she said, making no attempt to hide her annoyance. "Only in his mind."

In his mind. Well, how was he supposed to do that? He formed Everan's name in a thought.

"Say something," she said.

"Give me a moment! I am."

"No, you're not."

Cyrus gritted his teeth. This woman. *Everan*, he thought.

Still nothing.

"Imagine the sound of your voice when you say it," she told him.

He could easily imagine his own voice. "*Everan.*"

He heard Everan's chuckle.

Cyrus jerked his eyes open. "You heard me?"

"You sound different, but yeah."

"How—in what way?"

Everan shrugged. "I don't know, a little deeper. But it's you. I can tell."

"Talk back to him," Essandra told Everan.

"*Took you this long to figure out how to do this, you dumb fuck.*"

Cyrus's eyes flew open again.

Everan laughed. "He heard me."

"Do me," Kord said with a grin, grabbing Cyrus's hand and taking a small smear of blood for himself.

"*Fuck off,*" Cyrus said in his mind.

Kord let out a hearty laugh.

"Are you boys done playing now?" Essandra asked sternly.

They all quieted.

"Send your scouts," she told Cyrus. "They can call you through the blood bond when they find something." Then she shook her head. "We should have done this sooner."

She was right. They should have done this the moment they portaled in. Cyrus could have sent scouts in both directions along the route. Now they were into the fourth day, and if they'd missed the Mercian queen, then Cyrus would miss his opportunity at Alexander.

Kord and Ram each took a vial of blood and rode ahead, and Cyrus kept with the larger group, following at only a slightly slower pace. His unease grew as the sun moved across the sky, and he rode in silence.

The pull came sooner than he'd expected—that afternoon. He pulled his horse up and slid to the ground, wavering slightly.

"What's wrong?" Essandra asked, just behind him.

"It's Kord." Holding the side of the saddle for support, he closed his eyes and let his blood lead him to Kord's mind.

"*I found them,*" Kord told him as soon as he entered.

The beat in his chest leapt to his throat. He'd found them. He'd found Alexander.

"*Looks like someone else had the same idea we did, though,*" Kord added. "*And they beat us to it.*"

Cyrus stilled as his pulse raced even faster. "*What?*"

"*The queen's gone, but her army is still here.*"

He didn't care about the queen. But Kord's next words stopped him cold.

"*They're dead, Cyrus. All of them.*"

Chapter Twenty-Six

The Mercian soldiers lay where they'd fallen, their throats slit. Cyrus stepped through the bodies with his sword in hand, moving slowly, as if in a dream. They'd been lined up on their knees and executed. The smell of death hadn't yet set in—they hadn't been here long.

"Do you think the queen escaped?" Kord asked him.

He shook his head. "No. No one would have taken the time to line up these men and execute them if they were still in pursuit of a queen."

"So they have her, then. Who do you think would have done this?"

The Shadow King was the most obvious answer, but it was hard to imagine he'd have been informed of the Mercian queen's travel plans or have been able to get inside Mercia to attack her.

"Every wearer of a crown has a long list of enemies," he replied. But the thought that this was the work of the Shadow King seeded an anger deep in his stomach. He turned over the body of a Mercian soldier with his boot. They'd been efficient killings. Experienced.

"We've checked all the bodies," Kord said. "No one here has the same face as you."

Scavengers had started to steal the soft tissue—eyes and inside the mouths. It would have been hard to recognize everyone, but Cyrus didn't doubt what Kord told him. He could still feel the weight of Alexander in his chest—alive.

"Maybe they've taken your brother too," Kord added.

With everything the Shadow King had already taken from him, if he'd taken this opportunity from him too...

A rage swelled within him. He let out a roar and arced his sword, cleaving the dead Northman's head from his body. What he wouldn't give for it to have been the Shadow King's.

But as quickly as Cyrus had lost control, he got it back again, and he straightened, drawing a long inhale and letting it out slowly.

"Cyrus," Brant called from behind him.

He turned.

Brant reached him with a dark navy box in his hands. "We found this among the trunks in the carriage." He held it out.

Cyrus took it.

"Not much else, though," Brant added. "Dresses. Women's personal effects."

Cyrus pulled off the top of the box. Inside was a crown. It had a smooth base, with a sculpted floral top edging. A queen's crown. And he'd seen this floral petal style before. As a child. This design...

The Mercian queen had definitely been here.

He surveyed the site around him again. She'd also definitely been taken. But he was too late. He'd missed it. He'd missed his chance at Alexander. He snapped the box shut and pushed out a frustrated breath between his teeth.

"What do you want to do now?" Kord asked him.

What was there to do? The only thing he could. "Return to Rael," he said bitterly.

As he stepped to his horse, he almost tossed the crown but instead paused and toyed with the weight of the box in his hand. He opened it again. This was the first thing he'd touched in over twenty years that was connected to the life he'd once had. And despite the contempt that curdled in the pit of his stomach, something about it still called to him.

Cyrus closed the box again. He wanted to throw it. Crush it. Destroy it.

But something wouldn't let him.

He slipped it into his saddlebag.

"Let's head out," he called to his men.

"So, that's it?" Bravat shouted out, pushing through the men to the front. "We just go? With nothing?"

Cyrus didn't like it either but... "What do you propose, if nothing's here?"

Bravat grinned. "I say we find us a Northern temple. You know what's in Northern temples?" His grin grew wider. "Gold." He glanced back over his shoulder at his old arena teammates. "I have a few men who I think would love to pay some homage."

Cyrus certainly didn't mind the men collecting some spoils to make up for their fruitless journey, but... "It's too much of a risk. If you're caught—"

"We won't be caught."

Cyrus stifled a growl. He hadn't come to cause petty trouble in Mercia, but Bravat had been the first to support Cyrus in coming after his brother when he'd faced heavy opposition from his new council. And Cyrus cared about Mercian temples no more than he cared about Raelean temples, especially ones that Alexander was responsible for safeguarding.

Fine. "Two days," Cyrus told him. How much trouble could Bravat get himself into in two days' time? He handed him two vials of his blood that Essandra provided from her satchel. Cyrus had kept his curse hidden from everyone except those closest to him his whole life; to be more open with it now, to actually use it, was a strange feeling.

The large fighter took the vials warily. When he'd first learned of Cyrus's ability, he'd reacted the same as many of the men—not necessarily afraid, but cautious.

"You can't be caught," Cyrus warned him again. "Use the blood to call to me in two days, when you're ready to return, and Essandra will open the portal to bring you back."

Bravat slipped the vials into his pocket, looking at Cyrus with a wary eye.

"Two days, Bravat," Cyrus stressed.

"Yeah, I heard you."

The big fighter mounted his horse, giving a last look at Cyrus, and with several of his old teammates, they spurred their mounts into a gallop to go find their temples of gold.

Cyrus watched them as they disappeared. He hoped he wouldn't regret this lenience. He turned and walked through what was left of the Mercian company once more before mounting his horse.

As he settled into his saddle, the warmth that Essandra had cast in him days before suddenly evaporated, leaving a sharp cold in its place. He glanced at Everan and Kord, who both clutched their chests, feeling it too. Then he looked at Essandra.

Her expression was one he hadn't seen before: fear. And worry.

Her emerald eyes locked with his, and an even deeper cold ran through him. "Something's wrong," she said. "We have to get back to Rael. *Now.*"

Chapter Twenty-Seven

Cyrus crossed through the portal to find the capital in chaos. Smoke filled his nose, and violence filled the streets. Somewhere in the distance, bells clanged wildly. He immediately reined his horse closer to Essandra as his men flooded through the portal around them.

"Stay together!" he ordered, until he could figure out what was going on.

An arrow *sipped* by his ear. "Look out!" he shouted at Essandra, jumping from his horse and pulling her down with him.

The portal wavered, and she pushed Cyrus off.

"Stay focused!" she called to Tomel, her portal witch. Together they wove their hands rhythmically through the air to steady the magic supporting the portal. The arc shimmered like stretched glass, rippling with every shift of wind and violent rift.

Another wave of arrows came, and Cyrus jerked Essandra back again.

"I need to help Tomel keep the portal open!" she snapped.

"Well, you can't do that if you're dead!" Which was exactly what they would all be if they didn't find cover. They needed to get out of the open, but his men were still coming through from Mercia.

Tomel nodded to Essandra. "Go!" he told her and Cyrus. "Get to the palace. I'll keep it open until everyone—"

He stopped abruptly, midsentence, then looked down at the arrow that had buried itself in his chest.

"Tomel!" Essandra cried.

The witch dropped to his knees, then fell forward onto the ground. The portal slammed shut, severing the path for the men still in Mercia, and severing everything split between the two kingdoms. Two horses screamed as they fell without their back halves.

"Tomel!" Essandra cried again.

Cyrus barreled back to where the portal had been, his heart in his throat. None of his men had been hurt, but there were still quite a few of them stranded in Mercia, including Jaem and Kieve.

"Open it!" he shouted at Essandra. "They're not all through!"

"I can't!"

"Cyrus, get down!" Kord bellowed somewhere behind him.

"Open it!" he roared at her again.

"I can't! Not without Tomel!"

Another *sip* of an arrow. A thud. Pain pierced his shoulder. He staggered sideways.

"Cyrus!" Kord grabbed him and dragged him down behind a fallen horse for cover.

He was stunned for only a moment. "I'm fine," he rasped, and broke off the arrow shaft close to his flesh. "We have to get the portal back open!" He winced between words. "Not everyone made it through!"

"They're better over there right now! Focus on yourself."

The arrow wasn't too bad, and thankfully not in the shoulder of his sword-wielding arm. He'd manage until he could get to Teron. What he couldn't manage was staying out in the open. They needed to get to the palace.

Another onslaught of arrows came. One of his men was hit in the leg, and another horse fell. Cyrus gritted his teeth. It would be a long run—

Essandra stepped out, unprotected, her hair wild in the wind around her, her face twisted with fury. She was too far for him to grab. An arrow buried itself within paces of her feet, but she didn't even flinch.

Cyrus's heart leapt to his throat. He got that she was upset right now, but this woman was going to get herself killed. "Get down!" he shouted.

She paid him no mind. Instead, she clapped her hands together, chanting words he didn't understand, then threw her arms wide, as if casting something away from herself. The ground shook. Cyrus struggled for his balance as the earth erupted in front of her and a series of trenches snaked in multiple directions. One slammed through the embankment under a cluster of buildings from where the arrows were being fired. Men screamed as the buildings collapsed in on themselves.

Cyrus gaped at her in surprise. It wasn't that he'd forgotten he had a witch with him; he was just starting to realize how powerful she actually was.

And she wasn't finished. Essandra threw up a wall of thin rock, splintering it into a thousand jagged pieces, then flung out the shards like possessed arrowheads. At the same time, the illusion witch cast a cover over them. It was a sloppy one, the outer edges frayed, but it was better than nothing.

"Let's go!" Essandra shouted.

Cyrus rallied his men, and they charged toward the palace. The illusion shimmered over them, blurring edges and warping light. They tried to move quickly, but the cobblestone street beneath their feet had been broken and scattered in heaps—from Essandra's geomancer. There had been fighting. And a lot of it. One of his men stumbled over a body, barely catching himself.

As they reached the denser parts of the capital, they had more cover and dropped the illusion; however, Essandra again started ripping through earth and stone in counterattacks against the nobles. The enemy fell—tens at a time. Those Essandra's destructive magic didn't claim, Cyrus's men did.

The fighting thinned as they made their way closer to the palace. When they reached it, they were met by Hephain. The dogs were with him, and they shook their hinds when they saw Cyrus.

"Is the palace secure?" Cyrus asked him.

Hephain nodded quickly. "Yes." He'd stayed in Rael instead of going to Mercia—Cyrus had left him in charge of palace security. Clearly that had been the right decision.

"All walls and gates are reinforced," he told Cyrus, "but they didn't come for the palace. They came for the witches."

Both Cyrus and Essandra snapped their eyes to him.

"They what?" Essandra demanded.

"The nobles came for the witches. They attacked the fields first, but we were able to get the hedge witches out. Then they attacked the east side, where the rebuilding efforts have been focused. Necross held them so everyone could fall back to the palace, but we did lose Merene."

Necross was the geomancer, but Merene...

"Your fire witch?" Cyrus asked.

Essandra clutched her chest and gave the slightest of nods. "She was the youngest in the coven," she said quietly.

Hephain gave her a regretful dip of his head. "I'm sorry," he told her. "The palace is secure, though, and everyone is inside."

Essandra glanced at the young witch with them. "Go inside," she told her.

Hephain motioned them toward the doors as he said to Essandra, "You can shelter with them until we push back the—"

"I'm not sheltering," she said firmly. "I'm fighting."

Cyrus wanted to object, but he had seen what she could do. He needed her. "Where are we positioned?" he asked Hephain.

"Everything to the west and south is clear. The men from House Aramine are near the temple, corralling everything east. Houses Lycus and Akim are doing the same from the north."

"You said the rest of my coven is in the palace?" Essandra asked. "All of them?"

"All but Tomel."

The portal witch.

Her expression darkened. "Make sure they stay here," she ordered. Her voice had sharpened—clear, clipped, commanding. The grief that had blanketed her face just before was gone now, replaced by pure fury.

She turned to Cyrus. "We're not done."

And her eyes turned black.

They fought well into the evening, and as the sun slipped below the horizon, they'd driven the last of the nobles' army into a villa on the east side of the capital. It was a stronghold, fortified by high walls, with the men inside well armed.

Cyrus surrounded it, careful to keep his men far enough back from the reach of arrows. The dark of night covered them, but he didn't want to take chances.

"How are we going to get in there?" Kord asked as he and Cyrus eyed the iron gates. They could rush the villa, overtake it with numbers alone, but that would cost a lot of men, and Cyrus wasn't willing to do that. Not yet.

He shook his head. "I don't know yet."

Essandra snorted beside him. "Have you learned nothing?"

"You can bring it down?" he asked.

She looked out at the villa. The torchlight danced in her eyes. She didn't look at him when she spoke. "When all this is finished, I want men."

He frowned. "For what?"

"For my coven. For protection."

"She has the power to rip apart this city but wants men for protection?" Kord scoffed.

"Because we're vulnerable," she snapped back, "especially when we're focusing on using our powers. I can't lose another witch."

"So, you want guards?" Cyrus asked.

"Protectors, at least two per witch. And not just any men. I want your bloodsport fighters." She cut Kord a daggered glare. "Not him."

"Good," Kord snapped back. "Because I'm not guarding some fucking witch."

Cyrus flashed him a warning glance. If Essandra lost power every time she lost a witch, that would be bad for everyone, including Cyrus. And what did she have—fifteen, maybe twenty, witches in her coven? He could spare forty men.

"I'll give you men," he said.

Satisfied, she held out her hand for his.

"I'm already bleeding," he protested.

She wrinkled her face. "Old blood? I'm not putting that filth in my mouth."

"She has standards," Kord said sarcastically.

Essandra ignored him. "Give me your hand," she told Cyrus.

Finally, he gave it to her. She pulled her dagger and sliced the flesh across his palm.

His jaw tightened. She liked to take his blood from his palm, which was frustrating because it made it difficult to use his hand until Teron healed him, but she could collect it easier, whether into a bowl or directly into her mouth. She held his hand up and let it drip onto her tongue.

The pull came immediately—not a pull to enter her mind but a pull of power as she drew it through him.

A phantom wind rose from nowhere, fierce enough to make a man stumble. "Give me your sword," she told Cyrus, her voice hauntingly low, not entirely human.

He pulled it from the sheath across his back and held it out to her.

Grasping it by the hilt with both hands, she lifted the sword high, the blade pointing down, and plunged it into the earth in front of her.

The wind collapsed into silence, and quiet settled over them. The sword rocked back and forth slightly with the tip of the blade buried in the earth. Then it stilled.

Kord snorted. "That was incredible."

Cyrus shot him another glance, and Kord shrugged.

Murmurs rippled through the men.

"If you've got something else," Cyrus told her, "now might be the time to use it."

She said nothing.

Cyrus looked around. Had something happened to their geomancer? Had they lost that power too? He felt his impatience growing.

"I say we scale the wall," Kord said. "We have the cover of night."

"We'll lose the benefit of darkness when we reach it, though," Cyrus said. "They have it lit up with torches pretty well."

"Your witch can use her illusion charm, unless she's lost that too."

Yes, there was that.

Suddenly, the ground rumbled underneath their feet, and they widened their stances to keep their balance. Cyrus's sword sank farther into the earth, almost to the hilt. Ram held a torch closer. A small crack gave way, and they took a step back.

The crack snaked from the blade out toward the villa and disappeared into the darkness. Cyrus and his men all glanced at one another, then turned their eyes back to the villa with bated breaths.

All was quiet.

Until it wasn't.

A thunder boomed through the air, so loud the vibration rolled through him, then the ground quaked again. Cyrus and his men struggled for balance. However, their attention was quickly snatched from the ground underneath them back to Cyrus's sword, where the small crack split wider. Wider, still, it grew, trenching toward the villa wall, sending plumes of dust against the torchlight. Then, along the base, small cracks spidered from the ground to the top.

They grew darker. Deeper.

The wall buckled and collapsed.

The thick stacked-stone entryway of the villa burst apart, then the sidewalls, filling the villa with the panicked shouts of the men inside as the roof started to fold.

The large structure crumpled to the ground, sending a tidal gale of sand and dust in all directions.

Then, the tremors ceased.

As the air settled, Cyrus's men let loose a series of cheers and laughter. They'd never seen anything like that before. Cyrus couldn't help a smile himself. It *was* actually incredible.

Ram pulled his sword. "Now to make sure they're dead," he said.

The men moved to advance, but Essandra snapped, "Stop."

They stopped and quieted, confused.

She lifted her arms, and the rubble of the villa started to tremble. Slowly, the broken stone began to rise—massive boulders, fragmented rocks, debris.

Shouts echoed from beneath, the nobles still alive within realizing too late what was coming.

Essandra held one arm straight out in front of her, her hand spread wide with her palm toward the villa, as she stirred a circle in the air with her other hand underneath. She chanted words Cyrus didn't understand.

The rocks rose higher.

Kord and Cyrus glanced at each other.

Essandra brought them even higher, poising them, positioning them, then she wrenched her arms down, balling her fists as if ripping the air from the sky.

And the rocks came crashing down.

The nobles' screams were quickly cut off. Plumes of dust beat against Cyrus's face. The torchlight from within was snuffed, and everything went dark.

Everyone was quiet, in shock of it all.

"They're dead," Essandra said.

The capital was theirs again. Cheers erupted from his men.

She turned, and as their eyes met, he gave her a small smile.

The corners of her mouth hinted at a smile of her own. Until her gaze dropped to the arrow through his shoulder, and Cyrus realized that he couldn't feel his arm.

Then all hints of her smile fell.

Chapter Twenty-Eight

Cyrus roared in pain.

"If you kept still, it wouldn't hurt as much," Everan said as he helped hold him down.

Cyrus lay on Teron's worktable. He was glad the old healer had moved into the palace, making life much easier for one prone to injury. And Teron was there, prepared to heal him, but they needed to get the arrow out first. Cyrus had broken the shaft off too close to the skin, and it was nearly impossible to grab onto now. Kord straddled his stomach, practically sitting on him, trying to grip the small piece of broken shaft with a pair of pincers.

"Again," Kord said.

Everan and Ram held him tighter, and Kord pulled. The ends of the pincers slipped, snapping a nauseating pain through his shoulder. Cyrus roared again.

"There's too much blood," Kord said. "I can't get a grip."

"Let me try," Everan said. He swung up onto the table over Cyrus, and Kord dropped down to take his place holding Cyrus's left arm.

"I need light," Everan called, and Bash held the flame closer. Morning was still a long way away, made even longer by the pain.

Essandra watched them from where she stood in the corner. She didn't have any healing power. She probably wouldn't have offered it even if she did. Everan dug the edges of the pincers into his shoulder, driving Cyrus near mad with pain.

"I think you caught part of his skin," Kord said, dropping his face closer, trying to see.

Everan shoved him back. "Yeah, well, I have to get enough to grip the shaft. Hold him."

Ram and Kord gripped him tightly.

"Wait," Cyrus begged. "Wait!"

But Everan didn't wait and dug the pincers into his shoulder again. Cyrus bellowed. Everan pulled, and finally, the arrow came free. An ungodly sound ripped from Cyrus's throat, and he felt like he was going to pass out.

"Your turn," Everan told Teron, and he dropped down off the table.

Ram and Kord released him, but Cyrus didn't have any fight in him anymore. The pain left him shaking. His inhales came in ragged pulls. Sweat slicked his skin. For a few breaths, he just lay there, barely registering the sounds around him—the scrape of boots, the low murmur of voices—his eyes unfocused.

Then, warmth touched his skin as Teron's healing flowed into him. There was no flash of light, no dramatic swell of power—just a slow, steady warmth sinking beneath his skin and spreading through him.

It dulled the sharpest edges of pain first, then eased the stiffness in his chest.

Cyrus's breathing slowed. The shaking subsided. His body relaxed, and he sank back fully against the table. The haze behind his eyes lifted.

His mind began to clear.

Gods, he was tired, but there was no time for rest. He needed to figure out how to get his men back from Mercia. Nearly fifty were trapped there, including Jaem and Kieve. Bravat was the only one with his blood and the means to call him. Cyrus hoped they'd double back and find him.

"Is there no other witch who can open a portal?" he asked Essandra as he slowly recovered. "Even a small one?"

"No," she said. "It's a very specific ability."

Cyrus cursed. "Can we not find another?"

"Portal witches are rare, and even if I did find one, to get them to want to join the coven, to let me bond with them and use their power..." She shook her head. "It's not likely."

He swore again. "Can you not at least try?"

"Have I not tried enough already?" she snapped back. "Have I not given enough? Lost enough? Tomel and Merene are dead, just so you could chase after your brother, who *wasn't even there*!"

Cyrus sobered, and shame filled him. He'd been baited with the first opportunity at Alexander, and a lot of people had suffered for it, including his own men. Essandra had lost two witches. He swallowed.

"You're right. I'm sorry. You *have* done enough. More than enough. I'll find another way to get the men back from Mercia."

The room fell quiet and stayed quiet. It took a little longer for Teron to finish healing him. He'd been hit with a barbed arrow that had practically destroyed his shoulder, as well as had a few more injuries he didn't remember receiving. Ram, Kord, and Everan all took off for some much-needed rest once they'd made sure Cyrus was all right, but Essandra stayed.

Was she worried for him? He'd been hurt pretty badly.

He wasn't quite fully healed as Teron's power started waning, but he was healed enough.

"You can get the rest tomorrow," Cyrus told him, pushing himself up.

"I saw Everan and Kord with a few things to mend as well," Teron said.

Cyrus swung down from the table. His muscles were stiff and sore. "Kade too. He took an arrow to the leg."

"I'll see to them all."

Cyrus nodded. "Thank you, Teron."

The old man dropped a pile of bloodstained cloths into a large bowl and gave Cyrus a nod good night before retiring to his chamber.

Cyrus's eyes found Essandra. She was still waiting, watching him.

"You didn't have to stay," he said.

"You promised me men. I wanted to make sure you didn't forget."

Oh. Right. And here he'd foolishly thought she'd been waiting to see how he fared. He swallowed down the embarrassment knotting in his throat and gave a stiff nod. "You'll get them. I'll write the order in the morning."

"I'd like it now."

He nodded stiffly again. "Fine." He looked around Teron's workroom and found parchment and a reed pen and scribbled out his assignment of men to her cause. He paused. "How many witches do you have?"

"Twenty-two."

"So, forty-four men."

"And two for me."

His hand stopped midsentence. Why did that sting? Maybe because she was nearly always with him now. Was his protection not enough? No. She'd been with him so often lately only because they'd been traveling. Now that they were back, they'd focus on their own agendas and be together much less often.

"Forty-six, then." He finished the order and held it out for her.

She took it. "Thank you," she said, and waited a moment for the ink to dry before folding it. "Good night."

"Good night," he replied.

They started toward the door at the same time and then stopped at the same time. They both started again, then stopped. An awkwardness twined between them. He motioned her forward. "After you."

Cyrus followed her out into the hall and realized their chambers, both in the royal wing, were in the same direction. As if it weren't awkward enough.

It was a long walk—one made even longer by silence.

"Can I ask you something?" he said as he walked beside her.

"Nothing's stopping you." She was still upset. Fair.

"Tomel was a portal witch. When he died, you lost his power."

"Is that a question?"

"The same with your fire witch, Marlene."

She pursed her lips. "*Merene.*"

He cursed himself under his breath. "It was her power you used to warm us in Mercia, and you used your geomancer's power to take down the villa."

"Again, your question?"

"What's *your* power?"

Her step kept steady, but there was the faintest falter in her breath. Did the question bother her?

"Do you turn into a dragon?" he jested.

She shot him a daggered glance.

Or a viper. He kept that comment to himself. "Tell me. What is it?"

"What does it matter?"

He shrugged. "I'm just curious. Why won't you tell me?"

They reached the split in the hall that broke toward their different rooms, and she moved to turn down the one leading to her chamber. "It's not your business."

He grabbed her arm, stopping her. "Not my business?"

"You don't have a right—"

"I think I do." Anger ripped through him now. "I let you have my body, my blood, whatever this fucking power is that you pull from me. But every time I ask you a gods-damned question, you'd rather hurt me than give me an answer." His rage grew with his words. "What secrets do I keep from *you*?"

She shoved against him. "I *freed* you!" she snapped. "I made all this possible!"

"No, I freed *you*."

"I've done everything you've asked!" she shouted back at him. "And what secrets do *you* keep? A lot!"

"Like what? All you have to do is ask, and I'll tell you, like you're going to tell me now. What's your power?"

"Let me go." She tried to pull her arm away from him again, but he grabbed her around her throat, just under her jaw, and pushed her up against the wall.

"Tell me your fucking power." He was certain he was about to find out. She'd hit him with pain any moment now. The thought should have made him pause, but anger fueled him past thinking.

She struggled against him. He held her tighter. He wasn't sure why she didn't use her full force. He'd press her until she did, or until she just answered him.

"Tell me!" he demanded.

"I don't have a power," she finally cried.

He paused. She didn't have a power. That couldn't be true. He loosened his hold, but he didn't take his hand from her throat.

"I'm a bond witch. I have no power that belongs to me; I can only use the power of others." Her lip trembled in bitterness. "It makes me invaluable in a coven, but powerless on my own."

His anger evaporated. Was this why she was so guarded? Did she think herself weak?

"Are you happy now?" she hissed. "There you have it. I have no power."

"So, all this power you do have, you pull it all from others?"

She cast her eyes down.

And he realized—this wasn't a woman trying to be difficult; this was a woman who doubted herself. And a woman who didn't trust him.

He shook his head. She didn't see it. Cyrus drew her chin up to look at him. "Is yours not the greatest power of all, then?"

Her breaths came unevenly, and she softened.

He dropped his hand from her and took a step back, giving her space. The shift sent a stab of pain through his partially healed wound, and he winced. Her eyes dropped to his shoulder. She took a small step toward him as she sucked in a short breath to say something, but she caught herself, stopping abruptly, and bit back whatever words were on her tongue.

Cyrus would have liked to hear them, but he didn't press her. He imagined he'd done that enough already. He wasn't sure what else to say now, so he simply said, "Good night."

"Good night," she said, so softly it almost didn't reach his ears. Then she turned and padded down the hall to her chamber.

He stood there long after she'd disappeared from sight. *No power of her own*, she'd said, but damned if it didn't feel like he was under a spell.

Cyrus paced his chamber. Kieve and Jaem didn't have blood to call him through the bond, and Bravat hadn't yet used his vials. Cyrus was getting impatient. Bravat would call soon, he assured himself, and when he did, Cyrus would tell him about the others still trapped in Mercia.

After they found one another, they'd have to journey back the way men normally did, although it would be dangerous for them. Maybe he could ask Essandra to send the illusion witch for additional protection. *No*—he'd asked enough of her for this failed mission already. If they could make it to the Aged Sea, Cyrus could send a ship for them.

Shame and guilt filled him. He'd gone after Alexander, against his council, leaving Rael weak for the nobles' attack. They'd come after the witches, and Essandra had lost two members of her coven because of it. Everan and Kord had tried to convince him that the nobles would have attacked regardless, but Cyrus didn't believe that. His absence had given them the opportunity they'd been waiting for.

And he had nothing to show for it.

All that risk, and Alexander hadn't even been there.

A dog bumped against his leg with its nose, and Cyrus dropped his hand to its head.

Had his brother been taken with the Mercian queen? The mystery still remained of who had attacked her caravan, although Cyrus didn't particularly care, unless they'd also taken Alexander. But if it had been the Shadow King...

A knock pulled him from his thoughts, and the dogs wiggled at the door. He opened it to find Essandra, and he stepped back in surprise. She took that as an invitation and swept into his chamber, followed by several others—members of her coven.

Essandra carried a dark breastplate, and the rest carried what appeared to be a full set of armor. They set the armor on his bed, then turned and left. Only Essandra stayed.

"What's this?" Cyrus asked. He eyed her and the breastplate she still held.

"It's armor."

He snorted. "I know it's armor. Why do you have it?"

"I had Mal make it."

Mal. The forge witch.

"It can't be pierced," she explained.

He tilted his head. "You want me to wear armor now?"

Essandra set the breastplate down beside the rest of the pieces but kept her hand on it. Her green eyes were serious. "You were hurt pretty badly yesterday."

"I have Teron."

"You won't always have Teron, and you won't even let him completely heal you." She paused. "And it could have been worse. The arrow could have hit your heart, and then you wouldn't have made it to Teron at all."

If she held any resentment or offense from their encounter in the hall the night before, it didn't show.

"Are you worried for me?" he asked, risking a little jest to gauge her.

"I don't want you to die." She was still sharp with her tongue, but the tone of her voice, the way she looked at him, the angles of her face, were... a little less sharp.

A smile tugged at the corners of his mouth. "From you, that almost sounds like affection."

"Affection for the Aether. And your cock."

He snorted and had to glance away. *This woman...*

"You'll wear it," she told him firmly. "Whenever you travel, or fight, or while otherwise engaging in dangerous activity."

"Should I wear it with you?"

Her face was still fixed, but he thought he saw a faint flicker in her eyes. "That's not a bad idea."

Then she turned and swept out of his chamber, as abruptly as she'd come.

Chapter Twenty-Nine

The capital looked as if the gods had tried to destroy it. Cyrus and Essandra walked the city, surveying the aftermath of their fight with the nobles. He knew she'd wrecked quite a bit with the power of the geomancer, but now, seeing it in the daylight, he realized just how much. This would set them back in their rebuilding efforts.

Of course it wasn't her fault—he'd let her do it. More than let her, he'd wanted her to. They'd done what was necessary to protect the coven and to keep the city. All right, maybe a little more than what was necessary, but they'd both been fueled by their anger and loss. Now they'd have to work doubly hard to get the rebuilding efforts back on track.

Fortunately, only a few buildings had been toppled, mainly the ones the nobles and their men had been hiding in or using as cover. The damage to the streets was significant, though, given that Essandra had split the earth and catapulted the cobblestone.

People were still clearing the dead. One of Cyrus's dogs trotted by with a mangled hand in its mouth.

Essandra grimaced. "That's disgusting."

"Two, drop it," Cyrus called. When he'd named the dogs, he'd expected to still call them as a unit, or at the most, use the names interchangeably. But each dog gravitated toward a specific call, and Cyrus found himself noticing the subtle nuances about them. One was the largest, Two had a slightly longer bob of a tail, and while their coats were all a black brindle, Three bore a small white mark on his chest.

Two reluctantly let the hand fall from his mouth.

Cyrus couldn't help a smile.

As they rounded a bend in the street, he slowed. There was a set of buildings, all very similar—small, like mausoleums, but not ornate or marked. They had no windows, and heavy locks bound each of the doors. A stone wall stood tall around them, obviously to keep them from the public, but an inadvertent trench of destruction had collapsed both part of the wall and a corner of the building closest to the street.

"What's wrong?" she asked.

"Nothing, just... those are strange buildings."

She frowned. "King Orrid probably used them to lock people away to die in darkness, or for some other terrible reason."

That was likely. Something nefarious.

Still, he found himself wondering. If he climbed the corner rubble of the one closest to them, he could look down inside it, although exploring wasn't what he should be doing right now.

His curiosity got the better of him. Cyrus jumped up and over the buckled wall.

"What are you doing?" Essandra asked.

"Just taking a look inside."

Carefully, he climbed the fallen stone, gripping the corner of the building to keep from falling. Not so carefully, he reached up to the broken roof and pulled himself up higher. As he peered over the open edge, his eyes widened, and he let out a chuckle. Inside were shelves of coin—a lot of shelves, and a lot of coin.

"What is it?" Essandra called.

"Money. Loads of it." He worked his way back down. "These must be additional treasury storehouses."

"Why would Orrid keep money here?" she asked as she climbed over the crumbled section of the wall.

"I wouldn't keep all the money in the palace either. There are probably a few of these, spread throughout the kingdom." He glanced around. "It would have been heavily guarded—I'm sure they were killed when we took the city, though. Obviously, no one's discovered this yet, otherwise everything would be gone."

A heavy lock secured the door. He pulled his sword.

"Really?" Essandra asked, crossing her arms.

Oh. Right. He smiled sheepishly and took a step back to let her forward.

Reaching out, she put her hand on the lock. Her lips moved—words he couldn't understand.

The metal gave a brittle crack and then crumbled, a slow cascade of ash and dust falling like charred snow to the ground.

He'd seen her do that before, more than once, but it was no less impressive. Not just the magic, but the control of it. The quiet command of destruction.

"What?" she asked him.

He hadn't realized he'd been staring. "Nothing," he said quickly. Then he pushed open the doors. The hole in the roof let in the light, otherwise he would have needed a torch. He stepped inside, and Essandra followed.

They stood for a moment, letting their eyes adjust. He watched Essandra in the half-light. His mind wasn't on the coin anymore. It was on her power—power so easily lost—and what she'd told him the night before. She might wield the power of all the witches, but none of it was hers. If she ever lost her coven, she'd have nothing to fight with. Nothing to protect herself with.

"You know," he said as he slowly started down the center between the racks of gold, "I was thinking, you should learn to use a sword."

"I don't need a sword."

Rows of shelves stacked to the ceiling spanned the whole storehouse.

"Well, I would hope not, but it would be good for you to learn the skill, just in case. Aaron and Amiel, the two guards I've given you, were exceptional bloodsport fighters. Gold-tier. They could teach—"

"I don't need a sword," she said more firmly.

He paused for a moment and looked back at her. Her eyes combed the storehouse.

The shelves held mainly bags of gold and silver coins, but several also held odds and ends—maybe family treasures, religious trinkets, gods knew what they were. His gaze stopped on a solid-gold sword. He picked it up.

"You could have a pretty one," he teased, holding it up.

The daggered look she gave him could have cut him more easily.

He chuckled. A gold sword was useless anyway. Gold was weak against armor and weapons of steel. In fact, aside from the bags of coin, most of the items around them seemed useless or hardly worth taking up space in a private storage chamber. He picked up a bowl—it was odd to find a bowl here. It was gold, but nothing unlike what he'd already seen multiple times throughout the palace. He almost tossed it but paused as he glanced up to find Essandra staring back at him.

Still.

So still.

"Give that to me," she said, her voice barely a breath. Her eyes were fixed on the small bowl.

"Do you know what it is?" he asked.

She only stepped closer to him. Not casually, but like she was prepared to pounce.

He stepped back. "Tell me what it is."

She lunged for it, but he jerked his hand and held it high, out of her reach. "Is this what you've been searching for?" he asked her.

"Give it to me!"

"What is it?"

Her eyes turned black. "Give it to me," she demanded again with a demonic thunder.

He probably should have worn that armor she'd just given him, although something told him that even magically imbued armor wouldn't protect him—not when he stood between her and this... bowl. "You don't have to fight me for it," he said quickly. "I'll give it to you but tell me what it is."

Her breaths came clipped and fast. She was desperate for it, and the look on her face told him she didn't trust he'd give it to her after she told him what it was.

Trust.

He didn't trust that she'd tell him what it was, but he did trust her with things that were much more important to him than a stupid bowl. He wanted her to do the same.

Slowly, he held it out for her, and she snatched it from his grasp.

She turned it in her hands, her eyes wild, checking it, breathless. Then she clutched it to her chest and closed her eyes as a tear streamed down her cheek. She obviously wasn't going to tell him what it was, but he didn't really care, especially now that he knew it was just a bowl. But whatever it meant, it was important to her, and she'd gotten it.

Cyrus sighed and looked back at the coin. This would help continue to fund the capital's rebuilding, and whatever else a kingdom needed money for—like buying... things.

"It's the Amoran Cup," she said, and he looked back at her in surprise.

He opened his mouth, then closed it again. "The what?"

"The Amoran Cup," she repeated, as if he simply hadn't heard her.

"It"—he searched for words—"looks more like a bowl, but... it's very nice."

Her brows dipped, and her eyes narrowed. "Do you not know what the Amoran Cup is?"

He'd never heard of it.

"The Cup of Life?" she added.

He inhaled as he shook his head slowly.

"You don't know what the Cup of Life is?"

He was pretty sure they'd already established this. "Maybe you could try telling me," he shot back.

She crossed her arms, hugging the bowl to her. "It's believed that if you drink from it, it will give you eternal life, or eternal youth."

Cyrus recalled King Orrid, who was very much not alive, and who certainly hadn't been youthful when Cyrus had killed him. "Well, I don't think it works," he said. "Or maybe it's a fake."

Essandra shook her head. "No, it's real—I can feel its power—but that's not what this cup does. People are wrong."

The cup was a simple one, aside from being gold. It had no jewels affixed to it, no designs other than a foreign inscription that ran along the upper edge.

"So, what does it do?" he asked.

She raised it close to her face again, turning it in her hands as if she still couldn't believe she was finally holding it. "It brings life back. After death."

That sounded... not real at all. "How does it work—you just have the dead person drink from it... or... pour from it down their throat?"

"No. It's part of a spell. Combined with the bloom of an everlife tree, the cup will bring the person back to you." She drew her fingers again around the bowl's rim. "The spell won't work without the cup."

"Who are you trying to bring back?"

She pulled the bowl back to her chest but said nothing.

Of course. He sighed again. Well, at least the council would be happy about the storehouses, especially Fatim, his master of coin. He turned to head back out.

"My family," she said, stopping him. Her eyes met his, and they glistened. "I'm trying to bring back my family. My sister and my mother. This is why I came to Rael. This is what I've been looking for."

CHAPTER THIRTY

The council room was quiet. Too quiet for what had happened over the past few days. Not only had Cyrus pursued Alexander against his council's advice, but while he was gone, the council had also been a target of the nobles' attack. In addition to the two witches who'd been killed, three councilmen had been lost: Murius, Cyrus's master of law; his chief philosopher, whose name he still couldn't remember—perhaps he never knew it; and Pontil, his chief architect. The architect would pose a problem as they worked to rebuild the city. He'd have to find another with mastercraft knowledge of engineering and structural foundations.

However, these failings weren't what held his council's attention now. Instead, their eyes were on the letter that Cyrus held in his hand, bearing a red-and-yellow seal. A letter from Osan.

Cyrus broke the seal and opened it.

To King Cyrus of Rael,

I write with finality.

I have learned that your court not only tolerates but elevates those who walk in the shadows—witches whose hands bend the laws of nature and corrupt the balance that holds kingdoms in peace.

Osan stands upon a thousand years of tradition. We are a people of discipline, a people of honor, a people of principle. This darkness has no place in our halls, no seat at our tables, no voice in our counsel. To walk beside it is to walk toward ruin.

I extended an offer of alliance in good faith, believing your rise heralded a return of strength and honor to Rael. I see now that I was mistaken. A king who grants influence to such forces cannot be trusted with peace.

This offer is hereby withdrawn.

Osan does not bargain with darkness.

King Tagasi of Osan,

Keeper of the Eternal Flame

Cyrus flicked a glance toward Essandra at the far end of the table. She sat with her eyes on him, with that unreadable stillness she so often wore. He tucked the letter away.

"Tagasi has withdrawn his proposal for alliance talks," he told the council.

"On what grounds?" Verin asked.

"He's pursuing other options."

"Might you share the letter, Sire?"

"No. It's of no consequence. I had no intention of an alliance with Osan." He'd even forgotten the offer.

"We cannot continue to shuck potential alliances while at the same time provoking kingdoms we have no quarrel with."

"No one is provoking anyone," Everan countered, ever the mediator.

"That's exactly what that rampant bull Bravat is doing," Fatim said. "And when he's caught, Mercia will know Rael—"

"He's not going to be caught. He's simply trapped there with the others until we can find a way to bring them back."

"It's only a matter of time before they *are* caught," Verin said. "We should have never gone."

"But I did," Cyrus said. He said it matter-of-factly, hiding the weight in his chest. He wasn't sure if the shame that sat heavy in him now was the shame of failure or the shame of being foolish and careless enough to have made the attempt to begin with. Surely it was the failure, because if he'd had gotten Alexander, he'd have no shame at all.

And if he were honest with himself, if the opportunity at Alexander presented itself again, he'd absolutely take it.

However, his biggest regret was the loss of the two witches. Essandra sat quietly, making no effort to defend his decision to go to Mercia, and he didn't expect her to. She was still upset about it too, although finding the cup she'd been searching for seemed to have assuaged that anger a little. Without the attack and resulting destruction, they might not have found it at all.

Sharing the news of the treasury storehouses didn't win him back complete favor with the council, but it did finally help the conversation move forward as they discussed where to move the coin and how to allocate some of the funds to their rebuilding efforts. It would also help them purchase additional rice and grain to supplement their dwindling storehouses. The crop produced by the hedge witches was helping, but it wasn't enough. Cyrus didn't linger too long on this topic, as there was still the silent pressure to trade with the Shadowlands.

By late morning, he'd had enough and moved for them to break. They all agreed.

"Oh, Sire, one more thing," Fatim said as they stood. "Will *you* be the one to address the king's grievances now that Murius is gone?"

What grievances? "I don't have any grievances." Well, he had many grievances, but not ones he'd air.

Fatim awkwardly cleared his throat. "Not your own, Sire—the grievances of the people. Murius was fulfilling the duties of both master of law *and* justice. We might want to consider these as separate roles going forward and prioritize appointing a justice to manage grievances."

Justice. The mere word made his chest tighten. "I won't have a man by that title."

"But if you name a justice, you can leave judgments to—"

"I said I won't have a man by that title," Cyrus snapped.

Fatim gave a resigned bow of his head. "Yes, Sire."

Cyrus quieted. He hadn't meant to be so sharp.

"A justice of Rael is a very different role from the justice of Mercia," Essandra interjected, finally speaking, "and you do need one."

An uneasy silence stirred the air. Several of the councilmen shifted in their seats. Even now, even with her siding with them, they didn't like having a witch in the room—especially one that challenged Cyrus like an equal. She might have helped take Rael and stopped the nobles' attack to reclaim the capital, but her presence still made them uncomfortable. Wary.

Cyrus sat back in his chair. Essandra's emerald eyes returned his stare. He'd been a little concerned that she'd disappear the moment she'd found the cup, but she was still working to collect a few remaining pieces for her spell, and she still wanted access to his power, at least for a little while longer.

He wasn't sure why he was so inclined to listen when she spoke. Maybe it was because she recognized his aversion to the position of a justice even when she knew so little else about him. Or maybe it was because he was finding it increasingly bothersome to disappoint this woman.

She'd said he needed a justice. *Fine.* "Then call it something different," he said.

She looked around the table at the councilmen. "Assemble scholars of law for candidacy for the role of magistrate, formerly known as justice."

They all looked at Cyrus, shifting again.

"Why are you looking at me?" he asked them. "Did you not hear her?"

The councilmen bowed quickly.

Fatim paused. "And what about the current grievances, until the role is filled?"

Cyrus was about to tell him the grievances would wait, when Essandra said, "Those with grievances can assemble in the throne room in the morning, beginning next week. King Cyrus will listen to three per day until the role is filled."

Cyrus cut her a sharp look, but she only raised a brow at him with an air of finality.

Fine. He gave no objection.

Fatim bowed again. "Yes, Sire,"

And the councilmen made their way out of the room.

Essandra, Everan, and Kord all stayed.

After everyone was gone, Cyrus sat back in his chair. "Three per day?" he said irritably. "I don't want to deal with other people's problems—I have my own problems."

"You're king," Everan said. "Other people's problems *are* your problems. And it's just until you appoint a magistrate."

"Why don't you do it?" Cyrus asked him.

Essandra eyed him sharply. "Without a master of law or a magistrate, it's the king's responsibility to hear grievances. You'll be there."

No. He wouldn't. He didn't have time for this. Nor the care. He wouldn't.

Cyrus shifted uncomfortably on the throne—the last place he wanted to be sitting. But Essandra had sat him down squarely with the look of death in her eye should he even think about moving, and she now stood to his right to make sure he stayed through the grievances she'd committed him to.

It was his own fault he was here. Earlier that morning, he'd met with a group of men, all candidates for magistrate. Cyrus appreciated the speed at which the council had assembled them. Then he did what he usually did while in his finest form: told them he didn't care who was selected, solicited the council's recommendation, disagreed, then selected no candidate at all.

So here he sat, simmering in his annoyance. He also hadn't heard anything yet from Bravat, making him increasingly agitated. The recusant fighter was supposed to have used the blood to contact him two days after Cyrus had left him in Mercia. It had now been a week.

Cyrus shifted again. He didn't want to be here, but three grievances—that was what he had to get through. He could manage three grievances.

People filed into the throne room. A lot of people. The grievance process was open to the public, although for the life of him, Cyrus couldn't figure out why people would want to come and listen to other people's problems.

Essandra stood to his right, just off the dais, her hands clasped at her waist and her face unreadable. As the crowd settled in, a hush swept over the room—not exactly out of reverence for their king, but out of wariness for the witch beside him. Murmurs rippled through the crowd, heads turning, eyes darting. Cyrus caught more than a few people shifting uncomfortably.

They feared her.

Good. They should.

The first to come forward was a group of men who complained the wages offered by their employer weren't livable wages.

"Go to another employer," Cyrus told them.

"But, Sire," one of the men countered, "jobs are few. Employers know this and take advantage. There used to be a minimum wage, but King Orrid did away with it at the start of last year."

Cyrus looked at his councilmen nearby. "Why?"

"Employers complained it was eating too much into their profits," Fatim said.

Cyrus frowned. "But they were still making a decent profit?"

The councilman bobbed his head uncomfortably. "*A* profit, yes, but—"

"We'll bring back the minimum wage, then. If they're not making a profit"—he gave a pursed smile—"they can come with their grievance."

"But, Sire," Fatim said, "there will be implications for—"

"They can come with their grievance," Cyrus cut him off. "I do three a day." He shot an annoyed smirk at Essandra.

The group of men in front of him all smiled wide and bowed low, uttering repeated thanks.

Essandra stepped closer to him as the men shuffled out. "You need to take this more seriously," she whispered harshly.

"I am taking this seriously," he replied without looking at her.

"No, you're not."

He turned abruptly in his chair. "In what world did you think I'd be good at this?"

"No world," she hissed back, "but it's what you get for not picking a magistrate."

He gritted his teeth. The second group to air their complaints moved in front of him. They were a rough bunch—field workers maybe—but they all bowed respectfully, and Cyrus focused his attention.

"What's your grievance?" he asked them.

"Not really a grievance," one of the men said, stepping forward, "but still an ask."

"Go on."

"We want to know if the crown will buy back slaves that were sold to other kingdoms so families can be reunited."

Cyrus straightened in his chair, and any smirk that he'd previously been wearing fell from his face. The slave trade tore families apart, he was no stranger to this, but to have these families still trying to reunite with the ones they loved, for them not to have given up...

"Yes," he said finally. "Of course."

Loud murmurs rippled through the throne room.

"Sire," Fatim interrupted, quickly stepping closer. "We don't have that kind of money."

That wasn't true. "We just found quite a bit of money."

"Not enough. We'd bankrupt ourselves completely, and then some. Not to mention that that money is already earmarked to keep our grain and rice storehouses from emptying."

Cyrus shrugged. "We'll do a little at a time, then."

"Over what—the next hundred years? It would take an unfathomable amount of time, and the number of kingdoms that would entail cannot be confined to a small list. Do you know the resources it would require to track down all these people, find out where they are? We don't even know if they're still alive. There are no records. On top of all that, to have to purchase them back. We simply don't have the means."

So, Cyrus didn't have the means to go get them, but that didn't mean he couldn't help. "Make it known," he announced, "if people can find a way to get here, they'll be granted refuge and safety. Any slave, of any kingdom, anywhere."

The murmurs among the hall grew louder, and louder still.

"Sire," Fatim interrupted him again, "we barely have the means to support our own population. The kingdom isn't yet stable; we're still rebuilding."

"We'll figure it out. We can also help others overthrow their own kingdoms."

The hall grew even louder.

"Cyrus," Essandra hissed.

Fatim sputtered as if he might have choked on his own tongue. "You cannot so openly be talking about aiding rebellions!" he exclaimed.

Cyrus shrugged. "Why not?"

"What about Serra?" came a call from the crowd.

His skin heated at the mention of the slavers' kingdom. He stood. "I would destroy Serra," he said bitterly. His voice didn't sound like his own.

The reaction from the crowd hit him like a wave. Serra was the reason most of them were here, including Cyrus himself and nearly all his men. Rael hadn't captured their own slaves—they'd bought them from the slave traders.

"What about the Shadowlands?" another man asked.

Cyrus froze. *The Shadowlands.* His heart seized in his chest. Was it even a possibility to think about the Shadowlands?

"All right, I think that's enough grievances," Essandra called out, sweeping forward.

Her flurry broke him from the clutch that held him, and he glanced at her now in confusion. "That was only two."

"And one too many. You're supposed to be solutioning punitive complaints, not committing Rael to war. This was a mistake." She pulled at his arm. "Let's go."

He moved to follow, but a woman's yell caught his ear. "No!" cried the voice.

Cyrus's gaze shifted to a commotion toward the back of the hall. He couldn't see the woman, but he could definitely hear her.

"I need to see the king!" the woman shouted. "He said he'd see three—I'm not leaving!"

"Let her through," Cyrus called, and he waved the crowd to quiet down.

Essandra pinched the bridge of her nose and sighed.

A petite woman bumped her way forward. She was older than Cyrus, perhaps in her sixties. Her dress was simple yet well made, and she wore a pair of large spectacles that she pushed up as she stepped in front of him.

"What's your grievance?" he asked her.

She straightened, as tall as her small frame would allow. "I've come to ask for my father's house."

"What about your father's house?"

"When my father passed several years ago, ownership was given to my husband. When my husband passed away this last year, the home became property of the crown, instead of reverting to me or to my daughter. As you're seizing land now, I ask that you give it to me." She held up a thin finger, not pointing but clearly making a point. "My family has *never* owned slaves—one of the very few who can say that in Rael—and this house has been in my family for six generations. Please, Sire. I ask that you grant it to me."

This seemed easy enough. "Give her the house," he said to his master of records. He turned to go.

"Thank you, Sire," the woman said, breathless, but then added quickly, "It's just... to do that, you would also have to amend the law that women cannot own property."

He paused and turned back to her. "There's a law that women can't own property?"

"Yes. It's all listed in the Accords."

Cyrus narrowed his eyes on her. He knew that there was something *called* the Accords—the laws of Rael—but he didn't know what was in them. Mostly because he didn't care. "Do you practice law?"

The woman pursed her lips. "No. Women aren't able to practice law. But I studied while my husband was alive. He afforded me the opportunity to pursue many of my interests." She calmed a bit and swallowed. "He was a very good husband." She paused. "I miss him."

Cyrus nodded, still looking her over curiously. This was an interesting woman. "I'll strike these laws," he told her.

Murmurs rippled through the hall again.

She clutched her chest. "Thank you, Sire! And for these women who are now able to own property, might you change the law so that a wife may keep her property that she brought to the marriage, should she choose to divorce her husband?"

He shrugged. "Sure."

The murmurs grew.

"Then you'll also strike the rule that prevents women from divorcing their husbands."

The hall became so loud he could barely hear anything else.

Cyrus held up a hand to silence them. He couldn't help the hint of a smile that came to his lips. He liked her. "A woman won't be held a slave to her husband. If she wishes to leave him, she may do so and be protected by the law."

The quiet hall became even quieter—the quiet of shock.

The woman stood as still as a statue, staring at him in silent realization of everything she'd just heard him agree to. Her eyes welled.

But he did have one question... "If your husband is dead, why are you asking about divorce?"

"I merely wish to make this kingdom better for my daughter, for Rael's daughters. For Rael."

He genuinely believed that, and she seemed like a woman who could do it.

Suddenly, a pull came in his mind—the pull of the blood bond. *Bravat.* He needed to wrap this up and get out of here. Quickly.

"You want to make this kingdom a better place?" he asked the woman.

"Of course."

"Perhaps you'd best do that as magistrate."

Gasps rippled through the throne room, and the woman's mouth fell open. "Me, Sire?"

He shrugged. "Do you not know the law?" She obviously knew it better than he did.

"Well, yes, but I—"

"Do you not have an understanding of what needs to be changed to make Rael fairer and more equitable for all its citizens?"

"Perhaps, Sire."

"Do you not want the job?"

"I would be honored, but I am not nearly qualified—"

"Welcome, Magistrate." He paused. "What's your name?"

"Ruth, Sire."

"Well, Ruth, settle things with your father's house—*your* house—and return to the palace tomorrow to start listening to these gods-damned grievances."

Cyrus turned and strode from the throne room. He waved off everyone who tried to talk to him as he left, and he didn't even look at Essandra. He knew her scowl would pierce him straight through. He slipped into an empty drawing room, closing the door, and let his mind chase the bond to Bravat.

Only it wasn't Bravat.

It was Kieve.

"*Brother,*" he said in surprise as he entered Kieve's mind.

"*I went back and found Bravat,*" Kieve said. "*He gave me one of his vials.*"

"Is he with you?"

"No. When I told him the portal had been cut, he decided to take advantage of the additional time to plunder another temple." Of course he had. When Cyrus saw Bravat again…

"Jaem's with him," Kieve added.

Well, at least Bravat had one responsible person with him. That was good. Cyrus needed to break the news that he didn't yet have a way to get them home.

However, before he got to that, Kieve said, *"I found out who captured the Mercian queen."*

Cyrus's curiosity instantly quieted him.

"The Shadow King," Kieve said.

Both Cyrus's body and his mind froze. So, the Shadow King *had* taken her.

A chill crept up his spine as a faint memory flickered. His dream—the Mercian queen seated on the Shadow throne. That hadn't been a dream, just as seeing her going to Aleon hadn't been a dream. He was sure of it now.

But how could she take the Shadow throne if she was now the Shadow King's captive?

Had he seen the vision? Did the Shadow King have a seer of his own, and had they seen the vision too? Maybe that was the point of the attack, of taking her.

That would mean the Shadow King was trying to change his fate. Which wasn't possible.

Was it?

"*Are you still there?*" Kieve asked.

"*Yes, I just... that doesn't make sense. She takes the Shadow King's throne from him—I saw it.*"

"*Well apparently not before she's captured by him.*"

Maybe she'd find a way to escape, join with Aleon, then overthrow him. Or maybe she'd find a way to kill him while in his hold. Cyrus was envious of the opportunity.

"*Also, I don't think the Shadow King has your brother,*" Kieve said. "*I haven't seen him. But, Cyrus, the queen wasn't the only one taken.*"

Who else would the king have bothered with? He wasn't aware—

"*I'm caught, Cyrus.*"

Cyrus's blood ran cold. *What?* Kieve was caught?

"*We came back to where the portal was, and we were waiting to see if it opened again. The Shadows came upon us in the night.*"

"*How? Where are you now?*"

Kieve gave a sad chuckle. "*You can't help me now.*"

"*Tell me where you are.*"

"*No. You can't confront the Shadow King. He has a whole army with him. Thousands, Cyrus. Tens of thousands. There's nothing you can do. And you already had a failed mission—a mission not supported by your council, I'll remind you.*"

The Shadow King had Kieve. Cyrus's breath shook with fury. But Kieve was right—what could he do? He didn't have a way to get to him. He didn't have a proper army. Rael was a wreck; the dust hadn't even settled after reclaiming it—Cyrus hadn't even told him about the nobles' attack yet.

But none of that mattered. "*Where are you?*" he demanded again.

"*I couldn't even tell you.*"

Cyrus pushed against Kieve's mind, trying to see through his eyes.

"*No, Cyrus.*"

How was he pushing him out? "*Let me in, let me see.*"

"*No.*"

Cyrus had thought Kieve the weakest among them, especially over the past few weeks, but somehow, he was summoning the strength to push back against him. "*Kieve, I'll come for you. I'll bring you back.*"

"*I don't want to come back.*"

Cyrus stilled, and his chest tightened. "*What?*"

"*I'm tired of this world.*"

A sinking feeling hit his stomach. "*Kieve,*" he whispered.

"*Bravat has most of the men—they split off yesterday after he heard there was a second temple nearby. He'll probably call through the blood bond tomorrow; you'll have to tell him what happened.*"

"*I will,*" he promised. "*And then I'll send him back for you.*"

"*We won't be here.*"

What did that mean? Cyrus's heart thrummed heavier.

"*Only a few men are with me,*" said Kieve. "*We've all agreed.*"

The weight of Kieve's words threatened to crush him. "*Whatever you're thinking—*"

"*The Shadow King doesn't know who we are. And he won't.*"

"Kieve, what are you going to do?"

"I don't have much time. Listen to me. I know you gave me everything you could in this life. None of this was your fault. I know you'll blame yourself, but I'm glad I came. I'm ready."

"Wait—wait!" Cyrus begged. *"I'm coming for you."*

"You can't."

"Tell me where you are."

"I'm blessed to have known you." Even in his mind, Kieve's voice cracked. *"You were a good brother, and a good friend. The best."*

"Kieve—wait!"

"Goodbye, Cyrus."

"Kieve—"

Everything went silent.

"Kieve?" But he wasn't in Kieve's mind anymore.

Cyrus stood with his eyes tightly closed. He refused to open them, desperately trying to recover the bond.

"Kieve!"

But the pull was gone. He was back in his own mind now. A cry ripped from his lips. "Kieve!"

Chapter Thirty-One

Cyrus beat on the witch's door. "Essandra!" he bellowed. He'd tried to force it open, but it was locked. He beat harder.

She ripped it open, her face fixed in fury. No doubt she was still angry with him for what had happened earlier in the throne room, but when she saw him, her mouth slacked, and her brows lined a dip above her widening eyes. "What's wrong?"

He pushed himself into her chamber. "Bring him back!" he begged. "Bring him back now!"

She stumbled backward. Her mouth opened and her lips moved as if to form words, but no sound came. "What's wrong—what happened?" she finally managed to get out. "Bring who where?"

"Kieve!"

"I've been working on an alternative to the portal magic, but I haven't—"

"No, get your bowl and bring him back!" He grabbed her. "Get your bowl and bring him back!"

She froze as she realized what he was saying.

"Where is it?" He whirled around, searching. *"Where is it?"* He moved to the chest of drawers along the wall, ripping them open and pulling the clothing out from inside. It wasn't there.

"Cyrus—"

He whirled back around and scanned the room. He moved to the open shelves, knocking things as he went—jars filled with herbs and liquids, candles, it didn't matter. He swept it all out of the way. "Where is it?!"

Then he saw it.

The bowl sat on the small table by the bed.

Essandra didn't move to stop him as he grabbed it. She only shook her head. "Cyrus—"

He pushed it into her hands. "Bring him back," he begged.

"It doesn't work like that."

"Then, however it works, whatever you need. Tell me—I'll get it."

"Cyrus—"

"Please!" He pressed her hands tighter against the bowl, cupping them in his own. "Please. Bring him back." He dropped his forehead against her hands, begging, praying. She was the closest thing to a god; he knew she had the power. She could bring Kieve back.

"Cyrus—"

"Please!"

"Cyrus!" She dropped the bowl and grabbed his face. "Look at me." He quieted and raised his eyes to hers.

"I need the flower of an everlife tree," she said, "grown over his body."

His heart beat heavily and he nodded as he swallowed. He'd find Kieve's body, and get the bloom from this tree—

"No, Cyrus, listen to me. An everlife tree takes twenty years to flower, at least."

He stilled. *Twenty years...*

"And I'd need his blood, and the blood of a family member still alive to create the life bond to anchor him to the world of the living."

He glanced down, trying to remember. Did Kieve have any other family? Anywhere? *No.* "What if he—what if he doesn't have family?"

She shook her head sadly.

"We can't bring him back because he doesn't have family?" No, that couldn't be right.

"No, I'd have no way to bond him to the living world. And we don't have his body, or his blood—"

"I'll get those!" He'd get them himself.

"Or the flower from his everlife tree—we have nothing. I can't bring him back because we have *nothing*."

Cold rippled through him. A deathly cold.

"I'm sorry," she said.

That couldn't be the answer. No. He couldn't accept that.

"I'm sorry," she whispered again.

Cyrus just stood there, staring at her. But not seeing her, not really. Essandra, with all her impossible power, with her spells and her shadows of defiance—if anyone could bend the rules of life and death, it was her.

But there were things even she couldn't do.

His hands fell from her. His eyes burned, but no tears came. Not yet.

"That's it?" he asked quietly. But it wasn't a real question. He already knew the answer. A hollow beat passed between them. She didn't try to fill it.

His shoulders dropped.

Then, without a word, he turned and walked from her chamber.

"Where are you going?" she called after him.

He didn't know. He didn't know where he was going or what he was doing. He didn't know anything anymore. All he knew was that his friend was gone. So many of his friends were gone. Even as king, this world kept taking from him. The Shadow King kept taking from him.

He passed a large wall mirror and paused, staring at his reflection—at his face looking back at him. Alexander's face looking back at him. Mocking him.

Anguish ripped from his throat as he clasped the top edge of the mirror and tore it from the wall. The glass shattered on the marble floor. It felt good, and he needed more. Everything fell in his wake—vases, tapestries, the glass panes on the interior doors.

The halls were mostly empty of people, but the few poor souls he did pass quickly scurried out of his way.

"Cyrus!" Essandra's voice came behind him, but he didn't stop. He let the tempest within him rage.

He stormed the palace. As he passed the council room, he slid to a stop and then stormed back to it. This room—he hated this room. He ripped the paintings from the walls. He'd left them before because they weren't self-indulgent portraits of rulers past. They were landscapes and flowers—*but there would be no fucking flowers here!* A marble horse head sat atop a display column in the corner of the room. It took all his weight, but he toppled it to the ground. He caught sight of Essandra. She'd given up trying to stop him and just followed.

Back out in the hall, another large mirror sat mounted against a wall, and he ripped it off, sending hundreds of glass shards exploding around him. He broke another mirror, and another. He'd break everything in this palace. The way he was broken. He couldn't hold it together anymore. He didn't want to.

Finally, exhausted, he stopped, panting. His body hurt; his head hurt. And suddenly, he couldn't stand anymore. He sank to the floor. The broken glass bit into his skin, but he didn't care.

"Cyrus," Essandra said as she stepped carefully through the glass toward him.

"Don't," he told her wearily. "You'll cut yourself."

But she didn't listen and made her way to him. Quietly, she dropped down in front of him.

"Come on," she said softly, and took his hand.

Slowly, he got to his feet and let her pull him from the hall.

She led him to Teron's workroom. When they reached it, Teron wasn't there, but Essandra pushed Cyrus to sit on a stool and then searched the room's drawers for supplies. She found some pincers and some clean linen. She cut the leathers around his thighs with a pair of shears and pulled them from his legs to work on the small shards of glass lodged in his knees.

Cyrus sat, hollow. He didn't even feel the glass pulled from his skin. The room was quiet, save the clinking of glass shards as she dropped them into a small, metal bowl.

Finally, he broke the silence. "He didn't want to come back," he said. "I told him I would come for him, but he didn't want to come back."

She paused for a moment, glancing up at him before continuing with the glass.

"I thought he would get better," he said. "I gave him Pyro so he would get better." His lip trembled. His whole body trembled. "Why didn't he get better?"

She put the bowl on the table. Then she stepped forward and put her arms around him.

A silent sob escaped him as he buried his face in her neck. "Why didn't he get better?"

She tightened her hold around him. "What does revenge heal?"

"Everything."

"Cyrus." She stepped back, making him look at her. "*Nothing*," she whispered. "Revenge heals *nothing*."

He shook his head. "No, that's not true."

She gave a sad frown, but she didn't argue.

"That's not true," he said again.

Teron entered and stopped abruptly in his step in seeing Cyrus. Then quickly he came. "What happened?" he asked.

Cyrus couldn't answer.

"We lost Kieve," Essandra said.

Teron grew quiet. His eyes traveled to Cyrus's bloody knees, then he spotted the small bowl of glass shards on the table. "Did you get them all out?" he asked Essandra.

She nodded.

"I'll take care of the rest." The cuts were shallow, and Teron's touch healed them quickly. Then he went to the counter and stirred some herbs into a drink. Returning to Cyrus, he held it out to him.

"What's this for?" Cyrus asked. Teron had never given him anything medicinal before.

"For the mind."

Cyrus shook his head. "I'll be fine," he said, and pushed it back toward him

But Essandra stopped him. "Take it."

"I have things to do—"

"That can wait." She nodded to the herbs again. "You need more sleep, and you probably won't get it otherwise. Drink it down."

Cyrus eyed the mixture. She was right. He hadn't slept, and he wouldn't sleep. Not now, even though he was exhausted. Maybe just a couple of hours. Yes, just a couple of hours, and he drank deeply.

Cyrus blinked his eyes open slowly. Where was he? He tried to focus his vision against the sea of red around him.

Blood.

No, not blood. His eyes sharpened. Crimson sheets. On a bed—a rather large bed. He moved to sit.

"Easy," a voice called softly. He turned to see Essandra sitting in a chair by the window. She put down the book that she'd been reading on the small side table and rose, moving toward him.

"Where am I?" he asked.

"My chamber."

His brows dipped, and he blinked back the fog in his mind. The royal room was different from when he'd last been in it. "Why am I in *your* room?" he asked.

"Because the herbs worked faster than expected, and Teron and I could only manage to carry you so far. This was closer."

Teron. Everything came flooding back: Kieve, Cyrus's wake of anger, Teron's mixture.

"And it's more convenient for me as I watch after you," she added.

"You didn't have to do that." He put his head in his hands. He felt sick.

"I know," she said matter-of-factly as she stepped back to the table and poured a small cup of hot tea. She moved to the bed, sitting down on the edge, and held it out for him. "Drink this."

"I don't want any more of whatever that is."

"There's nothing in here; it's just tea."

He eyed it suspiciously but accepted it. "How long have I been asleep?" he asked, then took a sip. It was hot, but good, and he drank it down.

"All day, and now part of the night."

"It's night now?"

She nodded. "The middle of it."

He sighed. "I should go, let *you* get some sleep."

She gave a small smile. "I'm all right." She took the cup back from him, but as she moved to set it on the side table, he caught her arm.

Cyrus didn't know what made him reach for her. Despite her taking his body when she wanted it, he hadn't felt comfortable asking for hers. He didn't feel comfortable now. He wasn't even lustful.

He wasn't sure what he needed, he just *needed*.

She seemed to understand. And to have pity for him. Slowly, she reached back behind her and loosened the lacing of her dress, then pulled it from her shoulders and let it drop to the floor. She left her chemise on but reached underneath to pull off her undergarments.

There wasn't a rush of desire. This wasn't for pleasure.

Cyrus stripped off what was left of his torn leathers as Essandra lay down beside him, and he pulled her underneath him. He moved between her thighs and strung saliva to coat himself. She didn't say anything, she didn't try to control him. She simply let him take what he needed.

He sank inside her. She was warm and soft, and felt good and real. Gods, he was so desperate for something good and real.

She rocked her hips to encourage him. But he couldn't.

His chest tightened. What was wrong with him?

He'd thought he needed her. He *did* need her, but not like this. He just needed to have her, to be close to her, to be close to someone.

He knew she didn't like for him to touch her, but he couldn't help himself. He wrapped his arms around her and laid his head against where her neck met her shoulder.

The smell of her calmed him.

Right now, he was weak, but she was powerful. She had enough power for the both of them. His racing heart slowed.

"There's something wrong with me," he whispered.

She was quiet for a moment, before she said, "There's something wrong with all of us."

The softness of her hands drifted over his back, running up into his hair. His body grew heavier, and he let himself breathe her in deeper.

Her warmth.

Her scent.

Her calm.

When he opened his eyes again, light poured through the window. It was morning.

Essandra lay asleep beside him. They weren't joined anymore, but her leg was draped over his hip, and his arms were still wrapped around her. Her hair spilled across the pillow, wild and dark.

Her skin called to him, but he didn't move. Didn't press his mouth to her shoulder. Didn't let his hands wander. Not for lack of want, but he knew there were boundaries—boundaries she'd let him cross in his anguish. But she wasn't his. She'd merely given him what he'd needed to keep from completely breaking. It wasn't something he could expect often, perhaps not ever again. He respected that.

He let his head rest back down for a moment, pulling strength from the touch between them—her strength. She was the strongest person he'd ever met, and right now, he needed that.

Eventually, he moved. Slowly, carefully, he slipped his arm from beneath her and pulled away. She didn't wake.

He rose, dressed in silence, and stood at the door for a breath. Just one. Then he stepped out into the hall.

The sunlight was harsh against his eyes, too bright, too clean. It didn't care about Kieve. It didn't care that Cyrus was broken, or that the Shadow King had taken from him yet again. He'd taken something dear. Cyrus made another promise to himself as he padded back to his chamber—the Shadow King would die.

Chapter Thirty-Two

No one said a word about the state of the council room.

They stepped carefully through the broken marble sculptures and over the torn paintings that had been ripped from the walls. Robes and shoes brushed against glass fragments as the councilmen took their seats without comment.

None of them looked at Cyrus.

Neither did they mention his hastily appointed magistrate. When Ruth entered, they all rose, bowing politely in quiet greeting before taking their seats again.

Ruth sat with her eyes wide behind her spectacles as she glanced around the room—from the scattering of stone and marble to the broken chandelier crystals glinting in the corners. Cyrus wanted to tell her that it wasn't normally like this, but he wasn't sure what normal even looked like anymore.

Nothing was normal. Nothing had been normal. Ever.

Grief still gripped him in its claws. His whole body ached—his arms, his legs, his chest, his heart. He couldn't fill his lungs. He couldn't think.

What had happened to Kieve was his fault. Cyrus should have never let him go to Mercia. Kieve hadn't been well, and he'd known it. But he'd been so fixated on the opportunity to get Alexander, so blind to what was happening right in front of him.

If he had made Kieve stay in Rael...

If Cyrus had never gone to Mercia at all...

And now, as he sat at the table looking back at his councilmen, all he could feel was pain. And regret. And shame. And rage.

His eyes caught on Essandra as she walked in. Her red dress was striking against her dark hair and fair skin. She took a sweeping look around the room, and her eyes stopped on him. It was everything he could do not to ask her to sit beside him. He desperately needed the calm that her touch brought—not that he could touch her, but maybe just the feel of her closeness...

"It looks like we have everyone, Sire," said Fatim. "There was something you wanted to share with us?"

He didn't actually want to share anything. In fact, it had taken everything Everan had to convince him to pull the council together. Cyrus suspected it wasn't so much that the news couldn't wait, but more that he needed to bridge the divide of his actions—going to Mercia, spontaneously appointing Ruth, publicly threatening to aid rebellion against other kingdoms. Threatening Serra and the Shadowlands.

Everan was trying to get him to move forward, and Cyrus wanted to move forward. He just also wanted to leave.

He tried to pull his mind together as he looked around the room. "I have news. It was the Shadow King who captured the Mercian queen."

The councilmen shifted back in their chairs in surprise.

"Is she still alive?" Naik, his chief physician, asked.

"I don't know, but she's been foreseen to take his throne and wed Aleon's king, neither of which has happened yet, so I'd assume so."

It still struck him strangely to speak of his ability so openly. The council had had questions when they'd learned about him in the early weeks, but their shock quickly dwindled as they discovered that visions couldn't be conjured on a whim, and rarely did they show anything useful or that he could even identify. It probably also helped that his power paled in comparison to Essandra's, which she made no effort to hide.

"The Shadow King also captured and killed a couple of our own men," he continued, "some of those who were trapped in Mercia when the portal collapsed."

The councilmen shifted in their chairs.

"Who?" Naik asked.

But Cyrus couldn't say it. Saying it would make it real, and he wasn't ready for it to be real yet.

"Does he know they're from Rael?" Fatim asked.

Cyrus shook his head. "I've still heard nothing from Bravat," he said, "so I still don't know the state of the rest of our men. I expect an update soon."

"So, councilmen," Everan said, standing. "Not a lot of news, unfortunately, but the king wanted to keep you all updated with as much as he had."

Everan tried so hard.

Cyrus almost felt guilty as he said, "I also want to discuss a move against the Shadowlands."

All heads snapped to him, including Everan's, as that wasn't a topic they'd discussed bringing to the council.

"With what?" Fatim asked incredulously.

"We already have almost forty thousand men." Cyrus hadn't initially believed it when Kord had told him, but with all the fighters from the churn houses, they had the start of a large army. "It will take time to build enough strength to move against the Shadowlands, I know," he added. "But we must have an end in mind—what we're working toward."

Lomas leaned forward. "We should be working toward stabilizing Rael, feeding our people, building alliances, and preventing further attacks from the nobles."

Cyrus cast his gaze on his master of public works. "I don't disagree with any of those things. I'm merely looking to the future. Our long-term plan."

"The Shadowlands is a feat that even the strongest kingdoms do not dare—we're fools to even speak of it."

"We're cowards if we don't," Cyrus said.

"If we make any move at all, it should be a move against Serra," Nevin countered. "That's what the people want." Nevin was his master of ships, and Cyrus wasn't sure why he was even here. He *was* certain now, however, that he had too many councilmen.

Cyrus stood. "The people have said they want the Shadowlands." It had been the Shadow King who'd sold Cyrus to Serra to begin with. It had been the Shadow King who'd killed Kieve. It was the Shadow King's head he'd take first.

"Serra has put significantly more people in chains, stealing them from their homes," Verin said. "Their kingdom's economy lives off it. The Shadowlands are but an enabler, a contributor."

"We shouldn't be talking about Serra *or* the Shadowlands," Fatim argued.

But they *were* talking, and talking all at once. Too much.

Everan interjected, waiving the room quiet. "There's obviously strong opposing opinions," he said. He looked at Cyrus. "Even if moving against the Shadowlands first is the right action, I think what you're hearing is that there are concerns for Rael. And people are weary of fighting, even the discussion of fighting. Let's table this for now. This isn't a topic that will be resolved in one sitting anyway."

Cyrus didn't want to table it, but there wasn't much he could do right now, even if his council had agreed with him. He needed a larger army. He needed a plan.

And he had every intention of getting both.

Everan called them to close, and the councilmen filtered out, as did his men. Everan moved to approach him, but Cyrus waved him off. "Not now." He already knew Everan was disappointed in him. He didn't need to hear it too. Instead, Cyrus moved to where Essandra still lingered. He was glad she waited; he had several things he wanted to say to her, but before he could start, she asked, "What are you doing?"

"What do you think I'm—"

"I know you're upset about Kieve, but you need to focus on Rael."

"I am focused on Rael," he argued. "I'm just looking at the future—"

"There's plenty of future right in front of you." Her words were chastising, but her voice was gentle. Sympathetic almost.

He didn't want her sympathy. "Is that all?" he asked.

She glanced down at her hands clasped at her waist. "No. There's something else I wanted to talk to you about."

Probably the same topic he had for her... "Me too, but you first."

"No, you first," she said.

He drew in a deep breath and let it out slowly. "Um, about yesterday... and last night. I wanted to say I'm sorry."

She stiffened as her brows dipped. "You're sorry?"

"I don't know why I did that. Took you. I shouldn't have used you like that. I wasn't thinking clearly."

"Oh." Her eyes narrowed, and she shifted her gaze down again. "Right." Her words came clipped now, and her face grew sharper. Was she angry? Why?

He swore under his breath. Because he'd been too free with her.

"It won't happen again," he assured her.

Her lips thinned. "Good," she snapped. She turned to leave.

"Wait. Was there something else you wanted to talk about?"

"No. Never mind." And she left him standing in the empty council room.

Cyrus moved to follow her, but the pull of the blood bond stopped him in his step. Hope sprang in his chest.

Kieve?

CHAPTER THIRTY-THREE

The disappointment was crushing.

It wasn't Kieve through the bond.

It was Bravat.

The shift gutted him, and Cyrus surged down the bond with a sudden rush of anger. "*Where have you been?*" he snarled as he raged into the fighter's mind. "*What took you so long?*"

"*Fucking gods, Cyrus, calm down, it's just been a few days.*"

Calm down. If Cyrus could have physically reached through the blood bond, Bravat wouldn't have had a face.

"*Kieve found us a few days ago,*" Bravat said. "*Told me the portal failed. He went back to wait. I gave him your blood. He should have called to you and told you—*"

"*Kieve's dead now.*"

Bravat went quiet.

"*He was captured by the Shadow King.*" Cyrus shook as fury filled him to the brim. "*Where were you?!*"

"*You think I would have been able to stop that?*"

No, he didn't. Cyrus was angry, though, and he still wanted to blame him.

"We haven't even seen any Shadowmen. I would have called you sooner."

He wasn't sure he believed that.

"I found another temple," Bravat told him. *"That's where we've been. We've got a shitload of gold to bring back."*

Cyrus didn't care about the gold. *"Is Jaem with you?"*

"Yeah, I have him. All the men are here."

"Keep everyone together. I'm still trying to figure out how to get you all back. Lie low. Call me through the blood in three days."

"Fine."

"Three days, Bravat," Cyrus warned.

"I said fucking fine."

Yeah. Fine. But if Bravat didn't call him in three days, he wouldn't be fine.

Of course, Bravat didn't call him in three days.

But Jaem finally did. Bravat had passed him the blood vial and, apparently, the responsibility of talking to Cyrus. And as angry and annoyed as Cyrus was, he couldn't deny—he preferred talking to Jaem anyway.

Jaem had been a thief before he was caught and sold into the trade. Not only was he a good fighter, but he was good at finding things, good at observing, and good at getting information. If there was anyone to keep an eye on Bravat and keep Cyrus apprised of what was happening, it was Jaem. He was also extremely loyal, and Cyrus trusted him implicitly.

Unfortunately, the news that Jaem brought him was not what he wanted to hear. Bravat was out of control, razing the Mercian outer reaches as he saw fit. And there was nothing Cyrus could do about it. He hoped that Bravat would grow tired, be ready to return to Rael with all the gold he'd collected.

But weeks passed. Three of them. And still, Bravat *wasn't* tiring. In fact, he was getting worse.

"Cyrus, he isn't just looting the temples," Jaem told him in a desperate call. *"He's completely destroying them."*

Cyrus swore. This fool was going to get himself caught. Essandra was still looking for portal alternatives, but it wouldn't be something available quickly, and he wasn't entirely sure she was prioritizing it. Now that she had the cup, she'd been working on gathering the remaining things she needed for the spell for her family.

Cyrus had previously considered the possibility of the men starting the journey south, back to Rael, but crossing the Horsemen Tribelands would be dangerous. Cyrus didn't think they'd all make it, and he could easily find himself with no men left at all. He wanted to wait for Essandra, but much more of this and he might not have a choice.

"*How do the men feel?*" he asked Jaem.

"*Well, most are Bravat's men, and they're just different from us, you know? They don't seem to care. They're just happy about their gold.*"

Cyrus couldn't let Bravat keep going—it posed too great a risk to Rael. But he had no way to stop him. Not now. And if he were honest with himself, if Bravat wanted to spend time wreaking havoc in a kingdom that his brother was responsible for safekeeping, Cyrus wasn't particularly motivated to stop him. There was something appealing about making a menace like Bravat Alexander's problem.

Still, it left a bitter taste in his mouth. Cyrus knew he needed to bring him back. He just couldn't yet. Until then, he also had plenty of other things to worry about.

"*You haven't seen anything of the Shadowmen?*" Cyrus asked.

"*Nothing. I'm having a hard time believing they were even here to begin with.*"

So was Cyrus, but he trusted what Kieve had told him.

"*We'll talk again in a few days,*" he told Jaem. "*Make sure no one gets caught.*"

Cyrus opened his eyes back to his own chamber. A pain in his chest still lingered at the thought of Kieve.

The dogs lay stretched in the beams of sunlight falling across the floor. Cyrus tried to turn his attention back to getting dressed, as he'd been doing when Jaem had called him.

He fastened the buttons of his shirt as he stared at himself in the mirror. It looked too stiff, and he unfastened the top four. It had been months since he'd taken the throne, and he still wasn't used to formal-cut clothing, but he was king now, and apparently it wasn't socially acceptable to walk around with his arms and chest uncovered.

He frowned. Now he looked disheveled. He refastened two buttons. Gods-damned, it was hot. He eyed the vest that was supposed to go over it. *Absolutely not.*

A knock sounded, and the door opened. The dogs jumped up but then settled as Everan pushed in his head. "Cyrus." His face was shadowed. "You need to see this."

Cyrus followed him down the hall to the central city overlook and outside onto the balcony. As he neared the stone railing, he slowed in his step. Crowds of people filled the streets around the palace—so many he couldn't see the cobblestone. Some carried large packs on their backs, others held little more than the clothes on their bodies, but most notable was simply the number of them.

"Who are they?" Cyrus asked.

"Slaves who've escaped their kingdoms and have come here under your promise."

"My promise?"

"A couple weeks ago, when you were listening to grievances, you said that if a slave could make it here—"

"I know what I said," he snapped. Everan quieted, and Cyrus sighed in frustration. He didn't mean to be short, but his council wasn't going to be happy about this. He was barely managing to sustain his own people.

"They also say they've come to support your cause," Everan added.

"What cause is that?" Cyrus looked closer at the throngs of people below and noted they were different in dress and style. They hadn't all fled from the same kingdom.

"To overthrow Serra."

Cyrus jerked his head up in surprise. His council *really* wasn't going to be happy. He opened his mouth to object, but he didn't have words, so he closed it again. What could he say? He'd meant it—if he ever had the opportunity to take Serra, he'd do it. And if he ever got the opportunity to take the Shadowlands...

"The council is assembling," Everan said. "They're looking for you."

Cyrus stifled the groan rising in his throat. He shook his head. "I can't." The last council meeting had been excruciating. And, really, what could they do about this situation now? The people were already here.

"You can't avoid them."

He was pretty sure he could.

Everan gave him a small push toward the door. "Come on."

They made their way toward the council room. Cyrus's mind turned. These people had come here not just because he'd promised them refuge but also because they wanted to join him against those who'd oppressed them. He slowed his pace.

"Is something wrong?" Everan asked.

"How many do you think have come?"

Everan shrugged. "It's hard to tell. Five thousand maybe?"

"And more on the way?"

"I'd expect so. At first it was a few hundred, then we had about ten ships show up through the night and this morning. Word is spreading. Are you tallying the heads we'll have to feed?"

"I'm tallying the heads we'll have for an army."

Everan stopped. "Cyrus." He glanced both ways down the hall, making sure their words were private. "Are you really going to push to start a war?"

"It's the same war."

"Cyrus—"

"*Be their vengeance.* Isn't that what you said?"

Everan shook his head. "No—that's not what I said. I said be their *justice.*" His voice quieted. "And not everyone even wants that. Some just want a life."

"Some as in *you*?"

Everan sighed. He leaned closer. "I know losing Kieve has taken a toll on you. It's taken a toll on all of us. But these past few weeks, you haven't been yourself. You've been rash and impulsive—more than usual. I'm worried about you."

"You don't agree with me?"

"It's not about agreeing."

Everan's eyes shifted over Cyrus's shoulder, and Cyrus turned to find Essandra quickly walking toward them. His jaw tightened. She'd be just as displeased as the council about their new visitors. She and her hedge witches were already working night and day to meet the harvest demands for Rael's current population. This would be an added burden—a *significant* one.

"I'm sure you saw outside," Cyrus started, bracing for her anger.

"Yes." She was slightly winded, as if she'd been running. "I need you to come with me."

Of course. No doubt to push him back into his kingly obligations. She'd probably give him a piece of her mind later.

"We're already on our way to the council room," he told her.

"Not the council room." Her cheeks were flushed, and she wrung her hands. "There's something else. I need your help. I need you to come. Right now."

Cyrus realized she wasn't at all focused on their new visitors, or on the council. "What is it?" he asked.

She shifted impatiently. "I've developed an alternative portal spell, but I need you to make it work."

There was a lift in his chest. "You've created a portal? We can bring everyone back?"

"Yes. No. I mean—it's complicated. Please. Just come."

"The council is assembling now—"

"The council can wait." There was desperation in her voice.

"Go," Everan told him. "I'll tell the council you'll meet with them later, and I'll start the men working on mass accommodations for the arrivals."

Cyrus didn't need too much convincing. "Thank you, brother."

Everan nodded, then turned and set to his task.

"So, you've created a portal?" Cyrus pressed as he fell in step beside Essandra, back toward her chamber.

"Not exactly a portal, but a way to travel, yes."

"And this will let us bring back Jaem and Bravat and the rest of our men?"

"Not yet," Essandra said. "First, I have to see if it works. And it's not like Tomel's power—you can't just travel anywhere." They passed the hall to her chamber, and his brow hitched. Where were they going?

"What do you need from me?" he asked.

"I need you to help me travel through the Aether, since only a seer can."

They reached a cross hall, and she turned the corner to the right. He followed, confused. "I didn't think the Aether was a place," he said.

"It's not, but I've employed... an unconventional magic to use it like a bridge between two points in the physical world."

"What do you mean *unconventional magic*?"

She swallowed. It took her several steps before she answered. "Dark magic," she said finally. She seemed to think he'd be troubled by that, but it held no meaning for him.

"Look, I'll be completely honest with you," she said. "This portal serves me and my agenda. I've linked it to a place that I need to go to gather an ingredient for my spell."

He didn't need to ask her which spell. He knew—the Amoran Cup spell.

"I had to link to a place of great power for the portal spell anyway," she explained. "This place is the only one I know, and even then, I'm not sure if it will be enough. If this *does* work, I still won't be able to create a different portal closer to your men. But where I'm taking us isn't terribly far from Mercia, and I think it will prove a reasonable solution for your needs too."

It was certainly better than sending his men through the Tribelands.

"So, what do you need from me?" he asked.

"A tether, or a bonding spell, and for you to come with me so I can travel through."

"What's a bonding spell?"

She reached a chamber and opened the door, and Cyrus followed her in. It was a study—no, not a study—a workroom, similar to Teron's. A large table sat in the center, and on every wall, shelves stretched from floor to ceiling. They were filled with all her witchy things: books and scrolls, stacks of bowls, bottles of tonics, and jars of bones.

"What's a bonding spell?" he asked again.

"Exactly what it sounds like," she answered shortly.

He caught her arm, pulling her to him and forcing her to look at him. Her green eyes flashed in challenge. When faced with fight or flight, he suspected she'd always choose fight, but he wasn't looking for a fight right now. He did want to help her—this was important to both of them. Maybe she saw that, because, slowly, she softened. He loosened his hold.

She swallowed. "I'm sorry. I'm just..." Her voice dropped, betraying her fear. "I haven't been able to get it to work, and if this doesn't work now, with you..."

He glanced around the room and noticed all the open and half-filled jars on the table and bowls with various mixtures and the ash of spells past. Books lay strewn open, with parchments of notes that had been stricken and rewritten many times over.

Evidence of prior tryings. And failings.

"If this doesn't work, you'll keep trying until you figure out what does," he assured her. She nodded, but he could still see her doubt. "Tell me what to do," he said.

"The tether works similarly to the bond you create when your blood touches someone's skin," she explained, "except this will be a bond of the body, not a bond of the mind. There are several uses for this specific bond. In this case, I'll use it so the power of the Aether sees my body the same as yours, which will allow me to travel through it as you do. For this, it's *you* who needs to take *my* blood."

"Do all spells need blood?" he asked. It seemed like quite a lot of them did.

She pricked her finger with the tip of her dagger, drawing a small crimson swell. "I can mix it in a bowl with wine, if that's easier." She glanced around behind her for a carafe. "Blood holds the most power—"

Her words stopped abruptly as he caught her hand and brought her finger to his lips, taking it into his mouth and sucking gently. He wondered if she felt how he did when his blood touched another—the instant bond. She certainly felt something, as she stared at him with her eyes large. Her gaze dropped to his mouth, and her lips parted.

Then she cleared her throat and quickly pulled her hand from him. "Blood, um, holds the most power, so, um, most spells that, um, require a lot of power need it." She stood awkwardly, very uncharacteristic of her, but snapped out of it as she shuffled him toward the center of the room. Facing him, she whispered, "Amana fasora." A spell.

Again, he expected a physical feeling, for *something* to happen, but nothing did. "Did it work?" he asked.

She pushed up the sleeve of his tunic and, with the flick of her wrist, made the tiniest of cuts on the inside of his forearm.

He flinched, and she winced. "What did you do that for?"

"It worked," she said simply.

His brows dipped. "How do you know?"

"I just do." She slipped the dagger back into its sheath. At least she was done cutting him. For now.

"So, I should be able to travel through and take with me those physically bonded or tethered to me?" he asked. If this worked, he could use it to bring the rest of his men back.

She nodded. "Yes."

"How many people can I tether at a time?"

She hesitated. "That comes with other risks. Let's just see if this works first."

He studied her for a moment—her deep emerald eyes, the flush of excitement in her cheeks. Her hope.

"All right," he said.

Essandra hurriedly moved around the table and took a bowl with a dark sand mixture inside. She poured it into a small sachet. "This creates the door," she said. "We'll pour a line and step over it. But we can't use all of it. We need some to create a door back as well."

He pushed out a breath between his lips. "All right." This was getting complicated, but he trusted her.

Essandra stood beside him. She poured a palmful of the dark mixture into her hand and drew a line in front of them.

"What if this doesn't work?" he asked. "What will happen?"

"We'll probably burn in the Aether."

He jerked abruptly. "What?"

"It's a very small possibility, though. *Very* small. I think."

"Well, I'm not sure—"

"It's fine. It's going to work."

She sounded confident enough.

"All right," he said finally.

Essandra sucked in a deep breath before exhaling, then she looked up at him. "I'm nervous," she confessed.

"*You're* nervous?" *What the f—*

And she pulled him through.

Chapter Thirty-Four

His foot touched grass. He didn't know why he'd thought it would be entirely different from traveling with the portal witch—probably because Essandra had him worried about burning in the Aether. But they both stepped through, and neither of them burned.

When Essandra had said she'd linked the Aether to a place of power, he'd imagined something more... majestic. A temple, maybe. Marble columns and altars. Not this.

They stepped into a circle of massive standing stones, each one weathered and lichen-streaked, their surfaces etched by time. They stood like silent sentinels, rough-hewn and ancient, the height of two men.

Essandra's eyes welled, and her lip trembled. Slowly, she sank to her knees, threading the grass between her fingers. He stood quietly, giving her a moment. Clearly, this place was important to her.

He combed the landscape around them. The stone circle was surrounded by trees, with a low layer of mist. His breath fogged in the air. It was cold—not as cold as Mercia had been, but cold enough that he would have appreciated warmer clothing.

As she stood again, she shivered. "I'm sorry. I can't warm us without..."

Her fire witch.

"It's all right."

She turned her attention outside the circle of stones and started into the trees. "This way," she said.

He followed.

They walked until the forest thinned and the trees were few and far between. The terrain became slightly sharper. Then it leveled out amid scattered heaps of stone. An eerie quiet lingered. No sounds of wildlife, no birds. Essandra walked like she was in a dream—slow, somber, with her hands slightly open in front of her, almost reaching. She'd said there was power here. Maybe she was feeling it. Cyrus felt nothing.

He followed just behind her, wary, watchful, taking in everything around them. As they walked, he realized these weren't just heaps of stone. They were ruins. Thick layers of moss and plants had grown over the rubble, making the structures difficult to recognize, but he slowly made out the stacked stone of houses that had been toppled. In what used to be streets or walking paths lay fragments of pottery and small metal goods that had withstood years of elemental wear.

He paused. There was something familiar about everything, although he was certain he'd never been here before. "What is this place?" he asked.

Her sad eyes moved over the ruins. "Home." She kept walking.

Home? He caught back up to her. "What happened here?"

"Invaders from Choan."

"Choan," he repeated. "I've never heard of it."

"Well, it's not a kingdom anymore. It was destroyed by the Shadow King."

"Why?" Probably purely for the sake of destruction.

She shook her head. "I don't know, but I like to think of it as a gift of fate." She smiled sadly to herself. "That's strange to say, isn't it? The Shadow King—a gift."

Cyrus stopped cold. "A *gift*?"

His pulse quickened. She thought he was a *gift*? After everything he'd done? "Do you support him?"

Essandra stopped and turned to look back at him. "No. But I don't have to support him to feel gratitude for him killing those who killed my family and destroyed my life."

"Gratitude doesn't make him less of a monster."

"It might not make him less of a monster, but it doesn't make him wrong either. I also won't deny a sense of indebtedness."

He stiffened as a chill rippled through him. Was this a warning? "Would you try to stop me from killing him?"

She stared at him for a moment. For a long breath, she didn't answer.

Then she shook her head. "No."

The tightness in his shoulders slacked, and he eased.

She cocked her head. "What if I'd said yes?"

He picked up his pace again, not answering. She didn't press him, and he was glad. He wasn't sure what he would have said, but a friend of the Shadow King couldn't be a friend of his. A friend of the Shadow King would share the king's fate.

They passed the last of the ruins, and the trees grew thick again. Essandra kept on an invisible path, knowing where she was going, and he followed.

The ground grew slippery. Somewhere along the way—he wasn't sure when—it became wet, but it wasn't raining.

"How much farther?" he asked.

"Not much."

Except it was.

Finally, they reached a clearing. The fog had disappeared, and light broke through the clouds of gray to shine down on two trees in the center. They were small trees, different from the trees of the forest. Their branches twisted wickedly, although the eerie unease he'd felt in the town was gone. The trees held no leaves, save each a single white bloom. And it was warmer here, somehow.

Essandra stood, staring at them. "They're everlife trees."

"That's what you said I needed to bring Kieve back." Just saying his name brought a pain to his chest.

She nodded sadly.

"These are trees you've grown?"

"Yes. They have to be grown over the bodies of the people who died. After Choan destroyed my village and left, I came back and found my mother and my sister. I buried them. I didn't know about the trees then, but when I learned about the Amoran Cup, about the spell to bring back the dead, I returned to plant them, in case one day…"

She swallowed.

"It takes twenty years or more for them to start to bloom," she said. "And then they produce one flower every month." She nodded at the one on the right. "That's my sister's tree." Then the one on the left. "That's my mother's. I planted them twenty-three years ago."

Twenty-three years.

That was how long she'd been working to bring them back. He stared at the twisted branches, each tree holding a single bloom. This was what hope looked like—fragile, hard-won, and painfully slow. This was also what defeat looked like—the realization that even if he could find Kieve's body, this was what he'd have to do. Would he be able to grow the tree? Would he even be alive long enough to see it flower?

"Two years ago, they started to bloom," she told him. "But I didn't have the cup."

"Now you do," he said softly.

Her eyes glistened. "Yes. I do."

She moved to the trees, pulling her dagger, and gently cut the bloom from the tree on the right. The flower turned red, and crimson sap beaded from where she'd made the slice on the branch. She did the same for the left tree—again, the flower turned red. Carefully, she wrapped each bloom in a white silk cloth and tucked them into the bag she wore over her shoulder.

She clutched the bag to her chest for a moment and closed her eyes. She'd waited a long time for this.

And he hated to break the moment, but he needed to ask...

"So, do you have to... dig them out?" What he was really wondering was if she was going to ask *him* to dig them out.

Essandra shook her head, her eyes on the ground beneath the trees. "No. These bodies are gone."

"Then... how..."

"The Amoran Cup will make them new."

Right. Well. That was helpful.

A light mist started around them, and she glanced up at the sky. "Let's get back."

He nodded, and they started their return toward the stone circle.

She walked beside him now, instead of in front of him. "Can I ask you a personal question?" she said.

"Sure." She already knew the most personal things about him. He wasn't sure what else was left.

"Why do you want to kill your brother?"

Except that.

Cyrus wasn't completely averse to people knowing about Alexander. He didn't lie about him. He just didn't talk about him. It was hard to—the memories were still trenched in loss and hurt. He'd thought that would go away with time. It never did.

He didn't know what made him answer. Maybe it was because he felt like he should. Or maybe he just wanted to tell someone who wanted to listen.

"He abandoned me," he said finally. "He was the person I was closest to in this world. I loved him, and he left me."

"Wasn't that a long time ago? Wasn't he a child?"

"He's not a child now. He could have come. He could have looked for me."

She frowned. "Maybe he did."

"Then he gave up too easily," he snapped.

Her gaze dropped to the ground in front of them.

"If I was in a position of power, and I knew Everan was trapped somewhere. Or Kord. Or Bash. Or Jaem. Or Ram." Or *Kieve*. The backs of his eyes stung. "If I knew they were suffering..." His voice broke as he clenched his fists. "Nothing would stop me."

He felt her eyes on him, but he kept his gaze forward.

"They're lucky to have that," she said softly. "To have you."

He slowed. No one had ever told him that.

"What about your mother?" she asked.

His chest tightened. "I don't want to talk about her." He never talked about his mother, not even with Everan.

Essandra pulled her bottom lip between her teeth. "I'm sorry. I didn't mean to pry."

He shook his head. "It's fine. I-I just don't want to talk about her."

"Okay."

A quiet fell around them, but it wasn't an uneasy quiet.

Essandra held her bag tightly to her as she walked. Seeing her so close to achieving what she'd worked so long for stirred something deep inside him. The joy and hope of being on the cusp—was this how he would feel when he reached his own moment? What moment would that be? And then what after?

"What will you do after you bring back your sister and your mother?" he asked her.

She didn't answer right away. He hoped it wasn't too personal a question, especially after he'd avoided her question to him. But as he glanced at her, she had a hint of a smile on her lips, and she was still clutching her bag to her chest again.

"I don't know," she said. "My mother was a teacher, and my sister always wanted to open a school for people with our abilities. I've dreamed about it a lot over the years—us doing that together. It made me feel close to them, I guess. Now it feels like something I need to do."

He could see how it would.

"I know that sounds silly," she added.

"It doesn't sound silly. You should do it."

She paused, and he paused with her. Her brows lifted slightly, and her lips parted. "Really?"

"Yes. Anywhere you want in Rael, it's yours."

She quieted and cast her eyes down. Had what he'd said bothered her? But she replied, "That's very kind. Thank you." She started them forward again, quickening their pace.

They reached the stone circle, and Essandra pulled the small sachet of her door-making mixture. But she paused before opening it. "Thank you," she said. "For coming with me. For everything."

"Of course. I'm glad I could help you."

The faintest of smiles touched her lips. "Now to see if we can get back." She poured the mixture into her hand and drew a line in front of them.

He watched her. "Yeah, so... you were joking before, right? About burning up in Aether?"

She paused for a beat. "No."

He nodded. "Right."

"Here we go," she said, and she pulled him through.

Returning was much like how they'd come: over the mixture and directly into Essandra's workroom. The stone circle faded behind them until it was only a wall, and they both stood, looking at each other.

She had a smudge of dirt across her cheek, but she was the most beautiful he'd ever seen her. Not because of the way she looked but because of everything she carried—strength, grit, grace. Hope.

"Are you going to try it now?" he asked finally. "To bring them back?"

She swallowed. "Yes."

"Should I stay? Can I help somehow?"

She shook her head. "No. I'd like to do it alone, actually."

He could understand that. "I'll leave you, then." He started toward the door, but paused, turning back to her. "I'm looking forward to meeting them."

Her eyes welled, and she gave him a smile—small, shaky. But a real smile.

The first he'd seen from her.

CHAPTER THIRTY-FIVE

Collective footsteps rang through the hall outside his study. Cyrus looked up from his desk just as Kord pressed through the door with Hephain right behind him.

Two of the dogs growled from where they were lying under the window, annoyed at the disturbance.

"Two, Three," Cyrus called to the animals, and they settled.

Cyrus was relieved it was Kord. His first thought was that it might be some of his councilmen coming by to discuss why he'd missed their council meeting. Again.

But that relief quickly evaporated when Kord reported, "Four grain wagons have been taken outside the Morset villages."

Morset was where the hedge witches had been maintaining the largest of their growing fields, which had just become ready for harvest. "Do we know who did it?"

"There are rumors it's the nobles," Hephain said. "I'm sure they're pressed for food, given that they don't have access to the storehouses anymore."

"I think it's safe to assume those rumors are true," Kord added, dropping a wrinkled leaflet onto the desk. "We also found these nearby." Another drawing of Essandra. Another call to burn the witches, masked as a plea to "cleanse Rael." It bore the same heavy text as the leaflets before, and his men were finding them scattered in pockets of the capital.

Cyrus's jaw tightened. Of course the nobles were still trying to drive fear. If they couldn't fight the witches head-on, they'd try to turn the people against them. And the people were already wary of the witches. He needed to put a stop to this.

"Was anyone hurt?" he asked.

Kord shook his head. "No, the wagons were taken in the night."

"No more waiting until we have a full caravan, then," he told them. "They're to come here right as they're loaded. Assign men to guard them. We've been too lax with security." He picked up the leaflet, crumpling it in his hand. "And I want these found and destroyed. All of them."

A pull came in his mind. *Jaem.*

"Jaem calls to me," he told them. "See to the guard assignments. I'll join you after."

Kord nodded, and he and Hephain left on their task.

Cyrus followed the pull of the bond to Jaem. He liked traveling to Jaem's mind because Jaem had more control than others. It wasn't a chaotic storm of all his memories and all his dreams. He kept Cyrus confined to the quiet of their conversation in dark peaceful pockets of nothingness. Kieve had been able to do the same. Cyrus had asked Essandra how they might have done this, whether they had some kind of ability. They didn't. Some simply could. Most couldn't.

Jaem was waiting impatiently. "*You're not going to believe this,*" he said as Cyrus entered.

Cyrus doubted that. He was rarely surprised now.

"*The Mercian queen has wed the Shadow King.*"

Cyrus froze, both in body and in mind. "*That can't be right.*"

"*It is. Gone to three pubs now, and it's all everyone is talking about.*"

He didn't believe it. He'd seen her. He'd seen her go to Aleon. It had been a vision, not a dream—he was sure of it. She would wed the king of Aleon, not the king of the Shadowlands. This wasn't right.

"*It stands to reason, though,*" Jaem said. "*I mean, he captured her.*"

"*How does that stand to reason? The Shadow King makes slaves of his prisoners, not wives.*"

"*Maybe he didn't take her by force.*"

"*The Northmen with their throats slit on the way to Aleon would suggest otherwise.*" Cyrus leaned his weight onto his forearms on the desk, thinking. "*Has Aleon reacted to this news?*"

"*I haven't heard anything yet, but I'll see what I can find.*"

"*Essandra found a way to make a portal. We haven't worked out exactly how to get everyone through it yet—there are limitations—but we're close.*"

"*That's good, because things are getting worse with Bravat. It's not just the temples; he's completely wrecking some of these small villages.*"

Cyrus swore. He needed to get Bravat back to Rael. Or figure out how to kill him.

"How much blood do you have left?" Cyrus asked.

"Plenty. I hardly use any at all. It will last me a while."

"All right. Keep your eyes on everything. Let me know if you hear anything else about the Shadow King. I'll update you when we talk next."

Cyrus opened his eyes back to the parchments on his desk. He stared at them for a moment, but his mind wouldn't focus on them anymore.

He left his chamber and, weaving through the halls, made his way out across the ambulatory. He wasn't quite sure where he was going, he just needed to walk. He needed to think.

The Mercian queen had married the Shadow King? That couldn't be right. Cyrus pushed through the palace doors and outside. *That couldn't be right.* Mercia had been at war with the Shadowlands for over a decade. The Shadow King had clearly captured her with malicious intention. What would a marriage gain them? Peace? What good was that?

Cyrus rounded a corner and slowed as he saw Aaron and Amiel, the two guards he'd assigned to Essandra's protection. They stood at the palace garden gates.

"Where is she?" he asked.

"Inside." Amiel motioned to the garden. "She bid us to stay here."

"Is there anyone with her? Two more women?"

They both shook their heads. "She's alone," Aaron said.

That wasn't a good sign. He stepped into the garden. It didn't take him long to find her on a bench by the fountain between two sunstone statues.

She didn't move as he neared, but she knew he was there. Silently, he sat beside her. Her eyes stayed fixed on the fountain in front of her.

Cyrus's gaze caught on her forearms. Cuts scored her skin from where she'd pulled her blood for the spell. Over and over again. They started neatly just below her elbows but grew longer and deeper—more uneven—as they moved toward her wrist, and finally, her hand. Each gave evidence of growing desperation. Blood stained her dress underneath where her arms lay, but he didn't say anything. He only waited.

"It didn't work," she whispered finally.

He'd gathered that. "What happened?"

She shook her head. "I don't know." Her lip trembled. "I don't know," she said again. "Maybe I'm not reading the spell right. Maybe I'm missing something, or there's a timing element."

He wasn't exactly sure what to say but felt compelled to say *something*, to reassure her. "Well, whatever it is, you have the bowl. The trees keep blooming. You have time—"

"I don't have time!"

He didn't react to her snap. She shook her head again. "I'm sorry. I just..." Her voice dropped to a whisper. "I know it sounds stupid, but I thought I'd see them today. I thought *today...*" Her eyes teared.

He wanted to touch her, to comfort her, but she didn't want that from him. That wasn't what he was to her. So, he just reassured her the best he could. "It's not stupid. And you'll figure it out. You'll bring them back."

"What if I can't?" She crossed her arms and clutched herself. "What if I can't?"

"Don't say that," he told her firmly. "Look at me."

She rocked herself on the bench.

"Look at me," he demanded.

Her red-rimmed eyes met his.

"You'll figure it out. You've already done the impossible—finding the bowl. Now it's just figuring out the smaller pieces. You'll get it. Do you hear me?"

She nodded and settled back against the bench again.

They sat.

"We should get you to Teron," he told her. He didn't like her cut and bleeding. He didn't like it at all.

"In a little while," she said. "I need the pain right now. It helps."

He understood that. He still didn't like it, but pain did help sometimes. They sat longer.

The bubbling water of the fountain was peaceful. He liked sitting here. With her.

"I hate to push you for this right now," he said after a little while, "but I just talked to Jaem. We're running out of time with Bravat. I need to get him back here. Have you figured out the portal?"

She shook her head. "Not yet," she said. "But I'm close. I'm just trying to figure out multi-tether bonding. I've never done it before."

He nodded. At least they were close.

"Jaem learned some news," he shared. "The Mercian queen has wed the Shadow King."

Her gaze flicked to him.

"I'm not sure how that's possible," he continued. "She's supposed to wed the king of Aleon—I saw her ride to Aleon. I saw her in Mercian colors on the Shadow throne, and the Shadow King was *not* by her side. It doesn't make sense."

Her brow dipped.

He sighed. "I'm sorry, I don't mean to trouble you with this. I don't know why I brought it up. You have enough to deal with."

"No, I'm glad you did," she said quickly. "Will you show me?"

His brows dropped. "What?"

"Show me the vision."

His brow tightened and he shook his head. "How?" How was he to show it to her?

She sighed. "I keep forgetting you don't know how to do any of this." Her words were chastising, but her voice was kind. "Some of it should come naturally, you know."

Well, it didn't.

She grabbed his hand. She was gentle this time, with a simple prick to his finger with her knife, and she dabbed a small smudge of his blood on her palm. He felt the bond immediately.

"Now," she said. "I don't know the traveler's blood spell, but you can still do it, you just need to focus."

"How am I supposed to do it without the spell?"

She frowned. "The spell isn't the source of the power. You are. Spells only help focus your power, and channel it. You can still do it. It just might be... a little all over the place. You'll have to work harder to control it." She shifted on the bench, getting more comfortable. "Now, when you close your eyes, relax. Let yourself drift and follow the call of your blood."

He knew how to enter minds. He wasn't a complete idiot when it came to his power. Cyrus closed his eyes and followed the pull.

Essandra let him into her mind. She stood in front of him in the center of a long hall, with doors lining each side.

"*What's with the doors?*" he asked.

"*Seer trick,*" she said. "*It helps compartmentalize visions. It doesn't have to be doors. It can be draperies, anything that helps separate them in the mind.*"

"*You seem to know a lot about seers.*"

"*I've known a few. Over the years.*" Sadness flashed across her face, but it disappeared as quickly as it had come. "*Now,*" she said, "*think about the vision you saw. When we open this door*"—she waved to the door on her right—"*that's what you'll show me. Since we don't have the spell to help structure it, you'll have to will it there.*"

That didn't sound too difficult. He brought forward the vision in his mind and opened the door, but the room was empty. He shut it again and looked at her.

"*You have to will it,*" she said.

What did that even mean?

"*Concentrate,*" she added.

Irritation needled him. He *was* concentrating. Cyrus focused on the vision of the Mercian queen sitting on the Shadow throne, and he opened the door again. Nothing. He closed it.

"*I don't think you're—*"

He opened it again. Still nothing. He closed it. His irritation grew.

"*Cyrus—*"

He flung it open again. Empty.

"*Okay, stop,*" she said firmly.

Cyrus paused.

"*We're in my mind,*" she said, "*but you have to know that you can control everything here. I'm showing you a hall of doors. You can turn it into a hall of windows, or have it not be a hall at all.*"

"*How?*" he asked, his irritation growing to frustration.

"*Will it. I think you have a reluctance to be in someone's mind, a reluctance to take control from them. You have to get over that. Take the hall from me.*"

"*And make it what?*"

"*Whatever you want. Take it.*"

He was growing even more frustrated.

"*Take it,*" she pressed.

Take it how?

"*At least try.*"

"*I am trying,*" he said shortly.

"*Take it!*"

Something snapped. A bolt of anger burst through him, the doors flew open, and the entire hall collapsed to rubble around them.

She stumbled backward, her eyes wide, her mouth open.

Regret immediately filled him. He wasn't exactly sure how he did it, but he quickly swept the hall back up and into place as it was. "*I'm sorry,*" he muttered.

But she didn't take her stare off him. He wasn't sure why she looked so surprised now. She'd told him to do it. Or was she upset? He couldn't tell.

Give her the vision. That was what she wanted. He used the same weight of want, gave the same will from his core, and opened the door again.

Inside, the Mercian queen sat on the Shadow throne.

Essandra still stared at him for another moment, before she peeled her eyes from him and finally shifted her attention to the vision. She stepped inside, and he followed.

The Mercian queen sat on a throne of Shadows, staring into nothing. Her long, icy hair swirled around her shoulders, and her dress moved as if caught in a gentle breeze, but she sat like a statue, captured in a moment.

Cyrus walked around her, studying her. "*She sits on the throne alone,*" he said.

Essandra examined the vision as well. "*That doesn't mean the Shadow King is dead.*"

"*She wears the color of Mercia,*" he argued.

"*Look again. Notice the details.*"

He was looking.

"*Look at her crown,*" she said.

Then he saw it—not a Mercian crown. It was dark and sharp. A Shadow crown. His eyes moved lower. On the center finger of her right hand, she wore a black ring.

"*That's a mortite ring,*" Essandra said. "*She would've had to have gotten it from the Shadowlands.*"

"*A Shadow ring and a Shadow crown...*"

"*For a Shadow queen,*" she finished.

"*But she travels to wed the king of Aleon.*"

"*Does she? Let's look.*"

Essandra started back toward the hall and another door, but he didn't need a door. Cyrus pulled the vision to them, right beside the one of the Shadow throne. Here, the queen rode a white horse under the blue banners of Aleon, with a flurry of rose petals around her. There was no crown on her head, but Northern forces accompanied her.

All except one...

"*That's a Shadowman,*" Essandra said of the dark beast of a man riding with the queen. "*But not the Shadow King.*"

No. Cyrus knew what the Shadow King looked like. But this man rode beside the queen, not behind her. Close, with an air of protection over her. "*He appears to be someone of importance, though. And in the queen's service.*"

"*Look at her hand.*"

His eyes dropped to the same black ring that she'd worn sitting on the throne. "*So, she sits on the Shadow throne before she goes to Aleon, wears a Shadow crown, and travels with a Shadowman of importance, under his protection. I've had it wrong.*" He pushed out a breath. "*Fate, you tricky bitch. She does wed the Shadow King.*"

A wave of disappointment rippled through him. He'd thought higher of Mercia, and higher of the Mercian queen. But no—she chose to wed the Shadow King. She chose to ally herself with him. After everything her people had suffered, after everything Cyrus had suffered, she'd chosen the man who'd profited from this suffering.

Disgust rippled through him. That made her complicit.

He walked back to where the Mercian queen sat on the throne. "*Why would she do this? How can she so easily cast aside what he's done? Not for love. He's over twice her age.*"

"*No, he's not,*" she said.

What?

Her expression changed, and her brows drew down. "*Oh... You don't know...*"

"I don't know what?"

"Rhalstad Ratha Shal died in the war several years ago. It's his son who sits on the throne now."

Cyrus shifted back. The Shadow King was dead? He shook his head as he took another step back. *No.* He shook his head again. He'd never truly thought vengeance against him was a possibility, but he'd wished for it. He'd dreamed about it. And now that he had a crown himself, he'd hoped for it.

But that had been stolen from him.

Anger swelled within him.

He shouldn't be angry, Cyrus told himself as he tried to will back his calm. There was no guarantee he would have been able to do anything. If the Shadow King was dead, he should be glad for it, regardless of how it had come to be.

But he wasn't.

The Shadow King might have died, but he'd led a full life. He'd gotten to leave a legacy—a legacy that his son now carried on. Fury flushed Cyrus's skin. The son had taken his father's place. He'd inherited his father's crown. He'd inherited his father's guilt. And he'd killed Kieve.

He was still responsible.

And now, so was his Shadow queen.

Cyrus looked back at her on the throne. The edges of the vision began to crack.

"*Cyrus.*" There was an urgency to Essandra's voice, and he looked to see her staring at him. "*Cyrus, stop,*" she said.

Stop what?

"*Come out!*"

Come out of where?

"Cyrus!"

Her voice was no longer in his mind but in his ear, and he opened his eyes to her shaking him on the bench in the stone garden.

It took a moment for him to get his bearings. "What's wrong?"

"Your nose," she said, alarmed.

He reached up and touched the trickle under his right nostril and pulled his fingers back to find blood. Alarm rippled through him, but he shook it off. He was fine; it was only a nosebleed. Yet, when he tried to stand, his legs buckled underneath him, and he dropped to a knee. Essandra jumped forward to help catch him.

"What's happening?" he asked as he clutched her.

"I'm not sure." The worry in her own voice did little to quell his. She held him as he tried to stand again, but his strength was gone.

"You probably used more energy than normal since you didn't have the spell, but seers have natural protections for the body—a shield—not to mention the staves I gave you."

She'd rattled off her thoughts so quickly he'd barely caught it all. And he wasn't sure what any of it meant, but he didn't really care about the workings of power at the moment. A second attempt at standing got him back on his feet. He gripped the bench for support, and slowly, he started to feel more stable. It was fine. He was fine.

His breaths slowed.

"I'm fine," he said.

"Are you sure?"

He nodded. And then he remembered—she *wasn't* fine. Her arms still bore the cuts from her spells, some of them deep. "Let's get you to Teron," he told her.

She gave a small scoff. "You're the one collapsing and you want to take *me* to Teron?"

He straightened, and his eyes met hers. "I want you healed. Now."

Her smirk disappeared and was replaced by a look he couldn't read.

"Cyrus!" a voice called, and he turned to see Bash walking quickly toward them. "Cyrus!" Bash broke into a jog to meet him quicker. "Fuck the gods, that was a long way," he said, panting, when he reached him. "I've been looking for you everywhere. Kord said you were in your study, but you weren't. Then I checked the sparring field." He took another labored breath. "You weren't there either." His eye caught Cyrus's face, and he paused. "You don't look so good." His brows dipped. "Are you okay?" He stepped closer.

"I'll be all right," Cyrus assured him.

Then Bash seemed to notice Essandra standing there. "Oh, hi," he said, and gave a small wave. Then his eyes caught her arms. "You don't look good either." The large fighter didn't bother with social-status norms, mostly because he always forgot. He just did what came naturally as a kind-hearted person. Cyrus didn't mind. He preferred it, actually. He also preferred Bash get to the point of why he was here.

"What do you need, Bash?"

"Oh. Right. The council sent me to get you. A ship's come. With a messenger."

A messenger? "From where?"

"I don't know. But he looks important."

Cyrus glanced back at Essandra.

"You go ahead," she said. "I'll be fine."

"Take her to Teron," Cyrus told Bash. "Don't leave her until she's healed."

"That's not necessary," she said.

But Cyrus's eyes stayed on Bash. "Not until she's healed," he said again.

"Got it," Bash promised.

Giving Essandra one last look, Cyrus struck out for the throne room. His steps fell harder, heavier.

A ship. A messenger.

No peace. No pause.

Whatever news had arrived, he was pretty sure it wouldn't be good.

CHAPTER THIRTY-SIX

Cyrus turned the letter over in his hand and eyed the green wax seal on the back as he sat on his throne. The throne he hated. But this was where he was expected to sit to receive visitors. A ship had unexpectedly arrived in the port, boasting banners of green and gold—a war galleon, manned by a full crew, a host of guards, and this one messenger, who now stood in front of him.

His councilmen aligned themselves closely behind the visitor, still within Cyrus's direct view, no doubt putting themselves in position to silently communicate their reactions in hopes of persuading him.

Best of luck.

Kord positioned himself among them, although for an entirely different reason. He waited, ready to act at Cyrus's cue.

"Gregor, king of Japheth?" Cyrus asked as he eyed the messenger who stood with his head bowed low.

The messenger bowed even lower. "Gregor the Lion, king of Japheth, king of Hetahl, king of Aleon and the united kingdoms, rightful heir and high king of the Aleon Empire."

That was a mouthful.

Kord's mouth tightened to suppress a chuckle.

Cyrus narrowed his eyes on the messenger. "I thought Aleon's colors were blue." It was an important distinction to make. Japheth was an ally of the Shadowlands. Aleon was not. This man claimed to be king of both.

"I've heard of the king of Aleon," Cyrus added. "His name is not Gregor. It's Phillip."

"Phillip is a usurper!" the messenger said.

"A usurper?" The faintest of smiles tugged at the corners of his mouth. "Those are the worst."

This time Kord did chuckle.

"Forgive me, King Cyrus," the messenger said quickly as he shifted. "I meant no offense, nor does High King Gregor question your claim to the throne."

Cyrus would have to *want* the throne to be offended. And there was something else he would find much more offensive. "Is the king of Japheth still allied with the Shadow King?" he asked.

"You should read the letter," the messenger said.

Cyrus was starting not to like this man. "Should I?"

The messenger caught on and quickly shifted again. "High King Gregor provides answers to all your questions."

"I seriously doubt that."

The king of Japheth wouldn't be so forward as to outline his full intentions in a letter before even meeting. However, it wasn't a stretch to assume these intentions. Cyrus had expected other kingdoms to reach out—to try to learn him, understand his motivations, explore the potential for political and trade relationships.

In the darkest corners of his mind, he'd imagined Mercia reaching out, sending their lord justice. Sending his brother.

Delivering Alexander directly to his sword.

And Cyrus would take his head. He wouldn't be able to resist, even if it meant immediate war. His blood heated again at the thought of it, but Cyrus steeled himself. He wasn't looking at Alexander right now, he was looking at this messenger from Japheth.

The messenger glanced nervously around the room. He should have been nervous the moment he'd set foot in Rael. His early confidence betrayed his assumptions—his king's assumptions. New kings were often eager to form alliances, to establish themselves and build their strength. No doubt this was what other kingdoms expected of Cyrus. But Cyrus wasn't interested in an alliance. He didn't want one more thing he was beholden to, and he wanted absolutely no association with an ally of the Shadow King.

In fact, an ally of the Shadow King was an enemy. Yes—this messenger should be nervous.

Councilman Verin subtly flicked his hands that had been clasped at his waist to prompt Cyrus to read the letter.

Cyrus ignored him.

"High King Gregor is most eager to explore a friendship with your majesty and Rael," the messenger said as he bowed again.

Kord gave Cyrus a brief jut of his head, and he finally broke the seal and opened the letter to find Gregor's words.

King Cyrus,

I hope this letter finds you in the best of health and comfort. I must admit, Rael's news came as a surprise, but Japheth celebrates with you! Let me be one of the first to warmly congratulate you on your coronation.

Did kings really talk this way? And *coronation* sounded so ceremonious for what had essentially been a massacre of the previous regime.

You may or may not be aware of the histories between our kingdoms, but Japheth and Rael have always—

Words, words, words. Cyrus skipped to the bottom of the letter.

As the world remains in a constant state of change, it continues to open opportunities for new pursuits and new friendships. I'd very much like us to meet and discuss what I'm sure will be a mutually beneficial friendship between Japheth and Rael.

I look forward to your acceptance.

That was presumptive.

Signed *Gregor the Lion, king of Japheth, king of Hetahl...*

Cyrus skipped the rest.

He caught movement from the corner of his eye and glanced up to see Essandra discreetly slipping in along the side of the hall. Had she seen Teron for him to heal her?

She wore a different dress. Had she had enough time to do that *and* see Teron? He hadn't left her for long. She held her hands clasped in front of her, her forearms hidden from view, and stared back at him with a raised brow. Defiantly? Had she not gone?

Kord cleared his throat.

Cyrus turned his attention back to the letter and folded it closed. "Is Japheth still allied with the Shadowlands?" he asked the messenger again.

The man hesitated, his mouth moving silently before he finally said, "While these may seem straightforward questions, there are many—"

"Are they still allied?" Cyrus asked a third time, more sharply now.

The man's throat bobbed, and he pinched the inside cuffs of his sleeves between his folded fingers and palms as he gave a short nod. "Yes, Your Majesty."

Cyrus stood. "Go back to Japheth," he said.

A couple of councilmen shifted, and the messenger glanced around in surprise before fumbling a response. "Would you like me to bring a reply to High King Gregor?"

"If I decide to reply to King Gregor, I'll send my own messenger."

"Sire," Verin said, stepping forward, "it's a matter of your convenience. We'll have the messenger stay the night, so you can think on it."

"No need," Cyrus quipped back. Firmly.

The messenger glanced around again, as if expecting the council to further intervene. Cyrus almost dared them to try. But no one did.

The man gave a stiff nod, resigning, and bowed. "I'll return, then. High King Gregor eagerly waits to hear from you."

Cyrus watched him depart the hall. It was interesting that the messenger portrayed the relationship between Japheth and the Shadowlands as not a straightforward one, but it didn't really matter. The fact that Gregor declared himself as king to a kingdom he didn't hold, and that he'd chosen to ally himself with the Shadow King to begin with, told Cyrus everything he needed to know about him.

"We'll wait for you in the council room," another councilman told him.

Cyrus almost told them just to stay, since everyone was already in the throne room, but there was something else he needed to do first. He took advantage of the break to head off Essandra, stepping in front of her before she reached the doors.

"Did you see Teron?" he asked.

"That was an interesting interaction," she said, ignoring his question. "Is that how you've always made friends?"

"I have no desire to make friends with the king of Japheth. Did you see Teron?"

"What do you have against Japheth?"

Cyrus grabbed her wrist and pulled her arm up to look at it.

The skin was healed.

Good.

"Satisfied?" she snipped.

He was. His hand lingered a little longer than it should have. He let her go before she could notice.

"Sire," Fatim called, prompting him to join everyone in the council room.

Cyrus sighed and followed.

The room had more people than he thought he had councilmen, but he didn't care enough to reconcile.

"Sire, do you really intend to not respond to High King Gregor?" Verin asked.

"He's not *High King* if he doesn't actually hold Aleon. And what does it matter?"

"What does it matter? We should be taking every opportunity to build relationships with other kingdoms, promote trade, fortify ourselves."

"Form alliances, you mean," Cyrus said.

"Yes, exactly."

Cyrus shook his head. "I don't want to be obligated to another person, let alone another kingdom."

"We're not talking about obligation," Fatim said. "We're talking about cooperation."

"I don't want to *cooperate* with the king of Japheth." His patience was cracking.

Verin sighed, exasperated. "We need trade relationships."

Cyrus slammed his fist on the table. "Not with the king of Japheth! Or anyone else who sees the Shadow King as anything other than an enemy."

The room grew quiet.

"We're done," he said firmly.

Cyrus sat on a grassy knoll on a cliff overlooking the Aged Sea. In the distance, he could see the harbor. It was a lengthy ride from the palace—out of the capital, past the port city, and up along the hills where the mountains met the coast. He liked it here. It was quiet and away from everything—a good place to think. And with the thick dune grass covering the sand, it felt different from the rest of Rael.

The dogs liked it too. One and Three rolled in the grass, while Two found a place to dig. Cyrus smiled as he watched them. It was easy to forget about the rest of life here, easy to slip into believing he was happy, or could be happy. But what was happiness, truly? He'd never known it, and he was pretty sure he never would.

The dogs perked at something behind him but didn't growl.

"Thought I'd find you here," Everan's voice called. He took a seat beside Cyrus in the grass.

"You're going to make me regret telling you about this place."

Everan chuckled as he pulled a blade of grass and rolled it between his fingers. Cyrus noticed his friend didn't have the same heaviness in his shoulders as he once did, and although Everan was rarely one to smile, he was doing it more and more. This was the life he'd always wanted, to just live free, with Visa. He was happy. And Cyrus was happy for him. Perhaps that was the closest Cyrus would come. And perhaps that was all right.

"I thought the port would look better from up here," Everan said, with his eyes on the harbor. "But I think it looks worse."

Ships stolen by incoming refugees filled the port, which was now at maximum capacity, and they'd started anchoring them along the shoreline. The docks were chaotic and bustling, and it was easy to forget what was anchored out of sight.

Some eight hundred escaped slaves had reached the palace that morning. The numbers were lower than the initial wave, but they came steadily, with a group arriving every day or every other day.

Sometimes, Cyrus imagined Alexander arriving. He never fantasized about the misfortune Alexander would have had to suffer to find himself as a refugee. He only dreamed of him actually stepping into Rael, looking for safety. Looking for mercy.

And Cyrus would give him none.

"How many are we up to?" he asked, pulling himself again from this fantasy.

"A little over fifteen thousand."

In terms of mouths to feed, that was a lot. In terms of adding men to his army, it wasn't a lot.

"We've converted slaves' barracks to open accommodation halls," Everan said. "It feels... not quite right... but everyone seems appreciative. And we've put them to work. Those who are unable to do so are still doing things like mending, looking after the children, contributing however they can. I don't know if it's sustainable indefinitely, but it seems to be working so far."

"How many more can we take?"

Everan shook his head. "I don't know. That depends on how much food your witches can grow."

The hedge witches had now become the most important of all the witches. Cyrus had given Essandra even more men to protect them, due to the growing threats from the nobles. Losing just one would devastate the kingdom.

"Are you coming to join the council?" Everan asked.

Cyrus sighed. It had been two weeks since the messenger from Japheth had left, but there was still tension from Cyrus deciding to ignore the king of Japheth's invitation. And it was one more thing on the ever-growing list of things his council was displeased about.

"Why bother?" Cyrus said. "I'm pretty sure we know how things will go."

"How do you expect it to go? You appointed a council and now you don't listen to them."

Cyrus snorted. "I'm not going to listen to someone who tells me that I should unite with an ally of the Shadow King."

"Or you could look at it differently. The messenger said their relationship wasn't easily defined. What if their alliance isn't as strong as one would expect?"

"The fact that they were ever allies to begin with is the problem."

Everan looked directly at him now. "What if it's not about uniting with Japheth at all but about *breaking* the Shadow King from his allies and resources?"

Cyrus paused. That was... a very good point. He looked down at the ships again. "How many men do you think I'd need to take the Shadowlands?"

His friend shifted uneasily. "Cyrus."

"What? We're talking about war."

"No, I'm talking about political action. *You're* talking about war."

"How can I not?"

"You know that's not the answer."

It was the only answer. Cyrus flicked away the blade of grass he held in his hand. "Does this mean you won't be by my side, brother?"

Everan sighed. "I'll always be by your side." He rubbed his temple. "I don't know how many men we'd need to take the Shadowlands. No one seems to have a sense of how big their army is, or what their capabilities are."

"I need to find out. I also need to know what to prepare for if Mercia and Aleon come to their aid."

Everan's head whipped up. "Aleon? Aleon is a hundred thousand strong."

Cyrus looked back down at the refugee arrivals below. "At this rate, we will be, too, eventually."

"Cyrus, these aren't fighters. If you plan to go up against the Shadowlands, you'll definitely need an alliance, and you'll need to strip the Shadow King of anyone who might come to his aid." He shook his head. "But that's not what you should be focused on right now. These people need you."

"This is what they've asked for! In my own throne room!"

"*One man* asked about the Shadowlands, and you've latched onto it like a star of fate. I know your heart beats for personal vengeance against the Shadow King, but those men"—he pointed down at the harbor—"those thousands of men want to see you move against Serra. They want to enjoy their freedom in a stable and thriving kingdom and see their captors fall."

Cyrus shook his head. He didn't believe that was all they wanted.

"You talked about the future," Everan said. "And I see a future where the Shadowlands fall. But it needs to be *the future*. A *distant* future." He pointed down to the ships again. "Right now, they need you. Rael needs you." His voice dropped lower. "I need you." His dark eyes burned into Cyrus. "Will you not put us first?" he asked.

Cyrus sighed. Gods-damned this man who could talk him into anything. He cut another look back over the harbor. "Fine. I'll focus on Serra first."

"And Rael," Everan added.

"And Rael. But then"—he turned his eyes to his friend—"I bring down the Shadowlands. No matter what."

CHAPTER THIRTY-SEVEN

"Where were you?"

Cyrus looked up from the parchments on his desk to see Essandra in the doorway of his study. He wasn't entirely surprised to see her. He'd expected someone would come after he'd ignored yet another council meeting. "Have you not found me?"

She pursed her lips, curving them upward but not smiling. "Let me rephrase. Why weren't you at the council meeting?"

"What's the purpose of having a council if I have to go to everything, and be involved in everything?"

"You certainly don't go to everything. And you're not involved in anything."

"They can speak their grievances to Ruth." Out of everyone on his council, he was most appreciative to have his magistrate. She wasn't just another voice in his ear; she actually did things. She saw something that needed done and she did it. Like Essandra.

"You can't just throw everything on Ruth," Essandra said. "And this isn't a grievance. The council needs you to make decisions. And the people want a present king; they need someone to help them."

Cyrus stood. "What else do people want from me? I've given them freedom."

Essandra sighed and moved across the room to him. "Cyrus, it's not enough to free them. We're talking about people who've been slaves their entire lives. They've been exposed to so little. They haven't been privileged like you—"

"You think I'm privileged?"

"You know how to read. You know how things work. You understand the dynamics of power. You know how to get what you want. Yes, that's privilege." She shook her head. "These people don't know how to live in freedom. You have to feed them, educate them, teach them to participate in society. They might be free from their chains, but they're not free from the shackles of unknowing and inability."

"What would you have me do?"

"Build this kingdom."

"I am!" he insisted, his voice growing louder.

"No, you're not!" she cut back, her tone matching his.

"You're leaving—why do you even care?"

"Because I don't want to see you fail!"

Her words quieted him. Still, he was frustrated. He leaned his weight onto the edge of the desk. "I gave them land."

"That doesn't even scratch the surface. It's not enough to sweep up dead bodies, throw up more buildings, give them homes, and grow crops."

"That sounds like a lot to me."

"They need to learn trades and commerce, learn to build lives for themselves. We need to provide training and open schools."

"I don't have time to teach people to read." It had been months now, and he was no closer to getting Alexander. Or the Shadow King. Anger burned across his skin. "You promised you would help me bring down the Shadow King."

"I did not—"

"You promised to give me a *world of kings*!"

"And then *you* went and promised refuge to slaves worldwide without the ability to support them!"

Cyrus quieted again and sat back in his chair. He drew in a deep breath and let it out slowly. He was angry but not at her. She spoke truly. He just felt... stuck.

She drew in a deep breath of her own. "I *will* help you. We help each other, remember? But there are things you have to do first, and those things take time."

He knew she was right; he just didn't like it. He didn't have time. He wasn't sure how long fate would give him.

Her voice came softer now. "You don't think I know how hard it is to wait?"

Guilt pooled in his stomach. Perhaps she knew the most.

"Fine," he said.

"And you have to work with your council," she added.

"All they do is judge me. And get in my way."

"All they do is try to get *you* to do what's best for Rael. Have you even looked at the proposed infrastructure changes?"

He almost groaned. So many requests were included in a thick stack of parchments that now sat in the corner of his desk. Parchments that he hadn't read yet.

"I'll look at them," he said.

"Cyrus."

"I said I'll look at them."

The fight between them faded.

"On one condition," he added.

She sighed. "What's that?"

"You build your school too."

Essandra stilled—still as the stone in the statue gardens. "What?"

"Your school for people with abilities."

She opened her mouth, then closed it. Then she opened it again. "I need to wait for my sister—"

"No." He shook his head. "Build it so that when you finally bring her back, it's here and it's ready."

"I can't."

"You can. As I've told you—wherever you want—it's yours. Inside the capital, outside the capital, it doesn't matter. Wherever you want."

There was still objection written all over her face. "It would take resources you need for—"

"It doesn't matter. Build it. If you need money, I'll let Fatim know."

"Cyrus—"

"If you need physical labor, we have hands arriving daily. Ram will arrange it for you."

"Cyrus—"

"Do it. Do it for yourself."

"I can't stay here," she blurted.

He wasn't sure why that knifed him so. She'd been clear from the very beginning. Maybe he'd thought she'd change her mind, although he wasn't sure when he'd started wanting her to change her mind.

"I mean, I'm not leaving yet," she said. "But eventually. You know?"

Right. He'd known this. He'd always known.

"And you don't even have a regular school," she added. She glanced at the stack of parchments. "It's in the infrastructure proposal."

His words wouldn't come right now.

She stepped to the desk, biting her lip. "If you do approve the council's request for a school, I'd like to be involved," she said. "I'd actually really enjoy it."

He nodded. "Of course. Maybe it will convince you to stay and build your own."

She smiled. A sad smile. "Maybe."

But he knew a lie when he heard one.

"Oh," she said, "I also wanted to let you know that I'm ready to bring your men trapped in Mercia through the portal. Or at least try."

"Really?" Cyrus stood. "You could have led with that."

"I could have." She gave a small smile. "But I wanted to scold you first."

He snorted. "Of course you did." He couldn't help giving a small smile back. "Truly, though, this is excellent." The council would be relieved. Cyrus certainly was. However, he wasn't looking forward to having Bravat back in Rael. Still, it would be a weight off his chest not to worry about more of his men being captured, or Rael being discovered and risking war.

"They'll have to meet us at the stone circle," she told him.

He nodded. "I'll tell Jaem."

"Good. Just let me know when they're ready."

He nodded again. "Can I walk you to dinner?"

She raised her brows. "I didn't realize it was that time. Sure."

As she stepped to turn, the edge of her gown caught on the corner of a stack of parchments, sending them to the floor.

"I'm sorry." She stooped to pick them up.

"No, let me," he said, and dropped to a knee in front of her. But after he'd gathered them, he paused, looking up at her.

Her eyes flashed with something he couldn't read.

"What? Are you enjoying this?" he teased. "A king kneeling before you?"

She pulled the corner of her lip between her teeth. "Maybe." Her eyes briefly fluttered shut before flashing the same look again. With more heat this time. And suddenly, Cyrus knew exactly what that look was.

Desire.

A smile crept across his face. He rose slowly, not stepping away from her, all too aware of how closely they stood now.

Her eyes followed him up, and her lips parted.

He leaned even closer to her to slide the parchments back onto the desk behind her.

Her gaze traveled his face, from his eyes to his lips. It stayed on his lips.

He leaned even closer. She didn't stop him.

Cyrus dropped his head to hers. "Can I kiss you?" he asked softly.

She gave ever the faintest shake of her head. "No," she whispered.

This woman...

Want clawed at him, but he forced it down.

"You can unfasten your belt, though," she said.

He almost laughed, but she was completely serious. Essandra shifted back slightly onto his desk, ruffling up her skirts and pulling off her undergarments. Cyrus didn't need to be told again. His whole body came alive, and his desire took over. He unfastened his belt and pulled loose the ties, freeing himself.

Essandra reached down and wrapped her hand around him, and his eyes dropped heavily as a wave of need coursed through him. She fought the layers of fabric and guided him to her. As he sank inside her, they both shuddered.

She stayed upright, leaning back slightly with one hand on the desk behind her, the other hand holding back her dress. She rocked her hips against him, and he started to move.

"Slowly," she told him.

Cyrus moved as slowly as he could. He gripped the edge of the desk, his hands on either side of her. He didn't touch her, but he leaned closer. He couldn't help himself. Everything about her called to him—her warmth, her scent, the sound of her breaths. He needed this woman.

She put a hand over his eyes. "Don't look at me like that."

Like what?

"Faster," she said.

He quickened, his own need building.

"Faster," she panted.

He moved even faster. Harder. Deeper. Her breaths came quicker, then she paused. She tightened around him, letting out a cry of his name. He was ready with his own release and came with her. Over the edge. Everything within him lit fire as a deep tremor shook through him. He chased it to the end. Then they stilled, panting.

It was all he could do not to put his arms around her. Not to give into the need to hold her close to him.

They cooled in the silence, with only the sound of their breaths. Until Essandra pushed him off. She slipped out from between him and the desk, quickly smoothing her dress and fixing her undergarments.

He couldn't help a chuckle. "It's amusing how you both want me and detest me at the same time."

She paused. "I don't detest you."

"Then why won't you let me kiss you?"

"Because I can't let myself fall in love with you."

She said it so matter-of-factly, yet it was so unexpected. She swallowed, quickly turning her attention back to herself, but as she fixed her clothing, Cyrus could only stand there, still leaning on the desk, staring at her.

The door to the study opened. "There you are!" Visa exclaimed. "I was just checking to see if you were going to make it to dinner."

Cyrus didn't turn, keeping his back to the door, but he hastily fastened his clothing and rebuckled his belt.

"Oh, I'm so sorry," Visa said. "I didn't mean to... interrupt anything—"

"No, you're fine." Essandra swept toward her. "We were just on our way."

They stepped out into the hall, and Cyrus took a moment to gather himself before he finally followed after.

The women chatted in front of him as they walked toward the dining hall. They'd become close over the past months, with Visa sometimes assisting Essandra in her work.

Cyrus heard their words, but he couldn't follow the conversation. His mind was still on what Essandra had told him. *She couldn't fall in love with him.* He'd be lying if he denied the disappointment, but this was how things had to be. It was better this way. Fate had given him an opportunity, and he couldn't allow himself to be distracted from that opportunity.

They reached the dining hall. It was alive with conversation. Cyrus remembered when he'd thought the table was possibly too big to fill, but over the months, more had joined them.

Hephain sat quietly across from Kord. He didn't talk much, although he wore a warm smile and was quick to laugh. Sergen usually sat beside him, another quiet one.

As for everyone else—they weren't so quiet. But Cyrus didn't mind. He liked the energy of all of them together. He liked their laughter. And it took the pressure off everyone looking to him for how to act or how to feel. It allowed him to sit in his thoughts. Especially when something occupied his thoughts.

His eyes drifted to Essandra, who took the seat to his right. It was her usual place. Cyrus had previously offered for her to invite her coven, although there was barely room for them all now, but Cyrus didn't care. They'd bring another table, more chairs. However, the coven preferred to keep to themselves, eating on their own, leaving Essandra the only one who took her meals in the palace dining hall.

Cyrus forced himself not to stare at her and instead focused his attention on piling food onto his plate.

If he tried, he could still feel her. No—he didn't even have to try. Her warmth still lingered on him. Her fire, her need, her scent.

She shifted in her chair, and he wondered if she still felt him too. She certainly had to feel the part of him he'd spilled inside her.

His body hardened again just thinking about it.

He didn't know how she could act like nothing had just happened between them, her hand around her fork as though it hadn't just been wrapped around the most intimate part of him. Her voice carried on in conversation as though it hadn't just cried out his name.

He understood one thing, though.

She wasn't going to let herself have feelings for him.

He couldn't either.

CHAPTER THIRTY-EIGHT

"Try to find at least one thing to agree with." Essandra showered him in a flurry of instruction as they made their way toward the council room. "And try *listening* to them," she added.

But Cyrus found himself barely able to listen *now*. He was still riddled with anger. Earlier that morning, Essandra had taken him through the portal to the stone circle, where they were supposed to meet Jaem and Bravat and the rest of the men to bring them back.

Except Bravat and Bravat's men hadn't come.

Only Jaem had been there to meet him, along with the men who'd been trapped when the first portal had collapsed.

"Bravat isn't coming," Jaem had said.

"Why not?"

"He just said *no*."

Cyrus knew why. Bravat was enjoying his newfound freedom, with no one to rein him in. And he was enjoying all the gold he was collecting with each raid on a Mercian temple. He'd probably never dreamed of such wealth. But the longer Bravat stayed in Mercia, the greater the risk of him being caught, and the greater the risk of Mercia discovering Rael and taking retaliatory action. Cyrus needed to pull him back, but really, what could he do? He had neither the time nor the ability to hunt Bravat down right then. He'd have to deal with him later. In the meantime, he brought the waiting men back through the portal. He left Jaem, giving him a few more vials of blood, to keep an eye on Bravat and keep Cyrus informed.

As they returned, Cyrus quickly found the limit of how many men he could tether to himself at one time. *Three.* He could tether only three men before the bond started to fall apart, leaving them with burns as they passed through to the other side. So Essandra taught him how to create the tether, and he traveled back and forth, shepherding three men at a time, growing increasingly frustrated as he went.

And now, after quite a long morning, he was late to the council meeting. They walked quickly. Essandra's footsteps were silent beside his own. Cyrus tried to push away his earlier frustrations and focus on the agenda. Things had been rocky as of late with the council, made even rockier by Cyrus ignoring them all together. He hadn't attended a proper council meeting since...

Kieve.

But he'd committed to taking things more seriously now. To trying.

Cyrus pushed through the doors of the council room. The councilmen stood in greeting.

"*Listen,*" Essandra whispered to him as a reminder.

He took his seat at the end of the table. She took her own along the far side, but still in his direct view.

Everyone seated themselves.

"Sire," Lomas, his master of public works, said, "we'd like to start with the recommendations we've put together. There are a few infrastructure changes that the council feels strongly about—"

"Do it," Cyrus said.

The councilmen all stilled and stared at him in surprise. Essandra's head snapped up.

"W-which one, Sire?"

"All of them." Cyrus's gaze locked on Essandra. She narrowed her eyes.

"All of them?" Fatim asked.

Cyrus's eyes traveled around the room. "Is there any concern with this? When you said the council feels strongly, I assumed you meant you feel strongly about *all* the recommendations."

"Y-yes, Sire... I mean no," Lomas stammered. "Yes, we feel strongly about all of them. N-no concerns, none at all."

"Good." Cyrus sat back in his chair. "What's next?"

The councilmen shuffled, clearly reeling from the expectation they'd need to argue each line item, and they prepared for their next offense.

Verin handed him a letter. "From Morak, King of Pryam," he said. "We suspect he holds the same intentions as King Gregor and wants to discuss potential alliance opportunities." He refrained from including the king of Osan.

Cyrus glanced at Essandra.

"*Listen*," she mouthed to him silently.

Cyrus broke the bronze seal on the back, and opened the letter, but as he read the words, unease rippled through him.

"What does it say?" Fatim asked.

Cyrus struggled for a moment. "He does want to discuss an alliance."

"Ah," Verin said. "As expected."

"With the possibility of his daughter's hand in marriage," Cyrus added. He tossed the letter to the center of the table for the council to read.

"Princess Miriel?" Fatim said as he skimmed it. "She's said to be quite beautiful."

Essandra scoffed. "Cyrus has already made it clear that he isn't seeking a marriage." She took the letter from the councilman, and her face grew sharper as her eyes traveled the penned lines.

She was absolutely right. He wasn't.

"Rael can't keep refusing alliance conversations," Verin said. "It's proper these alliances come by way of marriage, and Pryam would be a powerful ally. They're a small kingdom, yes, but they're part of the Etrean Union. A collective of six kingdoms—can you imagine the trade opportunity?"

"Etreus is a slaving kingdom," Cyrus said. Absolutely not.

"But the rest aren't—Faulken, Nayalour, Cosar, Nestrana, nor Pryam. Only Etreus."

"Etreus is as large as the other kingdoms combined. Why do you think it's called the fucking *Etrean Union*?"

"Cyrus," Everan said quietly.

Verin sighed. "If you cut out everyone with ties to a slaving kingdom, you'd have no alliance options at all."

"He's right," Kord said.

Cyrus glared at him. "You too?"

Kord shrugged.

Cyrus leaned back in his chair. "It's an inopportune time. I've just approved a massive amount of work across the kingdom, we're still facing challenges from the nobles, and the masses are demanding action against Serra."

"On the contrary—it's the perfect time!" Verin said. "This will alleviate some of that pressure—it would show the people that there are plans in motion."

"Would Pryam lend me their army?"

The room fell silent for a moment, then Fatim said, "I'm sure there are implications with the Union that would have to be considered."

Cyrus snorted. "That doesn't sound promising."

"You'll never know if you don't have a conversation, and this is an invitation to do just that," Verin stressed. "For trade and for military strength. And in reality, the marriage would be such a small piece."

Cyrus wasn't ignorant of the political strategies to build power, and marriage between royals for this reason was commonplace. He just hadn't expected it to be something he'd have to deal with. Yes, he was king, but he hadn't planned on being king. He hadn't planned to still be alive at all. But here he was—both alive and king. And expected to consider this possibility of a marriage alliance.

"He'll think about it," Essandra said. "A conversation, that is." Her shadowed eyes caught his in a look that felt like daggers. Was she angry? Did she think he wasn't taking this seriously? He couldn't bring himself to agree immediately; his mind was still reeling.

"Sire," Verin pressed, "it's just a discussion—"

"He'll *think* about it," Essandra snapped, then she folded the letter.

"I *will* think about it," Cyrus assured them.

The council broke for the day, and Cyrus followed Essandra out. She walked quickly, and he had to lengthen his stride to keep up with her.

"What do you think of Pryam's proposal?" he asked as he followed her into his study.

She spun. "Are you seriously considering it?"

"Of course I am. You told me to listen—"

Her eyes flashed to something near feral. "Yes, but I didn't say to agree to every idiotic thing they put in front of you."

"What was idiotic?"

She stopped abruptly. Her breaths came shallower, and her words clipped. "Y-you were just saying yes to everything. You didn't even read the recommendations—"

"I read them yesterday. Funds for masonry and agricultural training, four sessions per month over the next year. Two schools, one for children under ten and one for those aged eleven to sixteen. Two additional roads to make travel easier between the capital and outlying towns, a scholar of livestock planning, three additional water reservoirs, and a second infirmary."

Essandra stared at him, her eyes wide.

"Did I get everything?" he asked.

She gave ever the slightest nod of her head.

"And I'm going to think about this King Morak," he said. "I'm not interested in a marriage, but you're right. I have to take this more seriously, and I am. I promise, I really will consider it."

She swallowed. "Good." There was a crack to her voice.

"That is what you wanted me to do, right?"

She nodded and swallowed again. "Of course. I'm... glad you're taking this more seriously." But the way she said it sounded strange. Did she not believe him?

"I am."

She nodded again, biting her bottom lip. "Good." Then she left him standing in the hall.

Cyrus sighed.

"Sire," came a voice behind him, and he turned to see Verin, Fatim, and Lomas. Their postures were careful, but their eyes sharp. "Might we have a word?"

"What is it?"

Fatim bobbed his head. "We have some concerns about Lady Essandra."

Irritation seeded itself in his chest. "What kind of concerns?"

The councilman swayed slightly. "Her influence. Her access. Her knowledge of the kingdom's inner workings."

Verin folded his hands. "Do you really think it's wise for her to be so involved in Rael's politics, lending her voice to our decisions? She is a guest in this kingdom."

"She's my adviser."

"She's also a witch," Lomas added, "with loyalties we don't fully understand."

Cyrus's jaw tightened. "She's the reason you're even here."

Fatim gave a quick bow of his head as he swallowed. "Yes, of course."

"And it was because of her I have approved everything you've asked." Everything on that ridiculously long list of requests he'd have never looked at otherwise.

"We're only saying that—"

Cyrus silenced him with a gesture. Essandra was the reason he listened to the council at all. She believed there was value in what they had to say, although, right now, he struggled to see it.

Fatim stepped in again, more cautious. "No one here questions your trust, Sire, but it's the people—they don't see her as one of us."

No doubt the anti-witch campaign by the nobles wasn't helping. Did the council view her the same way?

Cyrus nodded slowly. "Consider this my official statement," he said. "Essandra is not a guest. She is a citizen of Rael and adviser to the king, until the time she decides to leave." His voice dropped, quieter. Deadly. "If anyone challenges her place, or my authority, with which she speaks, they'll deal with me directly."

Cyrus unbuckled his sword belt from around his waist and leaned the blade and scabbard against the wall beside his bed. For once, he felt like if he were to lie down, he might actually sleep. The dogs stretched across the floor, enjoying the cool marble over their bedding. Perhaps they had the right idea.

However, they hadn't quite gotten comfortable before they jumped up, their hackles raised. A heavy knock on the door followed, and before Cyrus could reach it, it swung open. Kord stepped in, his face shadowed and sharp.

"Cyrus," he said, his voice heavy with urgency. "Come quick. There's a fire in the courtyard."

Cyrus grabbed his sword and followed at a run, weaving through the halls and out the main doors of the castle. What was even in the courtyard to catch fire? It was open cobblestone with a bronze and marble fountain at its center. But then he saw it—the blaze, already dying, smoke trailing into the night sky. It had nearly burned itself out, but not before leaving its message.

Someone had roped together a crude pyre from splintered timber. Blackened cloth clung to the stake, shaped to resemble a human form—a witch. And nailed across the front was a sign, the lettering still visible through the ash.

BURN THE WITCHES.

A crowd had gathered, although no one stood close to it. No one spoke. There was no sound but the hiss of the dying flame.

"Who did this?" he shouted.

The onlookers backed slightly, shaking their heads.

"Who did this?" he roared.

Still, no one claimed it.

He would pull this kingdom apart brick by brick until he found out.

Chapter Thirty-Nine

They tore down the pyre before the sun rose. Every splinter of wood, every ashen ember. But Cyrus could still smell the smoke. Everything had been cleared, but the message still lingered in the air.

BURN THE WITCHES.

They spent the day chasing down who might be responsible. No one had stepped forward. No one had seen anything. No guards. No staff. There were no whispers.

Now, as the sun set, he stood at the window in the drawing room that overlooked the courtyard.

"It had to have been the nobles," Hephain said from where he stood near the door with Brant.

"They're still working to turn the people against the witches," Kord added.

"For which you do nothing to help," Cyrus snapped.

His friend took a step back. "I had nothing to do with this."

"You speak against Essandra at every opportunity."

Kord scoffed. "Wait, are you angry at *me*?"

Cyrus pushed out a frustrated breath, then shook his head. "No," he said. "I shouldn't have said that." He wasn't angry at Kord. He was just... angry.

"The nobles are the most likely party responsible," Everan said.

"How would they have gotten in? Into my own palace? My own courtyard?" Cyrus rested his hand against the window ledge, his knuckles white. After the fire had been lit, no one had tried to stop it. It had burned long enough to be seen. To matter. It had burned long enough for Essandra to see. His blood grew even hotter. He looked back at Hephain. "Double the guards throughout the palace. And double the guard for each witch."

"What about those outside the palace?" Brant asked.

"Have Bash take another unit to reinforce the fields. Who's managing the east side? Ryman?"

"Yeah, Ryman."

"Good." The prior lead of House Lycus was a solid man, an excellent fighter, well respected, smart. "When Sergen gets back, he can take two additional units and join him."

"I'll see to it now."

"Good." Cyrus gave him a nod. "Brant," he called, holding him back as Everan, Kord, and Hephain left. He pulled a letter he'd prepared and stared at the seal a moment—a sword sigil. Everan had thought of the idea, and Essandra had created it. It was so... official.

But this letter was official.

He handed it to Brant. "I need you to deliver this to Pryam. There's a ship preparing to take you tomorrow morning."

Brant's eyes widened. "Are you accepting the marriage alliance?"

Cyrus wouldn't go so far as to say that. But he needed legitimacy, something to hold against the nobles. And against others. He wasn't just being judged from within; other kingdoms were watching. His council was right—he needed an alliance—for the strength it brought, for the resources, and it would be proof he was taking the crown seriously, that he was choosing Rael, that he was trying.

And it would give him an army...

However, given Osan's withdrawal, an alliance might be increasingly hard to find now. He couldn't be so inflexible and discriminative.

"I'm accepting the conversation," he said. "We'll go to Pryam in two weeks' time, and I'll decide then." Two weeks would give him enough time to make sure Rael was stable, and Essandra protected.

Brant took the letter, then left to prepare for his departure in the morning.

Cyrus sighed. Despite his decision, the thought of marriage still felt like a blade down his spine. He was trying to manage rebuilding Rael while still looking for opportunities against Alexander and the Shadow King. Not only did he have no desire for a wife, but he had no time. Not to mention an arranged marriage was its own form of oppression. And how did this woman even feel about it? What even was her name again? Mary? Melody? M... something. He tried to push it from his mind. He needed some air. The fading light meant the high heat of the afternoon was gone. He bid the dogs to stay and made his way through the halls and outside the palace. A slight breeze blew through, and it felt good. He breathed it in deeply.

Cyrus walked the gravel path to a side street that ran parallel to the mainway into the city. Cracks of metal against metal sounded as city keepers struck flints for the street torches. This was his favorite time of day—when day was over. He kept his gait easy and casual. It was a nice evening. Perhaps he should have brought the dogs.

As the road curved, he slowed in his step.

Essandra stood on a plot of cleared land that would eventually hold one of the two new schools. Her dark brown hair hung long over her shoulders and down her back. In the fading light, it looked black against the ivory of her skin. Somehow, she still radiated light.

Would things change between them if he wed? His chest tightened. It shouldn't matter. She'd been very clear with him—she wouldn't be here much longer. It was why she kept her distance, why she pushed him to make decisions for Rael that would withstand her absence. And anything else between them would complicate everything.

Although Cyrus had never been deterred by complication.

But then there was the practical matter that she just didn't want him. And he couldn't want her.

So, it was settled.

"How is everything coming?" he asked as he approached.

She moved with a start.

"Sorry," he said.

"No, it's fine." She waved it off. "It's going well. Everything's been cleared, and we expect to start building in the next two weeks or so."

"Great. That's great." He glanced around. Was she out here alone? "Where are your guards?"

"I dismissed them. I'm headed back now, anyway."

After what had just happened? He didn't like that at all. "I'll walk you."

"I'm perfectly fine."

"I know." And he waited.

Even under the shadows cast by the darkening sky and mainway torchlights, he thought he saw the faint trace of a smile. Was it a smile? Perhaps wishful thinking on his part. It was so easy to imagine.

She brushed a lock of hair from her face with graceful fingers. He could still feel them—across his back and in his hair. Not from their recent joining, but from when she'd comforted him after he'd lost Kieve. She'd only acted from a place of compassion in his grief, but still, her touch... the calm that came from holding her, the feel of her underneath him, him wrapped up in her, inside her. He'd remembered it many times over. He'd needed her in that moment. He still needed her. But in a short time, she'd be gone. And she was pressing him to take the future of Rael seriously. She was frustrated that he wasn't.

He did want her to know that he was taking this seriously now, that he understood the obligation, the responsibility, and that he'd give himself to it.

"I wrote to Morak," he told her.

"Oh," she said. They stepped out onto the mainway from the side street. The flames of the street torches lit the cobblestone, but the side buildings faded into black.

"I'll go to Pryam in two weeks' time to talk about an alliance."

Night shadowed her face. He couldn't tell if she was satisfied with that. Probably not. How much satisfaction could really come from him doing something he should have done already?

"I haven't been fully present," he said, "but I am now."

She only looked down at the ground in front of her. Was she not pleased to hear this? Why did she look disappointed?

"I know you've been frustrated with me," he said.

She looked up at him. "Cyrus." Her pause was heavy. "I know I said—"

His attention shifted to movement in the shadows. Cyrus grasped her wrist, stopping them both. Every sense sharpened—his eyes, his ears, his skin against the air.

"What is it?" she asked quietly.

He combed the darkness around them, listening.

Something wasn't right.

"Get inside the palace," he said. He kept hold of her, sliding his hand from her wrist to her upper arm and walking her forward.

But their path was cut off by two silhouettes in front of them.

Then there were four.

Cyrus pulled Essandra behind him but quickly realized they were surrounded. His hand dropped to the hilt of his sword.

"Sabine Laveau," one of the men said.

Essandra's body stiffened as she gripped him, and Cyrus felt something he rarely felt from her—fear. Real fear.

"What do you want?" Cyrus demanded.

"Easy now," the silhouette replied. "We've only come for the witch."

Cyrus drew his sword as fire lit under his skin. "Then you've come to spill your own blood."

A second silhouette chuckled. "Careful, soldier. You don't want trouble with us, especially once your king learns who we are."

It was Cyrus's turn to chuckle. "He doesn't give a fuck who you are."

"Oh, I think he will," the first man said, "but we're not here for trouble; we just want to talk."

Cyrus pulled Essandra closer, holding her against him. Men who said they just wanted to talk never just wanted to talk. As they stepped into the light, he was better able to see them. He'd assumed they'd been sent by the nobles, but their clothing was the color of night, and they wore wraps covering their faces.

No. These were *Shadowmen*.

The anger within him turned to rage, and Cyrus splintered. He attacked, launching himself forward.

The men fell back, caught by surprise at his speed of assault, and they clawed for the swords in their back scabbards.

"Stop!" one of them bellowed.

He would not stop. He would not wait. No more questions, no restraint—he went for their heads. They spun away, narrowly missing his blade's call for blood, and rapidly shifted to defense.

Essandra threw up a wall of stone, splitting the surrounding men so Cyrus could focus on the four in front of him. It wouldn't keep the others for long—he had to be quick. He lunged with a series of blows, each with the power of death. The men were good at evading them, but not good enough as Cyrus's blade caught one across the thigh.

"Back!" the largest of them barked at the other three. They weren't fully engaging. If they weren't planning to kill him now, that was a mistake.

"If you were sent by the Shadow King," Cyrus snarled, "I have a message for him."

"We're not from the Shadowlands," the man snapped back.

"Then I suggest you spit out pretty quickly where you *are* from," Everan said as he appeared from the darkness, his sword to the man's neck.

Kord and Hephain appeared as well, their swords drawn, with even more of Cyrus's men.

Everyone came to a halt.

"Drop your swords," Everan told them.

The intruders all looked at the largest man in front, who slowly lowered his sword to the ground. The rest followed.

"Take them," Cyrus said.

"Wait!" the leader quickly called. "We're just here to talk to the witch."

Cyrus glanced back at Essandra. She made no attempt to speak. No gesture of peace. Just the same unreadable stillness. He looked back at the man. "You'll get no talk here."

"Cyrus," Everan said. "Do you want us to put them down below?"

"Cyrus as in *King* Cyrus?" the man said. The men with him all cast quick glances between one another.

Cyrus didn't blink. "What have you come for?" he demanded.

The man pulled up his sleeve, revealing a rune-type marking on the inside of his wrist.

Behind him, Essandra drew in a breath. Her hand gripped his arm.

"The mark of the Jackals," she said, her voice low. "They're assassins."

Chapter Forty

It was going to be a long night. Cyrus sat on his throne, still brimming with the heat of fight. He rested his hand on the hilt of his sword, the blade still unsheathed with its tip sharp against the stone between his feet.

The assassins stood in front of him. He hadn't realized there were so many—twelve. Not that it mattered. Cyrus's own men were with him, and he had the strength of both numbers and fury.

He stared at the group of assassins as Everan and Kord stripped them of their remaining weapons and uncovered their faces. He was surprised to see a mix of skin colors. Clearly these men weren't all from the same kingdom. Their clothing was simple but well made, fitted to their lean bodies. They covered not just their faces, but also their bodies and arms. These men weren't Shadowmen, as he'd previously thought.

"Did you light the pyre?" Cyrus asked them.

"What pyre?" It was the same man who'd mostly spoken for them before. He was light-skinned—likely from one of the Northern kingdoms, although Cyrus couldn't place his accent. His hair was cut short, with a faint sheen of copper mixed with blond, matching the shadow of a beard across his face. His gray eyes stayed leveled on Cyrus. They were piercing, like steel.

"Don't play games—the one in the courtyard."

"We didn't light a fucking pyre."

Cyrus narrowed his eyes at him. "Who sent you?"

"We're not here on an order. We came on our own."

They hadn't come on an order to kill. That tempered his anger only slightly. "For what?"

"Help."

Cyrus snorted. "Interesting way of asking for it."

"You attacked *us*." The man's eyes blazed in defiance, but he checked himself, then added, "It was never our intention to bring harm." He was fearless. Cyrus could have liked this man... if he didn't want to kill him.

"The more questions I have to ask you, the less inclined I am to listen," Cyrus told him. "Say why you're here or your next words can be to your gods as you meet them."

"We need the power of your witch." He glanced at Essandra. "That is, if she has the ability to do what we need her to." His gray eyes rolled back to Cyrus—eyes too cocky, too proud. "In exchange, we offer our services."

"I don't need your services."

The man scoffed. "All kings need assassins, and the Jackals are the best you can get."

"I already have dogs, and I handle my own matters."

The assassin's gray eyes narrowed. "Men pay a life's earnings for our talents. It will be well worth your while."

"Why do you need a witch?" Essandra asked.

The men turned their heads to her in surprise. Cyrus found himself a little surprised as well. She'd remained heavily silent so far.

"Assassins are bonded to their duty by the guild witch's magic," the man said. He held up his arm and pulled the cuff of his sleeve back, again showing the mark on his wrist. "We need another witch to break it. A powerful one."

"How do you know I can?"

"We found a bond witch who was willing to help us, but she wasn't strong enough. She said the only witch she knew who could do something like this was Sabine Laveau, and if she had to bet money, she'd wager you'd be in Rael, that there was something you were looking for here."

The cup.

And *Sabine.* The assassin had called her that before. Where else had Cyrus heard that name?

Essandra stood deathly still.

"Then," the man continued, "in Etreus, we heard the new king of Rael had himself a witch that he used to take the throne. Heard that she had power that could level a kingdom." He tilted his head. "Put two and two together." The look on his face was entirely too smug. "So, can you do it?" he pressed. "Can you break the bond?"

"I can. Not to be confused with *I will*."

The man looked back at Cyrus. "Name your price."

"I do not belong to him," Essandra snapped—as she liked to remind Cyrus.

He almost chuckled. She stepped closer to the man, and Cyrus's urge to laugh quickly evaporated. He didn't like her this close to an assassin who wasn't going to get his way.

"Essandra," he warned.

"I make bargains of my own will," she said coldly. "But you can't afford my price."

The assassin stared back at her. "Essandra?" he repeated. "Is that what you're going by?" A smile tugged at his lips and his eyes narrowed. "Are you hiding from someone, Sabine?"

Essandra's only movement was the faint lift in her throat as she swallowed. Her face was fixed, sharp and shadowed.

"Ah, you are." The assassin's smile widened. "Then I'll offer you something else. You help us, and we won't breathe a word of it. No one knows you're here. They'll continue to not know you're here."

That offer sounded more like a threat. It was interesting that this man thought he was in a position to make threats.

"Or I'll just kill you," Cyrus said. "Same outcome."

"Hey, now." The assassin held up his hand. "I offer this in goodwill."

The worst fucking goodwill.

"Take them," Cyrus said. Everan, Kord, and the rest of his men swept forward, wrestling the assassins' hands behind their backs and binding them tightly.

"Wait!" the assassin said.

No waiting.

"You can't keep us here!" He fought against Everan's hold. "If you're not going to break the bond, you have to let us go."

No, Cyrus wouldn't be doing that. Not if it put Essandra at risk. He gave Everan a nod to take them.

The man looked desperately at Essandra, but she offered no intervention.

"Just let us go!" the man bellowed as Cyrus's men dragged them from the hall and toward the dungeons. "You don't understand—you can't keep us here!"

Cyrus could do as he liked.

The throne room grew quiet.

Essandra stood so still she could have passed for stone. Even after they were alone, she didn't look at him. Her eyes stayed on the open doors of the throne room, where the assassins had been dragged out.

Cyrus waited for her to explain.

She didn't.

"What was that?" he asked her.

"I don't know those men."

"You thought they'd come for you, though."

Her face remained fixed. "Have you forgotten the nobles? There are many who want to harm me. That's the nature of power."

"You aren't afraid of the nobles, but you were afraid of these men. Who did you think they were?"

She didn't answer him.

Cyrus stepped closer. "You act like I don't know what it means to bury your past and become someone else."

Still, she wouldn't look at him.

"Who are you hiding from?" So, this was why she wouldn't stay. She was running. "Who is Sabine Laveau?" he pressed.

She gave a slight tremble but quickly recovered, her cold veneer snapping back into place. Ever so slowly, she turned her head. "Sabine Laveau is dead."

Sleep evaded him yet again. Cyrus lay in his bed until he couldn't stand it any longer, then he rose and paced the room. He knew the assassins weren't Shadowmen, but seeing them, believing it was them—even if only for a moment...

It brought back the rage.

The fire clawed at him from the inside, burning away all logic and reason. He needed to calm down. He lay back on his bed again, inhaling deeply the cool night air, but it didn't help. Nothing helped. He twisted in the sheets that were too hot against his body, turning and seething, feverish and feeding his anger more with every thought of how he could do absolutely nothing against those who deserved fate's wrath most. Alexander. The Shadow King. They deserved a punishment worse than death. They deserved pain. But they weren't in pain. They were carrying on with their lives, attaining status and commanding armies, ruling kingdoms and taking wives. Being happy. Because fate was so unjust. He turned again, the silence pressing too close—

Suddenly, a scream ripped through his mind. "*No! Please! No!*" the woman's voice begged.

Essandra's voice.

"*No!*" she screamed.

Cyrus bolted up from his bed, grabbing his sword. He tore out of his room and down the hall.

CHAPTER FORTY-ONE

"*No!*" Essandra screamed again.

Cyrus raced faster toward her chamber. "Essandra!" he roared. He reached her hall and barreled down it.

Aaron and Amiel stood at the end, at their posts outside her door. When they saw Cyrus, they both straightened and dropped their hands to their swords.

"Where is she?" Cyrus thundered.

"Inside, sleeping," Amiel said quickly.

Cyrus collided with her door, but it was locked. "I heard her scream!" He beat on it with his fist. "Essandra!"

"I've heard nothing," Amiel told him.

But Cyrus had. And she wasn't screaming now. *Now, there was only silence.*

He threw his weight against the door, but this had originally been the king's chamber, and it couldn't be forced open by one man. "Essandra!" He beat again. "Help me open it!" he snapped at them.

Just then, the door swung open.

Essandra stood in front of him in her nightgown, her eyes squinting against the hall torchlight. "What is the matter with you?" she practically yelled. "Why are you beating on my door in the middle of the night?"

Cyrus pushed inside.

"You can't just come in here!"

Amiel followed in with a torch, lighting the room.

The empty room.

"I heard you scream," Cyrus told her.

"What?" She shook her head. "I was sleeping! I was—" Her breath caught, and she stopped abruptly. Her eyes widened as they locked with his. "You heard me?"

"So, you did scream?"

"No!"

He was even more confused. He pressed his fingers to his head. He thought he'd seen a flash of a vision as well, but in his hurry, he hadn't caught what it was. No, that couldn't be right. It couldn't have been a vision. He couldn't hear in visions.

Except once before.

And then the words that she'd spoken a few moments ago sank in a little more—*you heard me.* He *had* heard something. And she knew it. He paused as a thought came to him.

"Were you having a nightmare?" he asked. Was that what it was? Not a vision, not a memory.

She crossed her arms in front of her, backing away slightly. "I'm perfectly fine. You can go."

"How could I hear you?"

She shook her head again. "I-I don't know. I used your blood earlier."

"So, it *was* a nightmare."

"I don't want to talk about it."

"Essandra—"

"I said I don't want to talk about it. Get out!"

He stared at her, not sure what he could say to get her to talk to him. She wouldn't. He already knew.

"Get out," she said again.

He sighed, then nodded to Amiel to go. Cyrus followed.

Stepping out into the hall, he turned back to Essandra, but she promptly closed the door. He stood without words as he heard the lock slide into place, his sword still in hand, his pulse still racing with the heat of fight. Her scream lingered in his mind. But there was no threat, nothing for him to do.

"We'll be right here," Amiel assured him as he and Aaron assumed their posts again.

Cyrus couldn't do anything but return to his chamber. He lumbered back down the hall. Whatever the assassins' visit had stirred within him, it had also stirred something within her, whether directly related or not. But he wouldn't be getting any answers from her.

He reached his chamber; however, he didn't go back to bed. Instead, he paced the floor.

Something about the assassins' visit had scared her. Something that now brought her nightmares. He was going to find out what that something was.

Right now.

He quickly pulled on his boots and a tunic and strode from his chamber and out of the palace.

The corridors of the cells below the arena were dark, and his skin prickled. Not that he was afraid. *He* was the monster in these halls. They belonged to him now.

The air was cool, damp with a slight mustiness. It wasn't a comfortable place to be kept. He'd said these cells would never be used again. But that was when he'd been naive to the world. Naive to what was required of him to keep those he cared for safe.

Cyrus stopped in front of the cell that held the assassins.

Their leader quickly got to his feet and met him at the bars. "You have to let us out of here; you have to let us go," he said, his voice tinged with urgency.

"Who are you?" Cyrus asked him.

"My name is Orion Rome."

Cyrus wasn't sure why he'd asked. He didn't care. "Why did you call her Sabine Laveau?"

The assassin shifted, and his brow twitched. "Because that's her name. But it doesn't matter. We'll call her whatever she wants, you just have to let us go."

"Why does your arrival bother her?"

"My arrival usually *does* bother people."

Cyrus was in no mood for games. "You know what I mean. Answer me. Who is she hiding from?"

"Look—I don't know."

"I think you do."

Orion snorted, his frustration showing. "I told you everything. The witch in Faulken gave us her name."

"You said *Etreus* before." Now he knew this man was lying.

"No, we first heard about her in Faulken, but we didn't find out you took the throne with a witch until Etreus."

Cyrus didn't believe him.

The man stepped forward and gripped the bars of the cell. "If you're not interested in our bargain, fine. Just let us go."

That wasn't going to happen. If Essandra was hiding from someone, he wouldn't risk her being discovered. "You're not going anywhere."

"Then you condemn us!" He jerked up his arm, revealing the rune marking on his wrist again. "When the guild's call comes, and we don't go, these marks will kill us." He glanced back at one of the other men in the cell. "Mace just got a call. He can't stay here. None of us can."

"Maybe you should have thought about that before you came." Cyrus's voice held no sympathy, but surprisingly, he wasn't completely without it. There was something in the assassin's words, in his circumstance, eating away some of his hatred. Coerced obedience, a slave to another man's cause, compelled to kill or be killed. Is that not what Cyrus had been? Were they that different?

It didn't matter. He'd killed men like himself before. And he would again. The only thing keeping him from doing it now was that there was something else going on, something Essandra wasn't telling him. Something she was afraid of. He had every intention of finding out what that something was.

He turned and headed back the way he'd come.

"Cyrus!" the man called after him.

His plate sat untouched in front of him. It wasn't the food. Despite Cyrus significantly scaling back palace storehouses, his master cook, Portia, still managed to make feasts of simple things. Juniper-marinated beef—a favorite. Maidenroot vegetables—also a favorite. Still, he couldn't eat.

Cyrus's gaze traveled around the table from Kord to Everan to Visa to Essandra.

No one spoke. Not even the rest of his men. They seemed to sense something was amiss.

Essandra had refused him any answers about the assassins or what was upsetting her. He'd pushed her again until she'd refused him any conversation at all. And now he had an angry witch, and still twelve assassins in the cells under the arena that he hadn't yet decided what to do with.

And that was only one of his problems. Under the weight of the crown, each day seemed longer than the last. Building a kingdom took time. Rebuilding a destroyed kingdom took even more time, especially with an active resistance working against him and growing bolder, and Cyrus was running out of time.

Yes, he'd committed himself to rebuilding Rael, and he was trying his damnedest, but the need within him chained him like no manacle ever could—the need for blood. He blamed the assassins for stirring that need again. The only things that filled his mind were Alexander and the Shadow King.

And then there was Serra. The masses grew more vocal each day. He'd committed to moving against the slavers' kingdom, and it made sense the people were pressing him for action. They would make no progress in their cause if Serra kept stealing people from their homes, putting them in chains, and selling them to the highest bidder.

However, the worst part of it all was that he wasn't actually *doing* anything. Not against Serra, not against Alexander, not against the Shadow King.

Each day that passed whispered that the longer he waited, the more he risked missing the opportunity to do anything at all. But he hadn't yet had an opportunity. Alexander wasn't accessible to him—protected deep within Mercia—and spending resources to go after his brother in a kingdom that wasn't an enemy would upset the people, especially if it came before taking action against Serra. And to take Serra, he needed an army. To take the Shadow King, he needed an even larger army.

He'd have an army eventually, with each day bringing a new wave of refugees.

But they weren't really an army.

They'd become one.

He couldn't ask this of them.

They expected it; it was why they'd come. They practically fell at his feet, offering their lives for the cause.

They flocked to him.

They trusted him.

This wasn't just for himself anymore. He owed it to them.

But their fervor was for Serra.

He pushed out a long sigh. He also needed to focus on Rael. Rebuilding. Providing. It was what his council pressed him for. It's what Essandra pressed him for.

He just needed more time. He needed strength.

He needed her.

Not just for her power, though the kingdom was standing on it. Not just for her mind, though half the council's momentum came from her voice in his ear. He needed the way she pulled him forward.

Did she need him too?

She looked at him, and their eyes met.

"It's time for me to leave Rael," she said.

Chapter Forty-Two

It's time for me to leave Rael.

Cyrus nearly dropped his chalice on his plate as he tried to wrap his mind around Essandra's words.

Visa almost did the same. "Do you really have to?" she asked.

"What? Why?" he pressed.

"You know I only ever meant to be here for a short while," she reminded him. "It's been months."

"But we're relying on the coven to feed everyone," Cyrus said. "And there's still so much left here for you. We've just begun building the schools—"

"You've always known the support of the coven was temporary. And the schools will be fine without me. As will everyone here."

Cyrus shook his head. "I won't."

The room grew quiet.

Kord rose slowly. "I'm… not hungry anymore. And I have… stuff to do." He eyed the plate, then picked it up. "I am going to take my food, though." And he quickly left the room.

Everan and Visa rose too. "We're going to go help Kord do his stuff," Everan said, and they followed. The rest of his men quickly did the same.

When Cyrus and Essandra were alone, she finally turned her gaze on him.

"Why are you really leaving?" he asked.

"It's time. I should have left already."

"That's not an answer." He sighed as he shook his head. "What are you afraid of?"

She set her table linen down beside her plate and smoothed it flat. Of course she wouldn't tell him.

"I know you're reacting," he said. "I know you're scared of something. But you're safe here. I would never let anything happen to you."

She gave a soft laugh. "You are so naive to this world."

"Whatever it is, don't let it win. Don't give up on getting your family back because—"

"I'm not giving them up!"

Cyrus sat back in his chair. "You need my power. You need me to take you to the trees."

"I don't need your power for the spell, and I'll figure out another way to get back to the trees."

"You're only making it harder on yourself." Cyrus stood, leaning his weight over the table. "Can you really tell me that you don't want to stay?"

"Of course I want to stay," she said. "I just... I can't."

"You can at least stay until you get the spell to work. You still have time."

She shook her head. "I don't."

"Whatever you're running from isn't here now. Twenty-three years you've spent trying to bring back your family. Give yourself a little more time."

"I don't have time!"

"And if you leave and set yourself back, you'll have even less time."

She shook her head again.

"You're so close," he said.

Her green eyes stared back at him.

"Just a little more time," he repeated. "You're so close."

She swallowed as she looked back down at the table linen. She smoothed it again.

"You can do this," he said softly.

Her eyes moved to her chalice, back to her plate, then finally back to him.

"Essandra. Stay. Just a little while longer."

She pulled her lip between her teeth. "A little while longer, I suppose," she whispered.

Cyrus lumbered out of the council room, feeling like it was the only place he ever was. He knew he'd committed to this, but if he had to sit through one more meeting where they talked about land distribution...

He paused when he saw Kord and Hephain striding toward him.

"Where were you two?" Cyrus asked. If he had to sit through dull-as-fuck council meetings, they did too.

"You need to come," Kord told him. "Something's wrong with one of the assassins."

"What is it?" Essandra asked, coming up alongside them.

"You have to see," Kord insisted.

The corridors weren't any brighter during the day. The weight of the arena kept them dark, and they were lit only by the torchlight along the main walls. Cyrus and Essandra followed Kord and Hephain to the assassins' cell, where Bash stood waiting just outside.

Orion, the lead assassin, met them at the bars. "I told you that we couldn't stay here!" he said angrily.

Cyrus ignored him and looked inside to where one of the men lay curled on the damp stone ground.

"Do you see now? This is what happens!"

But Cyrus didn't see. A man on the ground meant nothing.

Kord opened the cell with his sword drawn.

If this was a ploy, Cyrus would just kill them all and be done with this.

But none of the assassins moved.

"Get him up," Kord told Bash.

Bash entered the cell and pulled the man up, who stood unsteadily and needed help to remain up.

Even in the torchlight, Cyrus could see the sweat beading across his brow.

Bash dragged him out into the corridor and pulled up the man's sleeve to show his forearm.

Then Cyrus saw it.

The assassin's mark wasn't the crisp rune symbol it had been before. It was spreading, as if bleeding poison into his skin. Half the man's forearm had turned black.

"This is what happens when we don't answer the call," Orion said. "You have to let us out! This is a warning. If he doesn't go, he'll die. The mark bonds us. He only has a matter of days."

Essandra's eyes were on the man's arm. She remained silent, her face giving away nothing.

"You have to let us go," Orion pressed again. "At least let *him* go."

Cyrus wouldn't be letting any of them go. He gave a nod toward the cell, and Bash shoved the man back into it.

Essandra stood with her arms crossed.

"Are you all right?" Cyrus asked her quietly.

She didn't answer.

"Come on," he said and walked her toward the exit.

"Please," Orion called through the bars. "You have to let him go!"

Cyrus ignored him.

"Essandra!" the assassin called. "Essandra!"

Cyrus ripped his sword from its scabbard and had it to Orion's throat before he could utter another word. "You don't speak to her," he snarled.

The assassin swallowed, holding up his hands and stepping back from the bars. "I'm sorry," he said quickly. There was a desperation to him now. "Let my men go, and I'll stay."

Cyrus eyed him curiously. "Are you not afraid to die?"

"We're not afraid to die. We're afraid to die for nothing."

"Then you shouldn't have come here," Cyrus said.

Cyrus ran his hand roughly through his hair and over his face. His eyes couldn't focus on the parchments in front of him anymore. His body begged for sleep, but he knew if he let himself fall into his bed, it wouldn't come.

In the morning, he'd be on a ship for Pryam to pursue the opportunity for an alliance. Now that the time was here, he couldn't help but feel a little unsettled—not about the potential alliance, or the discussion of common goals. No. It was something far more insignificant or, rather, something that *should* be insignificant—the prospect of marriage. He shouldn't be anxious about the concept. People got married all the time. He'd fought in the arena. He'd overthrown a king. He could manage a woman.

But it wasn't just the woman. He feared the *changes* this woman would bring. Not changes to Rael, not changes to his plans. Just... other changes. Changes he didn't want. Changes with Essandra.

And he struggled under the weight of expectation. Was this just the *discussion* of marriage? Would he come back with a wife? Where would she sleep? If she wanted his chamber, where would he sleep?

He felt like an idiot, and he cursed himself.

Surely no other king worried about where he'd sleep or what to do with a wife. He should be focused on much more important things—this meeting with Morak or, even more important, how to build his army.

He cursed himself again and kicked out his stride through the main hall.

Who cared about the woman? If Morak would give him an army, he'd do whatever the king of Pryam wanted.

As he rounded a corner, he saw Hephain. "Where is everyone?" he asked when he reached him.

"Kord just left to tend to some things. He sent Brant and Sergen to check on our men guarding the fields, Bash and Ram are assessing the wagon routes, and I haven't seen Everan."

"All right."

Hephain smiled.

Cyrus eyed him. "You seem in a good mood." He'd rarely seen Hephain in a bad mood, but today he seemed particularly bright.

Hephain's smile widened. "It's just a good day."

Cyrus nodded slowly. He supposed people could have good days. He turned.

"Cyrus."

He stopped.

Hephain shuffled, glancing at the ground, then back up at him. "I just wanted to say thank you. For taking a chance on me, for giving me this opportunity. I'm living a life I'd never dared to dream of, with a love I never thought I'd have, and I just… I just wanted to let you know that it's because of you."

Cyrus lost his words for a moment. "I…" He smiled and nodded. Cuffing Hephain on the shoulder, he said, "This makes me happy to hear. I'm happy for you."

Hephain nodded back.

A call sounded behind him. "Cyrus!"

He turned to see Kord walking quickly toward him.

"Do you know about the assassins?" Kord asked before he'd even reached him.

Cyrus wasn't exactly sure what he was talking about. "Is the one dead?"

"Uh, more like… healed."

Cyrus stilled.

"Their marks are gone."

Chapter Forty-Three

"What do you mean the assassins are *healed*?"

"The witch removed their marks," Kord told him.

"Essandra? How did she get into the cell?"

"Well, the men aren't going to stop her."

Cyrus couldn't fault them for that. He could still be angry about it, though. "Why would she remove the marks?"

Kord shook his head. "I don't know. She was leaving just as I arrived. She didn't say anything, and I didn't find out until after she'd already gone."

"Did she break the bond for all of them?"

"All of them. Oh, and, uh—if you thought that one guy was a smug bastard *before...*"

Cyrus's jaw tightened. "Are they still in the cells?"

"Yeah. Want to see them?"

"No." He had other things to do, like find Essandra. "Make sure no one else goes down there."

"You really want me to try to stop her if she comes again?"

As if Kord could.

"Just come get me," he said. Then he turned and made his way toward Essandra's workroom.

Thunder rippled through him as he walked. He wasn't quite sure why he was angry right now—he didn't even know her reason. Maybe part of him had hoped these markings would rid him of the assassins without him having to do anything at all. Now, if he wanted to be done with them, he'd have to kill them himself.

Essandra was exactly where he'd suspected her to be. He didn't come to her workroom often, and he usually knocked at the door and waited. He didn't knock now.

She was standing at her table and turned with a start as he entered.

"You removed their marks?" he asked, not bothering with a greeting.

She cut him a steely glance, then returned to the task he'd interrupted—crushing a mixture of herbs with a mortar and pestle.

"Why?" he asked.

"Because they were dying." Her voice was stiff and cold.

"What do you care? And wouldn't that solve your problem?"

Essandra only emptied the contents of the mortar into another bowl.

"Did you make a deal with them?" he asked. "You want to use them for something?" He stepped around the table, nearer to her. "What do you need from them? I'll give it to you."

Her body sagged slightly as she leaned against the edge of the table. "I don't need anything from them," she said quietly.

Then all of this made even less sense.

Essandra turned her back to him, smoothing her hands along the grain of the table wood. "You wouldn't understand."

"Then help me understand!" He reached out, but she pulled away.

Why couldn't she tell him?

"Essandra," he said softly.

She set her bowl down, staring into it.

His shoulders dropped as the weight of defeat settled onto him. She wasn't going to tell him. He sighed, nodding. He couldn't force her to open up to him. Even if he could, he didn't want to. He wanted her to trust him. But she didn't.

He'd leave her be. He turned to go.

"I used to belong to a coven," she said, stopping him, "led by a powerful witch, one of the most powerful witches in the world." She gave a long pause. "Soroya Fey. She's the one I'm hiding from."

He turned back to her.

"After Choan destroyed my village, I was alone," she continued. "I was a child, a girl, on my own. I wasn't bonded to anyone, and I was powerless, completely reliant on the mercy of strangers. Some were kind. Some weren't." She swallowed. "Some took advantage."

Her eyes welled, and his chest tightened. He stepped closer.

"When I got to the Free Cities, I met a witch," she told him. "She took me in, brought me to her coven. Soroya's coven. I thought I'd been saved. Soroya was powerful, and she made me feel powerful. She opened my eyes to what a witch could really do."

Her eyes glazed, staring into the past.

"I was one of three bond witches," she continued, "but I was the most powerful. I was able to bond other witches against their will so that Soroya could use their power."

"You did this willingly?"

"No." Her words were laced with bitterness. "But it doesn't really matter, does it? It's all the same. I tried to refuse, but she used dark magic to compel me. I had no choice. And that's how I spent the next twenty years—finding and bonding witches to Soroya's coven, helping her grow her power—power that she used to hurt anyone who opposed her."

She stared down at the mixture in her bowl. "All the while, I searched for the Amoran Cup."

"How did you know it was here?"

"I heard the king of Rael had found it. At the same time, the everlife trees had started to bloom, but I was afraid to leave the coven. Then, one day, Soroya brought me a seer. A young girl. Jessenia. She was the strongest seer I'd ever met. Until you." She crossed her arms as she rocked slightly. "Soroya wanted me to bond their power so she could access the Aether. Free, uncontrolled access. No blood, no limits." She glanced at Cyrus. "But Jessenia knew Soroya would become too powerful." Her voice dropped to a whisper. "I knew too." She shook her head. "Jessenia fought me like a rabid beast—a wild, chaotic, desperate fight. It didn't matter. It wasn't her choice."

Her throat dipped. "But when I tried to make the cuts for the spell, she was fast. She grabbed the knife and stabbed it into her own chest." Essandra's voice wavered, and her eyes welled. "She killed herself. She took her own life to keep her power from Soroya. And the world is safer for it."

Essandra pushed out a long breath. "That's when I knew I had to leave," she said. "Her fight gave me the courage. It took me months to figure out how to break the bond. I had to use dark magic to do it."

"You escaped," he said. "Then you came to Rael for the cup."

She nodded. "I didn't have Tomel at the time, so I traveled like useless people do."

He snorted.

"But I met witches along the way, and they joined me. I formed my own coven. I lead them. They've allowed themselves to be bonded with me, but it's all of their own free will. Anyone can leave at any time." She sighed. "Orion and his men want to leave the Jackals, but the assassin's guild is like Soroya's coven—no one leaves. Even without the mark, they're not safe. They'll be hunted. Like me. They can change their names too. It won't matter."

"You're safe here."

She shook her head. "Soroya will find me eventually, and when she does..." It was so slight, but he heard it—the faintest tremble in her words.

His chest tightened, and he stepped nearer. *This* was what she was afraid of.

"At first I thought the assassins had come for me," she said, "that she'd sent them. But Soroya wouldn't send assassins. She'll come herself to kill me."

He moved closer, dropping his voice. "I won't let anything happen to you."

She smiled sadly. "You shouldn't make promises you can't keep," she whispered.

Her words knifed him, and he moved even closer—so close there wasn't space between them. Her breath hitched as he lifted her chin to look at him. She raised her eyes to his.

"Essandra," he said. "If someone comes for you, I'll kill them."

Her breath caught.

Her lips parted.

Her lips, her lips, her lips. The want to kiss her—the pull—it was overwhelming, too powerful. But he knew he couldn't. She'd been very clear he couldn't. She wasn't his to kiss. Still, he dropped his head lower.

He'd meant every word. He would never let anything happen to this woman. If someone came for her... the heat of fight flamed under his skin just thinking of it.

But what if he wasn't here? He almost swore. He just remembered—"I have to go to Pryam tomorrow," he said. He didn't want to leave her.

Her face fell. "Oh," she said softly. "Right."

"I won't be gone long. A few days."

Maybe he shouldn't go. He didn't know what reason he'd have. No one was coming for her right now; she wasn't in danger. Yet...

"Cyrus," she breathed. Her mouth opened with unspoken words on her tongue.

Did she want him to stay?

He waited.

All she had to do was say it. All she had to do was tell him to stay.

He'd stay.

Say it.

Please say it.

But she didn't.

She wouldn't.

He peeled his gaze from her lips, fearing his body would betray him and he'd make an even bigger fool of himself. He focused on the table, on the parchments strewn across it, her materials, anything to distract himself.

His eyes landed on an open book, and he paused. The bottom of the page had a drawing of the Amoran Cup. The writing beside it wasn't in a language he knew, but he'd seen it before.

"What is that?" he asked. "Did you write it?"

"Um..." She shook her head as if to clear it and followed his gaze.

"Is that the spell you've been working on?" he asked.

"Um, yes." She quickly shifted, slipping away from him and moving around to put the table between them. "No, I mean. I didn't write it. I'm translating it. But I've obviously made a mistake somewhere."

His pulse quickened. Finally, something he might be able to give her. Something that might help her. "Teron has books like this."

She stopped, and her eyes grew wider. "He has books written in Old Nehalem?"

Cyrus nodded. "I'm pretty sure. The lettering is consistent. He might be able to help you."

Her breaths came clipped.

"Let's go talk to him. Get your book." Cyrus didn't care about the assassins anymore.

"N-now?"

"Yes, now."

She quickly scraped the loose parchments back into the book, holding it closely against her chest as Cyrus led her to Teron's workroom.

They found the old healer hunched over his manuscripts, scratching notes with a thick quill.

"Teron," Cyrus said as they entered.

The old man bobbed his head up.

"We have a book we're hoping you can help with. A spell we're trying to translate."

Essandra opened it and laid it on the table for him to see.

Teron's mouth opened in surprise. "Written in Old Nehalem?"

Essandra gasped. "Yes! You know it?"

"Yes, of course I do."

She covered her mouth, and her eyes teared.

Cyrus couldn't help a smile.

Teron read through the script, drawing his finger down the page. He looked up, his eyes wide. "You're trying to do this spell?"

She swallowed hard. "You know of it?"

"I've only ever heard of it. It's never been successfully done. It requires things not of this world." He eyed her again. "The Amoran Cup."

She glanced at Cyrus.

He nodded. She could trust Teron.

"I have it," she told him.

Teron's eyes grew even larger. "You have the Amoran Cup?"

Essandra nodded, practically shaking. "Yes. But I'm having trouble understanding everything else that I need. She moved around the table to his side, pointing to the first line of script. "A petal from an everlife tree."

His mouth dropped open, incredulous. "You grew an everlife tree?"

"Yes," she said, breathless, seeming to appreciate someone realizing the magnitude of the feat she'd undertaken.

Teron looked back at the book, touching it gingerly.

"I just need to figure out what I'm doing wrong." She pointed to the third line on the page. "This is the one I'm worried about—blood of the dead. I have their dresses, stained in their blood. I've been using cut pieces from it. Is this the problem, do you think?" She shook nervously. "I feel like it should work—in spirit spells you can use dried blood." She roughly brushed a lock of hair out of her face. "It should work, right? I-I don't have anything else. It has to work."

"Yes, that should be all right," he said.

Relief immediately washed over her face, and she started to calm. She closed her eyes for a moment, nodding, then swallowed. "Good. Good." Then I have all the pieces. She pointed to the fourth line. "I'm the familial blood for the anchor." She pulled back. "I must be saying the spell itself wrong."

Teron's brows shifted. His mouth pressed into a thin frown. "You cannot be the anchor for them both."

Essandra stilled. "What?"

"Have you been trying to bring them back together?"

Her breaths quickened again. "Yes."

"That's why it's not working. You must pick one."

"What?" She shook her head as her bottom lip trembled. "No."

Teron pointed to a word in the text. "This word—*anaktu. Each.* They each need an anchor. An anchor with power."

"No," she said again. "I just need more power." She glanced at Cyrus. "I'll use the blood to draw from the Aether."

"It won't matter how much power you can draw," Teron told her. "You need two anchors—different anchors, as one cannot be used for the other."

"No." She kept repeating it.

He shook his head sadly. "I'm sorry. This magic wasn't meant to be easy. It wasn't meant to be used by common men, or by men at all, for that matter. It's a dark power, needing many controls."

"I can't bring them both back?" she whispered.

"Not if you don't have another familial anchor."

The room began to shake.

"Essandra," Cyrus said warily.

She turned to him, her eyes rimmed red. "I can't bring them both back?"

The room shook harder.

"Essandra," he said again.

"I can't bring them both back," she whispered. She staggered sideways, letting out a cry, then dropped to her knees.

Bowls fell from a shelf on the wall. Jars crashed to the floor from the table. Cyrus jumped forward to cover her. Something hit him in the shoulder, and he winced.

"Essandra!" He needed to get her to calm, but her sobs racked her. All he could do was hold her.

Her whole body shook. Cyrus quit trying to stop her and only held her.

Finally, the room stilled.

He glanced at Teron, who'd taken cover under the table. The old man waved that he was all right, and Cyrus turned his focus back to Essandra.

Cries still tremored through her body. He needed to get her out of here—somewhere she could properly grieve. Carefully, gently, Cyrus scooped her into his arms and picked her up. Casting an apologetic nod to Teron, he grabbed the book and carried Essandra out of the workroom to her chamber.

She clung to him as she cried into his neck, and he held her tighter. When he reached her bed, he laid her down, then moved to pull away, but she held his arm.

He knew this grief. He knew the need for warmth to hold, the comfort of skin to skin. So, he crept into the bed beside her and wrapped his arms around her as she wept.

Sleep never came, not that he'd expected it to. Essandra woke two times in the night, then cried herself back into dreams.

Morning came slowly yet too quickly at the same time. His ship to Pryam would depart soon. He didn't want to leave her. She needed him.

No, she didn't. He wanted her to need him. The truth was, she'd been overcome with grief, and he was simply there. He shifted back slightly to look at her. Her arm was wrapped around his torso, and her legs tangled in his. Her pulse beat in the curve of her neck—slowly—the beat of a broken heart. He moved to dust his fingertips over her cheek but stopped just short of touching her. Gods how he *wanted* to touch her.

But he needed to go.

Carefully, so as not to wake her, he pulled his body from hers and slipped out of the bed. Then, quietly, he made his way to his own chamber. It didn't take him long to gather his things. Everything was ready.

He met Everan and Kord at the bottom of the stairs just as the sun spilled over the horizon and through the windows of the main hall.

"I stopped by your chamber," Everan said. "Where were you?"

"Just getting ready," he replied. Then he caught a passing servant. "Have breakfast sent to Essandra's chamber. Don't wake her, just leave it outside the door."

He couldn't shake the unease at just leaving her like this, but when she woke, she wouldn't want him there.

The docks were crowded, bustling mostly with those who would man the ship. Cyrus paused before he boarded. It had been over fifteen years since he'd sailed over water, and under very different circumstances. He'd imagined some of the feelings might return—the fear, the anxiousness. But right now, he was only anxious for what lay ahead. As he stepped aboard and they raised the anchor, he realized there was no turning back now.

The ship moved off, slow and steady. Men greeted him as he made his way up to the top deck. It wouldn't be a long sailing—they'd reach Pryam by the following evening.

Cyrus looked back toward Rael, and at the docks growing smaller and smaller. He thought he caught sight of a woman with long dark hair—Essandra—but he shook it off. It was his eyes playing tricks on him.

He tried to clear his mind as he turned his sight forward, east. To Pryam for an alliance. And a wife.

Chapter Forty-Four

The port was larger than Cyrus had expected. Pryam was a small kingdom, and he'd imagined a small port, but it was at least three times the size of Rael's. Ships filled the waters around them, slowing Cyrus's vessel to nearly a crawl as they drew nearer to the docks. Cog ships, he noted, used for either trade or war, and Cyrus was curious which they were used for here.

He stood on the bow, his impatience mounting, but not as much as Kord's, who stood pale as a ghost beside him. It had been a tough journey for his friend, who'd spent most of it with his head over the railing, emptying the contents of his stomach into the sea.

"Get me off this fucking ship," Kord muttered.

Cyrus half expected him to jump the railing and swim the rest of the way to the docks. He smiled sympathetically.

"It didn't seem to take that long to get here," Everan said, joining them from behind.

Kord snorted weakly. "Speak for yourself."

But Cyrus felt the same. He'd thought they'd reach Pryam's ports nearer to nightfall, but it was only midday. If he could wrap up this meeting with Morak quickly, he could leave earlier than anticipated—maybe even tonight. Then he could get back to Rael. It was interesting—all the time he'd dreamed and fought to get out of that cursed kingdom only to be looking forward to getting back.

Cyrus swept his eyes around the harbor and, now that his attention was on it, noticed the air hung heavy with an eerie stillness. "That's strange," he muttered.

"What is?" Everan asked, now beside him.

"The ships. They're empty."

There was no lively clamor of sailors at work, no clanging of chains and crates from cargo being raised and lowered, no boatmen's calls. All the decks were barren and quiet, save the echoing lap of waves against the hulls as the vessels rocked silently in the water.

"Where is everyone?" Kord asked.

It was a good question, and Cyrus warily dropped his hand on the hilt of his sword.

The chapping wind of the sea tamed to a gentle breeze as they drew closer. Salt mingled with the earthiness of weathered wood. The ship came to a stop against the worn wooden pylons, and the gangways creaked as they extended to the dock.

At first glance, Pryam wasn't entirely unlike coastal Rael—a semi-arid rocky desert. There were a fair number of palm trees that sprang up along the golden coastline—something Rael didn't have—and Pryam lacked Rael's crippling heat, although it was still hot.

Despite the early unease, Kord was the first one off the ship. Cyrus waited for Ram to join both him and Everan at the bow before following. They'd brought a fair number of men with them—a couple hundred. Visiting another kingdom always carried risks—risks that seemed a little greater now. Essandra had made Cyrus promise to bring his armor, and he had, although he had no intention of wearing it. He fought better without scraps of metal hindering his movement.

Scraps of metal. He should be more appreciative. It was probably the finest-made armor in the world—crafted by a forge witch, flawlessly fit to his body, and impenetrable.

Still, he wouldn't wear it. And he hadn't told anyone about its power. Not even Everan and Kord. It felt pretentious to even say.

Cyrus's men followed him down the gangway and the empty docks and up the stairs between the seawalls. They wore their blades sheathed but kept their hands on the hilts of their swords.

When they reached the top of the wall, they paused. Rows of guards lined both sides of the port's mainway, clearly laying out a path. It was an orchestrated display—perhaps one for welcoming an arriving king, although they didn't particularly feel welcoming.

He eyed the guards, who were strapped with more blades than one carried into battle. Not the best sign. Their faces were covered, not by wraps like the Shadowmen or the assassins but with golden masks. They wore ornate, sand-colored clothing—more ornate than his own—embroidered and heavy but fitted to their form.

Cyrus stood, sweating in his linen tunic. How did these men breathe? Although that was the least of his questions.

He glanced at Everan, whose sword-arm shoulder dropped and coiled as his hand tightened even more around the hilt of his blade.

But Cyrus reminded himself he was here by invitation. Of marriage. This was more likely a grandiose display rather than overt hostility.

And if it was hostility, Cyrus knew how to be hostile.

He led his men forward, alert and ready, following the path laid for him. As they made their way deeper into the city, it started to *feel* more like a proper city. People bustled through the streets, although they stayed clear of the path made by the guards. A young child toddled close, but his mother grabbed him and then quickly brushed the shape of a circle over her chest.

"What was that?" Kord asked.

"It's a physical prayer for protection against evil spirits," Ram said from just behind Cyrus. "It's of the Verinian faith."

Everan glanced back at him. "Is that what you are?"

"What my mother was," Ram answered.

Ram was from the Ballard Isles off the coast of Nayalour, which shared common languages and religions with the other five kingdoms of the Etrean continent, including Pryam. Cyrus had offered him to return after the rebellion, but there was nothing left after the Serran attacks that had enslaved or killed most of the people and had left the islands in ruin.

Kord snorted. "So, they think we're evil spirits?"

"Not *us*," Cyrus said, as he noted the people's wary eyes on the masked guards. "Them."

"Well, this is getting even more interesting," Kord said.

That it was.

They continued. The line of guards continued. On and on and on.

Cyrus and his men were easily outnumbered now. His men kept close—Kord and Everan so close that their shoulders brushed his own.

The mainway curved, and they followed the guards' path, but as they rounded the corner, Kord stopped abruptly, and so did Cyrus, as there, with a party of people who all wore varying shades of gold and cream and white, waited a girl—perhaps the most beautiful girl he'd ever seen.

Cyrus stared at her, not in a way of lust or want, he'd just never seen anyone quite like her. Perhaps it was how her golden mane contrasted against the dark hue of her skin, or her striking large wheaten eyes that sat under her long lashes. Maybe it was her high cheekbones, or the fullness of her lips, or the way her perfectly proportionate face tapered to her chin. And there was something else...

She gave a bow of her head and a curtsy. "King Cyrus," she said. "Welcome to Pryam." Her voice was soft and melodic. "I'm Princess Miriel."

Princess? The subject of his betrothal? That couldn't be right. This girl couldn't be more than fourteen or fifteen.

Maybe he hadn't heard her right; she'd said *princess*, but maybe there was another.

"Is there... another princess?" he asked.

Her mouth opened slightly, then she closed it again. There was a faint bob of her throat as her lips thinned. She smoothed the front of her dress.

"I am the only heir of King Morak," she said.

Cyrus stood, staring at her. No, that couldn't be right. She was a *child*. And why was *she* here meeting him? A king wouldn't send his daughter to meet a bloodsport fighter usurper he didn't know, especially his only heir.

Unless this wasn't *really* his daughter...

A decoy, perhaps. To test him.

"Where is King Morak?" he asked.

She swallowed. He knew nervousness when he saw it... Something was afoot.

"He's indisposed," she said. "But I'll take you to the palace, where you can freshen up from your travels."

Indisposed? The sinking suspicion in his stomach grew.

She waved a hand, and the guards parted, allowing a carriage forward—a very small carriage, meant only for two people, obviously to get him alone.

He glanced at Everan, and Everan cut him a wary eye in return.

Cyrus looked back at the girl. "Why are *you* greeting me?" he asked. Did Morak think she'd be able to persuade him away from his men?

Her large eyes darted to Everan, then Kord, then back to him. She swallowed again, and her breaths came even faster. "I'm sorry you're displeased," she said, clutching the sides of her gown between her fingers. She was beyond nervousness now, into what Cyrus recognized all too well—fear. Something was certainly going on here, and Morak was using this girl.

"I'll walk with my men," he said.

"It's a rather long walk," she countered.

"I like long walks, especially after being on a ship for two days."

Her eyes traveled over his men. She swallowed yet again. "Very well," she said, and turned, extending an arm in the direction of the guard-lined mainway. "This way, Majesty."

They walked silently, Cyrus beside the girl, with Everan and Kord and the rest of his men just behind. Every time the girl looked as if she were about to say something, she glanced back at them, then didn't.

It wasn't a far walk, fueling Cyrus's suspicion of the need for the carriage even more. He'd lost count of how many guards they'd passed. It didn't really matter anymore. Cyrus and his men were heavily outnumbered. He walked within an arm's reach of the girl. He wasn't above using her if things ran afoul, although, if she had been sent as part of a plot, she likely meant nothing to Morak. Cyrus would find out when he put a blade to her throat...

The palace was as palaces were—opulent, beautiful, wasteful, especially in contrast to the humble commoner-filled port city. Its stone matched the rock of Pryam's landscape, gold and sand, with marble accents throughout. It seemed to glow in the light of the sun, but what kept Cyrus's eye more were the rows of guards still on either side of the golden brick mainway. How many men did Morak have? Even more lined the sweeping stairs of the palace to the carved double doors that stood at least three men high.

Two footmen—not guards—pushed open the doors as they approached, and a third came quickly from inside with a tray of drinks. The girl took one of the chalices from the tray and turned back to Cyrus, holding it for him.

"It's rose water," she said, pushing it into his hands. "You'll love it. It's so refreshing, especially after the heat." Then she turned and swept forward again.

Cyrus handed Everan the chalice, who handed it to Ram, who set it on the pillar of a bust at the entry. They continued.

The girl took them through a series of halls, each growing even more elaborate, if that were possible. Everything was over-the-top, from the crystal chandeliers to the gold-spun tapestries, to the life-size statues centered between windows that stretched from the floor to the unreachable ceiling. And all along the way—golden-masked guards.

The girl stole several glances at Cyrus and his men before she finally asked, "Are these men that are with you the ones that helped you take Rael?"

A seemingly innocent question, but he knew what she was doing—she was trying to tell if they were all fighters. Why would that matter? Unless she was expecting a fight...

"They are," Cyrus answered.

"Are these all the men you brought?" she asked. "Or are there more on the ship who will need accommodations?"

Cyrus cut a glance at Everan, whose eyes narrowed.

"Actually, we won't have need for accommodation," Cyrus said. "I don't want to impose."

There was the faintest air of relief in her breath, although she quickly said, "You're no imposition. We're excited you've come. I've had the grand suite prepared for you."

She smiled and stopped at a large alcove with gilded doors, nodding to a footman outside, who pulled one open.

"I'll stay with my men," Cyrus said. "Should I need to stay the night, I'll stay on the ship."

She paused, her smile fading, and her large eyes flickered quickly as the wheels of her mind turned. Did she know how obvious she was? "That... hardly sounds comfortable," she said.

"I'm not a man of comfort."

She wrung her hands in front of her. "Well, at least take the opportunity to freshen up. I'll also call for some wonderful samplings of Pryamese foods and drinks for your men."

"They're fine," he said. "As am I."

"Oh. Okay." Her nervousness returned. "Perhaps I'll just leave you here, then. It won't be long until dinner."

"Why don't you wait with me, *princess*? I'd like to hear more about Pryam." This girl might be a pawn, but she was the only thing he had right now if things went sideways, and he didn't want to let her get away from him.

The girl took a step backward. Did she sense it? "I have to make sure everything is ready. I'll send someone shortly to bring you to the dining room."

She gave a small curtsy. As she turned to leave, his men didn't move for her. Shakily, she turned back to face him. "Is there anything else you need?" she asked with a small hitch in her voice. Her hands trembled as she clutched the fabric of her gown.

He could hold her, not let her go. Then he'd force Morak's hand—perhaps even force violence. Here. Now. But if he was wrong, if there were no foul intentions at play, he'd succeed in beheading alliance talks before they'd even begun. Something was going on, but was he confident enough that there was ill intention to risk it all?

Morak had no reason to hold ill will against him, at least not that he was aware of. And Cyrus *had* come with hopes of partnership. He *needed* an alliance.

"No," he said finally. "Thank you for your hospitality. I'll see you at dinner."

She swallowed and forced an uneasy smile. "Yes. I'm looking forward to it." His men parted to let her pass, and she quickly turned and briskly made her way down the hall. Her guards followed, leaving Cyrus and his men alone.

Cyrus watched her, cursing himself. He shouldn't have let her go. But then what? He cursed himself again. He'd come for an alliance, which was *not* likely to happen if he took the princess of Pryam prisoner in her own palace. No—she wasn't the princess... but the effect would be the same.

Kord and Ram stepped back out into the hall from the chamber. "The room is clear," Kord said.

Everan frowned. "But something's weird here. I don't like it."

Cyrus shook his head. "Neither do I."

"Why do I feel confined to this chamber?" Cyrus paced the stretch of room between the double doors that led to a bath chamber and another set of doors that led to a secondary room with a bed. This suite was at least twice the size of his chamber back in Rael. It could hold all the men he'd brought, although most of them stood post in the hall.

"Because you are," Everan said. He stood by the arched tri-panel windows that looked out over a somewhat-out-of-place garden of lush topiaries and florals. The line of the city sloped slightly, allowing views of the harbor in the distance, but not a view of Cyrus's ship—strategic of Morak to put Cyrus in this room.

Cyrus's jaw tightened. "Is this how kings are normally received?"

Kord snorted from his seat at a six-chair table with Ram, who sat opposite him. "I don't think there's anything normal about this kingdom," Kord said.

Cyrus was still angry with himself for allowing the girl to leave. He should have asked her for a tour of the palace. He should have asked more questions in general.

A knock sounded on the door, but as he moved to answer, Everan stepped in front of him, making him pause. His friend reached around and slid another dagger into the back sheath of Cyrus's sword belt that he normally kept empty.

Everan's eyes were dark and serious. "If this goes to shit, Ram and Kord will help you get back to the boat. Do *not* wait for anyone, including me. You leave. Do you understand?"

"I'm not leaving you here."

"Cyrus"—Everan gritted his teeth—"the first priority is to get you out. The rest of us will find a way to follow."

Cyrus sighed and looked at Kord and Ram, who were both checking the reach of their own weapons. They nodded at their assignments.

"Fine," Cyrus said. He had no guilt in lying.

Kord opened the door, and a waiting footman bowed.

"Dinner is ready, Majesty," the man said politely to Cyrus. "I'll escort you, if you're ready."

He knew what the man meant—to escort him alone—but he acted like he didn't. Cyrus had no intention of going alone. He had no intention of fighting alone. "Lead on," Cyrus told him. "We'll follow."

The man opened his mouth slightly but then closed it without voicing his objection. He glanced at Everan, Kord, and Ram, but then only said, "Of course," and turned on his heel and started down the hall.

Kord cut Cyrus a slight smirk. "After you," he said.

Cyrus walked as if he were walking into battle—focusing, honing, listening, aware of everything around him. His men trailed quietly behind, or as quietly as two hundred men could reasonably move through a palace.

This wasn't the welcome he'd expected, but Cyrus recognized he wasn't a traveled man, nor a man familiar with the customs of royal diplomacy. He was eager to meet Morak and flush out this king's true intentions.

When he reached the dining room, Cyrus paused. A row of palace guards lined the back wall, but the only person present for dinner was the girl, who stood by her seat at the end of the table.

"King Cyrus," she greeted him, extending her hand to the chair at the opposite end. "Please."

"Where is King Morak?"

"He remains indisposed, but you mentioned that you wanted to hear more about—"

"What keeps him indisposed?"

She glanced at her guards along the wall. Their golden masks looked slightly more ominous as the light faded with the day, drawing shadows across them.

"Let's talk about Pryam," she said, trying to recover the conversation. She stepped to her chair to sit but remained standing. A prompt for him to take his own seat. "I'll take you to the king tomorrow—"

"You'll take me to him now." He had no intention of sitting for dinner, and he was done with the games. Then something caught his eye. A stitch, a ripple, at the outer edges of the room.

Cyrus stilled.

It was so faint, virtually unnoticeable. But he'd noticed. He'd seen this before.

With Essandra's illusions.

Were the guards an illusion?

He eyed them closely—their impractical garb, their masks that showed no eyes. Their sheer number. If it was an illusion, it was an elaborate one and well beyond what Essandra could do. But there was no mistaking the slight fray where the illusion met reality.

He was sure of it now.

This girl wasn't the princess; *she was a witch*.

And if this was magic, it wasn't showmanship. It was a misdirection—something to trick him, perhaps until it was too late...

"Where is King Morak?" he asked more firmly.

Her breaths came faster, and she didn't answer.

Cyrus started toward her.

The guards put their hands on their hilts in unison and stepped forward, but Cyrus ignored them. Illusions were harmless. He moved around the corner of the table.

The girl stumbled back quickly and bumped up against her chair, almost knocking it over. "Don't come any closer," she demanded. The guards pulled their swords from the scabbards.

"Cyrus!" Everan called, and he and Kord pulled their own blades.

The guards swept forward. The girl turned to flee, but Cyrus was faster, and he caught her. As he seized her, she screamed, and the images of the guards—all but one—vanished.

They weren't real. The one guard remaining was quickly pinned by Everan and Kord.

Cyrus gripped the girl tightly at the base her jaw. She whimpered under his bruising hold.

"Who are you?" he demanded.

A sob escaped her lips. "I told you; I'm Princess Miriel."

He didn't believe her. "Where is Morak?"

She didn't answer.

"Where is he?" he snarled, tightening his hold.

"He's dead!" she cried.

They all stopped.

Cyrus stared at her. "What do you mean *he's dead*?"

Chapter Forty-Five

Cyrus angled the tip of his knife against the base of the Pryamese girl's throat as he held her pinned against the wall. No more games. If this girl didn't think he'd kill her...

Her sobbing breaths told him that she did.

"You'd better start talking," he demanded, "and every word that comes out of your mouth better be true. Now, where is Morak?"

"The king is dead," she said, her words clipped by her cries.

"How? And when?"

"Consumption." Her breaths shook her body. "A little over a month ago."

Cyrus dug his blade into her skin as he shook his head. "No. I just received a letter from him two weeks ago."

She squeezed her eyes shut, spilling tears down her cheeks. "I wrote it. The letter was from me."

His eyes narrowed. "Who are you?"

She blinked back more tears and sucked in another breath. "I haven't lied to you. I really am Princess Miriel."

"Why not write to me truthfully, then? Why not tell me Morak was dead?"

"Because no one knows," she said.

His brow stitched. "What do you mean *no one knows*?"

"I haven't told anyone. Not even my kingdom. The only people who know are the few who remain of my castle staff and royal guard, and Amish, who was my father's personal guard and friend." Her eyes moved to the man Everan held at swordpoint. Kord pulled off his mask. Cyrus couldn't tell how much the man's hair was graying through his prominent blond, but the creases on his forehead and the lines around his eyes aged him well beyond Cyrus, by fifteen or twenty years perhaps.

"They've been helping me keep the secret until I can figure out what to do. Please," she begged, and struggled with a swallow. "I wrote because I need you. I need your help."

Cyrus didn't believe her, or rather, he didn't *want* to believe her. He glanced at Everan, who had lowered his blade from the older man's neck and raised a brow back at him, subtly urging him to do the same.

Cyrus glared at her. "What did you do with him? Where is Morak's body?"

Her eyes darted to the man she called Amish, and he nodded. Looking back at Cyrus, she said, "We've put him in the crypts, below the castle."

"I want to see him."

She glanced back at Amish, who nodded again.

Cyrus stepped back and gave her room to collect herself, but he didn't sheath his knife. If she was lying...

Shakily, she led them from the dining hall. She walked with her head down and her hands at her sides, clutching her skirts.

Everan pushed Amish in front of them, and he, Cyrus, and Kord followed. As they stepped into the hallway, four guards against the wall pulled their blades and moved toward them, but the girl waved them to stay.

"It's all right," she said.

So, *they* were real... apparently. Where were the rest? They'd all disappeared.

"The whole army was an illusion?" Cyrus asked her.

She gave a shaky nod. "Pryam's never had an army. We've always relied on the protection of the Etrean Union. But then we were expelled."

Wait... "Pryam was expelled from the Union?" His council certainly wasn't going to be happy about that. The connection to the Union was the whole reason they were even pushing an alliance with Pryam. "Why?"

"My father wouldn't tell me."

Cyrus sighed. This was just getting worse. "How many do you have in the royal guard?" he asked.

Her voice dropped to a whisper. "Twenty-four."

"Twenty-four units? And each unit is a hundred—"

"No, twenty-four men."

Cyrus balked, rocking back on his heel. It took a moment before he could speak. "Twen... Twenty-four *men*?"

She kept her eyes down. "We never had many to begin with, but... well, my father released most of them from service, sent them away."

Cyrus snorted in bewilderment. "Why would he do that?"

"To protect me."

Then she turned and started again down the hall, her pace quickening now, as if running from where the conversation was heading.

Cyrus looked at Everan and Kord, who both stood speechless as well. This kingdom was absolute madness. But what else could Cyrus really do but follow her?

They reached another hall, which took them to a stairwell. The girl led them down another lengthy hall below and then to yet another stairwell. A very narrow stairwell.

Cyrus grabbed the girl's upper arm, jerking her to a pause. "Where are we going?"

"I told you—the crypts."

"No one is carrying bodies down this stairwell."

"There's a processional way," she said quickly. "But this way is shorter."

Cyrus narrowed his eyes. It could be the truth, or she could be quick-witted. He released her, only because he couldn't hold on to her and walk down the stairwell at the same time. "Go on, then," he said.

They descended farther down, and when they reached the bottom, the narrow stairwell opened to a dimly lit room.

Amish pulled a blazing torch from the wall beside the stairwell and made his way around, lighting more torches to illuminate the room.

And Cyrus saw it wasn't just a room. The massive hall spanned almost twice the size of Rael's great throne room, but the hall's low ceiling made it feel smaller. Columns ran throughout, supporting the myriad arches that stretched the entire space above them. Whether they were for structural support or adornment, he wasn't sure—perhaps both.

The girl led them past another hall—no, not a hall, a deep alcove that opened to a vaulted bay. They passed several of these. Within each bay lay a stone sarcophagus in lavish baroque. Cyrus assumed each of these held a king.

But the girl didn't stop at one of these bays. Instead, she led them behind a dividing wall to an unmarked sarcophagus. Her lip trembled and another tear spilled down her cheek. "We haven't engraved it yet or placed him in his chamber," she said quietly, "for fear of someone seeing."

Cyrus nodded to Everan and Kord, and the three of them clasped the top of the sarcophagus and pulled back the heavy stone from its place. Everan handed Cyrus a torch, and Cyrus held it close to view the man inside.

It was certainly a man a month dead, although some kind of embalming had been done, staving off signs of decay and the smell of death. He was an older man, with features similar to the girl's, and dressed in Pryam's colors of white and gold. The tassels that lined his embroidered tippet sash had been meticulously straightened and evenly spaced. Small flowers, long dead, had been scattered around him. His arms lay folded, with his hands clasping a crown that had been placed on his chest.

Cyrus sighed as he slid his knife into the sheath at his back. He had no doubt about the girl's story now. "Why did you write to me?" he asked.

"My father wanted to write to you with the offer months ago, but I was scared, and I begged him to wait. I..." She paused and moved her eyes to the old man in the sarcophagus. "I thought he had more time."

"But why me?"

"We heard how you took Rael with the help of a witch. We'd lost support of the Union, and we needed protection, and"—she cast her gaze to the ground—"we thought that maybe... you wouldn't be so unsettled by me, like everyone else is. They call *me* a witch, which is utterly ridiculous."

"You are a witch," Cyrus said.

Her eyes darted up to him and her mouth opened in objection. "W-what? No! I can only project images, I have no power—"

"Projecting images *is* power. And you do it very well, so you likely have a lot of power."

Her objections still sat on her tongue, but she didn't say anything else. She only stood, gaping at him with her eyes wide.

"And it's true; I'm not unsettled by you," he said. "But I can't help you."

Her eyes widened even more. "Why not? You don't want to be king of Pryam?"

"I don't even want to be king of Rael."

He saw his words sink in, and the devastation his answer brought. He pitied her, but there was nothing he could do. He was struggling to rebuild Rael; he couldn't take on another kingdom that needed support. "I'm sorry," he said.

He nodded to Everan and Kord, who helped him move the lid of the sarcophagus back into place. Then he started back up the narrow stairwell.

"Where are you going?" she cried.

"Back to Rael."

In his chamber on the ship, Cyrus lay on the mattress made of layers of wool and down. It would be another night of no sleep, he was sure. This trip had been a massive failure and a waste of time. They'd set sail in the morning, back to Rael, where he'd tell his council that he had not, in fact, secured an alliance with a child of a crumbling kingdom.

Commotion outside his door pulled him from the bed. Bash's voice carried through, not yelling but forceful. Then came a rush of footfalls. When Cyrus opened the door, he took a step back in surprise to see the girl, and Ram and Bash trying to hold her back without actually touching her.

"It's all right," Cyrus told them. His brow stitched as he looked at the girl. "Princess"—what was her name?—"Myrel," he said, half greeting, half questioning.

"Miriel," she corrected him, and she pushed inside.

His mind hadn't quite recovered from the surprise enough to stop her.

"What are you doing here?" he asked.

Her lips were pursed and firm. "I need to talk to you."

Cyrus glanced out at the gathered men, who wore faces of equal exasperation. Then he looked back at the girl. There was something different about her—a look of determination. *Fine*—he could at least have a conversation with her. He let go of the door and it swung closed, but as he turned, he found her pulling the straps of her dress off her shoulders.

"Oh, wait, no." He quickly stepped forward and scooped them back into place. "Let's just leave those right there." He realized his fingers were now touching her skin, and he flattened his hand, turning his touch into an awkward pat.

Her lip trembled, and her eyes welled.

"Mariam..."

"Miriel," she corrected him again.

"Miriel." He drew in a sharp breath. "You are... a very beautiful girl. But I..." He struggled for words.

"I screwed it up, didn't I?" she cried.

He stopped. "What?"

A tear spilled down her cheek. "If I'd just been honest with you right away, instead of lying. I just didn't know how to tell you. I thought if we got to know each other a little better first—"

"Look," he interrupted her. "The truth is, it wouldn't have gone well with your father either."

Her eyes widened with dismay.

"I came here because I thought you had an army I could use," he said. "And you don't."

She quieted. "Oh."

"I'm struggling to rebuild Rael, and soon, I'll move against Serra and the Shadowlands. I have neither men nor resources nor time to spare. So, you see—I can't help you."

She swayed and lowered herself to sit in the side chair nearby. "What am I supposed to do?" she whispered.

He sighed and shook his head. "I don't know. Where is your mother?"

The girl quieted, and she shifted her eyes to the floor. "My father exiled her." There was a long pause before she added, "After she tried to kill me. She said there was an evil inside me."

Cyrus froze. Cold rippled over his skin. Those words...

"It was several years ago," she said, "when I first started showing signs of my ability. She tried to get Amish to do it—to throw me from the south cliffs into the sea."

The weight in his chest threatened to crush him.

Her eyes welled, and her lip trembled. "I was lucky it was Amish she asked. So many others wouldn't have hesitated. The thought still gives me nightmares."

Cyrus couldn't speak.

"But you know what's worst of all?" Tears spilled down her cheeks now. "I begged my father to forgive her, to let her stay. But she said she'd rather be exiled. Even as she was leaving, I cried for her to come back." The girl lifted her red-rimmed eyes to him. "Even after what she did, I still didn't want her to leave me." Her voice dropped to a whisper. "How shameful is that?"

Cyrus still couldn't speak. He knew that shame.

"Do you have any other family?" he asked finally.

She shook her head. "No. Do you have family?"

He was quiet for a moment. "I have a brother." He wasn't sure why he told her that.

"Are you close with him?"

"I'm going to kill him when I see him again."

"Oh," she whispered. "So, no."

Cyrus didn't want to talk about this anymore. "Why did you get expelled from the Union?"

"My father wouldn't tell me." She bit her bottom lip. "But I know why. It's because of me."

His brow stitched. "Because of you?"

"After what happened with my mother, my father reduced the staff to only those he trusted—those most loyal," she said. "They're who remain now. I fortified their numbers with illusion to try to keep us all safe, but it didn't quite go as I'd planned. People thought I'd raised an army of demons." She nervously rolled the edges of her golden sash between her fingers. "But I can't take the illusion away now, and it's only a matter of time before the trick is discovered. Then they'll come for me. If not the Etrean Union, then my own people."

"I won't let that happen." The words spilled from his mouth before he could even consider what they meant.

She gaped at him as she jumped up from the chair. "You'll wed me, then?"

Cyrus shook his head. "Oh, gods no."

Her face fell, and she swallowed, a deep crimson of embarrassment flooding her cheeks.

He hadn't meant to insult her. "I would be a terrible husband," he added quickly. "The absolute worst. And I'm almost twice your age."

"That's not uncommon."

He grimaced. "It should be."

She just stared at him with her doe eyes.

"Anyway," he said, taking a step back and putting more space between them, "I'd be gone. All the time."

"Where?"

He paused. Where?

...

"Places. And Rael is terrible too. It's fucking hot. And people are still trying to kill one another."

Mariel's face fell. "Oh."

"But we don't have to be wed to be friends," he told her.

She pulled her bottom lip between her teeth. "Well, how will this work?"

Cyrus pursed his own lips. "I don't know yet. But I'll figure something out."

"You'll stay for a while, then?"

He sighed. "A little while, I suppose." Until he could figure out what exactly he was promising.

A grin spread across her face. "Then come back to the palace. You'll love it, I know you will!"

Cyrus certainly didn't think he'd love it, but he also didn't expect to hate it. And her face was filled with genuine excitement. He sighed again and opened the door. "Get Everan," he called.

Everan was in the room within moments.

"We're going back to the palace with Princess Miriam," Cyrus told him.

"Miriel," she said.

He was really going to have to remember her name. "Princess Miriel," he corrected himself.

Everan gave a quiet sigh of complete unsurprise, then left to gather everyone to head back to the palace.

Cyrus led his men off the ship, following the girl. This girl who needed him.

CHAPTER FORTY-SIX

The sound of insects filled the night. Cyrus should have been in bed, but he knew he wouldn't sleep. So instead, he sat in the oversize chair in the oversize royal guest room, mulling the oversize mess of a situation he now found himself in—promising to help this girl when he had no plan how and no resource to do so. How had he let himself get pulled into this?

He knew how—with her story that rang so similar to his. Her words, her shame, her fear.

And now he was committed.

His council would be disappointed. More than disappointed. But they could add it to the long list of disappointments he was curating for them.

Cyrus pushed out a long breath.

A soft knock on the door tore him from his thoughts.

He jerked his head up. Did he really just hear a knock? It was the middle of the night...

The knock came again.

Cyrus rose, pulling his sword, although he suspected he didn't need it—he was fairly sure of who might be visiting him at this hour.

And he was right.

As he opened the door, he found the princess staring back at him with a lantern in her hand.

"I couldn't sleep," she said, and she brushed past him into the room.

He gave a small snort. "So, you'll see to it I don't either?"

She popped around, her eyes wide. "Did I wake you?"

Cyrus leaned his sword back against the wall. "No."

She smiled as she set the lantern down. "Oh, good. I didn't think I had. I mean, you don't look like you sleep." Her eyes darted over him with a slight flicker of judgment. "Ever."

That didn't sound like a compliment.

"I don't either," she said, her voice quieter now. She sat on the small settee by the window.

His brow drew down deeper. *Make yourself at home.* Well, he supposed it was technically her home.

"I can't sleep when I'm scared," she chattered on, "which is... most of the time."

Cyrus felt for her. She really was just a child. "Are you scared now?"

She paused, rolling the cross trim of her dress between her fingers. "Well, not *right* now, but for what happens after you do whatever it is you're going to do."

"You don't even know what I'm planning."

"Do you?"

She'd meant it as a genuine question, but it came as a slight insult, because he had no idea what he was going to do yet.

Her eyes stayed on him, probably because no one had ever taught her that it was rude to stare. He didn't mind, so long as she didn't try to take her clothes off again.

Cyrus crossed his arms and leaned back against a pillar inset into the wall.

She cocked her head, still studying him. "Amish says you're a seer."

"How does Amish know?"

She shrugged. "He knows lots of things. So, are you?"

He was still coming to terms with it. "I suppose I am."

"What does that mean? What can you do?"

He thought the title was self-explanatory. "I see visions. Of the future."

She raised a brow. "What's my future?"

"It doesn't work like that. I can't control what I see."

"So, you just get inundated with random visions of things?"

"Well, not inundated. They come when they want to. Sometimes." He cleared his throat.

"Oh." She frowned.

All his life, this curse had been overwhelmingly too much. Now, somehow, it seemed not enough. "I can travel into the minds of others, when my blood touches their skin."

She leaned forward on the settee, perking up. "Can you take over someone's mind?"

"Well, no. But I can talk to them and show them the visions I see."

"The visions that have come only a couple times?"

He wet his bottom lip. Why was this bothering him so much? "Yeah."

Her nose crinkled slightly. "Is that all?"

"I *can* take over the minds of *animals*." He cursed himself under his breath. Why did he even share that with her? It wasn't even *his* power—it was the power he had access to through Essandra. He cursed again. He didn't have to impress this girl. Although, here he was, feeling pressure to do just that.

Her eyes widened. "Really? Like how? You talk to them?"

"Well, not exactly."

Her smile faded. "Oh. What, then?"

"With my blood, I can travel into their minds, see through their eyes, and take control."

"So, what do you make them do?"

He stood, stumped for a moment. "Nothing really. I mean, the only animal I need already obeys me—a horse. What other uses would I have?"

Her mouth popped open as she sat up abruptly and flopped her hands onto her lap. "What uses?" She scoffed. "The possibilities are endless!" She sighed as she sank back against the settee again and smiled dreamily. "You want to know what I would do if I were you?"

He didn't, but he had a feeling she was going to tell him anyway.

"I'd bewitch the birds." She stretched her arms out like wings. "I've always wanted to know what it was like to fly. Can you imagine? If I could see through their eyes, it would be like I was with them, looking down on the world. Exploring, seeing everything there is to see." She gave a small giggle. "Spying, even."

Cyrus stilled. *Birds.* He stared at the girl. "That's... actually a really good idea," he said finally.

Her eyes widened. "Are you going to try it?"

"I think I will."

She grinned with a clap of her hands. "I want to see!"

"I'll think about it." But he had no intention of thinking about it, because he had no intention of letting her see him try. He didn't want an audience. It was bad enough to struggle with his ability in front of Essandra. Now a girl? No.

"What else can you do?" she asked.

"That's it," he resigned. "The truth is, Essandra is the one with true power."

She straightened and rocked forward again, her small hands now at her sides with her fingers pinching the edge of the settee cushion. "That's your witch?"

"I can't call her mine, but yes."

"Is she a powerful witch?"

"Very powerful. And beautiful." He hadn't meant to add that last part.

Her large eyes didn't blink. Cyrus suspected this was really what the girl wanted—to hear about someone like her. It was what Cyrus would have wanted, what he did want, and still wanted...

"What can she do?" the girl asked eagerly.

"Well, she has a coven, and they bond their powers so they can share them. This gives her many abilities."

"Illusion?" She leaned forward even farther. Cyrus half expected her to topple off the seat.

He nodded. "Yes. That's one."

"That's how you figured me out."

He nodded again. "It is, although, I have to say—you're quite powerful yourself. How are you able to project so many men, in all their detail?"

The girl beamed. Cyrus was fairly certain she'd never felt her ability appreciated, much less heard it complimented.

"Well, I don't have to imagine each one," she told him. "I just imagine a few, then replicate that. And it's also easier when I have someone to copy. I usually use Amish and whichever guards are with him."

Cyrus couldn't help a small smile. How clever.

The girl let herself relax a bit. Then she asked, "Have you decided what we'll do yet?"

We. Like they were in this together. He supposed they were now, with his commitment. Cyrus sighed. He'd hoped to have had more than a couple of hours to come up with a plan.

"I haven't figured it all out yet," he said. "We have to announce your father's death and see to your coronation. Once you're queen—"

"Wait… I can't be queen!" She jumped from the settee as if this were the first time she'd heard of such a concept.

He stared at her with a stitch in his brow. "Well, that's typically what being a princess leads to."

"I mean, I'm not ready!"

That, he could relate to. "I don't think anyone ever is."

"But I don't know what I'm doing!"

"I don't either."

She stopped and gaped at him in surprise.

"Half the time, I'm struggling just to rebuild the kingdom and feed my people," he told her, "and the other half, I'm fighting the nobles, who are trying to take back control, or debating with my council, who rarely approve of my decisions. And I can assure you they certainly won't approve of what I'm doing here now—committing resources to a kingdom and gaining no army for it."

She slowly sank back onto the settee. Her eyes drifted, traveling around her but not actually looking at anything. What he'd said upset her, but it was a harsh truth—

"Your people are hungry?" she asked, her voice barely above a whisper.

That wasn't what he thought she'd catch on, but perhaps it was a challenge for her as well.

"They are," he admitted. "Rael doesn't have the climate for farming. The coven has hedge witches, which help, but even they have limits on expediting harvest. Then add the challenge of escaped slaves from surrounding kingdoms arriving every day, seeking refuge. The number of mouths to feed continues to grow, while our provisions... don't."

Slowly, her eyes rose to meet his. "We have rice. Lots of it."

Cyrus stilled. "From the Shadowlands?"

She shook her head. "From the Horseman tribes. They use our ships to trade across the seas and get their heavy stock from the Emerald Isles. In exchange, they give us rice."

He narrowed his eyes. That didn't sound right. "The Horsemen breed their own horses."

"Their standard stock, yes, but not their destriers that they trade with the world." Her eyes widened, hopeful. "We have more food than we need—you can have it. Will that please your council?"

It wouldn't *displease* them, which would be a nice change. And there was something else he could use...

"Would Pryam also welcome slave refugees?" he asked.

"Of course!" Her face sobered. "Many people have left these past several months."

He nodded slowly as the plan formed. "Then I'll train men and send them to join your army and your guard. In return, you'll supply Rael with rice and take some of our refugees."

"What about the Etrean Union? If they come for me—"

"I told you; I won't let that happen."

Relief washed over her face. He almost thought she might hug him, and he shifted away to dissuade her.

"We'll finalize everything tomorrow," he said. "But now, we both should get some sleep."

She nodded, standing, and moved to the door. Turning back, she said, "I know you said you'd make a terrible husband, but I think you make a really good friend." Then she gave him a soft smile and slipped out of the room.

He wasn't sure he could afford to be a friend. But what was the worst that could happen?

CHAPTER FORTY-SEVEN

When he'd first arrived, Cyrus had expected to spend a day in Pryam. It had now been a little over two weeks. He'd stood by Miriel's side as she announced the passing of her father, and he'd stayed by her side before the masses of the throne room as the crown was placed atop her head. Her doe eyes were constantly on him, looking for reassurance. He'd nod, and at times, even found himself moving closer.

She'd smile.

He liked her smile—so full of innocence. He told himself he wasn't getting attached to this girl, but he knew he'd fight to protect that innocence.

Cyrus spent a lot of time with Amish, who he found to be a loyal and respectable man. What was not respectable, however, was Amish's skill with a sword. Miriel had said Amish had been her father's personal guard and friend. The description of *guard* was generous, and Cyrus assumed him to have been more of a friend and an adviser, committed to her protection rather than actually *able* to keep her protected. He'd continue to be a good supporter for Miriel, but to help Amish, Cyrus charged Bash as the princess's personal guard and put under him a little more than a hundred men, about half the number Cyrus had brought with him. Pryam had a royal guard, but only a mere twenty-four men. Bash would keep Miriel safe until they established a more robust palace unit.

Cyrus assigned Kord to evaluate Pryam's defensive resources and see what they had to work with, and to determine what else needed to be built. Kord would also stay in Pryam until they established a structure Cyrus was confident in.

Satisfied, at least for the time being, Cyrus could return to Rael.

He stood on the docks as his men prepared their ship to depart. Three additional ships would come with them, laden with rice. They'd be the first of many. Cyrus was grateful he'd be returning with something to offset the hundred-plus men he was leaving in Pryam, and the many more he'd committed to sending.

White flashed in the corner of his eye, and he looked to find Miriel walking toward him, her long dress billowing with the light breeze.

"I wish you didn't have to go," she said when she reached him.

He almost said he wished the same, but he'd be lying, so he didn't. The truth was, he was eager to get back to Rael. But he'd also be lying if he said he hadn't come to care about this girl. Essandra would love her. That sparked a thought.

"Miriel," he said, "when things are settled here, and you can get away for just a little while, I'd like for you to come to Rael and spend some time with Essandra. She'd love to meet you, and I think she can help you."

A smile lit her face. "I'd like that."

He smiled back. "I'm glad that you wrote to me."

Her eyes glistened. "I'm glad that you came." She snaked her arms around him and pulled him into a tight embrace. Cyrus stiffened, but he didn't stop her. He couldn't remember the last time someone had hugged him. He'd held others, comforting them in their grief and their defeat. But the last time he'd felt the affection of an embrace freely given... He couldn't remember, yet he remembered the feelings that came with it—warmth, care. Happiness.

A bell rang through the air, giving notice that it was time to depart.

She released him and took a small step back. "Thank you, Cyrus. For everything."

He quickly blinked away the emotion in his eyes. "Goodbye, Miriel." His gaze shifted to Bash, who stood behind her. "Remember your charge," Cyrus told him.

Bash gave a small bow of his head. "I'll keep her safe."

Cyrus nodded. He knew he would. Giving one last look to Miriel, he turned and strode up the gangway to the deck.

Everan and the men that Cyrus was taking back with him had already boarded. Cyrus joined them on the bow, where he came to a rapid halt when he noticed four large square cages, stacked on top of one another, filled with birds.

His brow creased. "What's this?" he asked.

"A departing gift," Everan told him. "From the new queen of Pryam."

He pulled the sealed note that was tied to one of the cages and opened it to find Miriel's words.

I'd wager these will show you more than your visions. When I see you again, you will have to tell me what it's like to fly.

Journey safely back to Rael. You take my love and friendship with you.

Miriel

Cyrus shot his gaze back to the dock where Miriel stood. She waved with a large grin on her face. He couldn't help a smile in return. She watched as the ships were pulled through the harbor, until Cyrus lost sight of her.

Then he set his eyes on the open sea. For Rael.

Sailing into the main port of Rael brought a feeling Cyrus hadn't expected—one of coming home. It had only been a little less than three weeks that he'd been gone, but he found himself eager to get back. He couldn't deny some of that eagerness was to see Essandra again, although he doubted she'd given him more than a single thought in his absence. He was a little worried she might not be there at all. She'd said she'd stay until she figured out the spell to bring back her family, but he wasn't sure if that had changed.

He also couldn't deny the small weight of worry about what else he might be returning to. The last time he'd left Rael, the nobles had tried to retake the capital. While he'd trusted the council to run things in his absence, Cyrus had tasked Hephain and Brant to oversee the safety of the kingdom—Hephain to keep the capital, Brant to manage the protection of the rest. In the arena, Brant had been the lead of House Akim and a gold-tier fighter. Men respected him, and Cyrus trusted him. Eventually, Cyrus would probably send Brant to take Kord's place in Pryam.

Cyrus rubbed his temples. At sea, he'd taken the opportunity to try his ability with the birds. He'd brushed them with a smear of blood and set them to the sky. And it had been one of the most incredible things he'd ever experienced. Not only could he see through their eyes, but he could also somewhat control them. He wasn't sure if that was his own ability, or something that lingered from Essandra's power. Regardless, it was an asset that he was sure would prove useful. However, it had also left him with a crippling ache his head, and he'd spent the remaining time trying to sleep off its effects. But the rising sun found him standing at the bow of the ship as they pulled into the harbor.

His headache ebbed slightly when he saw Brant standing on the pier. Cyrus let his shoulders relax. The fact that Brant was standing alone, his sword sheathed, at least meant the kingdom wasn't falling apart.

As he made his way down onto the dock, Brant met him with a smile. "Welcome back," he said.

They clasped arms. "Things are well, it seems," Cyrus said.

Brant nodded. "The nobles made another move, but Ryman stopped them before they even reached the hills. We didn't lose anything, nor was anyone injured. I think they're testing us."

Cyrus pushed out an irritated breath but nodded. "Good work." He was glad to have the Lycus House lead managing the men on the east side. Ryman was on top of things, but these nobles were proving to be a problem that likely wasn't going to go away.

"I brought horses," Brant said, and he led him to two waiting mounts. They took to the saddles and urged the animals toward the palace.

"Do you want me to call together the council?" Brant asked as they reached the front courtyard.

"Yes, shortly." He needed to do something first. "Is Essandra here?"

"I don't know. I've spent hardly any time here—I just came by this morning to check in with Hephain before I went to the port."

"Assemble the council," Cyrus said. "Tell them I'll be there in a moment."

Brant nodded, and Cyrus struck off for Essandra's workroom. He silently prayed that she hadn't left.

As he turned down her hall, relief rippled through him to see her walking toward him.

They both stopped as they reached each other.

But instead of the greeting he'd been expecting, she delivered a sharp slap across his cheek. "Where were you!" she demanded.

The force wrenched his head, but he caught himself. Confusion flooded him. "You knew I was going to Pryam—"

"For *weeks*? You were supposed to be back within *days*. And you left without even saying anything! Anything at all!"

"I told you I was leaving!"

She turned from him and wiped her face with her hand.

He honestly hadn't expected her to be angry. Or upset. At all. He also hadn't expected his absence to bother her so much.

"Essandra," he said softly. "I'm sorry. I should have sent word. I should have returned sooner. It's just that there was a lot—"

Rapid footfalls came behind him, and he turned to see several members of his council hurrying toward them.

"King Cyrus!" Fatim called. "So glad to have you back!"

Essandra quickly wiped her face again and resumed her countenance of cold perfection.

"You were in Pryam much longer than we expected," Verin said.

Cyrus nodded. "It was longer than I expected too."

"And Princess Miriel—"

"Queen Miriel, now," Cyrus corrected him.

Essandra stilled, her stare snapping to him with an expression he couldn't read.

The councilmen erupted with clapping.

"Sire!" Verin exclaimed. "We thought there was a possibility you might come back wed, but we weren't—"

"Excuse me," Essandra mumbled, and slipped away down the hall.

"Essandra," he called, "wait." But she didn't.

He moved to follow her—

"Let's go to the council room," Verin said as the councilmen surrounded him. "Tell us everything."

Cyrus looked around for Essandra. But she was gone.

He lingered for a breath longer, then turned back toward the council.

He'd come back with an alliance...

But he couldn't help but feel it had cost something far more valuable.

CHAPTER FORTY-EIGHT

They swept him toward the council room like an ocean tide. Cyrus let himself be pulled into the chamber, where Everan, Kord, and Brant had also made it.

"I'm surprised that with you now wed, you didn't bring her back with you," Verin said.

"Wed?" Cyrus stopped abruptly. "Oh, I didn't marry her. Morak's dead. In fact, that's why I stayed so long, to see her properly set up. But we're... not wed. Nor will we be."

The councilmen all paused, their brows dipping and their mouths open. And Cyrus set to explaining. It was well into evening by the time he'd recounted everything that had happened, from the awkward arrival, to finding out about Morak, to the agreement he'd made with Miriel for rice and his plan to help her and Pryam. He left out her advances—desperation should be private.

The council was happy to hear of the rice shipments, but they weren't happy about Cyrus's promise of men and protection or about Pryam's expulsion from the Union.

Lomas, his master of public works, sighed. "We haven't even fortified Rael and we're already committing ourselves to another kingdom that has its own troubles."

"But is that not what an alliance is?" Cyrus argued. "Is it not what I would have done under a marriage arrangement?"

"Well without a marriage, it's a shaky alliance at best."

"So, what are you upset about?" Cyrus challenged. "That I committed us to another kingdom or that I haven't committed us enough?"

"Fair, Sire," Lomas said, "but we're just reacting to the news. We were under the impression that Pryam was in a different circumstance. Now we're committed to a kingdom who can't come to our aid when we need it."

Cyrus folded his arms. "What do you think supplying food is? That's the greatest aid we need right now."

Verin nodded. "Very true," he admitted. He looked around at the other councilmen. "We should consider this a successful venture. We've built an alliance of friendship with Pryam, bolstering our provisions and helping feed our people, and we're still in position to secure alliances with other kingdoms."

"Speaking of other alliances..." Fatim pulled a letter from his robe pocket and held it for Cyrus.

Cyrus immediately recognized the king of Japheth's green seal. He almost rolled his eyes. This man again. Cyrus hadn't responded to his previous letter. A man of pride wouldn't have pursued him.

"He's said to have a beautiful niece," Fatim said.

"Is that all you ever observe about potential marriage prospects?" Ruth cut in.

Fatim quieted.

Cyrus snorted. His magistrate didn't speak often, but when she did, Cyrus loved it. "A niece, huh?" he questioned. "Of the man who killed one brother and is at war with the other?"

"A niece on his wife's side," Verin said.

This time, Cyrus did roll his eyes. "Has Pryam not shown you that I'm not motivated by marriage? It's merely a means to an end."

"Sire, Japheth is not a kingdom to be ignored. At least read it."

Cyrus took the letter, breaking the seal, and skimmed the words.

King Cyrus,

I know the initial weight of the crown is both overwhelming and all-consuming of one's precious time, both night and day.

Cyrus wasn't sure if that was an underhanded jab or if Gregor was offering an excuse for his lack of response in effort to continue to pursue talk between them.

I'm unsure if my previous letter reached your hands.

A lie.

If it did, it grieves me to think my previous missive may have failed to capture the full extent of my admiration and respect for all that you have accomplished in Rael. Your reputation now precedes you and casts a luminous glow on what I'm sure will be a long and prosperous reign.

It wasn't a jab earlier, Cyrus realized, but a willful overlook and complete forgiveness of Cyrus's slight. Perhaps Gregor needed this alliance more than he did.

If, by misfortune, my letter did not reach you, let me reiterate the profound honor a potential friendship between our two kingdoms would be. Your Majesty would bring unparalleled insights and perspectives, which will, without question, serve to enlighten our shared path forward.

More flattery. Cyrus skipped to the bottom.

I would happily pay a visit to Rael, which I'm sure, under your sovereignty, has become even more glorious than when I last visited.

Cyrus glanced out the window at the toppled administrative offices that had been destroyed during the rebellion. They'd fix those. Eventually. He looked back at the letter.

I eagerly await your reply.

Signed, *Gregor the Lion, king of Japheth, king of Hetahl...*

Cyrus tossed the letter onto the table for his councilmen to read. "This man reeks of desperation."

"Rich desperation," Verin added. "Do you know how much money Japheth has?"

He didn't. Nor did he particularly care. Something didn't feel right about Gregor, and Cyrus wanted no part of him.

"Cyrus," Everan said, "this is how you break the Shadow King's alliance. It's not about what you stand to gain here. It's about what the Shadow King stands to lose—what you can take from him."

Cyrus's lips tightened. It did annoy him how often Everan was right sometimes. "Fine. Write this: *King Gregor. I appreciate your offer of friendship.*"

Verin scribbled the words quickly, pausing when he finished, then stared up at him. "Is that all?"

Cyrus's eyes traveled the table to see all the councilmen looking at him, expecting more. He sighed. "Add: *I'll consider it.*"

Verin's mouth formed as though to speak, but he remained silent.

Fatim cut in. "Sire, might I suggest something a little more approachable and amicable to meeting?"

Cyrus could read the room. He waved a dismissive hand as he stood. "Everan, work with him on something better. Make it sound like something I would say."

The corner of Everan's mouth hinted at a smile. "I think the key is to make it *not* sound like something you would say."

Small gusts of wind broke the heat, although any reprieve was erased by the abrasive sand they carried. The sun sat low on the horizon, and Cyrus prayed it would hurry and dip below. After three weeks gone, he'd almost forgotten how hot this forsaken kingdom could get. But he wasn't thinking about the heat now. He'd spotted Essandra in the sparring field, practicing sword work with her guardsman, Aaron. It was a surprise that had brought a smile to his face. He'd wanted her to learn the sword, but she'd been adamantly against it. He didn't like that she relied purely on magic—he didn't trust magic, but he did trust a blade, and he was pleased to finally see her using one. And by the looks of it, this wasn't her first lesson.

He was glad he'd found her, though. They hadn't had an opportunity to catch up. And he was curious if there were any further developments with the assassins.

As he approached, Essandra broke from her spar, and both she and Aaron paused. It felt like a lifetime since Cyrus had used his sword. *Really* used it. He pulled the blade from his back scabbard and gave her a mischievous smile.

Essandra didn't smile back. He nodded at Aaron, who bowed to let Cyrus take over. Cyrus contemplated whether he should ask if he could impose but then decided if she really didn't want him here, she'd let him know pretty quickly.

He stepped forward with an easy swing, testing her, and she stepped back.

Her eyes narrowed. Then, she moved forward, cutting in with her sword. He mildly swung a counterstrike and stepped out.

"Is that all you have?" he teased.

Her face was hard. Was she still angry? Had his apology not settled her even slightly?

She tightened her hand around the hilt of her sword, and her lips thinned. She was no match for him with a blade, but he wasn't trying to beat her.

They circled for a moment, each waiting for the other. Her eyes sized him up. Then she lunged forward, not holding her attack. He fought defensively as she took ground—she actually fought pretty well, but she still had a lot to learn. He pivoted with a series of offensive counters, now pushing her back. The flurry of their weapons sliced through the morning air. He pushed her back farther, but as they almost reached the railing, he eased off, offering her a breath. Cyrus smiled, but she only reciprocated an icy gaze.

She *was* still angry.

Essandra held her sword in front of her and brought her other hand up to its hilt, then she pulled a second blade from it—turning one sword into two.

Now *that* was a trick he needed to learn.

She attacked. She swept the two swords in unison, trying to take ground back with a fury. He could feel her anger, the heat radiating off her. It made her sloppy. He easily parried, thwarting her strikes.

He couldn't help a laugh.

But she wasn't laughing. She hit him with a burst of power, almost dropping him to the ground, and launched a full-fledged attack.

A real attack.

His body switched to defense. He met one blade with a force that almost knocked it from her hand, but her second blade sliced upward from below and skimmed his face, splitting open his left cheek and narrowly missing his eye.

Cyrus stumbled back in surprise. He reached up to touch his cheek and pulled his hand away dripping with blood. His nostrils flared, his smile gone. Her eyes blazed back at him. He wasn't sure if she'd intended to do that, although she didn't seem to have intended *not* to. What was wrong with this woman?

Essandra stood, her chest heaving, her hair wild in the wind around her. She shoved both swords into Aaron's hands, apparently finished now, and whirled back toward the palace.

"Essandra!" Cyrus called after her.

Of course she didn't wait.

He flung his own blade, lancing it into the ground, and stormed after her. "Essandra!"

She still didn't stop.

He quickened his stride and caught up to her just as she stepped inside the palace. "Essandra!" He grabbed her arm and stopped her to face him.

She shoved him back. "Get off me!"

"I said I was sorry!"

"Well, it's not my job to make you feel better about your failings anymore, it's Miriel's!"

He stopped abruptly. Miriel's? His brow dropped. "Why would it be Miriel's?"

She turned away from him and fixed her gaze out the window of the small sitting room they'd nearly overturned.

"Why would you say it's Miriel's?" he asked again, softer this time, as he stepped closer.

"She's your wife now," she said shortly.

"My wife?" He shook his head. "I didn't marry Miriel."

Her head snapped back to him as her eyes locked with his, and she stared at him for a moment. Her lips parted. "You didn't?"

"I told you; she's a child. I saw to her coronation. I helped—"

He stopped. He hadn't told her; he'd told his council. And Essandra hadn't been there. "Wait, are you angry because you thought I married her?"

She scoffed. "Of course not." She swallowed.

"But that's what I went to do, or at least to discuss."

"I know, and I said I wasn't."

She *was* angry, though. It was written all over her face, all over her body. On the lips he wanted to kiss, in the hair he wanted to touch. All over her flamed a fire that threatened to burn him.

And damned if he wouldn't let her.

Cyrus found himself being shoved backward into a chair. Essandra clawed at his belt as she climbed on top of him and straddled him. He wasn't exactly sure what was happening, but he didn't stop her. Did she want to hurt him? Was she trying to take him? When she pulled his cock free from his leathers and sank down onto him, he was beyond asking. He didn't care—whatever this woman wanted, she could have it.

She took him deep, shifting to angle him how she needed him. His hips rolled to meet her, but she tightened her hold, pinning him. She had more control over his body than he did.

Her skin burned like fire. He pushed his hands up her thighs under her dress but then stopped. Even in the thick of the chaos of her, he knew the rules. He simply let his head fall back as she settled into her rhythm.

Slow and deep, she took him, rubbing herself against him with each drop downward. Everything about her drove him closer to the edge—the look of her, the smell of her, the feel of her. The sound of her breaths. His mouth hungered for her, and it was all he could do not to devour her.

Her body blazed hotter. She clasped his shoulders and rocked faster. Cyrus struggled for control, trying not to lose himself. Sweat beaded them both. He wanted to lick it from her skin.

Harder still, she ground into him. She dropped her head, their cheeks touching, her mouth so close to his. The warmth of her breaths dusted his ear. He couldn't help himself, and he turned, needing her kiss.

But she clasped his jaw, keeping him. The bond snapped into place as his blood on his face touched her skin, but she didn't allow him inside her mind. She denied him. She denied him everything. She held her lips over his, not touching, allowing him nothing. Only taking more from him, and more, and more.

Until she shattered.

She tightened around him, arching her back and gripping him between her thighs, pulsing and shaking. Then she stilled, gasping in release.

Two more thrusts and he'd join her.

But she pulled herself from him and stood.

Cyrus jerked his head up. "Wait," he panted. A stitch cramped his brow. "Are you leaving? Where are you—"

"You should know that I freed the assassins," she said, still breathless as she reached under her skirts, fixing her undergarments before smoothing out her dress.

He gaped up at her, his mind in a fog, his chest still heaving. "What?"

"And sorry about your face," she added shortly. With that, she turned and left him.

Cyrus stared at the empty doorway she'd disappeared through, his leathers still open, his body still begging for her.

This woman. This woman was going to be the death of him.

CHAPTER FORTY-NINE

Teron washed the last of the blood from his hands in the basin, then dried them with a towel.

Cyrus looked at himself in the mirror under the candlelight. It had taken Teron a few hours, but there was no sign of the gash that had split his cheek below his eye.

"You have to be more careful," Teron had chastised him through the healing. "I can't bring back an eye."

Cyrus was well aware of Teron's limits—limits that he'd pushed many times through the years. And here, in the darkness of night, receiving Teron's healing touch, it almost felt like they were back at the villa again.

The healer sank into his chair in the corner of the room, and Cyrus knew he felt it too.

Looking at him in the reflection, he asked, "Are you all right?"

The man waved off his concern. "I'm getting old, that's all."

"You're not that old." Cyrus started washing the blood from his face.

Teron gave a faint scoff. "I'm eighty-three. I'm probably older than everyone else in this kingdom." He grew quiet for a moment. "I don't have much time left. I'm glad I got to see you rise. I only wish I could stay longer to watch how you grow."

Cyrus stilled in the mirror, his eyes still on Teron. The thought stung him. Teron was more than a healer, more than a friend. He was family. Cyrus turned. "Don't say things like that. You're going to live longer than me, old man."

The sun had barely risen, and Cyrus was already bothered. Jaem had called him through the blood bond. Bravat still refused to return. He refused to even talk to Cyrus, and Cyrus was beyond trying to get him back to Rael and was now more of the mind to just figure out a way to kill him. He'd briefly thought of tasking Jaem, but Bravat was a more skilled fighter. The risk to Jaem was too great. Still, if Cyrus couldn't figure something else out, he might not have a choice.

Cyrus was even more bothered by the news that followed. The Mercian queen was in the Shadowlands. Apparently, she'd been there since her wedding.

He'd already judged her for marrying the Shadow King and had written her off accordingly, but for her to stay in the Shadowlands—to *choose* to live there—meant it might be beyond a political arrangement. He wasn't sure why this bothered him so much. Perhaps something made him still want to believe that she'd married this monster out of some extreme necessity. Perhaps he wanted to believe that she was better than this—that *Mercia* was better than this. Or maybe it was because Cyrus wanted to strip the Shadow King of everything he had, but instead the fiend seemed to be building more.

Perhaps Cyrus was annoyed that he needed to expand his list of fated enemies. But he would need to be careful. He couldn't commit to yet another war with another kingdom, especially a kingdom that his people didn't see as an enemy.

Cyrus's footsteps echoed in the halls as he made his way toward the council room. What irritated him even more were these damned council meetings. He'd spent nearly the whole day prior with his council, and somehow, they needed to meet yet *again* today. And coming on the heels of... whatever that was that had happened with Essandra the night before... his mind still reeled. He needed to talk to her, although he wouldn't get the chance until after this cursed council meeting.

When he rounded the corner, he saw her. Essandra.

And his chest tightened even more at the sight of the lead assassin standing beside her.

Orion. He had lost the short beard and was now clean-shaven, but Cyrus recognized him. He recognized the hair of copper mixed with blond, the steely gray eyes, the lithe build of a deadly assassin—one Cyrus had incensed and who was now freely roaming his kingdom.

Orion let his head drop, almost in a bow, but kept his steely eyes on Cyrus as he approached. It felt like a challenge under the guise of respect.

Cyrus returned a piercing glare. "I thought you said you let them go, and they left," he said angrily to Essandra when he reached her, not taking his eyes off the assassin.

She stiffened. She didn't appreciate his tone, but he didn't care.

"No, I said I freed them. I must have forgotten to mention I also told them they could stay in Rael."

Cyrus's hand dropped to the hilt of his sword. They should have left when they'd had the chance.

"Good morning, Sire," one of his councilmen called as a small group of them shuffled toward him. They slowly came to a stop as they sensed something amiss.

"Is everything all right?" Verin asked.

Everything wasn't all right. Not even close.

Essandra nodded to Orion. "I'll find you when we're done," she told him, dismissing him. She turned to the councilmen. "Everything's fine," she said.

But tension hung heavy in the air.

Orion glanced at Essandra, then back to Cyrus. He said nothing. He only backed away slowly before turning and leaving the hall.

Cyrus's eyes bore into the departing assassin as the councilmen shuffled warily past into the adjoining room. He caught Essandra before she could follow.

"So not only did you let them out, but you let them stay," he said between his teeth.

She wrenched her arm from his grasp. "Where else would they go?"

"Literally anywhere. They were so desperate to leave."

"They had no choice before, but now they do. And they have skills—we could have a use for them."

"I've already said I don't need them."

She crossed her arms and pursed her lips. "That was before you committed to giving half our men to another kingdom."

"It wasn't half."

Her emerald eyes blazed. She wasn't backing down. Did she really think keeping the assassins around was a good idea? And trusting them to protect her secret? They shouldn't be free; they should be dead.

"You think you can trust them? With what they know?" Anger flushed his skin. "And what—they so willingly pledge themselves now? To help us against Serra? Against the Shadow King?"

"Not if you keep acting like this," she snapped. "But who do you think sold them to the Jackals to begin with? It was the Shadow King."

He shifted back. The Shadow King had sold men to the Jackals? Even so, that didn't mean they could be trusted.

Essandra turned and headed into the council room.

Cyrus pressed close behind her. "Any more surprises since I've been gone?"

"I don't want to spoil it for you," she hissed over her shoulder.

They stepped into the council room, and Cyrus took his seat at the end of the table. Essandra sat to his left, as if they hadn't just debated a heavy threat walking around the kingdom.

He hardly followed the meeting conversation—an update on the communication back to Gregor, which he couldn't care less about, defense updates, the status of provisions and expected harvests, other odds and ends. But nothing that could take over the churning already in his mind.

The meeting finally broke, and the councilmen filtered out. Essandra tried to slip away, but Cyrus grabbed her and pulled her down a side hall, pressing her back against the wall and leaning close. The past hour had done nothing to calm his irritation. "You put me in an uncomfortable position."

"Do you mean with the assassins, or yesterday evening?" Her face was as cold as stone, her voice cutting.

He thought they were past this. "Why are you still angry? I told you I'm sorry."

"You think that fixes everything?"

But what else should he have done? "I don't know what you expected me to do. Miriel needed me, Pryam needed me—"

"*I* needed you!" she cried.

Her words stole his.

Her lip trembled. "Damn it," she breathed, and she shielded her face with her hand. She hated to show her emotion.

He shifted to the side, leaning his shoulder on the wall beside her to block any prying eyes from the main hall.

Her voice dropped low in defeat. "I needed your power for the Amoran Cup spell, but I didn't have your blood."

"I thought you didn't need me for that."

"Now that I'm working on alternatives to the original spell, I do."

So, she was still trying to get the spell to work. Relief filled him, but it did little to ease the guilt. "I didn't know," he said. "I'm sorry."

"And I needed to travel to the trees," she added. "And you weren't here. I've missed this month's bloom."

She'd needed him. She'd needed him and he hadn't been here. And he didn't know how to make it better now. His voice dropped to a whisper. "What do you want from me, Essandra? Whatever it is, I'll give it to you."

She lifted her gaze to his. Her face sobered, and the stiffness in her body eased. Her lips moved slightly. Then she covered her face as she breathed deeply. "You didn't do anything wrong," she said finally. She shook her head. "I don't know why I'm blaming you."

"Because I wasn't here, and you needed me."

She dropped her hands from her face.

"I'm sorry," he said again. He didn't know what else to say. He didn't know what else to do. Then he paused.

"Bond our power," he said.

Her eyes flicked to his, and a line trenched her brows. "What?"

"Bond our power. You said that Soroya brought you a seer to bond to her, that it would allow her to access the power of the Aether without needing the blood. Do that with me. Bond our power."

"No." She shook her head. "I can't."

"Why not?"

"Because there are implications, implications that Soroya didn't understand."

"Like what?"

"The power goes both ways. I would have limitless access to the Aether, and you'd have limitless access to my power and anyone bonded to me—limitless access to the power of my whole coven."

"And you're worried about this." It wasn't a question.

She was quiet for a moment. "It would make you a very powerful man."

"Do you not trust me?" he asked.

"I don't know," she whispered.

That felt like a dagger to the chest. "Can you just break the bond after?"

She shook her head. "No. It's a bloodline bond. It would be broken only when one of us dies."

"If you don't want me to wield your power, I won't."

"You would if it allowed you to take your brother," she whispered. "Or the Shadow King."

He quieted and dropped his gaze to the ground. He couldn't deny that.

"So, you see?" she said somberly. "You'd be a powerful man driven by vengeance. No controls."

She had no idea just how much control she had.

"I am also driven by other things," he said.

"Like what?" she asked him.

But he couldn't say it.

"Right," she said softly. Then she stepped around him and left him, and he watched her walk away.

Chapter Fifty

Cyrus drew in a deep breath and let it out slowly. He wasn't sure if he was relieved in his decision, or disappointed in himself. He'd intended to order Jaem to kill Bravat. The out-of-control fighter now posed too great a risk to Rael, and he was killing innocents, which he'd been doing for some time. It soured Cyrus's stomach, even if they were innocents under his brother's protection, which he was inclined to subvert.

It would be a suicide task for Jaem. After he killed Bravat, assuming he could, Bravat's men would kill him. And if he couldn't, Bravat would kill him himself, then Bravat would be even more dangerous.

As Cyrus heard Jaem's voice in his mind, running down his updates, he found himself unable to give the command, unable to ask this of his friend. His brother.

Jaem would do it. He'd do it without question.

But Cyrus couldn't ask him.

Now, afterward, he was left twisted in relief and frustration with himself. He needed to get this under control, just as he needed to get the growing disquiet of his people under control. They called for action against Serra and had now started various protests through the capital, with a vocal few delivering quite passionate orations to rile people even further.

He needed to discuss it with Everan, but first, there was something else he had to do. He gave an awkward knock on the chamber door with his elbow.

As Essandra opened it, her eyes widened. He held the blood vials out for her in his linen-wrapped hands.

She blinked. "What is all this?" she asked.

"It's several days' worth, but I know you go through it quickly. I'll have it delivered to you regularly. You'll never be without."

"That's..." She shook her head as if unsure what to say. "I mean, is that really practical?"

When had he cared about practical? "I'll make sure you always have it." He held out the vials, and slowly, she took them.

Her hand brushed his as she gathered them, and she paused, letting it linger. "You never question me about what I use the blood for," she said.

"Do you want me to?"

She shook her head. "No."

He nodded. "All right, then."

She stood, holding the vials.

He stood, looking at her holding the vials.

"I'll leave you," he said finally. "I just wanted you to have it." He turned to go.

"I don't just use it for spells," she said. "I use it to see them. It helps me remember."

He paused, turning back. There was a space of quiet. Then he asked, "Your mother and your sister?"

Her gaze dropped, but she nodded. "I use the power to unlock old memories—things forgotten."

"Can you show them to me?" He regretted the words as soon as they left his tongue. It was too private. "I'm sorry," he said quickly. "You don't have to do that."

"Do you *want* to see them?" she asked softly.

Her invitation caught him by surprise. "It would be a privilege."

Essandra opened the chamber door wider, letting him in, and he stepped inside. Carefully, she laid the vials on a side table, save one, and moved to the settee by the window.

"We should sit," she said.

Cyrus sat down beside her, shifting to face her. His heart beat heavily in his chest. He was nervous. No, not nervous, but... something.

She handed him the vial.

She could have opened it herself, used the blood inside it herself. But allowing him to take it, allowing *him* to touch it to her skin...

He took her hand in his, using his thumb to press a drop of blood to her palm. She closed her eyes, and he did too. He didn't release her hand.

Cyrus followed the call of his blood, and Essandra let him into her mind. She brought him into the center of a village. There were people all around them, working, bustling about.

A group of young girls held hands, skipping in a circle. A man walked by a few paces away with a bundle of firewood on his shoulder.

"*I'd forgotten what all of this looked like,*" she told him. "*So long I'd seen it in ruin. But now...*"

Her words trailed off. She smiled as a boy carried by two sloshing buckets of water.

"*This way,*" she said, and led him down the center street to a side street of houses.

They came to a house on the end, with a small garden. As they drew nearer, Cyrus saw a woman working between the rows of green. She was only a little older than him, no more than ten years his senior, with a young girl beside her—twelve maybe, or thirteen.

Essandra walked toward the garden, her eyes fixed on them, and stopped at the edge, watching them.

"*Aren't they beautiful?*" she whispered.

The woman turned, and as Cyrus got a better look at her face, he stilled. He'd seen her before. His eyes darted around him. This village...

And suddenly, he remembered—the dream, the vision—the only vision he'd ever been able to hear. This was where it had been.

"*Is something wrong?*" she asked.

"*No,*" he said quickly.

Essandra looked back out at the garden. "*My father died when my sister and I were barely walking. I tried to uncover memories of him, but they're too far gone. I was too young. My mother raised us.*" She smiled sadly. "*She was an amazing woman. She always knew what to do.*" Her eyes welled. "*Teron said I can only pick one, but how can I choose between them?*"

She wiped a tear that had spilled down her cheek. "*I know my mother would have me choose my sister. And I love Indira, more than anything. But my mother—she made me feel safe. She made me strong. I need her. I know it's selfish, but I need her. I miss her so much.*" She hugged herself. "*To be able to see her like this again has been such a gift. I just wish that she could see me too. I wish I could hug her. Feel her.*" Essandra's lip trembled. "*Sometimes, I just need my mother.*" She covered her mouth to silence her cry.

Cyrus looked back out at Essandra's mother and sister in the garden. This was a memory. He wished he had the power to manipulate the image of a memory.

Maybe he did…

He channeled his focus, studying the memory, then slowly started replacing its pieces with copies of his own making, though they weren't perfect. Essandra glanced around, sensing the change.

"*What is that?*" she asked.

Piece by piece, he replaced it with his own re-creation, to something he could control.

She took a step back. "*Is that you? Are you doing something?*"

Piece by piece.

She took another step back. "*Cyrus.*"

It wasn't real. Could she see through it? Piece by piece. Person by person. Would she hate him for doing this? He wavered slightly.

"*Cyrus,*" she said again, her voice laced with alarm. She grabbed his arm. "*Whatever you're doing, stop!*"

But then she froze as her mother stood from the garden and looked straight at her. Essandra stared at her, and she sucked in a ragged breath. She took a step back. "*Can she see me?*" she whispered, her breath quaking.

He pulled the image of her mother forward, into a slow walk toward Essandra. He lit the woman's face with a look of joy, a look of love—one that he'd wished he'd seen from his own mother.

"*Can she see me?*" Essandra asked again, more desperate now.

He didn't want to lie. Fortunately, she didn't give him the chance. Essandra stumbled forward, toward her mother, practically running as she let out a cry.

And Cyrus poured everything he had into the woman. All his power, all his energy. *More than a vision*, he willed. It wasn't enough for Essandra to see; he wanted her to feel. She had to feel.

It had to be real.

He'd make it real.

Everything he had, he gave, channeling every scrap of will.

And he knew he'd done it as Essandra threw her arms around her mother and sobbed. They clung to each other.

Cyrus was quickly losing strength. He felt himself weakening, but he forced himself to hold. Just a little more time. But he couldn't. The vision started to fade.

Essandra stumbled back and snapped her eyes to him. "*Cyrus!*" she said in alarm.

He shook his head, breathing heavily. "*I'm sorry, I can't hold it.*"

"*Let it go.*"

Just a little bit longer...

"*Let it go!*"

He released the vision, opening his eyes back in her chamber. Blood spilled from his nose, and he wavered to the side.

She grabbed his arm, catching him. "Cyrus!"

"I'm fine." He tried to blink back the darkness closing in.

He just needed a minute.

When he opened his eyes again, he was lying on his back. Confusion flooded him as he focused his vision on the beams of the ceiling.

His beams. His ceiling.

His chamber.

How... What...

Cyrus pushed himself up. He was in his bed. Sun poured through the window. The room was quiet around him. He was alone.

The door to his chamber opened, and Visa swept in with a plate of food in one hand and a carafe in the other.

"Oh, you're awake!" she said when she saw him.

"What's going on?" he asked her. "What happened?"

"Essandra will be back shortly," she told him. "She was waiting in here with you, but she was an absolute mess. I sent her to clean up."

"But what happened?" he asked again.

"She said you overexerted yourself. She said if you woke up, you needed to eat"—she lifted the plate—"and drink"—she lifted the carafe.

"I'm not hungry." He pushed off the thin sheet covering him.

"No," Visa said firmly, setting the carafe down on the side table and moving to the bed to keep him from getting out. She pushed the plate into his hands. "You can't get up until you eat all of this."

"But I'm not—"

"Eat, Cyrus," she ordered.

Fine. He snapped up an apple and took a bite in irritation. She pursed her lips into a satisfied smile, then bustled around the room, straightening it.

The door opened again, and Essandra stepped inside.

Visa paused. "He just woke," she told her.

Essandra perked as her eyes found him. "How are you feeling?" she asked.

"Fine," he said. Fine enough. "How did I get here?"

"Aaron and Amiel carried you."

That was... great. More people seeing him weak.

"I'll leave you two," Visa said, and she slipped out of the room.

Cyrus promptly set his plate down on the bedside table.

"No, eat that," Essandra said.

He stifled a growl.

She moved to the far corner of the bed and sat down, her eyes on him.

They both stayed for a moment, neither sure of what to say first.

"I don't know how you did that," she said finally, "with my mother. But thank you."

It was a relief she wasn't angry at him. He'd been a little worried she would be.

"How did you make me feel her?" she asked.

His mind scrambled to remember everything. "Honestly, I don't know."

"It triggered more memories," she said softly, "ones I'm not sure I would have recovered otherwise. Feeling her. Holding on to her." Her eyes teared, and she blinked them back.

"I'm glad."

She gave a sad smile. "It's so easy to forget."

"I know."

"Do you remember much of your mother?"

He shifted.

"I'm sorry," she said. "I don't know what I was thinking. You don't have to answer that. I know you don't want to talk about her."

She rose and moved to the carafe on the table, filling a cup. She brought it to him.

"Are you thirsty?"

He was, but as he took the cup, he paused.

"I killed my mother," he said, a whisper so faint he wasn't sure he'd truly spoken it.

She stopped. So did her breaths.

"She left me to die," he said. "Alone in the dead of winter."

His voice didn't sound like his own.

"She said I was cursed," he told her. "Evil." It had been a long time since he'd let himself remember. Really remember. "She thought the cold would finish me." His voice dropped to a whisper. "That would have been a mercy."

He felt her eyes on him, but he couldn't look at her as he spoke.

"She was the only person I didn't need the blood to travel to. I threw my mind after her. I begged her to come back. I begged her to save me. Not to leave me." The backs of his eyes stung. "I told her I loved her." That was the shame that still crushed him, shame that it had been true. After everything she'd said to him, everything she'd done to him, he'd still loved her.

"I told her I wouldn't do it anymore. That I'd be a good son." He wiped the corner of his eye. "But she only screamed at me to stop haunting her." A silent sob racked him. "I tried. Over the next year. I tried to stop. But sometimes I'd think that maybe she'd changed her mind." His voice dropped to a whisper. "I'd travel back." He shook his head. "She never changed her mind. In fact, eventually she took her life to get away from me." He swallowed down the knot that threatened to choke him. He'd never told anyone that. "I killed her."

Cyrus finally dared to look at Essandra.

Her breaths were short and shallow.

"I suppose that does make me evil," he said quietly.

She shook her head. "You're not evil," she whispered. "You're one of the best men I know."

His eyes darted to hers. He hadn't been fishing for reassurance, but it felt good to hear it. Surprisingly good. He gave a soft chuff at the weight that fell from his shoulders.

Essandra sat slowly on the end corner of the bed again. "I've been thinking more about the bloodline bond."

He wasn't sure what she meant. "The what?"

"The bond we discussed, between witches and seers."

"Oh." He nodded. "Right." He wouldn't have called it a discussion.

Her throat bobbed. "I think I want to do it."

He let himself lean back against the headboard. "Are you sure?"

She nodded.

"What made you change your mind?"

She drew in a long breath and cast her gaze down. "Honestly, because I need it, especially after I leave."

After I leave.

Her words knifed him. It wasn't a surprise, so he didn't know why it felt like one. He knew she'd stayed as long as she had only because she needed his power.

"Also"—her eyes met his again—"I don't think there's anything you would do with my power that I wouldn't do for you. And I trust you, Cyrus."

He trusted her too, but he'd be giving her the ability to leave him. He sighed. He didn't want his power to be the reason she stayed.

"Do it," he said.

CHAPTER FIFTY-ONE

Cyrus found himself in the center of the throne room, surrounded by Essandra's coven. It wasn't the place he would have preferred, but they needed a space that would accommodate them all. There were more witches now. Many had arrived with the refugees, not necessarily escaping slavery but escaping persecution. They'd heard of Cyrus's promise of protection, and of the high witch by his side.

The room was cool—a nice reprieve from the sun. Everan and Brant stood in a corner with a few more of Cyrus's men.

Essandra faced him. She pulled her dress from her shoulders and let it drop to the floor, stepping out of it, naked. Despite what they'd shared, he'd never seen her body, but he didn't think now was the right time to appreciate the opportunity, and he quickly averted his eyes. He cut his men a harsh glance but was pleased to see they'd done the same.

"Take off your clothes," she told him.

"Is this some kind of... sex magic?" he asked quietly.

She pursed her lips to keep in a laugh. "No, that's not a thing. But unless you want your garments infused with power, for anyone to wear, you must take them off. Especially jewelry." She reached behind her neck, pulling off her necklace, and handed it to a blond-haired witch who stood beside her. Then she stepped into a large circle that had been chalked onto the stone floor.

Cyrus didn't think himself a shy man, but standing there, surrounded by a large group of people waiting for him to take his clothes off... he felt a little shy now. However, he did as he was bid and stripped down. He paused when left with only his braies but then stripped those off too. Now he stood infinitely more uncomfortable.

Essandra waved her hand for him to join her inside the circle.

He did.

She held her hands out, palms up, and nodded to him. He did the same.

Two women stepped forward, one on either side of them. They each delivered a slice across Essandra's palms with a blade. Then they moved to him and did the same.

Essandra took his hands, pressing her palms to his, and the coven formed a large circle around them.

Cyrus glanced around, until his eyes landed back on Essandra, who gave him a reassuring smile. Then the witches started chanting.

"What are they—"

"Shhh."

Cyrus quieted. He focused on Essandra, but he still kept his eyes from wandering down her body.

The chanting paused.

Essandra brought his hand to her mouth and drew her tongue across the line of blood on his palm. Then she took a smear of her own blood and dabbed it across his bottom lip.

He took it into his mouth.

The chanting started again. This time, Essandra joined in. She started quietly, whispering the foreign words, her eyes dropping closed.

The air shifted. A prickle crept up the nape of his neck.

A pressure grew in his veins. Pulsing. Building.

The chanting grew louder, and her voice did too.

His whole body thrummed.

They grew louder. And louder.

And then they stopped.

Essandra opened her eyes.

All was quiet.

She smiled.

He glanced around again. Were they finished? Was it done? Nothing felt different.

"Is that it?" he asked.

She nodded.

Quite... anticlimactic.

Essandra let go of his hands and stepped from the ring. The blond-haired witch swept a robe around Essandra's shoulders.

Cyrus followed, but as he stepped over the chalked line, something hit him like a battle clash. It slammed into him. His knees hit stone. His ribs locked as a force in his chest pushed the air from his lungs.

"Cyrus!" Essandra dropped down beside him.

But he couldn't breathe. He couldn't speak.

Darkness closed around him.

CHAPTER FIFTY-TWO

A heavy beating thrummed in his ears. Or maybe it was throbbing.

Loud. Everything was so loud. And painful. In his head, in his chest, throughout his body. It was as if he were being crushed and pulled apart at the same time.

"Cyrus!" Everan's voice called to him. *Was* it Everan's voice?

Cyrus couldn't see. He couldn't speak.

Essandra replied, but he couldn't understand her words.

"Cyrus!" Everan called again.

He couldn't answer.

Then came the fire—creeping over his shoulders and down his back. He tried to scream but couldn't.

It spread. Around his sides and up his chest. Scorching. Searing. Scalding.

"Why is he so hot? His skin is burning."

"Don't touch him," Essandra ordered.

Cyrus knew what it was. It was a pain he hadn't forgotten. She was giving him more markings—the same as she'd done in the arena.

Staves, she'd called them. She'd said it was to keep the power from killing him.

The burn spread farther, down his arms to meet the markings he already bore from his wrists to his elbows, and up his neck, choking him in a collar of fire. If the cursed bonding wasn't going to kill him, these markings surely would...

But then a cool settled over him.

His lungs filled with air, and he gasped desperately for it.

"Is it working?" Everan asked.

"I think so," Essandra replied. "But I don't know how effective the staves are when placed afterward."

"You should have given them to him before you did this," Everan snapped.

Slowly, his body started to respond to him. Cyrus was finally able to suck in a full breath, despite the stabbing pain that still clawed his chest. His arms, his legs—the skin pulled tight, threatening to split as he shifted.

"He's moving," Everan said. "Cyrus. Cyrus, can you hear me?"

He blinked his eyes open. Gradually, things came to him. He lay on the stone floor of the throne room. It was cool against his skin, and he desperately wanted to stretch across it. He reached up and squeezed his temples, where a pulsing pain refused to relent.

Essandra knelt over him. "Cyrus? Can you hear me? Can you stand?"

"I don't know," he rasped, testing his voice. He rolled to his side.

"Easy," Everan said, reaching for him, but Essandra pushed him back.

"I said don't touch him! The power is unstable." Despite her warning to others, her hand gripped his shoulder.

Cyrus pushed himself up and tried to stand, but his legs wouldn't hold him, and he dropped back to his knees.

Essandra caught him, still barking at Everan—who was desperate to help—to back up. She shouldered herself under his arm and pushed him up as he tried again. This time, he made it, although he swayed unsteadily.

Warmth trickled down his upper lip, and the taste of metal filled his mouth.

"He's bleeding again," Brant said.

Pain pierced his skin, just below his chest, and he groaned. *More markings.*

"Stop doing that!" he snarled. It took nearly all his energy to speak.

"Your body's overwhelmed by the power," Essandra told him. "You're supposed to have some natural protection, but it doesn't seem to be very strong, if it's even working at all."

He didn't even know what that meant. "It hurts" was all he could say.

"Where?" she asked. Her own breaths came in pants now, under the strain of his weight.

"Everywhere." But especially where she marked him.

"Get Teron," Everan said.

"Teron can't help him," Essandra said. "Not with this." She gripped him tighter. "You need to rest," she told Cyrus. "Let's get you back to your chamber."

With only Essandra helping him, the walk to his chamber felt like an eternity. She warded off Everan and Brant more times than he could count. When they reached the three-stair landing that joined the throne hall to the main hall, Cyrus stumbled, nearly dropping them both to the stone floor. But she caught him. Gods, she was strong.

They reached his chamber. Essandra helped him stagger to the bed, then she dropped him onto it. Cyrus's entire body protested, and he groaned again.

"He needs to rest," she said as she waved off Everan and Brant.

"We'll wait," Everan told her.

Brant added, "We'll be quiet."

"You'll be waiting a long time, then," she said shortly. "This will put him out for a while."

"It's all right," Cyrus told them through labored breaths. "You can go."

"I'll send for you when he wakes," she assured them.

Everan sighed, and Brant frowned, but they finally acquiesced and shuffled out of the room.

Essandra moved back to the bed and took a seat on the edge beside him.

Another trickle of warmth came from his nose, and he wiped it. More blood. "You're killing me, woman," he told her.

Worry lined her brow. "I'm afraid I actually might be." She put her hand on his chest, and the searing pain came again.

Cyrus twisted and snarled through his teeth. "No more!"

"Trust me, they're helping you."

They didn't feel like they were helping him. But as the pain abated, his body relaxed. The weight in his chest lessened.

Essandra moved to the side table, where she poured a little water from a pitcher into a basin. She dipped a clean linen into it, then wrung it out. Stepping back to the bed, she took a seat on the edge again and started to wash the blood from his face.

Inside him felt like a maelstrom. If there was a bond that came from her touching his blood, he couldn't feel it because of the noise. He tried to sit up, but she pushed him back down.

"The staves augment your natural protection to keep you from being consumed by your power," she told him. "But your shield seems... defective." She thwarted his effort to sit up again. "As is your brain if you think you're going to do anything but rest right now," she added. "Stay down."

"Why don't you need markings?" He wasn't sure if he'd asked a coherent sentence. A deep tiredness pervaded him.

"I draw the power of the Aether through you, which means your body takes the consuming chaos. I also have the protection of my magic. Unlike a seer's power, a witch's magic is protective magic." She paused. "Well, most of it is. Dark magic isn't."

Finished with the wet cloth now, she dropped it onto a small pile of clothing beside the bed. But she didn't get up. He hoped she wouldn't. He didn't want her to go. Perhaps she felt it. She brushed the hair from his brow. His eyelids grew heavier.

"Does that mean the Aether is dark magic?" he asked.

She paused for a moment. "Some people think so. Some kingdoms ban seers who are able to draw from its power."

Her hand rested on his chest. Her warmth permeated his skin. He let his eyelids drop closed as her sweet scent filled his nose. He breathed her in. She said something else, but he didn't hear it.

They attacked from all directions, a flurry of swinging swords. It was a battle the likes of which he'd never seen before. Not a battle—a war.

Havoc roiled around him, sprawling the rocky terrain like fields sown with violence.

Silent violence.

Snow covered the ground, but it was stained red by the dead and dying.

So many dead and dying.

But so many still fighting.

Shadowmen surrounded him. They didn't see him, and Cyrus moved through them like a phantom. They fought against an opposing army at the base of a mountain stronghold, an army he didn't recognize.

Then he froze.

Brant battled a Shadowman with a fury and desperation Cyrus had never seen from his friend—his face twisted, his eyes blazing. He bared his teeth in a silent scream at something behind Cyrus.

And Cyrus turned, just as another Shadowman who held Teron dragged his dagger across the old healer's throat.

"No!" Cyrus bellowed.

He bolted upright in bed, his chest heaving, his heart pounding.

Essandra startled beside him. "Cyrus!" She grabbed his arm to steady him. "You're okay," she told him. "You're okay."

"Teron!"

She didn't let him go. "You're okay. Teron can't do anything. You just need to rest."

"I don't need..." His words dropped as his eyes tore around him.

He was in his own bed, in his own chamber. Essandra sat on the bed beside him. A book lay overturned on her lap, its pages bent underneath.

Sweat beaded his brow. He wiped a rough hand over his face. It had been a dream. His recent conversation with Teron had to have prompted it. But it was just a dream. He tried to push it from his mind.

"How long have I been asleep?" he asked.

She picked up her book and smoothed the pages before closing it. "Two days."

He stilled. "Two days?" That couldn't be right.

"The bond creates a constant flow of power through you now," she explained.

He could feel it. It was like being filled and emptied all at once.

Essandra swallowed as she crossed her arms and hugged the book to her. "I underestimated how much power would come. I thought it would be the same as when I drew it from your blood, but it's more." Her fingertips absently kneaded the leather of the book spine, her nails leaving small crescents. "Exponentially more."

"Does that mean you're stronger than you thought you'd be?"

She swallowed. "Yes," she said quietly, almost guiltily.

"That's not necessarily a bad thing."

"It is when it comes at the cost of consuming you."

He glanced down at the markings that covered his skin. They ran up his arms to his shoulders and across his chest and stomach. He didn't need to look to know they spanned his back as well—he remembered feeling the burn there.

"It's too much for your body. Unfortunately, it's not something Teron can heal. But a lot more staves and some good rest seem to have done the trick."

Cyrus snorted. Then he paused. "Were you here the whole time?" He glanced around, and the realization came to him. "In my bed?"

She stood briskly and smoothed her dress. "Don't get ahead of yourself. You woke every time I tried to leave. Fortunately for you, I had a lot of reading to catch up on."

"For two days?"

Her lips thinned in irritation. "I said I had a lot of reading."

Cyrus couldn't help a smile. "What are you reading about?"

Her face grew more serious. He didn't expect her to tell him. She kept her work close, especially when it involved anything personal. But she surprised him when she said, "I'm looking for a few rare herbs. Some of them are found only a few places in the world."

"Any in Rael?"

She pursed her lips. "Rael can barely grow a blade of grass."

He snorted. There were no lies in that. "What are you looking for?"

"A few things. Serium, for one."

"Where is it?"

She shook her head. "I don't know. I wish I did, though. I have an entire book of spells it would unlock for me. A proxy spell that could provide alternatives to bringing back my sister, which would let me then be the anchor for my mother. Lifeblood spells, blood-borne spells, just... a lot."

He wasn't quite sure what those were, but they were important to her, so they were important to him. "When you find it, regardless of where it is, I'll send for it. Anywhere in the world."

Her lips parted, and her eyes brightened. She pursed her lips against the smile that came to her mouth and nodded. "Thank you."

"I'm glad you're still trying," he said softly.

A warm silence sat between them.

A glisten of emotion came to her eye. "The council wants to see you," she said, blinking it back.

He almost groaned. "Of course they do."

"What do you expect? You're king—things are needed from you."

He pushed himself up from the bed and ran his hand through his hair. "As you keep reminding me."

His muscles ached, protesting every movement as he stood. He reached up behind his neck and dug his fingertips into the cramp between his shoulder blades. His braies hung loose, and they dropped lower on his hips as he stretched.

Her gaze stayed on him, traveling his chest and shoulders. And down. When she glanced up to find him looking back at her, she quickly cleared her throat and dropped her eyes to the floor.

"Do you need something from me?" His voice came out low and husky. He hadn't meant it as an advance, but as her eyes drifted back to him again, he didn't clarify.

"I do want something."

A smile tugged at the corners of his mouth.

"I want you to employ Orion and his men."

That smile disappeared, quickly replaced by a flame in his chest. "Orion?"

"We could use them," she said.

"For what? Assassins aren't soldiers."

"No, but they're skilled nonetheless, and skilled men are something we're in short supply of." She stepped closer. "You have to take advantage of every opportunity. Kingdoms and crowns are a dangerous game, and the more capable men you have around you, the better."

"Yes, surrounding myself with aggrieved assassins—that would make me feel much safer."

"There's a difference between intentionally wronging someone and simply doing what you think you have to. Orion understands this. I've gotten to know him rather well these past few weeks."

"Have you?" If Cyrus wasn't sure he disliked Orion before, especially with the smile Essandra carried as she talked about him, he was certain of it now.

"He's a very genuine person. And enjoyable to be around."

And now Cyrus liked him even less.

His face obviously betrayed him, and she shifted. "We'll talk about it later," she said. "Right now, the council is waiting. Verin and Fatim stopped by to see you earlier, which I refused. But now that you're awake, we really shouldn't keep them."

He was *barely* awake. The cramp between his shoulder blades spidered up his neck, knotting his whole back. He wondered if he could put them off for a while longer, but Essandra's waiting brow told him no.

He sighed. "Fine. Let me put myself together."

A knock sounded on the door, and she stepped to open it.

Teron stood in the hall. He gave a small bob of his head as he clasped his hands in front of him. "I know I'm of little use," he said, "but I just stopped by to check in."

On seeing the healer, the raw emotion from Cyrus's dream swept through him again. "Teron." There was a crack in his voice. He moved quickly to the door and pulled the old man inside.

Teron's heavy white brows drew together. "What's wrong?"

Cyrus could only stare at him, holding his arm. Finally, he caught himself and shook his head. "Nothing. I'm just glad to see you."

"I'll leave you," Essandra interjected. "I need to freshen up. I'll be in my chamber when you're ready." She gave a quick nod back at Cyrus and then slipped out of the room.

Cyrus stared back at Teron. "You're all right."

The old healer's brows dipped. "Of course I'm all right. Are *you* all right?" He glanced down at Cyrus's hand, which was still holding on to his arm, then slowly looked back up at Cyrus. "What worries you?"

Cyrus opened his mouth, but the words lodged like a blade in his throat. He didn't want to say it. He didn't need to say it. It had just been a dream. Only a dream.

"Nothing." He shook his head again. "Nothing. It was just a bad dream."

The old man frowned, and the shadow of his brow grew heavier over his eyes.

"Really," Cyrus said, "everything is fine. But, come"—he pulled Teron toward the cushioned chair by the window—"you can sit while I get ready."

Teron let himself be seated, although he kept a suspicious eye on Cyrus. "Get ready for what?"

"The council has been waiting to speak to me." Cyrus moved the plate of fruits that sat on a sideboard on the far wall to the table beside Teron. "Just how I wanted to spend my day," he added sourly. "I also have to figure out what to do with these assassins. Essandra is pressing me to employ them."

"Yes, Orion," Teron said as he nodded.

Cyrus paused. "You're familiar with him?"

Teron shrugged. "He seems like a decent fellow."

Cyrus's lips tightened. "You too?" At the line of puzzlement that snaked Teron's brow, he added, "Essandra seems somewhat smitten with him."

The old man tilted his head. "Does that bother you?"

Cyrus paused abruptly. "Why would it?" He picked up the carafe on the table. "Are you thirsty?"

Teron's eyes narrowed as he watched Cyrus pour a glass and set it beside the plate of fruit. "Tell me about this dream," he said.

Cyrus paused, then he set the carafe down slowly. He was trying to push the image from his mind, not relive it. "I've already forgotten it," he said. He turned and stepped into the side dressing chamber, where he pulled out a clean tunic and leathers. "Have you seen Everan?" he called as he dressed.

Teron didn't answer.

Cyrus stepped back into the main room to find the healer's eyes on him. He avoided them and looked for his boots. Finding them, he sat on the edge of the bed to pull them on.

All the while, Teron watched him. Finally, the old healer said, "When I leave this world, you have to find the next healer."

Cyrus gave a small snort. "What?"

"Only one exists in the world at a time."

Cyrus didn't like where this was going. He pulled on the left boot.

"When a healer dies, the gift moves to another," Teron told him. "You must find them. It will be someone from the Opakanaku bloodline."

"I don't even know what that means." Nor did he care. Cyrus had no intention of finding another healer. He pulled on the right boot and stood.

"The Opakanaku were the first of the grassland tribes."

Cyrus paused. "The Horsemen?"

Teron nodded. "Many generations ago, Manak Anu, the first chieftain of the Opakanaku, fell in love with one of the three sister goddesses of the Wild. He wooed her for one year, two years, three years, four years, and in the fifth year, he finally won her heart."

Cyrus smiled to himself as he took a seat in the chair beside Teron's. "Some women are hard to win over."

"She had to become human to be with him. And she did. But when she left the Wild, she took with her the power of healing. This power still remains, moving from person to person. They need not be directly related, only a descendant of the original Opakanaku tribe."

Cyrus eyed Teron, his white hair and white beard. "I never knew you were a Horseman."

"Punaloan," the old man said with honor.

Cyrus hadn't heard of them, but he smiled in seeing Teron's pride.

The healer shook his finger. "When I'm gone, find the next."

When I'm gone...

Cyrus's chest tightened. "I won't need another."

Teron's face sharpened and he grabbed Cyrus's hand, clasping it in his own. His eyes welled. "You're a fool who's going to get himself killed without a healer. Find them. Promise me."

"I will," he said. But he had no intention of replacing Teron. Because nothing was going to happen to him.

CHAPTER FIFTY-THREE

Essandra was in her chamber, as she'd said she would be. She answered the door as she was pinning her hair back from her face.

Cyrus stopped when he saw her. She wore a green satin dress, the color of her eyes.

"There you are," she said. "I thought I was going to have to go back and get you."

He hadn't seen this dress before. It hung from her shoulders, showing the curve of her neck and the hollow at the base of her throat.

"Is something wrong?" she asked, and he realized he'd been staring.

"No, not at all. You just look... very nice."

She smiled. "Thank you." And she swept out of the room.

They walked with purpose. "Have you talked to Everan?" she asked.

He hadn't yet seen him. "Should I have?"

"He was helping Ruth deal with a bit of a vocal crowd earlier. The people are growing restless."

"About what?"

"Serra. It's actually one of the things—the main thing—the council wants to talk to you about."

Now this was a topic that Cyrus was looking forward to. He was eager to solidify a plan, also finding frustration in inaction. Serra needed to fall, and the sooner that happened, the sooner he could focus on other things. Other things like the Shadowlands. Other things like his brother. Was his council finally willing to act?

Cyrus stood at the end of the table in the council room, unable to handle the confines of the armed chair.

A tall man with gray-peppered hair leaned forward. "We can't wait much longer," he said. "The people grow restless."

Yes, exactly. Cyrus liked this man. He'd employed him for one of the council positions at some point, but he didn't remember when or which one. He also didn't remember the man's name. He'd ask Essandra later.

"And what are we to do with Serra?" Verin argued. "They're one of the largest kingdoms in the world, if not the largest! We haven't even stabilized Rael. How are we to be responsible for yet another takeover? And don't forget—we've also committed ourselves to Pryam."

"No one is talking about being responsible for Serra," Fatim argued back. "The people are only wanting us to help overthrow their rule." He looked at Cyrus. "You're king, you're obligated to the people of Rael. You've promised them, and they're waiting." He shook his finger. "But don't misconstrue my words as my support for this effort.

I think it's ill-timed. I just don't know if we have a choice to wait longer."

Verin threw up his hands. "So, what's the plan? Go in, wreak havoc, topple those in power, and leave?"

"That would suffice," Cyrus said, finally speaking.

"With what men?" Verin asked.

"We have the original forty thousand fighters from the arena," Everan said. "Then we're up to about twenty thousand refugees who've completed basic training. Ten thousand more in progress. That includes freed men of Rael who've volunteered to join. We also have new waves of about fifteen hundred joining each week."

"That's hardly enough to topple a kingdom like Serra."

Cyrus leaned forward, resting his weight on his fists at the ends of the table. "The point is that we *will* have enough, eventually. The army is growing quickly. But I don't even think I need an army. I could do it with Serran slaves."

All eyes turned on him.

"What?" Fatim asked.

Cyrus looked back at them coolly. "I could do it the same way I took the villas here."

The councilmen glanced at one another, still not understanding.

"And how did you take the villas?" one of the councilmen asked.

"Simply by setting foot into them," Everan said, "and pulling his sword."

The man shook his head. "I don't know how that would have—"

"It gave them the courage they needed to fight back," Everan interrupted. "Slaves easily outnumbered the nobles; they just needed something to rally behind. Cyrus gave that to them. It worked every time."

"But we're not talking about a villa here," the councilman said. "We're talking about a kingdom."

Everan leveled his dark eyes on the man. "It worked on Rael. Cyrus stood in the center of the arena and raised his sword, and everyone joined him."

Verin leaned back in his chair. "Are you really proposing a strategy of simply walking into Serra and trying to inspire a rebellion?"

Cyrus shrugged. "Sailing, more specifically," he said. "But, yes, I think I am."

Verin shook his head. "Sire, we have to build the army."

Fatim nodded. "And if people know we're building an army, they'll at least see it as action, and it will buy some time."

Cyrus pushed out a frustrated breath. He didn't want to wait to build an army. The longer it took him to bring down Serra, the longer it would be before he could focus his attention on Alexander and the Shadow King. But it didn't look like he had a choice.

The graying councilman leaned forward again. "It won't take long to build an army. In the meantime, we should properly plan—how big of an army we'd be up against, how many slaves might join us. We'll need to send some men to find this out. It will be a dangerous task, though."

Cyrus quirked his lips into a small smile. "I have the perfect person," he said.

"We're assassins, not spies." Orion's words were laced in venom. He stood across the desk from Cyrus in his study.

Orion's steely gaze was sharp enough to cut him. Spies were the lice of the assassin world, which didn't entirely make sense to Cyrus, as their work was just as important, if not more so.

"Your men are trained for stealth," Everan said from where he leaned against the wall. "You know how to get in and out of places, *generally speaking*. That's what we need."

"I need to know what we're up against," Cyrus told him, "what Serra has in terms of defense, and how many slaves there are. I need to know anything and everything about their army, how big it is, what their capabilities are."

Orion looked to Essandra, who stood behind the chair next to him with her hands clasped and resting on the high wingback. A lock of hair fell over his brow, blond with a touch of copper. He curled his fists against the edge of the desk and leaned his weight onto it as he contemplated. Lean muscle corded his arms. Orion was an attractive man, in face and body, lithe and chiseled, if one liked that sort of thing. Cyrus looked at Essandra. Did *she* like that sort of thing?

She gave Orion a nod. "You're in a unique position to get this information for us," she told him. "And you know we need it."

Orion cut Cyrus another sharp glance, then softened as he looked back at Essandra. Cyrus hated how he looked at her.

"Fine," the assassin said. "I'll ready my men. We'll sail in two days." He made no effort to hide his shadowed scowl before leaving.

Essandra gave Cyrus a quirk of her brow, then followed Orion out.

Cyrus sighed as he leaned back in his seat.

"I'm proud of you," Everan said, and he rocked off the wall and moved to the chair across from the desk, dropping down into it.

Cyrus snorted. "Why?"

"I know it's not Serra that you want. But you're putting Rael first."

"I *do* want Serra. I just don't want them the *most*."

"I'm still proud."

Cyrus chuckled with a shake of his head. "I'm sure I'll find a way to fuck that up."

CHAPTER FIFTY-FOUR

Cyrus strode quickly through the main hall and out through the courtyard. Everan and Kord fell in step beside him. Kord had just returned from Pryam the week prior, after Cyrus had sent Brant to take Kord's place in overseeing building the Pryamese army. He'd brought back a letter from Miriel. It had flowers drawn on it.

She'd also returned the vials of blood Cyrus had sent her so they could talk across the sea between them. *That's gross*, her letter had told him. And she said she liked writing letters. Cyrus didn't. But he'd write to Miriel.

Things were going well for her in Pryam. With the men Cyrus had sent her, she'd been able to lessen her own illusions that frightened her people so much and replace them with illusions of men from Rael. Slowly they'd replace those with real men from Rael. Rumors would fade. All and all, things were settling there for her, which was more than could be said about Rael.

"How many?" Cyrus asked as he stormed through the courtyard, his anger building from the news Kord had just delivered.

"Four," Kord said.

Four wagons they'd lost. The displaced Raelean nobles had attacked another harvest caravan a half day's ride from the capital. This was the third attack in the past two weeks, even with increased guard, and things were escalating. The wagons of grain weren't the worst of the losses now. This time, a hedge witch had been killed. It was a relatively new witch who'd recently joined the coven, but it was still a hard loss for Essandra and was a detriment to continuing harvests. And Cyrus's tolerance was gone. He'd root these men from wherever they were hiding and kill every last one of them.

"The nobles want to meet," Kord continued. "They want to discuss terms of peace."

"With what they've done today, they've ruined their chance at that," he replied darkly.

"If this will stop the attacks, I think we should consider it."

Cyrus halted abruptly, halting them all. "They've killed another one of Essandra's witches. For that, they'll pay."

"And how many more of our people will we lose while you're figuring out a way to make them pay? We don't even know where the nobles are. And the men loyal to them could very well be walking among us."

Cyrus stared at him. Kord had been different since coming back from Pryam. "What's going on with you?" he asked. "Did something happen in Pryam?"

Kord shook his head with a snort. "No. Nothing happened in Pryam. *Exactly nothing.* And you know what? It was nice to be in a kingdom with nothing happening."

Cyrus looked to Everan. His friend said nothing to agree with Kord. He also said nothing to disagree.

"Look, Cyrus," Kord said, "all I'm saying is that there's a lot going on right now. You're planning a strike against Serra, you want to go after the Shadow King—"

"I've agreed to wait on the Shadow King," Cyrus countered.

Kord tossed up his hands. "But we have to remind you of that every time you think about him. You're already fighting a war with famine, you've overcommitted our few resources—both in a free-for-all invitation for worldwide refugees, and now with Pryam. Add waging a civil war against the nobles?" He snorted again. "Thank the fucking gods you can't get to your brother in Mercia, otherwise that would be on the table too. Cyrus"—he shook his head—"you can't do it all. At least not all at the same time. Not to mention what you're putting yourself through. You just bonded yourself with this witch and nearly died."

"I didn't nearly die."

"A roomful of people literally watched you hemorrhage from your fucking nose and pass the fuck out."

"I'm fine now." Mostly fine, other than the storm of power that constantly eddied inside him and sometimes threatened his balance. He'd get it under control.

"Just... think about it. If we made peace with the nobles, it would be *one thing* resolved." His blue eyes burned with an icy fire. "Think about it?"

"I'll think about it," Cyrus said, but the words tasted sour on his tongue.

Cyrus sat at the end of the table in the council room. Disappointed. He'd been eager for this meeting, a little too eager, thinking it would be another discussion about Serra. Instead, he held an envelope in his hands that bore a green seal.

From Gregor.

The king of Japheth had sent a reply to Everan's very diplomatic response to his last letter. Perhaps Cyrus should just give it to Everan now to read and reply as he saw fit. He was better at these things anyway. But he broke the seal and opened it. His nonchalance quickly turned to annoyance as he read through. He tossed the letter onto the table for Everan to read.

"He invites me to Japheth," Cyrus said as Everan picked up the letter and skimmed it.

"Will you go?" Verin asked.

Everan passed the letter to Kord beside him.

Cyrus sighed.

"Cyrus," Kord said. "You can't really be thinking of *not* going." He passed the letter around the table.

Of course he was thinking of not going.

"Sire," Verin said, "this is an excellent opportunity to explore the possibilities between Japheth and Rael."

"And what of the Shadowlands?" Cyrus cut back. "What if he has no intentions of severing his alliance with the Shadow King?"

"It sounds like he does."

"By a vague comment from an overconfident messenger?"

"Very true," Verin said. "But we won't know for sure until you talk to him. He could come here, or you go there, but he has made the first invitation. I don't think we have a choice."

Cyrus looked around the room. His eyes stopped on Essandra.

"Do you think I should go?" he asked her.

She shifted in her chair, and her eyes darted around the table. "I..." She straightened. "I think you should. No decisions should be made. Meet with him, talk to him, return when you know more, and then we'll decide—collectively—where to go from there."

Cyrus rested his weight on his elbows against the edge of the table. "Fine." Then he leaned back in his chair. "Send a reply. I'll go in a couple weeks."

The councilmen filed out of the room in high spirits, but Cyrus walked with aversion knotting in his shoulders. There was something about this king of Japheth that bothered him beyond his current alliance with the Shadow King, but he couldn't quite figure out what it was.

Essandra walked silently beside him. It had been over a week since the nobles' attack that had killed the hedge witch, and while she wasn't outwardly grieving, she was quiet and withdrawn. Cyrus knew it wasn't just the loss. She was suffering the failure and shame of not being able to keep her coven safe. And Cyrus was suffering the failure and shame of not being able to give that to her.

Suddenly she perked up. "Orion," she said.

That name was like a fork dragged across a plate. Cyrus stiffened as he saw the assassin walking toward them, alive. Unfortunately. But he stifled the growl in his throat, as well as his want to dagger this man as he approached. Orion had just returned from Serra, and Cyrus was eager to hear what he had to say.

"Took you long enough," Cyrus told him, not bothering with a greeting.

"It's a massive fucking kingdom," the assassin cut back. Then he quickly nodded to Essandra. "Apologies for the language, Lady Essandra."

She gave a small shake of her head, but there was a hint of a smile on her lips.

Maybe Cyrus *would* dagger this man.

"My study," Cyrus said shortly. He led them all to the room. Inside, they swept around the large trestle table in the center that sat layered with maps.

"So how many slaves are there, and where are they primarily?" Cyrus asked, picking up a pen.

Orion pointed to the capital city by an inlet labeled *Slaver's Bay* on the east side of the kingdom. "I'd estimate seventy-five to a hundred thousand all in this area." His finger moved slightly north. "Another fifty thousand here." Then he trailed east and down to the southern coast. "And maybe sixty thousand spanning the east side."

"So, upward of two hundred thousand in total," Cyrus said as he noted the numbers on the side.

"That's double the size of Aleon's army," Kord said.

"But they aren't soldiers," countered Everan. "Aleon would decimate them."

"We're not fighting Aleon right now," Cyrus replied. He looked back at Orion. "So, the majority of the slaves are in the capital?"

The assassin nodded. "It's also the main port city, so it's where the majority of their slave trade comes in and out of. Another interesting detail—most common citizens don't keep slaves. They're primarily held among the nobles, located in and around the capital."

"Just like Rael," Everan said.

Cyrus nodded. That was good—centralized targets, and the slaves weren't as scattered as he'd feared. "What about the west?" he asked.

"The west is largely uninhabited," Orion told them. "If you think Rael is hot and barren, western Serra is even worse." He pointed to the center of the kingdom between two sets of mountains. "Once you get past here, there's not much you'll encounter."

Interesting. Cyrus nodded again. "So how many Serrans do you think there are?"

"People living in poverty? I don't know. A lot. But the size of their army is significantly less than the number of slaves."

Cyrus jerked his head up in surprise.

"Wait, what?" Everan said. "That can't be right. I was held in Serra for over a year. The capital's huge. And everyone knows it's one of the largest kingdoms."

"Largest in terms of wasteland," Orion said. "Once you get outside the capital, there's nothing."

Cyrus snorted. "Quite the ruse," he said. "It makes me think no one has ever visited Serra."

Orion frowned. "Who would want to?"

Fair. Cyrus had never been to Serra himself. He'd been purchased from the Shadow King and sold directly to a noble in Rael. Like an animal. He'd show them just what kind of animal he could become.

He stood as he looked at the numbers. *Two hundred thousand*, all held in this ruse of a kingdom—the kingdom he'd tear to the ground. And now he felt even more confident about everything. His army was growing rapidly, but he didn't even need it.

"I've made sketches of the capital and of the palace," Orion said, pulling parchments from a bag at his side. "I think you'll find them beneficial."

Cyrus took them and flipped through. They were probably the best drawings he'd ever seen. He looked back up at Orion.

The assassin's frown deepened. "What?"

"You do make a rather good spy."

Orion scowled at him.

Cyrus felt a pull come through a blood bond. *Jaem.* "Just a moment," he told them as he opened his mind and pulled Jaem in. He just needed to—

"*Alexander,*" a woman's voice called.

Cyrus froze. Ice rippled across his skin.

It wasn't Jaem he'd let in.

He traveled the bondspace to find the Mercian queen staring back at him. She looked a little more disheveled than a queen ought to, in a wrinkled and slightly twisted golden gown. Her hair was hastily tied back behind her, and mud streaked her temple.

What was happening? How was this possible? She didn't have his blood. She couldn't call him. She didn't—

Everything stopped as his eyes darted back to the streak on her temple.

It wasn't mud.

It was blood—blood of another that allowed Cyrus to travel into minds as if it were his own blood.

The blood of his brother.

Cyrus's heart seized in his chest.

Alexander's blood had touched the Mercian queen.

And the Mercian queen was in the Shadowlands.

That meant *Alexander was in the Shadowlands.*

Cyrus felt unsteady as he opened his eyes in his study again.

"What is it?" Essandra asked, stepping around the table to him.

His pulse beat heavily in his ears. "Alexander. He's in the Shadowlands."

Everan and Kord gathered closer around the table.

"Did you see him?" Everan asked.

"His blood touched the queen's skin." His eyes were locked on his desk, but they weren't focused on the maps strewn across it. His voice dropped to a whisper. "This is my chance."

"What do you mean by that?" Kord asked.

But Cyrus's mind was turning too quickly to answer. This was the closest his brother had ever been to him. Not only that, but he was in the same place as the Shadow King. If Cyrus had ever doubted fate, this was surely a sign. This was fate calling him...

"I have to go to the Shadowlands," he said.

Essandra's chin dropped and now she leaned forward too. "You can't be serious."

"Have you lost your mind?" Kord asked.

Possibly, but Cyrus didn't care.

"We're sitting here, planning a strike on Serra," Kord pressed.

Cyrus shook his head. He didn't care.

Kord gaped at him. "What makes you think you could even get into the Shadowlands?"

"They're allied with Mercia now. If my brother is welcome, and I wear his face..." Cyrus could pass for Alexander. His heart raced even faster. "Perhaps I can even get close to the Shadow King."

"Uh"—Kord frowned—"if your brother is bleeding, he might not be as welcome as you think."

"I have to go."

Essandra grabbed him. "You need to think this through."

"I have," he insisted. "I've dreamed it a thousand times over."

"You've dreamed of blood. I meant an actual plan," she said. "This could go very poorly very quickly."

"I can't not go. To have both my brother and the Shadow King in the same place, at the same time..." Fight flamed under his skin. *To have the opportunity to kill them both...*

"It's double the risk!" she stressed. "Focus on one, then the other."

"You shouldn't be focused on either one of those things right now," Kord interjected.

"And when will I have a chance at my brother if not in the Shadowlands?" he snapped. "I can't get to him in Mercia."

Essandra shook her head. "The council won't support this."

"I wasn't planning on telling them."

She looked at Everan and Kord in desperation, but they had nothing and were obviously still trying to put their own objections into words.

"Cyrus," she said, gripping her temples, "you can't go to the Shadowlands." She put both her hands flat on the desk and looked at him squarely. "You're king now. People depend on you. You can't go flinging yourself off on a mission of self-vengeance. It's too great a risk. We're still suffering attacks from nobles. You can't just leave Rael like this."

"I *will* deal with the nobles," he promised.

"When? *And* you've just agreed to visit Gregor in a few weeks. And Kord's right about getting into the Shadowlands. How would you even do that?"

"I'll be back before I have to meet Gregor. And I'll use the birds. I can be in and out through the Canyonlands in a matter of days." He'd be forever grateful to Miriel for giving him that idea.

"The birds give you sight but they're debilitating for you."

"I'll manage it. Worst case, it will only take me half a day to recover."

"In enemy territory? Cyrus"—she shook her head again—"absolutely not."

"I can't do nothing! My brother and the Shadow King are finally within my reach—"

"You can't kill the Shadow King," Everan said flatly. "Not yet."

Cyrus snapped his gaze to his friend.

"It would only result in a change of power," Everan said. "You know this. You know everything we're all telling you." His dark eyes bore into Cyrus as he shook his head. "If you're going to do an attack like this, it needs to be carefully planned. It needs to be a step toward bringing down the *whole* of the Shadowlands, something that you know for sure would crumble an alliance or throw them toward war, and *not with Rael*. Killing a lord justice isn't going to do that. It won't be enough."

A justice wouldn't be enough. What would?

"Killing a queen would," he found himself saying.

Kord threw up his hands. "What the fuck, Cyrus?"

"The Shadow King's alliance with Mercia would crumble," Cyrus said. "They might even retaliate against him if they think he's to blame." Cyrus turned and paced the room, his heart beating faster. "After, I'll come back, go to Japheth, break his alliance with Gregor. The Shadow King will have no one. If Mercia and Aleon move against him then, that would be the fall of the Shadowlands."

"That's a lot of steps that all need to work perfectly," Kord said. "You can't possibly think this is a good idea."

Cyrus didn't particularly like the idea of killing the Mercian queen. No, she wasn't just the Mercian queen any longer, he reminded himself. She was the Shadow Queen now, and she'd chosen her path. If she could forgive these atrocities, she was complicit in the crimes against him, against humanity, even if she hadn't put the manacles on Cyrus herself. And her death would wreck this kingdom that so greatly needed to fall. It would wreck his brother, whose job it was to protect her.

The idea had felt hasty as he'd spoken it, but now that he was thinking it through, it seemed the only viable option.

He had to kill her.

"Cyrus, it's too dangerous," Essandra said, still feverishly trying to dissuade him. "You can't seriously intend to go to the Shadowlands right now."

But he'd never been more serious.

"I have to," he said.

"Then send the assassins."

"I would go to the Shadowlands," Orion said.

Cyrus shook his head. "No. I need to see Alexander's face. I need to watch him die." He needed to go prepare, but Essandra slid between him and the door, stopping him from reaching for the knob.

"I can make that happen," she said breathlessly. "I can bond you. You'd be able to see through the assassins, speak through them."

"That's what a coward would do." He reached around her for the doorknob, but she grabbed his hand.

"It's what a responsible king would do!"

"I am not a responsible king!" he snapped back.

But she didn't quake under his storm. She only gripped him tighter. "Cyrus," she begged. Her breaths came short and desperate. "What if you don't come back?" She clutched him tightly. "You can't go."

His gaze moved back and forth between her pleading emerald eyes. He shook his head. "I won't stay just because I might not come back."

"Then do it because I asked you."

Her words stilled him.

"Stay," she whispered.

But he couldn't.

"I'll help you get your brother," she said. "I'll help you get the Shadow King. But I beg you—*don't go*." Her eyes flashed desperately. "*Stay*," she said again.

They stood, so close, unmoving. Her hands still gripped him. Tightly.

Cyrus turned, leveling his fiery gaze on Orion.

"Prepare your men," he told him. "You're going to the Shadowlands to kill the Shadow Queen. And you'll bring me the head of my brother."

THE BLOOD DUOLOGY

Continue the journey with:

BLOOD KING II

To avenge his past, he must sacrifice his future.
Blood or the heart—
Only one will prevail.

Author's Note

There's something deeply vulnerable about writing a story just for yourself.

From the beginning, the *Blood King* books felt like a gamble. They're darker. Angrier. Sharper around the edges. I didn't know if readers of the *Crowns* trilogy would want them. I wasn't sure they would connect. But I *needed* to write this story. It was clawing to get out of me.

Maybe that's because this story is tied to something personal.

For those of you who don't know, I was diagnosed with Stage II lobular carcinoma, an invasive breast cancer, in late 2022. I worked on *Blood King* throughout my treatment, and when these books release in September, it will mark two years of me being cancer free. That still feels surreal to say. There were days I struggled to imagine life on the other side of that fight. But I made it. I'm here. And writing these pages—building this world, giving these characters voices—was part of both my escape and healing.

Blood King will also be my first release as a full-time author. Something that once felt like a distant dream is now my actual, everyday life, and I still can't believe it sometimes.

So yes, this story is different.

And yes, this one is for me.

If you've made it this far, thank you for taking this journey with me. Thank you for embracing these books and for allowing me the space to keep creating in this world I love so much.

I'm so grateful to be here.

With love,

Nicola

About the Author

Nicola Tyche (TIE-kee) is a romantic fantasy author, weaving stories full of twisty suspense, fierce heroines, and villains you can't help but root for.

She lives in the Pacific Northwest with her husband and three daughters. When she isn't writing, she enjoys tacos, traveling, gardening, exploring the great outdoors, and other creative projects.

Visit her website at www.nicolatyche.com, join her reader communities on Facebook or Discord, and find her on your favorite social platforms through the link below!

Books by Nicola

North Queen

Shadow Queen

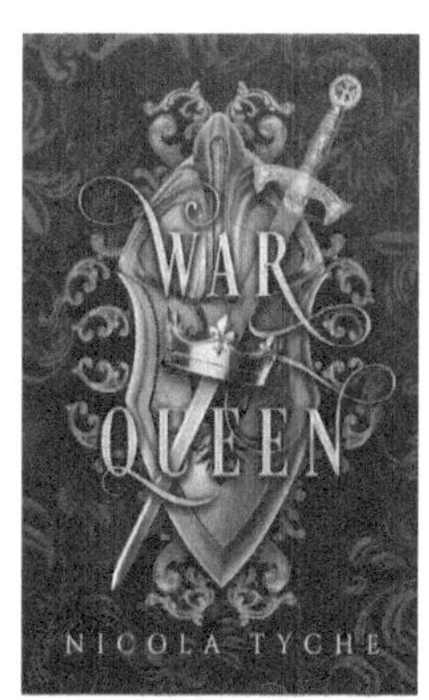

War Queen

Blood King I

Blood King II